The Hippocratic Heist

A Righteous Wrong Heist Novel

Walden Gray

waldengray.com

For my family, who give me the strength every day . . .

and

For those trapped in cycles of addiction and exploitation, who believe there's no way out—remember that recovery is possible, justice is attainable, and sometimes the most unexpected allies are the ones who understand your struggle best.

The price of anything is the amount of life you exchange for it.

Henry David Thoreau

Author's Note

Dear Reader,

As you prepare to join the *Righteous Wrong* crew on their next adventure, I want to address the sensitive themes that form the backdrop of this story. This installment explores the devastating impact of gambling addiction and the predatory nature of healthcare fraud—systems that often target those at their most vulnerable.

While this is a work of fiction, I have approached these topics with care, aiming to highlight the very real struggles faced by those caught in addiction's grip and those exploited by corrupt healthcare practices. Through our characters' journeys, we explore themes of accountability, redemption, and the complicated nature of justice when systems fail those they should protect.

My goal has never been to sensationalize these issues, but rather to examine them through the lens of characters seeking their own forms of redemption. As with the previous book, you'll find this story contains minimal profanity and no explicit content related to drugs, alcohol, or sexual situations.

If you or someone you know struggles with gambling addiction, please know that help is available. There are resources and support systems ready to assist on the path to recovery.

Thank you for continuing this journey with me and the *Righteous Wrong* team. I hope this story not only entertains but also illuminates how patterns of exploitation often share common roots, regardless of the industry in which they occur.

With gratitude,

Walden Gray

Contents

Prologue

Time doesn't heal wounds so much as it rearranges the scars—William knew this as his taxi crawled along the coastal road, the headlights briefly illuminating the unmarked path up to the cliffside gambling den high above, his sobriety chip heavy in his pocket like a bullet he'd dodged but couldn't quite forget.

William's finger tapped a frantic rhythm against his pen—click, click, click—each click a sharp beat against the silent anxiety building inside him. Through the taxi's window, the neon lights of the cliffside gambling den blurred into a kaleidoscope of temptation. The scent of salt air mixed with his cologne, a pungent cocktail that brought memories flooding back—nights of glory and shame, fortunes won and souls lost.

Click, click, click. The pen's rhythm was the only betrayal of his tension.

He had been here before, not this cliffside den of iniquity, but places like it. Places where neon lights promised hollow delights and where his addiction had once anchored him in its depths. It was an era best left behind, yet here he was, on the precipice of diving headlong into that world again.

Decision time, William.

The pen's incessant clicking punctuating his inner turmoil. Leave or go in? His hand paused, the pen now still as if withholding judgment. Then, with a resolute click, he pocketed the pen and stepped out of the cab. So much for Emerson's guidance today; this was purely Thoreau's *quiet desperation.*

A rush of cool air laced with sea salt greeted him as he walked uphill. He breathed it in, letting the familiar cocktail of excitement and repulsion fill his lungs. It was a scent he recognized all too well, a blend that whispered of excess and regret in equal measure.

His suit felt like a costume . . . camouflage among the gamblers and high-rollers who frequented these secretive gatherings. They were looking to score big, but William—he was mining his past for literary gold, digging through the muck of his experiences. Addiction had been his muse—always would be?—the driving force behind his decisions.

The doorman's gaze washed over him like a spotlight, scrutinizing, judging. William returned the look with a faint smirk before ascending the staircase, each step taking him deeper into the belly of the beast.

Inside, the air was thick with the scent of ambition and cologne, the kind that tries too hard. William's eyes registered everything—the tables heavy with silent tension, the multi-ethnic security detail with their coiled earpieces and stoic expressions, and the caterers who flitted about like moths drawn to the intoxicating flame of wealth.

As he skirted the periphery of the gambling frenzy, his gaze skimmed past the clatter of roulette wheels and craps tables. He dodged a server balancing a tray of bubbling champagne flutes . . . her smile as effervescent as the drinks she proffered. It was all glitz and glamor on the surface, but beneath the veneer, desperation clung like the stale scent of spilled liquor.

"It's not cards," he said under his breath, sidestepping a cluster of serious faces buried in hands of baccarat. The felt-covered tables with their kings and queens were mere jesters in this court; William sought the kingpin, the ace in the hole.

To his right, the caisse—cashier's desk—loomed like a fortress, its attendants the modern-day Charons ferrying souls across the River Styx of lost wages. But it wasn't the clickety-clack of chips or the mechanical whir of slot machines that held William's attention. It was the hidden door tucked away behind the cage, leading to what the regulars called *The Library*—where the real gambling happened, where fortunes and souls traded hands with equal frequency.

"Black plaque, please," he said when his turn came. The woman in glasses appraised him with the clinical detachment of a mortician, before pushing the singular black token towards him. William pulled out one thousand dollars in a wrapper—the price of admission to his personal hell. He watched her count his money with mechanical precision. Around him, other patrons collected their colored plaques like candy:

- White for $5,000

- Yellow for $10,000

- Blue for $25,000

- Red for $50,000

Each color represented a different level of desperation, a different shade of delusion.

But his was black. Black wasn't for the standard games of chance. Black was for the high-stakes private poker rooms where millionaires lost everything and smiled while doing it. Black was for the exclusive tables where luck wasn't so much a lady as a dominatrix with expensive tastes. Black was for the things that had once consumed his body and his soul.

"Welcome back, Mr. Prescott," the doorman said with a knowing smirk as William crossed the threshold. *The Library* was as he remembered—dark wood paneling, leather chairs that had absorbed decades of cigar smoke and broken dreams, and tables where men in bespoke suits played for stakes that could feed small nations.

He settled into a chair at the highest-stakes table, the black plaque his ticket to this exclusive dance with destiny. The familiar rush of adrenaline coursed through his veins as the cards hit the felt. *Research*, he told himself. *Just research for the book.* But the old hunger stirred in his gut like a hibernating beast catching the first scent of spring.

Hours passed in a blur of cards, raises, and carefully measured breaths. When he finally emerged, dawn was painting the sky in mocking pastels. His walk back to the taxi was slow, purposeful—each step a reminder of why he'd left this life behind.

Slumped in the backseat as his well-practiced facade was crumbling, William watched the cityscape blur past. The tendrils of his past addiction reached for him with familiar fingers. Was this return to the abyss truly research—fuel for his motivational speeches about redemption—or was he just another moth drawn back to the flame? Either way, the taste of it sat bitterly on his tongue, like ashes from a hand he'd sworn never to play again.

• • • ● • ● • • • •

The next morning, William strolled into the Los Angeles Convention Center with the confidence of a man who had read Adam Smith's *The Wealth of Nations* cover to cover.

Twice.

He was back—not that LA had missed him or he it—but this time as a grad student determined to unravel the mysteries of economic behavior like a modern-day Indiana Jones, minus the whip and fedora.

The hum of academia filled the conference rooms, a symphony of intellect and ambition playing out in PowerPoint presentations and vigorous nodding. William navigated through the sea of eager minds, his own brain buzzing with thoughts more complex than last night's Sudoku puzzle.

"Rationality," he said under his breath, "is just collective madness in disguise." He scribbled down this nugget of cynicism in his moleskin—because leather-bound screamed pretentious—as he settled into a chair that offered a view of both the speaker and any potential exits. One could never be too careful when trapped in a room with economists; the thrill of fiscal policy debates could turn lethal at any moment.

As the lecturer droned on about market equilibrium, William couldn't help but let his mind wander, pondering whether anyone else considered the irony of using paper—a dying commodity—to distribute their academic findings. Digital was the way forward . . . trees everywhere breathed a sigh of relief.

His advisor, a stern woman with a penchant for tweed and a stare that could melt steel, caught his eye from across the room. She arched an eyebrow—a silent challenge to engage or face her academic wrath later. William flashed her a grin that said, "I'm here physically, that's half the battle" and dutifully nodded along with the next point about behavioral economics.

As the session wrapped up, William rose, stretching his stiff limbs, a satisfying *crack* echoing the end of the intense mental workout. His eyes scanned the crowd, noting the subtle interactions, the posturing, the peacocking—all part of the socio-economic ritual. He smirked. These were the true behaviors worth studying, the unspoken transactions that no ledger could capture.

"Excuse me, are you enjoying the conference?" a voice asked, pulling him from his reverie.

"About as much as a root canal," William replied, his sarcasm slipping out before he could stop it.

The questioner, a young hopeful with a badge too shiny and a smile too earnest, blinked, then laughed awkwardly. "Good one!"

"Thanks, I'm here all week." And with a wink, he sauntered off, leaving the budding economist to wonder if he had just been insulted or enlightened.

It was going to be a long conference.

Later that evening, as William sat in his hotel room reviewing his notes, a familiar restlessness crept over him. He'd been working on a book—an ambitious project combining economic theory with his personal battle against gambling addiction. His publisher wanted more *raw authenticity*, whatever that meant. More importantly, William wanted to understand the psychology of the places that had nearly destroyed him, but from the other side of addiction. A sort of exposure therapy, he told himself, though he knew playing with fire was never entirely safe.

His fingers traced the outline he'd drafted: *The House Never Wins: Breaking Free from the Economics of Addiction*. The irony of using his economics degree to dissect his former addiction wasn't lost on him. But if his experiences could help others understand the mathematical certainty of destruction that awaited them at the tables, maybe some good could come from his past.

Decision made, William grabbed his jacket. There was a place nearby, the *High-Stakes Social Club*. He'd pay to watch, not play. Observer, not participant. The rational part of his brain knew the risk, but the writer in him needed to see it all again—this time through the lens of recovery rather than addiction.

• • • • • • • • • •

With the predatory grace of a man who knew the night too well, William navigated the seedy neon glow that clung to the club like cheap cologne. The underground casino was a half-mile journey into a world he'd sworn off, yet here he was again, another moth flirting with the flame.

The doorman's palm, as open and expectant as the house odds, absorbed the crisp hundred-dollar bill William handed him. A nod granted him entry, the door swinging shut like the last page of a chapter he couldn't stop re-reading.

Inside, the air was thick with desperation, each breath a cocktail of cigar smoke and shattered dreams. He made his way through the dark room, avoiding eye contact with the players at the tables and their vacant stares. His destination: a private poker room chosen for its obscurity—a lone island in a sea of lost wages.

"Sparkling water?" Her voice cut through the soft jazz, a dealer's siren call wrapped in a tailored vest that spoke of house prosperity. She was beautiful in the way of all things designed to separate men from their money—polished, precise, her smile a carefully calculated odds bet.

"Club soda. Lime," he replied, his voice betraying none of the storm brewing beneath his stoic exterior. As she turned to fetch his order, William allowed himself the briefest of reprieves, his gaze drawn to the hypnotic shuffle of cards at the nearby table, an echo of a life he'd abandoned.

She returned, the glass poised between manicured fingers, bubbles rising like the hopes of desperate men. Setting it down, she took her position at the table with the fluid grace of a card shark circling her prey.

"Looking for some action?" she started, but William's slight shake of his head cut the script short.

"Let's just deal." His tone was even but edged with a sarcasm that hinted at a thousand hands he'd played and a million more he wished he hadn't.

She seemed to weigh his words, the corners of her mouth tilting upward in what might have been amusement or understanding—it was hard to tell under the carefully calculated lighting. For a moment, they shared the quiet, two players finding an odd solace amid chaos.

"Silence is golden," she finally said, a private joke shared in a room where fortunes were won and lost in whispers.

"Or at least worth the price of admission." William's wit was as dry as the desert wind that swept through Vegas.

For the first time that night, a genuine laugh escaped her, a sound quickly swallowed by the soft shuffle of cards. And in that fleeting second, William found something akin to peace—not in the game or the stack of chips before him, but in the rare connection that defied the odds in such a place.

The table lights continued to illuminate the felt, the dealers moved with practiced precision, and William sat there, philosopher king of his small, dimly lit domain, contemplating not the economics of markets, but the intricate mathematics of probability and loss.

She shuffled, but William had seen this ritual too many times. He raised a hand, cutting through the smoke-heavy air with a gesture that brokered no argument.

"Listen . . . I'm not here to play. I'm here to watch. To remember why I walked away." His fingers traced the edge of the black chip—the kind reserved for the highest-stakes games, the ones that had almost destroyed him. "I know it's hard to understand. Most people come here looking for action, for the rush. I'm here for the opposite."

She met his gaze, her expression a cocktail of surprise and intrigue. Maybe she understood the weight behind his words, or perhaps she saw the weariness etched in the lines of his weathered face—a roadmap of all the bad bets he wished he could forget.

He extended his hand, the black chip pinched between calloused fingers. "I'll pay for the table, but I just want to sit. To observe. Nothing more."

Her lips parted, ready to offer the usual spiel about minimum bets and table limits, but his slight shake of the head was all it took for the words to die unspoken. She hesitated, then accepted the chip, as if touching it might shatter the fragile understanding they had just established.

The silent transaction spoke volumes more than the soft jazz from hidden speakers could ever hope to convey. William discovered Thoreau in his recovery program, the philosopher's words about simplicity and self-reliance striking a chord deeper than any jackpot ever had. His sponsor had handed him *Walden* after a particularly rough meeting, saying something about finding strength in solitude. William had scoffed at first—what could some long-dead hermit teach him about battling addiction? But here he was, three dog-eared volumes of transcendentalist philosophy later, finding wisdom in the most unlikely places.

In this moment, watching the desperate dance of cards and chips below, he wondered whether Thoreau had ever envisioned his beloved Walden Pond as a high-stakes poker room where one sought enlightenment in the stoic observation of human nature at its most raw and desperate. He couldn't help but appreciate the parallel—Thoreau retreating to the woods to *live deliberately*, while William sat here in this temple of chance, deliberately facing his demons without surrendering to them. Maybe there was something to this whole transcendentalism thing after all. After all, wasn't he practicing his own form of self-reliance by refusing to play, by choosing to watch and learn instead?

"Thank you," he whispered, not certain whether it was gratitude or something else that prompted the courtesy.

The dealer nodded, the chip now tucked away, hidden like the myriad tells that clung to amateur players. She stood, leading the way to a secluded observation area overlooking the high-stakes tables, and William followed, his footsteps echoing softly—a philosopher trailing probability through the labyrinth of what some called gambling, but he knew to be just another facet of human folly, dressed up in green felt and false hopes.

William, with the gait of a man who'd folded one too many winning hands in his past life, followed her; oblivious to his presence, the club buzzed with the soft murmur of bets placed and fortunes scattered below. He thought of Emerson and the friends one must be to have—the irony of seeking enlightenment in a place where everyone was a potential mark wasn't lost on him. But tonight, he would pay his dues to a different kind of economy, one where watching was the only game worth playing.

The dealer—she called herself Lady Luck, he noted her name with sardonic appreciation—positioned him at a private viewing alcove with the assurance of someone who'd seen every trick in the book. No words had been spoken since the exchange of chip and understanding; their contract was wordless, but binding.

From his vantage point, William could observe the dance of cards and chips below, the ritual he once knew so well now viewed through the lens of a recovered addict. His internal monologue waxed sarcastic about the VIP treatment he was receiving. *For the discerning gentleman who prefers his existential crises with a bird's-eye view of other people's bad decisions.*

Lady Luck remained standing nearby, her silhouette outlined against the dim light, a casino Mona Lisa with a smile that held secrets. She looked at him with an expression that bordered on understanding, as if she'd seen others return like this—not to play, but to remind themselves why they stopped.

As he watched the games unfold below, William couldn't help but contemplate his life choices, each one a bet placed on a table of missed opportunities and moral compromises. When the hour was up, the silence lingered, heavy and thick. It coated everything like the residue of stale cigarette smoke. William rose, straightening his jacket as if it were armor against the gambling tables' lure. He glanced at Lady Luck, offering a nod that served as both thanks and farewell.

Sixty Blocks and Counting

A week later, William found himself back on Omaha's campus, worlds away from the seaside cliff mansion and neon-lit temptations of the *High Stakes Social Club*, where probability and luxury intertwined behind heavy velvet drapes. The peaceful rustling of fallen leaves was a stark contrast to those temples of chance, with their shuffling cards and whispered promises. Here, among the red bricks and earnest ivy, William navigated the academic maze, a silent observer in a crowd of voices, finding a different kind of sanctuary in the mundane rhythms of campus life.

His *research* at the club had left him shaken. Even just watching the games, feeling the familiar pull of the cards, had proven more dangerous than he'd expected. The old hunger still lurked beneath his carefully constructed facade of recovery. Sure, he hadn't played—but the desire to do so had twisted in his gut like a living thing.

He sat in the back row of lecture halls, where the scent of chalk dust was heavy, and the presence of women was an intoxicating mystery he never quite solved. They were like puzzles wrapped in enigmas, draped in college sweaters. Their laughter was a melody that seemed tuned to a frequency just beyond his grasp—much like the siren song of the felt tables he'd sworn to resist.

With friends—the few that he had—William could summon a smile, command a joke to mask his discomfort, but alone or face-to-face with a female classmate, his words tangled like earphones in a pocket. He was the king of the non-committal shrug, the master of averting gazes—a philosopher without an audience, quoting Thoreau to empty bleachers.

Most men lead lives of quiet desperation, he'd think, watching a girl's hair cascade down her back as she turned a corner. But William led a life of silent observation, scribbling notes in the margins of his life that no one would read.

Now, as he stood at his own crossroads, those margins and careful observations felt like prologue rather than prophecy. Tonight would be another chapter, one that might finally lead him away from the shadows of his past.

· · · ● · ● · ● · · ·

William's wallet was a barren wasteland, not even a tumbleweed of a receipt rolling through its desolate compartments—a fitting reminder of his past life, where money had been nothing but chips to be wagered and lost. The campus sprawled before him, mocking his poverty with its manicured lawns and students who still harbored the illusion of disposable income.

"Game theory," he said to himself. "Or the art of predicting outcomes in strategic interactions. What's the point if you can't win at the game of life?" The irony stung—an economics major who'd once calculated odds for a living, now unable to balance his own checkbook. With a scoff, he bypassed the classroom where he should've been deciphering Nash equilibriums and, without really knowing why, instead laced up his trusty old Adidas that had seen better days—or at least less cynical ones.

He started running.

His mind churned with thoughts that surfaced the instant his feet hit pavement; the rhythmic pounding of shoes against concrete became a metronome for uncomfortable truths. Each step was an attempt to outpace his recent history of fleshly transactions. The soles of his shoes slapped against the pavement like the regretful claps of a solitary audience member who realizes too late that the performance deserves no encore.

Reaching the edge of campus, William halted, hands on his knees, breathing in fiscal responsibility and exhaling the remnants of last week's poor choices. "Who needs money when you've got oxygen, right?" he wheezed, his internal monologue laced with the kind of sarcasm that could cut steel or, at the very least, his self-pity.

Catching his breath, he set off again. One block down—where echoes of stoic wisdom battled the pulsating memory of neon lights. Another block—where philosophical quotes tried to drown out the bass line of club music that still thrummed in his ears. And another—where Socrates' unexamined life wasn't worth living, but neither was an over-examined bank account.

Keep running, Will. It's cheaper than therapy, and the sweat is just your body crying over your sins.

He smirked, knowing full well that his self-deprecation was as much a part of him as his shadow, which kept pace beside him, never judging, always following.

· · · ● · ● · ● · · ·

William had always found comfort in the blatant lies geography teachers spun about Nebraska. "Flat as a pancake," they used to say; he'd imagine himself atop a comically large stepladder, binoculars in hand, surveying the entire state from east to west in a single panoramic sweep. The thought made him chuckle—a brief, audible scoff—because if those educators ever set foot in Omaha, they'd eat their words.

The concrete beneath him rose in a mocking incline, his legs protesting their new purpose. *Ah, the famed mountains of Omaha.* A wry smile twitched at the corner of his mouth as he felt the burn setting into his calves, a tangible reminder of his all-nighters spent in less athletic pursuits. He felt the gravity of his vices with each upward stride. The morning sun climbed higher, his own shadow shortening ahead of him like regrets receding in the dawn light, yet somehow never quite fading away.

Who knew sin weighed so much?

Maybe I should've taken my philosophy classes here; Plato's 'Allegory of the Hill' or Nietzsche's 'Thus Spoke Zarathustra'—now with more cardio.

Emerson would've hated cardio. Something about 'the sublime and the beautiful' being sufficient exercise.

With each step, he continued his internal monologue, with no one around to appreciate the biting wit. As he crested the top of what felt like the umpteenth hillock—what kind of word is hillock, anyway . . . and why did it suddenly occur to him now?—he paused. It wasn't out of necessity but for dramatic effect, he told himself. Sixty Blocks.

Might as well be sixty miles.

From this vantage point, he surveyed the descent, the cityscape unfurling below, a tapestry woven from threads of urban sprawl and suburban monotony. William's lungs demanded tribute with each gasping breath as he contemplated the return journey—another 60 blocks stretching out before him like a penance. He launched forward, succumbing to the pull of gravity, allowing it to hasten his retreat from the summit of his temporary enlightenment. He recognized the irony; here he was, a man who dissected economic theories and pondered the rationality of human behavior, running as if chased by his own shadow.

Downhill. The direction of my life's ambitions.

Next time I'll find redemption in a place that doesn't fight back quite so hard.

But even as he thought it, he knew the hills weren't really the obstacle—it was the man attempting to run them into submission.

William's breath came in labored bursts, his feet pounding the pavement with a rhythm that was almost hypnotic. Up ahead, a crack in the sidewalk loomed like a challenge from nature herself—a silent sentinel daring him to conquer it or succumb to the obvious trip hazard. He could feel the muscles in his quads tighten with each downhill step, the lactic acid building up like unpaid debts.

Thoreau found solace at Walden Pond. I find mine in the torture of topography.

The descent completed, William turned on his heel, a sharp pivot that sent loose gravel skittering across the sidewalk. With the skyline of the university coming back into view, William quickened his pace. Each step now carried a touch of urgency, a desire to return to the flatlands of theory and contemplation. The journey back to campus had become a reverse pilgrimage through the same streets that had witnessed his struggle against both the tangible slopes and the intangible burdens he carried.

William staggered past the campus entrance, his stride now more of a shuffle. His body was a ledger of debts paid in sweat and soreness, and tomorrow's balance sheet wasn't looking any better. The rest of the day slipped by in a haze of ice packs and silent promises to never run again—a vow that lasted exactly as long as it took for the pain to dull into a memory. As he lay in his bed, the overwhelming quiet became a stark reminder of the noise within him, the restless cacophony that no amount of running could silence.

Tomorrow, I'll face the hills again. But for now, let's call it what it is—an exercise in futility, wrapped in the guise of self-improvement.

With a wry grin, William turned onto his side, allowing the weariness to claim him, knowing full well that surrender was only temporary. The road would be there in the morning, indifferent to his sarcasm and ready to challenge his resolve once more.

He didn't go to another class that day and, because he couldn't walk for the next two days, he skipped those classes as well.

On the third day, when every fiber in William's body screamed mutiny against his brain's draconian regime, he rose from the bed with all the enthusiasm of a man marching to the gallows. The sun hadn't bothered to put in an appearance yet; apparently, it had more sense than him.

He pulled on his Adidas with the care one might take handling live grenades and stepped out into the chill of pre-dawn Omaha, which bit at his exposed skin like a loan shark reminding him of unpaid debts. The streets were deserted, save for the distant rumble of a garbage truck making its rounds—another reminder that the world kept moving, whether or not you could feel your legs.

With each step, his joints offered their own brand of sarcastic applause, popping and creaking in protest. William acknowledged their complaints with a grimace that was almost a smile—if smiles involved more bared teeth and less joy.

Ah, the sweet symphony of self-imposed agony.

The sun had barely dared to peek above the horizon when William was already deep into his masochistic pilgrimage. He ran past the same old landmarks, each one a silent witness to his daily routine. *Sixty blocks of scenic monotony,* he mused, appreciating the irony of seeking solace in repetition when his life already felt like a broken record.

· · · ● · ● · ● · ● · · ·

Day four greeted William with limbs that felt forged from a blend of lead and leftover animosity. Yet, there he was again, lacing up his running shoes as if they were glass slippers, and he was Cinderella off to the ball—or, more accurately, Cinderfella off to indulge in another round of cardio penance. He shut the door behind him with a finality that echoed his resolve.

Glutton for punishment, party of one.

As he hit the pavement, the first rays of daylight cascaded over the quiet neighborhoods, washing them in a deceptive tranquility that belied the turmoil churning within him. Each inhale brought the crisp promise of a new day, each exhale expelled ghosts of yesterday's defeat.

Who needs therapy when you've got 'the agony of de feet'?

William joked to the silent houses that lined his route, but his humor was a thin veneer, barely concealing the truth that with each stride, he was outrunning demons dressed in memories—memories of dark rooms, whispered transactions, and the weight of choices made in desperation.

And so he ran, block by block, up hills and down valleys of asphalt, a lone figure tracing the contours of redemption with each determined step.

The Economics of Escape

There's something about the City of Angels that makes even the most pious feel like they've got a pocketful of quarters and an itch for the slots. But William wasn't here to gamble—at least not like he used to.

He stood backstage at the economics conference, trying to focus on the sound of his own breathing rather than the murmur of the crowd. It had been ten years since he'd last set foot in LA—a decade of cold showers and lacing up running shoes until his feet bled redemption. He was a different man now, or so he told himself.

Running . . . because nothing numbs the sting of life's poor choices like the burn of lactic acid in your calves.

The conference coordinator—a sprightly woman with a clipboard that might as well have been welded to her hand—gave him a curt nod. "You're up, Mr. Featured Speaker."

The auditorium stretched out before him, faces blurring into a tapestry of expectant scholars. A sea of intellect, bobbing on the tide of economic discourse. The parallel hit him with the force of a dealt card; once a purveyor of cards, now a purveyor of thoughts. The currency had changed, but the market . . . maybe not so much.

"Emerson said, *Life is a journey, not a destination,*" William began, the microphone carrying his voice like a secret whispered from ear to ear. "But I'll bet Ralph never had to navigate the freeways of Los Angeles."

A smattering of polite laughter rippled through the audience. Good, they were awake.

"Today, I'm going to talk to you about the economy of desire—the invisible hand that isn't so invisible when it's wrapped around . . ." He paused, grinning as he let the innuendo hang in the air. "Let's say, less traditional commodities."

As he delved into his lecture, each slide click was a familiar pen tapping open-shut, open-shut—a reminder of decisions made, paths taken, and a life that somehow felt both distant and uncomfortably close.

"Transcendentalists believed in the inherent goodness of people and nature," William said, projecting a slide of a serene forest. "Try telling that to someone who's spent too much time in Hollywood."

The audience chuckled again. This was going well. Better than well—it was going great. And yet, beneath the intellectual repartee and academic rigor, there was an itch, a twitch, a memory of neon-lit streets and whispered promises.

"Thankfully," William continued, "we're not trees rooted in place. We move, we change, we grow. Economics, like life, isn't static. It's about the flows, the cycles . . ."

And wasn't that just the truth? A cycle. Ten years clean, and still the city's pulse beat like a siren call in his veins. But this time, William wasn't listening. He had his own rhythm to run to.

· · · ●●· ● ● · · ·

The next morning's sun peeked over the horizon, casting an orange glow on the palm tree-lined streets of Los Angeles as William laced up his running shoes. The city was just starting to wake, the hum of early traffic blending with the distant crash of waves along the Pacific coast. He took a deep breath, the crisp air tinged with the faintest scent of salt and car exhaust, and set off at a steady pace.

Starting from the hotel in downtown LA, he ran by all the popular spots.

Walt Disney Concert Hall, its reflective surfaces catching the first rays of daylight and throwing them back into the sky like a challenge. He smirked, pushing his lean frame harder, moving through the awakening streets with the ease of a shadow.

Echo Park Lake, where the lotus flowers were still closed tight against the chill of dawn. He dodged around early risers walking their dogs and others like him—runners finding solace in the solitude of exertion. As he circled the lake, his reflection kept pace, a silent partner in this dance of determination and endurance.

Griffith Park—at over 4,000 acres, it is one of the largest public parks in the country—and he felt the burn in his calves as he tackled the incline leading up towards the Observatory.

His last stop was Mount Hollywood and the Griffith Observatory, which stands as a sort of sentinel overlooking the sprawling cityscape, offering breathtaking vistas that are particularly stunning as the sun dips below the horizon. This architectural gem, completed in 1935, has become as synonymous with Los Angeles as the Hollywood sign itself, its Art Deco design a testament to the era's aesthetic.

There's more; its significance extends beyond its role as a tourist attraction. During World War II, it served as a crucial training ground for pilots learning the art of celestial navigation. Later, in the 1960s, it played a part in humanity's greatest adventure, preparing astronauts for the Apollo missions that would eventually land men on the moon.

Today, visitors can explore a wealth of cosmic wonders within its walls. The Observatory houses a state-of-the-art planetarium, showcasing the mysteries of our universe. Various exhibitions offer insights into astronomical phenomena, while public telescopes invite stargazers to peer into the depths of space. The Griffith Observatory remains one of Los Angeles' most iconic landmarks.

He ran by the bust of James Dean who famously got in a knife fight here during *Rebel Without a Cause*. He glanced at the Hollywood sign, a white beacon of dreams made and shattered, and wondered if the letters stood for hope or hypocrisy.

Maybe H stands for 'Hypothetically Speaking.'

Runyon Canyon, the trail a mix of dust and determination beneath his feet. The views from the top were Instagram-worthy, but he didn't break stride to snap a picture. Instead, he savored the silent victory of reaching the peak and the luxury of letting gravity assist him on the descent.

Exhausted but energized, William found himself back at the hotel, the sun now fully asserting itself in the sky. He wiped the sweat from his brow, the salt stinging his eyes—or was that something else? A twinge of nostalgia, perhaps?

As the evening sun spilled over the Los Angeles Convention Center, William found himself alone on his hotel balcony, the city sprawled before him like a neon-lit circuit board of temptation. Below, the streets pulsed with life—people flowing from bars to clubs to late-night diners, all chasing their own versions of escape.

· · · ● · ● · · ·

Yesterday's conference presentation had gone well. Too well, perhaps. The rush of commanding the room, seeing recognition in the eyes of his peers—it left him with a familiar hollow feeling afterward. A void that once could only be filled by the green felt and clicking chips.

Ten years. Ten years of sobriety. Ten years of measured breaths and careful choices. Of running until his lungs burned and his legs trembled, anything to outpace the cravings that still lurked in the shadows of his mind.

William's fingers found the business card in his jacket pocket—smooth, expensive stock with embossed lettering. The Palace. A man at the reception had slipped it to him after his talk. *For when the intellectual stimulation isn't enough,* he'd said with a knowing smile.

Ridiculous. Yet he couldn't bring himself to tear the card in half or toss it over the balcony. Instead, he turned it over and over between his fingers, the motion hypnotic, soothing.

His phone sat on the table, innocent and waiting. William stared at it, feeling the weight of ten years pressing down on him. What would one night hurt? Just research for his book. A controlled experiment. He'd write about it, transform the experience into something useful—redemptive, even.

The rationalizations came so easily, slipping into his thoughts like old friends. That's how it always started, wasn't it? Just one hand. Just one night.

His heart quickened, the familiar rush of anticipation flooding his system. This was the true addiction—not the gambling itself, but this moment. The delicious agony of standing on the precipice, knowing he shouldn't jump but feeling the pull of the abyss.

William picked up his phone, his thumb hovering over the screen. Emerson would disapprove. Thoreau would suggest a walk in nature instead.

But tonight, William wasn't listening to the philosophers. Tonight, the old hunger clawed at him, amplified by the isolation of the hotel room and the lingering energy of a day spent performing for others. Tonight, he wanted to feel something real, even if that something was the risk of losing everything he'd built.

He grabbed the phone from the bedside table.

Stoics would say to resist temptation.

But his fingers were already dialing a number he'd sworn to forget. He hesitated. Ten years had passed; ten years of therapy in the form of adrenaline and asphalt. Yet here he was, the city's magnetic allure drawing him back to the edge of a precipice he'd sworn he'd never revisit.

Ah, hell . . . the words escaped him as he pressed 'call,' surrendering to the undertow of old habits.

"The Palace," a clipped voice answered.

"Where's the game tonight?" William asked, his voice rough with unspoken apologies and a decade's worth of restraint unraveling.

The response was brief—just an address and a time. No questions asked. In this world, anonymity was currency.

William stood there, alone with the weight of his decision and the echo of his own heartbeat. It was a rhythm he couldn't run from—not today.

• • • ● ● • ● • • •

The door shut, its click sharp in the quiet room. Her presence was a stark contrast to the musty air—a fresh current in a sea of lethargy. She moved like she owned the place, which, given her purpose here, wasn't far off the mark. William didn't turn to greet her; he remained a silhouette against the cityscape, his form outlined by the neon glow that never seemed to sleep.

"I'm here to collect, William." Her voice was assertive yet smooth, an auditory nudge.

"Over here." His tone was as warm as the view was cold.

She navigated through the semi-darkness, her footsteps muffled on the well-trodden carpet. William finally turned from the window, allowing the city to carry on without his watchful gaze. There was no mistaking the redness around his eyes—a testament to internal battles rather than external elements.

"I shouldn't have gone back to the tables," he said, sounding more like he was admitting to raiding the cookie jar than losing thousands at poker. "I don't know what I was thinking."

"Probably the same thing everyone thinks in this city: *It seemed like a good idea at the time*," she said, although debt collection rarely included passing judgment.

"Maybe," he replied, with a faint chuckle that held as much regret as humor. "Or maybe I was trying to outpace my own shadow. Turns out it's got a hell of a sprint."

"Shadows tend to keep up," she said, allowing a hint of playfulness into her voice. "But if you're looking for someone to run interference with the house, you've got the wrong kind of company."

"Story of my life," he sighed, the truth hitting harder than any punchline.

William sank into the chair by the window, the leather creaking under his weight like the sigh of a weary confidant. He glanced at Darby, her tall silhouette a svelte question mark against the humdrum backdrop of the hotel room's faded wallpaper.

"Where do I even start?" He ran a hand over his bald head as if to summon memories from the polished surface. "The beginning is cliché, and the middle is a melodrama . . . could this be the end, I wonder?

"The end? Really? Let me hear it." She crossed her arms, her posture radiating an aura that was equal parts enforcer and therapist.

"Picture this: A young man, convinced that the road to nirvana was paved with green felt and lucky streaks. That was me," William said, the sound bitter as a bad beat. "I thought I was mastering probability, but really, I was just excavating my own grave."

"Sounds less like mastery and more like mayhem," Darby interjected, her tone laced with the kind of sarcasm that could slice through steel.

"Mayhem, mathematics . . . tomato, tom-ah-to." William shrugged, a ghost of a smile flickering across his lips. "All I found at the end of that rainbow was a stack of markers and a heap of regret."

"Rainbows are overrated. Especially in LA. Here, they're just smog halos."

"True enough. But I managed to claw my way out of that pit. Started running—not away from anything, but towards something better. Wrote a book. A real page-turner for the insomniacs."

"Let me guess, the tale of a fallen gambler, rising from the ashes. How very Phoenix of you."

"More like a bald eagle, all scrawny and squawking." William's eyes twinkled with self-deprecation as he locked gazes with her. "Thanks to running and a generous helping of stoicism, I've been clean for a decade. Until tonight."

"Stoicism? Let me guess, *with a dash of Seneca and a sprinkle of Epictetus?*"

"Ha! You've got me pegged. But the irony isn't lost on me. Here I am, in Las Vegas West, calling for markers. And for what? To relive my mistakes?"

"Or to remind yourself why you made them in the first place," she said, tilting her head as if pondering the enigma before her. "Sometimes, we need to dance with our demons to appreciate the angels."

"Could be, but ten years clean . . . I thought I had it licked. But I called the house, and here you are." William sighed, his gaze drifting back to the window where the city lights flickered like false beacons. "This is the lowest I've been, my last bet. One final hand against my own greed."

"Then consider this your wake-up call. One with questionable timing, but it'll get you out of the game. And you made it ten years."

"Yes, I suppose."

"You've done the hard part, you can do the rest—"

"I probably can . . ."

"—and I won't let you fail now. I just won't."

"Thank you, Darby, for everything," William said, the words heavy with a gratitude that felt like an anchor in his chest.

As she walked to the door, Darby's heels clicked a staccato rhythm on the hotel room's hardwood floor, each step a deliberate echo in the charged silence. She felt William's gaze—it was tangible, a weight pressing against her spine, tracking her progress like a spotlight she neither craved nor could escape.

At the door, she paused—a statue carved from the evening's confessions and unpaid markers. Darby turned, her movements slow, as if underwater, and found his eyes still on her. Those windows to a soul that had seen too many bad beats were clouded with complexities she couldn't decipher.

Her lips curled into a wisp of a smile, one that carried this shared experience, a brief flicker of camaraderie in a world that had too often been cruel. The moment hung between them, fragile as a poker chip balanced on its edge, shimmering with the residue of words left unsaid and bets not taken.

Darby's fingertips brushed the cool metal of the knob, a lingering touch as though bidding farewell to more than just a room. The click of the door latch sang a soft requiem to the intimacy of shared truths and vulnerability.

"Goodbye, William," she said, her voice a murmur lost in the cavernous space between them.

Runner's Justice

William's lanky silhouette, a stark contrast against the golden hues of the setting sun, cut through the throng of eager runners with the grace of an antelope that had somehow wandered into a herd of buffalo. Each step he took was measured, his lean muscles honed from countless miles of pounding pavement and trails alike.

The Tuesday evening run was the highlight of his otherwise regimented week—a chance to escape the suburban fortress he had built around himself, keeping the sirens of his past at bay. Because Tuesday nights at the running club meant a speed workout. Though it had never been his favorite type of training—he preferred long, slow runs and even weight training to speed days—it was the one running modality that made the biggest difference in his race results.

As he arrived at the night's session, he noticed a new runner. Her dark brown eyes were alert and intelligent, scanning the crowd as she approached the other runners. She moved with quiet confidence, dressed in form-fitting black running tights and a breathable neon yellow tank top. Her long, straight black hair was pulled back in a high ponytail, secured with a bright blue elastic band. As the track session was about to begin, her movements became infused with a frantic energy. She fumbled with her GPS watch, her fingers trembling slightly as she tried to set her desired pace and distance for the upcoming run. She hunched over, brow furrowed, poking at the device with slender fingers, trying in vain to make it submit to her will.

"Excuse me," he William said as he approached, his voice carrying the gruff timbre of a man accustomed to solitude, "can I help? These gadgets can be more temperamental than a philosopher on a bad day." With the practiced ease of a seasoned con man, the words tumbled from his lips, a smooth cascade.

"Lexi," she said with a slight accent, glancing up from her battle with the fancy new watch. "Well, Wang Mei, actually. But everyone calls me Lexi." Her name, Americanized, hung in the air—another subtle heist, identity snatched and replaced with something more palatable to Western tongues.

Many Chinese women, especially those living in Western countries or interacting frequently with Western cultures, adopt Americanized or Western names. This is especially common with Chinese students studying abroad and professionals working in international environments. Why? Pronunciation. Blending in. Professional and educational advantages. Personal choice. Not all Chinese individuals do this, of course. Many proudly use their Chinese names in all settings. But Lexi chose Lexi.

"William." He extended a hand not just in greeting, but as an olive branch from one runner seeking connection with another. He took the watch, fingers deftly dancing across buttons, changing the settings to improve communication with the GPS satellites.

"Running is the simplest sport, until you add satellites and sensors," he said. "Next thing you know, you'll need a degree in astrophysics just to log a 5K."

Obedient at last, the watch sprang to life with a beep and a green blink. Lexi's face brightened as William handed back the timepiece, his stoic facade cracking just enough to let a sliver of camaraderie shine through.

As the runners began stretching and chatting to prepare for the run, William felt an unfamiliar warmth bubble within him. It wasn't the flush of pre-run anticipation, but the glow of having reached out, bridging the gap between isolation and intimacy, if only for a moment.

· · · ●· ● ▮ · · ·

The crisp, early autumnal air was a welcome companion to William's stride as he paced alongside Lexi, the rhythm of their footfalls a metronome to his racing thoughts. Their running partnership began a month before during a running club speed workout and grew from there. What started as occasional training runs soon became a thrice-weekly ritual, their conversations evolving from breathless small talk to deeper discussions about life, ambitions, and the challenges she faced at school. As they rounded the bend on the trail, the skeletal trees stood sentinel, their leaves a mosaic of decay that crunched underfoot—a fitting soundtrack for the plot taking shape in his mind.

Over several weeks, William noticed changes in Lexi's behavior during their running club sessions. Her usual enthusiasm waned, replaced by a nervous energy. Her running gait, always a little different—why was that?—became even more awkward. Dark circles appeared under her eyes. She often arrived late, her eyes darted around as if looking for someone. Her performance suffered, and she'd fall behind during runs, lost in thought.

One day, William casually asked how her classes were going. Lexi's response was evasive, her smile forced. "Oh, you know, the usual," she said, quickly changing the subject.

The next week, Lexi's distress became more apparent. As the stretching subsided and the collective pace and pulse of the running club quickened, William noticed Lexi lingering on the outskirts, her body shadowed by a cloud of unease. He sidled up beside her, his long strides slowing to match her hesitant gait. During a particularly grueling hill workout, she lagged behind, clearly struggling.

William slowed his pace to run beside her. "Everything okay, Lexi?" he asked gently.

Lexi's eyes welled with tears, but she blinked them back. "I'm fine," she said, but her voice cracked.

He left it at that as they finished their run, but afterwards, as other members dispersed, William noticed Lexi lingering, reluctant to leave. He approached her cautiously. "Lexi, if you want to talk, I'm here to listen."

Lexi hesitated, then seemed to crumble inward like a house of cards caught in a draft. "It's not the running," she began, voice barely above the whisper of rubber soles on pavement. "It's my professor—he . . . can we go somewhere private?"

They walked to a quiet corner of the park. Lexi sat on a bench, her hands fidgeting in her lap. William waited patiently, giving her space to gather her thoughts.

"It's . . . it's about my Applied Multivariate Analysis professor, Dr. Scofield. John Scofield," Lexi began, her voice barely above a whisper. She paused, struggling to continue.

William nodded encouragingly, his concern growing.

Slowly, haltingly, Lexi began to share her story, revealing the professor's inappropriate behavior and escalating demands.

Sexual demands.

As she spoke, her composure crumbled, and the full weight of her distress became apparent. "He was more than some professor. He was a mentor. He was someone I trusted. I thought he was looking out for me."

William listened, an internal switch flipping as he tuned into her frequency—an empathetic ear amidst the cacophony of footfalls and breaths. He'd heard such confessions before; the sordid tales that accompanied late-night whispers and tear-streaked faces. It was a familiar darkness, one he'd grappled with in others and himself, etched across pages both literal and metaphorical.

"That's a heavy burden for such a light runner," he said, his own experiences fueling a deep-seated loathing for coercion.

She looked at him, uncertainty etched in the furrow of her brow, searching his face for signs of judgment or disbelief. What she found instead was the steady assurance of someone who had walked through fire and emerged not unscathed, but understanding.

"I believe you," William said, his words slicing through the ambient noise, affirming her truth in a world too often inclined to dismiss it.

"Lexi, it's so hard for me to imagine that intellect and power could be used for anything less noble than personal gain. The universe sure has a twisted sense of humor at times. It grants wisdom to some and leaves others to run laps in moral mediocrity." The sarcasm laced through his comment was as biting as the wind against their skin, a humor that belied the gravity of his intent.

In the space between them, an unspoken promise of action took shape. William knew this path well; it was littered with obstacles, each demanding a toll. But unlike the runs he often spoke of, this was not a race against time, but a stand against injustice—one he would not take lightly.

Lexi got up, and they began walking along the paved bike trail. They talked for nearly two hours. She was the only daughter, born in one of China's hutong, *Jiuwan*.

Though much less common now, hutong date back to the Yuan dynasty of the late 1200s. These narrow streets or alleys were most often seen in northern Chinese cities, especially Beijing. Each hutong residence is linked to another; this weaving of the streets and courtyards results in frequent gossiping and informal communication among locals, fostering a connection and a bond that is deep and warm.

"I remember riding on the front of my dad's bike or the back of my mom's to and from school."

Lexi's home, with its twisty lanes and varied shops, was *Jiuwan* hutong—meaning nine curve road—was in southern Beijing, about half a mile from Tiananmen Square.

"After I moved to the US for university, my parents moved to a high-rise in central Beijing. When I visit, it doesn't have the same feel as home, but it is nice."

After earning an undergraduate degree at Cal-Berkely, she came to the university in Omaha to pursue a PhD in Biomedical Informatics.

This wasn't her first exposure to sexual coercion and harassment.

"When I was eight, I began training at the Chinese Gymnastics National Training Center in Beijing. The abuse you've heard described is real. I experienced that, too. But there was more. Three coaches, at different times, assaulted me. I was 10 years old, and I experienced pure terror. During one of my weekend visits with my parents, I told them. I was one of the lucky ones; my parents cared. Though it meant the loss of a monthly stipend, they removed me from the Center and I moved back home.

"We couldn't really do anything about it, but at least I was safe. I felt loved.

"The Midwest is quite different from Beijing and from Berkely. But I have grown to love it. I thought people were nicer here . . . that I had escaped all that. Guess not."

William was quiet during their visit and shared with her some of his own history. Of gambling addiction. Of wanting to help. As he listened to Lexi's story, a familiar fire began to burn in his chest—the same righteous anger that had fueled his own recovery and transformation. Here: An abuser, hidden behind authority and power, saw himself as untouchable, just like many others. William knew all too well how such men operated, and more importantly, how they could be brought down.

"Lexi, can we meet next week to discuss this further? I want to look into some things to see if we can find a way to help you and end this, this, this . . . predatory behavior."

As the semester was winding down, William decided it was time for action. Determination hardened his tone, dispelling the chill.

"Bring anything you have . . . emails, messages, anything that might shine a light on the darkness of Dr. Scofield's actions," he continued, each word measured and deliberate. The suggestion hung between them, an invisible thread weaving the fabric of their alliance.

"Documentation is our ally," he added, his tone carrying the weight of someone who had learned the hard way that truth alone was seldom enough. The shadows stretched long across the path as the sun sank lower, mirroring the shadowy nature of their undertaking.

"Like Thoreau once mused about the price of anything being the amount of life you exchange for it," William said, his philosophical leanings surfacing like a reflex. "And I assure you, this man will pay dearly for the lives he's tried to bargain with."

His wit, dry as the fallen leaves, was not lost on Lexi, who managed a small smile despite the gravity of their conversation. William's assurance was a cloak she wrapped around herself, a shield against the vulnerability that threatened to seep through her resolve.

"We'll pen this plan with precision," William said, almost cheerfully sardonic at the thought of engineering the professor's downfall. "After all, revenge, much like economics, is all about proper allocation of resources."

Their eyes met, and in that moment, there was a silent understanding that they were not just running side by side on a trail but towards a shared goal—justice.

• • • ● • ● ● • • •

The morning sun spilled through the blinds of a coffee shop a mile from the bike trail, casting striped shadows over the linoleum floor. It was the kind of place where the barista knew your order by heart and the pastries were always suspiciously fresh—as if they'd brokered a deal with the dawn itself.

Settled into a corner booth, William's form was almost camouflaged against the faux-leather seat, his lean frame and bald head reflecting the light like a lighthouse beacon for the morally righteous. A steaming mug of black coffee sat in front of him, untouched, its bitter scent mingling with the sweet aroma of baked goods—a sensory contradiction not unlike the situation at hand.

Lexi arrived, her presence a stark contrast to the retirees and freelancers that populated the cafe. She slid into the booth opposite William, her eyes scanning for eavesdroppers. There was a delicate air about her that belied the steel in her spine, a juxtaposition William silently applauded.

"Confrontation is both an art and a science," William began, his voice low enough to blend with the hum of idle conversation around them. "An art in gauging human reaction, a science in precision timing and irrefutable evidence."

Lexi nodded, absorbing his words as she toyed with the paper napkin in front of her. He admired her resolve, even as he felt the tug of responsibility for the plan they were crafting.

"It's like chess. We're setting up the board, and our dear Dr. Scofield will soon find himself in check—with nowhere to move but straight into a resignation letter."

He laid out the potential fallouts with seasoned precision: the precarious balance of power within academia, the ripple effects on the professor's career, and the inevitable scrutiny they would both endure.

"Retaliation is a possibility," William warned, his gaze steady on Lexi's. "But fear not; every philosopher from Zeno to Aurelius has faced adversaries. We'll simply be joining a long line of stoic warriors."

As they spoke, William was aware of the irony at play. Here he was, a man who'd spent years in the throes of vice, now plotting the downfall of another's indiscretions. But redemption was a funny thing—it could turn a life of running away into one of running towards something greater.

They rose from the table, their plan etched in hushed tones and determined nods. William felt the familiar rush of adrenaline, the kind that used to accompany his more sordid exploits. Only this time, the stakes weren't just personal—they were principled.

As Lexi stepped out into the sunlight, William lingered for a moment, watching her go. He turned back to his coffee, finally taking a sip, the bold flavor a fitting endnote to their clandestine meeting. The taste was strong, unsweetened . . . and perfect.

• • • ● • ● • • • •

As William headed home, his mind was still spinning with plans to help Lexi. When he walked in, he flipped open his laptop and went to a news site for some background noise. A TechTruth live stream just started; he turned up the volume, momentarily distracted from Lexi's situation by a fascinating, disheartening story.

INVESTIGATIVE REPORT: America's Healthcare Crisis

TechTruth News with Anie Chen

Transcript from broadcast

[Theme music—serious, journalistic opening]

ANIE: Good evening. I'm Anie Chen, and tonight on TechTruth Investigative, we're examining the troubling trend of corporate takeovers in America's healthcare system.

Across the country, community hospitals that have served their neighborhoods for generations are closing their doors or being absorbed by massive healthcare conglomerates. The consequences for patients and healthcare workers have been devastating.

LUCAS: Over the past decade, more than 120 rural hospitals have closed nationwide, leaving vast regions without emergency care. Medicare reimbursement rates have fallen by nearly 20% in inflation-adjusted dollars, pushing many independent facilities to the brink of financial collapse.

ANIE: And waiting in the wings? For-profit healthcare systems like Coastal Beacon Health, or CBHS, are ready to swoop in and "rescue" these struggling institutions.

LUCAS: [sardonic] Their version of rescue might need rescuing itself.

ANIE: We spoke with Dr. Margaret Wilson, former Chief of Medicine at Lincoln Memorial Hospital in Ohio, which was acquired by CBHS three years ago.

DR. WILSON: Before the acquisition, we were struggling financially, but patient care always came first. Now? We're understaffed, equipment repairs are delayed for months, and critical medications are often unavailable because bills haven't been paid.

ANIE: Dr. Wilson isn't alone. We've spoken with healthcare workers at twelve former community hospitals now owned by CBHS.

NURSE RODRIGUEZ (identity obscured): They cut our staffing to the bone. I'm responsible for twice as many patients as before. Some nights, I don't even have time to check on my most stable patients. I'm terrified something will happen to them.

LUCAS: Internal documents obtained by TechTruth reveal that after CBHS acquires a hospital, staffing is typically reduced by 30% within the first year, while executive bonuses increase proportionally with every "efficiency improvement."

ANIE: We reached out to CBHS CEO Vincent Blackwell for comment. His office provided this statement:

STATEMENT (read by ANIE): "CBHS is proud of our record of salvaging struggling healthcare facilities. Our efficiency measures ensure these institutions can continue serving their communities rather than closing entirely. The healthcare industry faces unprecedented challenges, and difficult decisions must sometimes be made."

LUCAS: Those "difficult decisions" have real consequences. In Lakeside, Michigan, 82-year-old Harold Jenkins suffered a heart attack just weeks after CBHS closed the cardiac unit at his local hospital.

JENKINS' DAUGHTER: Dad had to be transported 67 miles to the nearest cardiac facility. The doctor said those extra minutes made the difference between recovery and permanent damage. Now he needs full-time care.

ANIE: Financial records show that in the same month Lakeside's cardiac unit was shuttered, CBHS approved the purchase of a second private jet for executive use.

HEALTHCARE ANALYST: What we're seeing is a fundamental tension between the mission of healthcare—to heal and protect patients—and the profit motive of these corporations. When hospitals become investment vehicles, patient outcomes often suffer.

LUCAS: The crisis extends beyond rural America. Even in major metropolitan areas, hospital consolidation has led to higher prices and reduced access to specialized care for vulnerable populations.

ANIE: Dr. James Beard of the Healthcare Policy Institute explains:

DR. JAMES BEARD: When a single corporation controls all the hospitals in a region, they can effectively set whatever prices they want. Insurance companies have no choice but to pay, and those costs get passed on to consumers through higher premiums and reduced coverage.

LUCAS: And patients aren't the only ones suffering. Healthcare workers report deteriorating conditions across the board.

ANONYMOUS PHYSICIAN: They monitor how many minutes we spend with each patient. There's literally a stopwatch running. If I take too long with someone who needs extra attention, I get called into a meeting about my "efficiency metrics."

ANIE: Meanwhile, CBHS reported record profits last quarter, with CEO Vincent Blackwell receiving compensation of $27 million—a 40% increase from the previous year.

LUCAS: The company has announced plans to acquire an additional fifteen community hospitals in the coming fiscal year.

ANIE: As America's healthcare system continues its transformation from community service to corporate asset, the fundamental question remains: Who benefits from this new model of care? And at what cost?

For TechTruth Investigative, I'm Anie Chen.

[Theme music fades out]

The Perils of Hubris

William closed the laptop, the troubling healthcare report lingering in his thoughts. Another system failing those it was meant to protect—just like the university's handling of Lexi's situation. The parallel wasn't lost on him. But one battle at a time. Right now, Lexi needed his help, and Dr. Scofield needed to be stopped.

· · · ● ●· ● ● · · ·

A brisk wind, carrying the scent of a recent thunderstorm, nipped at William's skin as he stepped out, a welcome contrast to the stuffy, musty air of his office. He had chosen their meeting point with care, a quiet corner of the university's library café. It was public enough to deter any outbursts yet sufficiently private for a conversation that required discretion.

He had reached out to Lexi's (tor)mentor and used the idea of multi-center research collaboration as bait. Publishing and securing funding was on nearly every professor's mind. What do they say?

Publish or perish?

No money, no mission?

Scofield went for the bait.

William arrived early, grabbing a table with a view of the door and ordering a black coffee—no sugar, no cream, much like the truth he intended to serve. His fingers drummed lightly on the table, the only outward sign of his agitation. To any casual observer, he appeared to be just another professor preoccupied with his thoughts, perhaps contemplating the economic theories he often lectured about.

At precisely 3:15 p.m., Dr. Scofield arrived, a man whose academic prowess was only eclipsed by the rumors of his moral bankruptcy. With a nod that bordered on cordial and a smile that didn't quite reach his eyes, William gestured to the seat across from him.

"Thank you for meeting me, John," William began, his voice measured. "I trust you've found the semester invigorating, if not exhausting?"

"No doubt," the professor replied, easing into the chair with a confidence soon to be tested. "Always exciting to shape young minds, but I'd be lying if I said that part of me doesn't look forward to our semester breaks."

"Speaking of shaping young minds," William interjected smoothly, "it appears there's been some overzealous . . . mentoring going on." The words hung in the air, a velvet glove masking the iron fist beneath.

"John, I'm here to discuss your inappropriate relationship with one of your students," William said, his tone firm yet devoid of malice. The statement landed with the weight of inevitability, and the blood drained from the other man's face as if he'd witnessed the ghost of his career passing before his eyes.

A silence descended upon them, punctuated only by the distant hum of student life outside the café. In that moment, William watched the play of emotions over the professor's features—a silent symphony of guilt, fear, and the dawning realization of consequences.

Ah, the perils of hubris, William thought, quoting Thoreau—*There are a thousand hacking at the branches of evil to one who is striking at the root.* Today, he would be that one, and there would be no ivied walls or pretentious titles to hide behind.

William unfolded a crisp sheet of paper, the edges sharp enough to draw blood—a fitting metaphor for the cutthroat truth it bore. He laid it on the table between them, his movements deliberate, like a chess grandmaster positioning his queen for the inevitable checkmate.

"Let's talk specifics," he began, his voice as steady as a metronome in a silent room. "April 3rd, 10:23 PM. A message sent, shall we say, *encouraging* personal engagement beyond the academic purview." Dr. Scofield tried to maintain an air of nonchalance, but William could see the facade crumbling like the walls of Jericho at the sound of trumpets.

"May 15th," William continued, tapping a finger on the date as if punctuating the gravity of the moment, "a *study session* that lasted well into the night. Odd, considering the library's documented closing hours."

He leaned back, allowing the silence to swell and fill the space with its accusatory tone. "I have testimonies from multiple students," William pressed on, each word wrapped in the velvet of concern but laced with the steel of resolve. "Their experiences weave a troubling pattern, John. And this," he gestured to the innocuous smartphone lying dormant on the table, "this is Pandora's box—its contents equally damning."

The professor's eyes flicked toward the device, anxiety etching lines upon his previously smug visage. William resisted the urge to smirk; after all, there was no joy in witnessing a man meet his downfall—only the somber satisfaction of justice being served à la carte.

"Corroborating accounts," William added, almost as an afterthought, though they both knew it was the nail in the proverbial coffin, "are funny things. Like breadcrumbs leading back to the gingerbread house. And, like Hansel and Gretel's story, the witch won't fare so well here, either."

He let the words hang, a pregnant pause following suit, its due date immediate and uncompromising. The professor opened his mouth, perhaps to protest or plead, but William raised a hand, halting any semblance of defense before it could take root.

"Save it. The time for excuses has passed, much like the age of discretion you seemingly skipped."

There was no need for further speech; the documents and digital missives spoke volumes more than any soliloquy could. William watched the professor absorb the reality of the situation, his own internal monologue reciting Marcus Aurelius: *The best revenge is to be unlike him who performed the injustice.*

And in the quiet battle waged across that table, with evidence as his sword and integrity as his shield, William had become the embodiment of that philosophy.

Dr. Scofield's mouth clamped shut as if his lips were auditioning for a role in the *Zipper Olympics*. The man was clearly gearing up to launch into a well-rehearsed monologue of innocence, probably with dramatic pauses for effect and all the sincerity of a cardboard cutout. But William didn't give him the opening.

"Forty-eight hours," William said, his voice devoid of any trace of the warmth he reserved for his running anecdotes. The professor's eyes widened slightly—a silent acknowledgment that his academic tenure was sprinting towards a cliff. "Resign your position, citing personal reasons. I'd suggest perhaps a sudden passion for Tibetan throat singing or competitive dog grooming—anything vague and unverifiable."

William continued, unfazed by the attempted interruptions that died before reaching the air. "And let me be perfectly clear," he said, leaning forward just enough to watch the reflection of fear dance across the professor's pupils. "If I so much as catch wind of another student squirming under your lecherous gaze, not even Carl Lewis could outpace how fast I'll act."

William sat back in his chair, feeling an odd kinship with the GPS watches he often tinkered with; he'd just recalibrated the professor's moral compass, whether he liked it or not. For a man who'd built his life on exploiting the desires of others, the shift to becoming their champion felt like a bizarre, jarring discord, a dissonance that echoed in the heavy silence of his new resolve.

"Consider this your starting gun," William said, a wry smile briefly breaking through as he imagined the professor on a starting block, poised for the race of his life. "I would say *may the best man win*, but we both know that ship has sailed—and I'm pretty sure you're not on it."

William stood, feeling the familiar rush of endorphins he usually experienced at mile five. There was no physical exertion here, but the thrill of the chase—the hunt for justice—was its own kind of high. And as he exited, leaving the professor to digest the ultimatum, William couldn't help but think that this was one finish line he wouldn't mind crossing first.

The moment carried poetic weight; a formerly impulsive man now steered others from the brink he once frequented. As William turned to leave, he couldn't resist one last jab, a wink at his former self.

"Remember, it's not just the swift who win the race, but the vigilant. And, Professor, when it comes to vigilance, I could give a night watchman a run for his money." With that, William exited stage left, his mind already racing ahead to the next scene in this play of justice.

· · · ●· ● ● ·· ·

In the shade of an American linden tree, William watched Lexi cross the finish line of her latest 10K race—a very underappreciated racing distance wedged between the popular 5K and half marathon distances. There was an undeniable spring in her step, one that spoke louder than any victory chant could. She lifted her arms triumphantly and for a moment, as the sun broke through the leaves, it seemed like she was running beneath a spotlight designed just for her.

"Looking at you now, no one would guess there was ever a storm cloud above your head," William said when Lexi approached, her face glistening, not just with sweat, but with the glow of newfound emancipation.

"Thanks to you," she replied, her gratitude washing over him like the first warm shower after a long run in the cold. "You didn't just believe me; you acted. You ran the extra mile when others wouldn't even tie their laces."

William gave a half-smile, his lips twisting in wry amusement. "Well, I'm more of a marathon man myself. Sprints are too much like fleeting pleasures—intense and over before you know it. I prefer the enduring satisfaction of a long-distance win."

He looked away from her, his gaze landing on the horizon where the sky met the urban sprawl of Omaha's suburbs. He'd found a peculiar comfort here, away from the tantalizing neon lights of downtown life. The suburbs were his monastery, and economics, his scripture.

His new home here, chosen for its lack of urban temptations, was as bland as unsalted popcorn, but it was safe. Yet safety often flirted dangerously close to boredom, prompting William to consider his recent victory with Lexi's scourge. Was there something to this?

"By the way," Lexi said, holding out her GPS watch to him, "I think this thing is finally in sync with my pace, all thanks to your initial calibration."

"Ah, the wonders of modern technology," William replied, taking the watch and pretending to inspect it. "Ensuring that every step of our journey is monitored and quantified. It's the perfect metaphor for life, isn't it? We keep chasing the satellites, hoping they'll validate our existence."

"Is that what we're doing?"

He handed her watch back.

"Perhaps. Or maybe we're just trying to ensure we don't get lost on the way to the finish line."

William turned his attention back to the dispersing crowd, each runner basking in the afterglow of their morning exertion. This was his new tribe—the Omaha Running Club—a band of weekend warriors battling against nothing more than their own limitations.

"Remember," he said, locking eyes with Lexi, "the power you reclaimed today isn't just for crossing finish lines. It's for starting new races, too. Ones where you set the pace."

"Thank you, William." Her voice held a muted strength. "For everything."

As she walked away, mingling with the other runners, William allowed himself a rare moment of self-congratulation. He had crossed many finish lines, written chapters of his life that were both sordid and sublime, and yet none felt as significant as this.

"Sometimes the longest journey begins with the shortest stride," he said aloud, recalling a line from his book—a tome of confessions and lessons learned. In helping Lexi, he had taken more than a stride; he had leaped forward, closing the gap between his past and present.

"Emerson said, *To be great is to be misunderstood*," William whispered to the trees. "But perhaps *to be good* is simply to understand."

As laughter and chatter filled the surrounding air, he started walking towards the parking lot, feeling a different runner's high—one born from the knowledge that today, he had been part of a different race, one where the stakes were human dignity and justice.

As he drove away, the sun dipped below the horizon, painting the sky with streaks of orange and pink—nature's own flamboyant bow after a well-performed act. And William, ever the reluctant protagonist in his own story, couldn't help but take a bow, too. He couldn't help but think that for a recovering addict who once lived only for the next high, he had found a far more potent drug: the art of being truly, profoundly useful.

Mr. Johnson's Hat

The arrival of summer in William's suburban neighborhood brought with it the rumble of a moving truck and the promise of change. As the vehicle lumbered down the street, neighbors peered from behind curtains, curiosity piqued by the prospect of new faces in their midst.

William, ever the observer, leaned against his white picket fence, watching the drama unfold across the street. Amidst the chaos of boxes and furniture emerged a small figure that caught his eye—a young girl, no more than eight years old, with dark, searching eyes that seemed to absorb every detail of her new surroundings.

"Ella," he heard her mother call, "come help with this box, please."

The girl—Ella—moved with a reluctance that spoke volumes. Her body language screamed of someone uprooted, transplanted against her will into foreign soil. William felt a pang of empathy, remembering his own struggles with change and adaptation.

Days passed, and William's curiosity grew. He'd see Ella sitting on her front porch, nose buried in a book or fiddling with what looked like a small computer. She seemed a solitary figure, an island unto herself in a sea of suburban conformity.

One sunny morning, as William returned from his daily run, he spotted Ella attempting to dribble a soccer ball on her driveway. Her frustration was obvious as the ball repeatedly escaped her control. Without thinking, he jogged over.

"Need a pointer or two?" he called out, his voice friendly but not overly familiar.

Ella looked up, her gaze wary but curious. "Depends," she replied, her tone matching his own. "Are you some sort of soccer savant?"

William chuckled, caught off guard by her quick wit. "I'm more of a runner, to be honest. But I've kicked a ball around in my day."

What followed was an impromptu soccer lesson, punctuated by banter that grew more comfortable as the morning wore on. William found himself impressed by Ella's sharp mind and dry humor, a refreshing change from the often-mundane conversations of suburban life.

· · · · ● · ● · · ·

Later that afternoon, as William watered his lawn, Ella's father approached, his expression a mix of gratitude and parental concern.

"I'm Jim," he said, extending his hand. "Ella's dad. I saw you helping her with soccer earlier."

William shook his hand firmly. "William. And it was my pleasure. She's got quite the sharp wit for an eight-year-old."

Jim chuckled, though a shadow crossed his face. "That she does. Look, I wanted to thank you. The move's been tough on her. She didn't want to leave her friends, her school . . . her whole life, really. My company's transfer was sudden, and while it's a great opportunity . . ." He trailed off, running a hand through his hair.

"Change is hard at any age. But especially when you're young and don't have a say in it."

"Exactly. And Ella, well, she processes things differently than most kids. Books, computers, always thinking, always analyzing. Sometimes I worry she thinks too much."

William nodded, understanding blooming. "Well, she's welcome to come kick the soccer ball around anytime. Sometimes physical activity helps quiet the mind."

"I'd appreciate that," Jim said, relief clear in his voice. "Just . . . she's my little girl, you know?"

William smiled. "Jim, you've got quite a daughter there. Smart as a whip and not afraid to tell me when my soccer tips are completely wrong."

• • • ● • ● • ● • •

As days turned into weeks, a routine began to form. William, free from teaching duties for the summer, found himself spending more and more time with Ella. Their soccer sessions became a regular occurrence, evolving from simple passing drills to complex maneuvers that left them both breathless and laughing.

Cupcake outings became another staple of their growing friendship. They'd walk to the local bakery, debating the merits of various flavors with the seriousness of food critics. Ella insisted on trying a new flavor each time, her choices growing more adventurous with each visit.

"*Cookies & Cream of the Crop* today," she'd announce, her eyes sparkling with mischief. "I read it's good for contemplation."

"Ah," William would reply, stroking his chin in mock seriousness. "And here I thought *red velvet* was the flavor of deep thinkers."

Their bike rides through the neighborhood were perhaps William's favorite activity. They'd set out in the cool of the evening, Ella on her fire-engine red bike and William on his more subdued blue mountain bike. As they pedaled, they'd trade observations about the world around them, their conversations ranging from the mundane to the philosophical.

"Why do you think Mr. Johnson always wears that hat?" Ella would ask, nodding towards a neighbor tending his garden.

"Perhaps it's his armor against the judgment of the world. Or maybe he's hiding a really bad haircut."

Ella's laughter, bright and uninhibited, would ring out, a sound that never failed to bring a smile to William's face.

As the summer progressed, William found himself reflecting on the unexpected turn his life had taken. At 40, he'd thought he had a clear picture of who he was and what his life entailed. But Ella's presence had shifted something within him. In her, he saw not just a child in need of guidance, but a kindred spirit—someone who challenged him, made him think, and reminded him of the joy of discovery.

Their friendship, always appropriate yet deeply meaningful, gave William a sense of purpose he hadn't realized he'd been missing. He found himself looking forward to their time together, planning activities and thinking of new ways to engage Ella's quick mind.

One evening, they sat on William's porch enjoying popsicles after a particularly grueling bike ride. Ella's dad, Jim, was finishing a walk and approached the porch. Ella turned to him with a serious expression as her dad began walking up the stairs.

"William," she said, her voice quiet, "thank you for being my friend this summer. I was . . . I was really scared about moving here."

William felt a lump form in his throat, touched by her candor. "Thank you, Ella," he replied, his own voice soft. "You've been a wonderful friend to me, too. You've reminded me of how exciting the world can be when seen through fresh eyes."

With that, she hopped on her bike and rode the short distance home.

Jim stayed behind and said, "I heard what Ella said to you."

William looked into Jim's eyes, surprised to see them welling with tears.

"You have meant the world to her this summer. She was nervous—frightened—during our move here. Away from her friends . . . new town . . . and all that.

"She's good at making friends, so I expected that to abate once the school year began. But in the two summer months she's been here, you've been a role model . . . a friend . . . her best friend, really. And I—we—can't thank you enough."

"Jim, Ella is a good person and I'm happy to know her. She means a great deal to me and I look forward to being her friend and supporter whenever she needs it."

They were both crying now. The two shook hands, and Jim began walking home.

· · · · ● · ● · · · ·

As July drew to a close and the back-to-school sales began in earnest, William found himself both grateful for the summer they'd shared and apprehensive about the changes fall would bring. Would their friendship survive the structure of the school year? Would Ella, surrounded by peers her own age, still have time for their adventures?

But as he watched Ella pedal away after their last summer outing, her red bike a blur of motion and her laughter trailing behind her, William felt a sense of peace settle over him. Whatever the future held, this summer had been a gift—a reminder that connection and growth could come from the most unexpected places.

He turned back to his house, his mind already whirring with plans for their next adventure. After all, who said the fun had to end with summer? There were still so many cupcake flavors to try, so many philosophical debates to be had over bike rides and soccer matches. And William, rejuvenated by his unexpected role as mentor and friend, was looking forward to every moment.

Every Lazy Password

Conferences never got old for William. Though unbelievably expensive, Boston was his kind of town. Sure, it's an incredible sports town, but for him, its history was the major draw. Boston is one of the oldest settlements in the United States, though not as old as New England's Plymouth, Gloucester, or even Salem. (St. Augustine in Florida, Jamestown in Virginia, and Sante Fe in New Mexico all pre-date New England settlements.)

While he loved traveling the touristy Freedom Trail, running along the Charles River—besides maybe Central Park, is there a better place in the US to run?—and visiting the newer Seaport area, it was Salem that provided the highlights of this trip. This quirky town on Boston's North Shore provided the right amount of interesting colonial and Federal-style architecture, sites, pirate museums, history—more than just witches—recreation, coastal beauty, and solitude.

He'd return.

***

William arrived back in Omaha with the subtle throb of discontent that always followed him when he left a conference. The city greeted him with its usual charm, which is to say, it didn't.

OK, that's not true.

It's popular to say that Omaha is boring . . . ho hum . . . charmless.

But there is actually a lot to do and a lot of magic. But it takes an open mind and heart to see it and to appreciate it. William fell in love with the Missouri River and the pedestrian bridge that connects Nebraska to Iowa. While it may not have the sheer number and volume of restaurants larger cities have, the quality is on par with—and often surpasses—most of them. And while its history *only* dates back to the mid-1800s, it's a pretty cool history of transportation—think Lewis and Clark, covered wagons, and more modern railroads—stockyards—smells and all—organized crime, unseen wealth, and insurance.

Well, the insurance piece isn't all that exciting, but all the rest adds up to a pretty cool place.

William needed to get out after flying all morning. So he began pedaling his way through familiar streets, noting that even the potholes hadn't changed since his departure.

The afternoon sun teased the back of his neck as he rode, and he thought about the closest cupcake shop—*The Whimsical Whisk*, a place where flavors like *Existential Crunch* and *Mint-Conditioned Life* pretended to offer more than just a sugar rush. He headed there and, as he approached the shop, he spotted Ella outside, her silhouette as thin and rigid as the bike she leaned against. She was staring at nothing in particular, or perhaps at everything in general; it was hard to tell with her. Her dark eyes had a storm brewing in them, the kind that warned of trouble on the horizon.

He dismounted with the grace of a man who'd rather be running. As he approached, her gaze flickered towards him, a silent acknowledgement that carried weight.

"Rough day?" William asked, hoping to see the flicker of a smile. But today, her frown was etched deeper than usual.

"Something like that." Ella's voice was flat, betraying none of the sarcasm that usually seasoned her words.

Inside the shop, they sat across from each other at a table that felt too small for the conversation ahead. Ella's outfit—a blend of modern chic and *I couldn't care less*—seemed oddly appropriate for spilling secrets.

"Spill it, then," William said after a beat, pushing aside his *Espresso Yourself* cupcake. "You look like you've seen a ghost, or worse, an honest politician."

Ella's lips twisted into a wry smile, but it vanished as quickly as it appeared. Her tone turned frosty. "Worse. Mr. Rissler."

· · · ●· ● ·· ·

Ella's demeanor had shifted over the past few months. The spark in her eyes dimmed, replaced by a wary, haunted look. Her usual witty retorts became less frequent, often giving way to long silences or abrupt changes of subject.

It began subtly. Mr. Rissler, her 5th grade PE teacher, began paying extra attention to Ella, praising her athletic abilities and offering to help her improve her skills. At first, it seemed like genuine mentorship, something Ella, always eager to learn, welcomed.

But the attention changed. Mr. Rissler started finding reasons to keep Ella after class, insisting on one-on-one coaching sessions. He'd place a hand on her shoulder, leaving it there a bit too long, or stand uncomfortably close while demonstrating techniques. The compliments became more personal, less about her abilities, and more about her appearance.

Ella found herself dreading PE class, her stomach knotting with anxiety as she approached the gym. Mr. Rissler's gaze followed her constantly, making her feel exposed and vulnerable. He started sending her text messages, innocuous at first, but growing more frequent and familiar.

The grooming extended beyond the gym. Mr. Rissler began showing up at Ella's other extracurricular activities, always ready with a smile and an offer to drive her home. He'd bring her small gifts—a new water bottle, a fancy stopwatch—items that seemed thoughtful but carried an unspoken weight of expectation.

Ella's friends noticed her withdrawal from their usual activities. She stopped joining them for after-school cupcake runs, making excuses about extra studying or feeling tired. In reality, she was avoiding situations where she might encounter Mr. Rissler outside of school.

At home, Ella became more secretive, password-protecting her phone and jumping whenever it buzzed with a new message. She struggled to concentrate on her computer coding projects, her usual refuge no longer providing the escape it once did.

The final straw came when Mr. Rissler suggested a special weekend training camp, just for his "star athletes." The thought of being alone with him, away from the relative safety of the school, filled Ella with dread.

As she sat across from William in the cupcake shop, Ella felt the weight of her secret pressing down on her. She knew she needed help, but fear and confusion had kept her silent until now. Meeting William's concerned gaze, she realized it was time to break her silence and seek the support she desperately needed.

· · · ● · ● · ● · · ·

William's face darkened as he listened to Ella's story, his usual wry smile replaced by a grim, tight-lipped expression. His hands, wrapped around his now-forgotten cupcake, tightened until his knuckles turned white. He took a deep breath, struggling to calm the storm of emotions brewing within him.

"Ella," he began, his voice low and controlled, "I want you to know that what's happening is not your fault. Mr. Rissler's behavior is completely unacceptable, immoral, illegal, wrong . . ."

He paused, considering his next words. "I'm proud of you for telling me. It takes a lot of courage to speak up about something like this."

William leaned forward, his eyes meeting Ella's with a mix of concern and determination. "We need to take action, but I promise you, you won't have to face this alone. I'm here with you every step of the way."

He then outlined a plan of action, his words measured but firm. Thinking back to Lexi, he said, "first, we need to document everything—every interaction, every text message, every time you felt uncomfortable. Then, we're going to report this to the school administration and the police. Mr. Rissler needs to be stopped, not just for your sake, but for all the other students he might target."

William's tone softened as he noticed Ella's apprehension. "I know it's scary, but remember, you're not alone in this. We'll face it together, just like we tackle our bike rides and soccer matches. And Ella? You're much stronger than you realize."

"I don't want to report this. At least not yet."

"But we need it to stop. For you, Ella. And for everyone else he's doing this to."

Ella knew he was right, of course. After a few minutes, she said, "Maybe there's another way."

He reached out, laying his hand on the table, palm up—an offer of support without intrusion. "Ella, we need to stop this, but as you say, going through official channels might not be enough. Your skills . . . they could be our secret weapon here."

Ella's eyes widened, a spark of her old self returning. "You mean . . .?"

"Exactly," William nodded. "Can you do it?"

· · · ● · ● · ● · · ·

"Okay, so we're up against Goliath with a chalkboard," William said as he observed her, his arms folded across his chest. He could see the gears turning in her head, each click bringing them closer to retribution.

"More like Goliath's sleazier cousin," Ella shot back without missing a beat, finally pausing to look at him. She exhaled sharply, the breath of someone ready to dive into treacherous waters. "We'll need to be invisible . . . and invincible."

"Right. A ghost with an unbreakable shield," he said, knowing full well the seriousness of their endeavor.

William moved to the cluttered table, where a laptop sat open among stacks of papers and energy drink cans. He ran a hand over the keyboard, feeling the keys that would soon serve as their weapons. "We start with surveillance. You crack into his email, socials, any digital footprint that makes this creep tick."

As the night enveloped the city of Omaha, two silhouettes hunched over glowing screens, orchestrating the downfall of predators who lurked in the shadows. Their mission was clear: expose, dethrone, and ensure no more lives were tainted by those meant to nurture and protect.

Ella had tunneled into the depths of Mr. Rissler's phone backup, expecting to find more incriminating files, but nothing could have prepared her for the horror that greeted her.

Images, hundreds of them, cascaded across her screen in a relentless tide of depravity. Each one was a silent scream, a moment stolen and twisted into a grotesque souvenir of innocence betrayed. Ella's heart thrashed against her chest as she clicked through them, her face a mask of revulsion.

"God, what an exhibition," she said to herself, the words tasting like acid on her tongue. These were pictures you'd expect to find locked in a vault, not just floating around in the cloud—every pixel pointed to the ugliness lurking beneath the veneer of a trusted educator.

The videos were worse; moving tributes to Mr. Rissler's monstrous appetites. Ella pressed play on one, and within seconds, her stomach revolted against the scene unfolding before her eyes. The acts depicted weren't meant to be witnessed—especially not by the young souls who were their subjects.

Ella's methodical keyboard clicks were a symphony to their clandestine movements, a background rhythm to their silent war. Breaking from the music one evening, she said in a whisper, her face pale with dread. "His home computer, his phone . . . William, it's worse than we thought."

William's jaw clenched. "How many?"

"Over twenty other people that I've counted so far. And . . . and there are pictures. Videos." Ella's voice cracked, tears threatening to spill.

William placed a comforting hand on her shoulder. "You're doing fantastic work here, Ella."

"Got something else," Ella said, not looking up. "Looks like he has a penchant for encrypted chats."

"Charming." William placed his coffee on the table and leaned over her shoulder.

"Chat logs, meet-ups, the usual slime trail. Enough breadcrumbs to bake a loaf of evidence." She minimized the window and opened another. "And here we have an anonymous survey for the students. Time to let the victims speak without fear."

"Thoreau would approve of this civil disobedience," he said, nodding sagely. "Let's hope it's as effective as Walden was inspiring."

"Hope is for Vegas and lottery tickets. We deal in certainties."

Their operation spanned several more days that melted into nights, each bringing its own shade of darkness. They spoke with victims, voices hushed, stories whispered like confessions. Ella recorded everything, her relentless typing a testament to their resolve.

"Another email account cracked," she whispered with a snicker, "If I had a nickel for every lazy password . . ."

"Save your nickels for something worthwhile," William said, his voice a low rumble. "Like a decent cup of coffee after we're done here." He leaned back in his chair, legs outstretched, the epitome of relaxed vigilance despite the tension thrumming through the room.

· · · ● · ● · ● · · · ·

Ella pedaled furiously down the streets of Omaha, her dark hair whipping behind her like a flag of defiance. The wind was a partner in her escape, urging her on as she put distance between herself and the school, the lair of Mr. Rissler. William was waiting at their agreed-upon rendezvous—a nondescript café that always smelled of burned toast and ambition.

In the quiet of the café, amidst the clinking of porcelain and the grumbling of the espresso machine, a predator's empire began to crumble. And outside, the world spun on, blissfully unaware—for now—of the storm brewing in its midst.

"We—mostly you—have gathered a lot of data. Are you ready to serve up some cold, hard justice?" William asked, knowing full well the answer before the words left his lips.

"Justice served with a side of public humiliation?" Ella replied, preparing the incriminating payload for delivery. "It's been a lot of work, but it was almost easy. It was like shooting fish in a barrel—if the fish were sleazy predators and the barrel was a pit of everlasting shame."

"Then let's not keep our audience waiting," William said, a smile tugging at the corner of his mouth. "After all, revenge is a dish best served viral."

They executed their plan carefully. Anonymous tips to the police, the school board, local media . . . each recipient selected to ensure maximum exposure. But they didn't stop there. They drained his bank accounts, distributing the funds to the families of his victims.

With a deft click, Ella sent the evidence soaring into the digital ether. It was more than a takedown; it was a declaration, a testament to what two resolute souls could accomplish when driven by a shared purpose.

Ella powered down her station. "Now, about that coffee . . ."

· · · ● · ● · · ·

As news of Mr. Rissler's arrest broke, William and Ella sat in silence at a new cupcake shop, *Flour Power*, the weight of their actions settling around them.

"Was it right?" Ella asked, her voice small.

He nodded, his jaw set in a hard line. There was no quote from Thoreau or Seneca to neatly package his rage. "What he did to you, what he was planning to do with Sidnie, and—" William stopped himself. He didn't need to finish the sentence; they both knew the weight of unsaid words.

"Let me guess," Ella said, despite the darkness that hung over them, "you wanted to go for a run to clear your head? A quick marathon across the Midwest?"

"Ha," William snorted, a humorless sound. "I wish a run could fix this mess." He leaned back against the cold metal chair outside the bakery, an island of normalcy in a sea of chaos. The flavor of the day sign mocked him with its chipper promise of *Strawberry Fields Whatever*.

William sighed. "Sometimes, Ella, justice needs a push. What we did . . . it wasn't just revenge. It was protection for all those who couldn't protect themselves."

Ella nodded, a determined glint in her eye. "There are others out there, aren't there? Other Mr. Risslers?"

William met her gaze, understanding the unspoken question. "Indeed, there are. And perhaps . . . perhaps we're just the ones to stop them."

"Maybe we should start doing yoga," Ella said with a sidelong glance, the corner of her mouth twitching in a half-smile. "Find our inner peace, channel our *om*, and somehow magically zen all the Mr. Risslers of the world into jail cells."

"Or," William said, the gears turning behind his steady gaze, "we use that brilliant brain of yours to ensure all those like him wish we'd chosen the yoga route."

"Sounds more appealing than *downward dogging* my way through this scandal." Ella leaned forward, her eyes now alight with a mix of mischief and determination.

"Besides," William added, a sardonic edge to his voice, "who needs chakras when you've got Wi-Fi and a disdain for injustice?"

"Exactly." Ella smirked, swiping away the remnants of tears with renewed fervor. "Let's get to work."

There was no looking back now, only forward, into the eye of the storm they had conjured. As other cupcake connoisseurs passed by, he could almost hear the clink of digital handcuffs snapping shut on wrists that had signed off on too many secrets.

"Your brain's like a Swiss Army knife for modern-day Robin Hood antics," William observed, the ghost of a smirk playing on his lips.

"More like Robin Hood meets the digital age. We're not stealing from the rich; we're redistributing the wealth of wickedness," Ella said, her sarcasm a velvet hammer hitting the nail on the head.

They paused for a moment, the hip suburb's pulse syncing with theirs. The shadows seemed to lean in, listening, as if the very night itself was complicit in their next caper.

"Let's call it social engineering with a side of payback. Charity with a side of vengeance." Ella finally broke the tableau, her silhouette cutting a sharp figure against the backdrop of the decades old strip mall.

"Sounds dangerous without even trying," William said, though his tone remained serious. It was all business—the kind that didn't make it onto balance sheets or boardroom agendas.

Ella's gaze flickered across the faces in the bakery, each one a story untold, a potential canvas for the kind of justice the courts sometimes missed. "It went off without a hitch. No violence, just simple revenge for a"—she paused to glance at one of the bakers passing by, considering—"for a world that could use a little less sweet talk and a lot more action."

"Speaking of action . . ." William nodded toward a street artist who was skillfully coaxing the likeness of a local politician onto his canvas, the caricature dripping with satire.

"Looks like we're not the only ones painting outside the lines," Ella noted, the corners of her mouth twitching upward. It was a silent nod to their shared truth: sometimes you had to color outside the lines to capture the full picture.

Walking home now, Ella nodded; her long hair swayed as a cool breeze teased it into wild swirls, as if attempting to unravel the secrets tightly coiled within her mind. With each step, the echo of their footsteps whispered promises of justice served cold, coded by a girl who'd seen too much and a man who refused to close his eyes any longer.

In their own way, William and Ella had transformed into artists, painting a picture of others' disgrace so vivid that it would hang in the galleries of public opinion forever. Their brushes were keystrokes; their palette, digital proof of monstrosities that could not be unseen or forgiven.

Thus began their crusade, a summer of digital vigilantism that would change both their lives forever. Neither could have predicted where this path would lead, or the dangers that lurked in the shadows of their noble intentions.

• • • • ● • ● • • • •

The neon sign of the pawnshop jeered, its erratic pulse a beacon for those peddling desperation or stolen goods. Ella's fingers fluttered over the keyboard like hummingbird wings, the clacking a staccato accompaniment to the hum of nocturnal insects. "You know, I always thought *pawn* was just chess jargon," she said, her eyes never leaving the screen.

"Ah, but in life, as in chess, pawns have the potential to become queens," William replied from his perch on a dilapidated bench, watching the street with hawk-like intensity. He chuckled, a low rumble that matched the distant thunder. "Or in our case, give checkmate to the kingpins of sleaze."

Ella smirked, her code slicing through digital defenses like a hot knife through butter. They were onto their next mark—a loan shark masquerading as a benevolent lender. The kind who'd liberate you from your kneecaps if your wallet ran dry. "Speaking of sleaze, this guy's about to learn that interest rates can indeed be too high—especially the moral kind."

"Sometimes I wonder if Dante missed a circle in his Inferno," William said, glancing at the screen. "One specifically designed for white-collar criminals."

With each line of code, they peeled back layers of deceit and treachery, revealing the rot festering beneath. It wasn't just the loan shark; there were others—a smorgasbord of society's underbelly. Their targets numbered a dozen—a rogues' gallery of the corrupt who preyed on innocence, plundered charity, and celebrated their own cruelty.

"Got him. And look, he even invested in some . . ." Ella squinted at the screen, ". . . unethically sourced art. How avant-garde."

"Picasso once said, *Art is the lie that enables us to realize the truth.* Our friend here is about to become quite the patron of reality."

"We've prepped the canvas. Time to paint him into a corner."

"Make it a masterpiece," William said with encouragement, his gaze returning to the shadowy street, where the guilty walked with the swagger of the untouchable. But tonight, their touchstone would crumble, their confidence shattered by the very tools they wielded with impunity.

"Masterpiece?" Ella echoed, her lips curling into a half-smile. "More like a mosaic. You know, pieces of his life rearranged to reveal something new."

In the city's symphony, their operation was a muted note—a harmony of justice that hummed beneath the surface. Where the law was impotent, their brand of sarcasm-laced retribution thrived, a vigilante waltz composed by two unlikely partners. They weren't heroes, not in the traditional sense. Theirs was the path of gray—twisting, turning, and sometimes dark—but always leading toward the light of restitution.

· · · ● · ● · · ·

In the years following their first takedown of Mr. Rissler, William and Ella's bond had deepened beyond their summer friendship into an unlikely alliance, a duo of digital vigilantes operating from the heart of the Midwest. Their weekly cupcake outings and bike rides continued, but now these innocent activities often served as cover for planning their next mission. What began as a singular act of justice blossomed into a crusade against corruption, their targets ranging from small-town predators to corporate giants with shadowy practices.

Ella, once a precocious 8-year-old, had blossomed into a formidable hacker by age 12. Her keyboard maneuvers were done with a prodigy's virtuosity that left William in awe, her ability to navigate the digital realm bordering on the supernatural. Together, they had orchestrated the downfall of 12 wrongdoers—pedophiles, embezzlers, abusive authority figures—each victory a notch in their moral belt. Their reputation grew in underground circles, whispers of their exploits spreading from Omaha to Chicago, even reaching as far as the coasts.

William found an unexpected purpose in this clandestine partnership, even as their friendship continued to ground them both. He marveled at how Ella's intellect had sharpened, her hacking skills becoming increasingly sought after in certain circles. Yet, with each successful operation, a nagging fear grew in the pit of his stomach. They were playing a dangerous game, and William couldn't shake the feeling that their luck might run out. Little did he know his worst fears were soon realized, altering the course of both their lives forever.

Is This What You Call Transcendence, Margaret?

The morning sun hadn't yet mustered the strength to burn through the mist clinging to Salem's cobblestone streets as William, now a local fixture for half a year, bent over his well-worn running shoes. The laces, frayed at the edges from his countless tying and retying, threaded through his fingers with an intimacy reserved for favorite books. He pulled them taut, each loop and knot a silent mantra of determination.

The day Ella vanished, a part of William died. The vibrant, precocious girl who had brought light to his life was gone, leaving behind a void that seemed to consume everything. For weeks, his life became a frantic, desperate search—plastering posters on every lamppost in Omaha, questioning anyone who might have seen her, working with law enforcement and private investigators. But Ella had vanished without a trace, as if swallowed by the earth itself.

After six months of fruitless searching, William made the agonizing decision to leave Omaha. He chose Salem, a city steeped in history and far removed from the painful memories of the Midwest. It wasn't an escape, he told himself, but a strategic retreat—a chance to regroup, to heal, and to continue the search from a new vantage point.

In Salem, far from Omaha's haunting memories, William found a different kind of solace in running. What had once been his path to redemption now became his anchor to sanity. He became a streaker in the running sense—someone who runs every single day without fail. Through rain, snow, and blistering heat, the physical discomfort became a welcome distraction from darker thoughts.

Emerson's words, *What lies behind us and what lies before us are tiny matters compared to what lies within us*, took on new significance. Thoreau's assertion that *I went to the woods because I wished to live deliberately* resonated with William's choice of Salem as his sanctuary. The Transcendentalists' emphasis on self-reliance struck a chord with his solitary quest. Margaret Fuller's conviction that *Very early, I knew that the only object in life was to grow* became his daily mantra—even in grief, even in seemingly hopeless circumstances, he could choose to grow, to learn, to push forward.

Thoreau's musings on the spiritual benefits of nature resonated as he ran each morning. The simple act of moving through the world, feeling the earth beneath his feet and the wind on his face, became meditation.

With every punishing incline and treacherous descent, William's determination did not waver. He ran because it was the purest metaphor he knew—a relentless journey towards a horizon that promised, if nothing else, the chance to outpace the shadows of yesterday and greet whatever tomorrow held with open arms and a weary, yet still beating, heart.

Nature always wears the colors of the spirit, he thought, his breath fogging in the early morning air. Here, amidst Salem's natural splendor, William found a semblance of peace that had long eluded him. The earthy scent of fallen leaves mingled with the briny tang of the nearby sea, anchoring him in the present. His stride was a metronome, each footfall a rhythmic echo on the pavement. Running was more than mere exercise; the rhythmic pounding of feet on pavement was his personal rebellion against life's cruel jests. And now, he was not just running from something but towards a tangible goal.

· • ● • ● • ● • • ·

New York City's Fifth Avenue on the Upper East Side spread before him, a concrete jungle that had tested the limits of his endurance. He entered Central Park, surrounded by people—so many people—for some non-bridge hills to break up the mostly urban route. As he was about to turn right onto 59th Street along Central Park South, his body was a symphony of aches, playing out the final movement of his New York City Marathon effort. He re-entered the park and the finish line loomed . . . a ribbon of redemption stretched across the path of the fallen and the triumphant alike.

Never bet the devil your head, Poe had mocked, but here William was, betting his soul on the breadth of his stride and the strength of his will. As he crossed the threshold, the clock blared its verdict: 3 hours, 9 minutes, 52 seconds. A moment stretched into eternity, the taste of victory sweeter for the bitterness of past defeats.

He had done it.

He broke 3:10.

He'd qualified for the Boston Marathon, the hallowed ground of the running world. It was more than a race; it was a testament to his journey, a middle finger raised to the demons of his former life. He recognized the irony—a gambling addict turned philosopher-runner, finding purpose in the pounding of the pavement.

"Transcend, my friend," he might have said aloud, had he been one for speeches at such times. Instead, William let out a breath that seemed to carry all the weight of his past, watching it dissipate into the cold air of triumph.

· · · ● · ● · · ·

A philosophical framework gave structure to his days, infusing his runs with a purpose beyond the physical. Each mile became an opportunity for reflection, for communing with the *oversoul* that the Transcendentalists believed connected all beings. In this way, William felt he could maintain a connection to Ella, even as the physical distance between them remained unknown.

William's breaths came out in misty spirals as he settled onto the weathered bench at Marblehead's Fort Sewall, legs stretching before him with the lassitude of a marathon done and dusted. His gaze meandered over the Thanksgiving Day ocean, where the undulating waves seemed to flirt with the horizon. The Marblehead Light Tower stood stoic, an unwavering sentinel amidst the capricious tides of Marblehead Harbor and Children's Island.

He was alone in this Revolutionary War fort turned park. The town's high school football team was in nearby Swampscott, playing their rivals in what had become one of the oldest Thanksgiving Day games in Massachusetts. Most of the town made the short trek to the Big Blue's Blocksidge Field hoping the Marblehead Magicians would win, continuing to lead the historic series.

He let his eyes linger on the expanse of water, the same way one might observe a beautiful stranger across a crowded room—appreciating from afar, knowing the distance was part of the allure. He sought solace in the arms of the Atlantic, a vast blue confidante for his thoughts.

The crisp morning air was semi-flirtatious, nipping at his skin with a freshness that bordered on mockery. *A little cold for your old bones, eh William?* it seemed to say. With each wave that lapped against the shore, it whispered secrets he could almost grasp—secrets of redemption and the folly of man's greed, like a siren call wrapped in Transcendentalist prose.

Nature always wears the colors of the spirit, Emerson had mused, and here nature donned a gown of blues and grays, reflecting William's inner tumult—a cocktail of triumph, regret, and an unshakeable sadness. It was as if the entire scene were painted with the same brushstrokes that colored his soul.

His mind replayed the marathon, each footfall a drumbeat against the pavement, a rhythmic echo of Thoreau's message of self-reliance, the sounds and vibrations reverberating deep within him. Each mile, a silent testament to his resolve, was marked only by the rhythmic thud of his feet on the trail and his ragged breathing; the stillness afterwards made him question if this was victory or escape.

Is this what you call transcendence, Margaret? He pictured Fuller's stern countenance softening into understanding. He snorted softly, the sound lost in the wind. Yeah, right. As if she'd give a damn about a washed-up gambler turned runner.

He noticed the irony of it all. Here he was, a man once enslaved by fleshly desires, now seeking something purer, yet still finding himself alone with his conquests. A cynical chuckle rumbled in his chest, the sound as dry as Poe's wit. *Metaphor-run mad*, indeed.

In this solitude, the salty air and cries of gulls underscored William's grief over Ella's absence. Her abduction was an open wound, and no amount of philosophizing or physical exertion could staunch the bleeding.

"Running towards something, or from it?" the sea seemed to ask, its voice an echo of his own introspection. William is often asked that question. He lacked, lacks, and will likely continue to lack an answer; all he knew was the run itself, the constant motion that both propelled him forward and kept him suspended in place.

As the sun peaked, casting a golden light over the scene, William rose from the bench. This was not the end, but merely another marker on his path—his quest for redemption, a marathon with no clear finish line. He turned his back to the ocean, a solitary figure silhouetted against the awakening day, and walked away, carrying his contemplation, regret, and sadness as closely as the shadow trailing behind him.

Economical
Transcendentalism

L ife had a way of writing its own peculiar stories, William mused as Boston's reluctant sunset painted the sky. Eight years since Ella's abduction, one since the
California operation, and here he was—an unlikely literary sensation, his gruff wisdom
now filling bestsellers more captivating than watching paint dry.

From running shoes to book tours, William often thought, the irony not lost on him. A year
out from their most daring escapade, he had traded the adrenaline rush of con artistry for
the thrill of the pen—or the keyboard, because who even uses pens anymore?

On this particular evening, the light jog from North Station to meet Ella served as a
prelude to their weekly ritual. The tradition: cupcakes, her treat—an MIT sophomore's
way of saying, "Thanks for not being a terrible influence." They'd pick a place, ranging
from hole-in-the-wall bakeries to the posh places made famous by trendy social media
posts . . . places where the cupcakes cost more than a good steak.

OK, not really. But close.

Today's venue of choice was a small boutique—*The Wry Baker*—near Boston Common
that boasted flavors inspired by classical literature. William couldn't help but snort at the
pretense: *Sylvia Plath's Sweet & Salty Existential Crisis*—a salted caramel cupcake that
pairs perfectly with poetry and contemplating your life choices . . . yes, please. Yet, secretly,
he loved it—the cupcakes and the company.

Ella was waiting outside when he arrived, a vision of awkward grace leaning against the
iron railing. Today's outfit was a quirky ensemble that somehow blended MIT geek chic

with runway rebel. She'd always had a knack for making thrift store finds look like haute couture.

"Late by two minutes, William," Ella deadpanned, without looking up from her phone. "Your commitment to punctuality is about as reliable as a weather forecast in this town."

"Ah, but isn't anticipation the purest form of pleasure?" William replied, quoting someone or other. He could never resist the urge to turn life into a living bibliography.

"Or the purest form of torture, depending on who you ask," Ella shot back with a wry smirk, finally locking her dark eyes with his.

They stepped into the cupcake shop, a bell tinkling overhead like a chime of gentle mockery. Vanilla and pretension perfumed the air inside, a scent William found oddly comforting. Choosing their flavors was a silent dance they both knew well—Ella went for the *Cookies & Cream of the Crop*, while William, ever the iconoclast, skipped the Sylvia Plath-inspired creation and instead opted for plain old chocolate—OK, it was called *Midlife Crisis By Chocolate*. Ironic? Timely?

"Really branching out there, William," Ella said as they took their cones. "I'm surprised you didn't just ask for a scoop of stoicism on a sugar cone."

"Ah, but Ella, one must appreciate the foundational flavors of life to truly savor its complexities," William said, giving her a wink that crinkled the corners of his wise eyes.

They strolled through the Beacon Hill neighborhood streets, the city lights twinkling like distant stars fallen to earth. Their conversation meandered through philosophy and computer algorithms, each finding amusement in how their different worlds intersected. William would quote Thoreau; Ella would counter with Python code logic. He'd muse about the nature of existence; she'd explain how quantum computing might unlock those very mysteries. As they walked, Boston's historic facades provided a fitting backdrop for their unlikely but perfectly balanced debate society of two.

• • • ● • ● ● • • •

The next morning, William began his day as he always did. He laced up his running shoes with the precision of a man who measured life in breaths and strides and he ran ... through Salem Common, right on Essex St, and paused in front of Wicked Good Books. He was a runner, yes, but these days, William was known as much for his words as his miles.

From Addiction to Inspiration: A Runner's Journey sat prominently displayed in bookstore windows, its cover boasting a silhouette of a solitary figure against a dawn-streaked sky. Within its pages, William bared his soul, charting a path from the clutches of gambling addiction to the liberating embrace of long-distance running. It was a tale of redemption, every chapter infused with the Transcendentalist teachings that had become his lifeline—a narrative steeped in self-reliance and the pursuit of a higher purpose.

Running with Emerson: Finding Wisdom in Every Step was there, too. This was a natural sequel, a lean volume where prose met philosophy at a crossroads. Here, William trod alongside Emerson, delving into essays as one would into personal correspondence with an old friend. It was an exploration of the intersection of body and mind, each step a meditation on the intrinsic value of growth—personal, spiritual, and intellectual. It was transcendence in motion, or so the glowing reviews claimed.

Shaking his head in amazement and a bit of disbelief, he started running again.

As the sun crested the horizon, casting a golden glow over the waterfront, William slowed to a stop, hands on hips, breathing in the salty tang of the sea. Because he was focusing more on his writing, his books had become more of his legacy, not just bound paper and ink, but artifacts of a journey from the depths of human frailty to the peaks of potential.

With a wry smile, he thought of how his readers envisioned him—a modern-day philosopher king in moisture-wicking fabric. If only they knew the truth: that every word he wrote was another step away from who he had been and a stride closer to who he might become.

· · · ● · ● · · ·

Later that day, William surveyed the Harvard Business School audience from behind the stage curtain, his bald head reflecting the soft backstage lighting like a beacon of intellectual promise. In his hand, a copy of his latest brainchild, *The Transcendent Econ-*

omist: Applying Thoreau's Principles to Modern Economics—an ambitious concoction of highbrow economic theory and Walden Pond musings. It was as if Thoreau himself had decided to don a suit and tackle Wall Street, armed with nothing but civil disobedience and a keen understanding of diminishing marginal utility.

Who knew self-sufficiency could be so . . . lucrative? he thought, the irony not lost on him. The book was an oddity, a juxtaposition of naturalistic simplicity and complex fiscal systems that somehow resonated with the minimalist CEO and the overworked barista alike. He'd stitched together Thoreau's teachings with modern economics to tailor a unique perspective on financial well-being that didn't require selling your soul or investing in dubious cryptocurrency schemes. Personal fulfillment, according to William, was about as much about knowing your net worth as it was about understanding the value of laying in a field, staring at the sky—preferably without checking the Consumer Price Index on your phone.

As the host introduced him, William stepped onto the stage, his lean frame moving with the understated confidence of a man who'd run marathons in his mind just as often as on the asphalt. Today's keynote presentation, *Running Towards Transcendence: Finding Equilibrium in a Chaotic Market,* promised yet another packed auditorium full of eager souls searching for enlightenment between supply and demand curves.

"Equilibrium," he began, his voice even, "is not a static state. It's moving through life with purpose and poise, much like navigating a volatile market without the existential dread of wondering if you've diversified enough."

Laughter rippled through the crowd.

"Life is chaotic. But so is the free market," he continued, images of serene forests juxtaposed with bustling stock exchanges flashing behind him. "Yet every firm finds its niche amidst the chaos. It doesn't try to branch . . . I mean, merge unnecessarily."

More laughter. William's wit was as dry as the aged pages of the books he revered, yet it carried a touch of sexiness—like an economist who could explain the Laffer Curve and wink at the same time.

"Today, we sprint through our routines, hurdling over opportunity costs, sometimes stumbling, occasionally face-planting into negative externalities," he said, pacing the stage with the deliberate steps of a man accustomed to measuring miles by footfalls. "But we rise, we internalize the costs, and we keep moving. Because the finish line isn't maximizing shareholder value; it's optimizing personal utility at any age."

Nods of agreement met his words. They came for advice, for stories, and maybe, just maybe, for a glimpse of the man who'd turned personal catastrophe into a philosophical crusade against the modern-day rat race of infinite growth.

"Transcendentalists believed in the inherent goodness of people and nature," he said, wrapping up. "I believe in the inherent sense to know when the marginal cost outweighs the marginal benefit. So let's lace up our shoes, metaphorically speaking, and run towards a simpler, more Pareto-efficient existence."

Applause thundered as he took his bow, the echo following him offstage like the afterglow of a well-run race. William might not have all the answers, but he certainly knew how to pose the questions that got everyone lacing up their proverbial sneakers, ready to chase down a life less dictated by the invisible hand.

• • • ● • ● • • • •

The next month, William stood before the eager congregation of the Transcendentalist Society's annual convention, an unlikely prophet in his well-worn sneakers and a crisp, untucked linen shirt. The murmur of the crowd hushed as he began weaving the timeless threads of Emerson and Thoreau into the fabric of modern-day capitalism. *The Power of Self-Reliance in Achieving Financial Freedom* wasn't just a topic; it was a siren call to the overworked souls searching for an escape from the corporate hamster wheel.

"Nature," William offered, pacing before an oversized projection of Walden Pond, "isn't just a pretty backdrop for your Instagram selfies. It's a brutally honest stock market, where the currency is energy and the investments are literally life and death." A chuckle rippled through the audience. William's knack for grounding high-minded philosophy in the gritty soil of reality had earned him not just accolades, but also a certain celebrity within circles that found C-SPAN riveting.

"Thoreau said, *I went to the woods because I wished to live deliberately*," he continued, pausing for effect as the image behind him shifted to a dense thicket of trees. "Now, thanks to cutting-edge technology, you don't have to get your shoes dirty to find your inner hermit. There's an app for that." Smirks and knowing glances crisscrossed the room like silent fireflies signaling their amusement.

It was during one such engagement, under the lofty ceilings of an auditorium filled with financial gurus who made a living peddling advice at the cost of personal connection, where William delivered his pièce de résistance—a tale so steeped in irony that it left the audience both charmed and chastened.

"Let me tell you about the time I met the Dalai Lama of Wall Street," he said, a mischievous twinkle lighting up his eyes. "Man had a heart of gold—24 karat, to be precise. He told me his secret to success was detachment. So I asked him how detached he could truly be while wearing a Rolex that could feed a small village."

An eruption of laughter followed, the sound bouncing off the marble pillars like a tennis ball volleyed by pros. William's point landed with precision: enlightenment couldn't be bought or worn, and wisdom often came packaged in the guise of paradoxical humor.

"Remember, folks," William concluded, his voice a blend of sincerity and satire, "self-reliance means more than just being able to change your own tire. It's about knowing when to step out of the race altogether and ask yourself if the prize is really worth the chase."

A standing ovation greeted his last sentence, and as he walked off the dais, there was no doubt that William's message had resonated. In a world cluttered with complicated investment strategies and relentless pursuit of more, his calls for simplicity and introspection struck a chord. And perhaps, just maybe, they would think twice before buying that next status symbol—or at least check if there was an app for it first.

As the applause receded into the fabric-lined walls of the lecture hall, William made his way through the throng of admirers and skeptics alike. Each step he took seemed to echo with the weight of his words, the impact of his message reverberating not just in the room but beyond its confines, across campuses and into the cozy, overpriced coffee shops where the next generation debated economic theory and philosophy.

William's tenure as an adjunct professor had been an unconventional trajectory—gambling addict to philosopher king of economics. His classes were less about supply and demand curves and more about the curvature of human aspiration, bending toward meaningful existences rather than opulent emptiness. He wove Thoreau's wisdom through the threads of modern fiscal policy like a skilled tailor, crafting bespoke suits of thought designed to fit the contours of his students' minds.

"Professor," a young man called out, notebook clutched with the kind of fervor usually reserved for religious texts or limited-edition smartphones. "Your lecture . . . it's like you're saying we should aim to be economically transcendental."

"Hit the nail on the head, didn't I?" William replied, his voice laced with the sort of dry humor that could sap moisture from the air. "On one hand, it's simple: live deliberately in your means, not vicariously through your screens.

"Economical transcendentalism also refers to an economic philosophy that goes beyond traditional metrics of success and wealth, incorporating spiritual and personal fulfillment into economic decision-making.

"In our pursuit of economic understanding, we often become entangled in the web of GDP, inflation rates, and market indices. But what if we transcended these material measures? An economically transcendental approach asks us to consider the true value of our economic choices—not just in dollars and cents, but in personal growth, community well-being, and harmony with nature.

"For instance, when we talk about utility in economics, we typically think of the satisfaction derived from consuming goods or services. But a transcendental economist might argue that true utility comes from experiences that enrich our souls: the joy of creating something with our own hands, the peace found in a moment of solitude in nature, or the fulfillment of helping others.

"Similarly, when we discuss opportunity cost, we shouldn't just consider the monetary value of our next best alternative. We should also weigh the cost to our inner peace, our relationships, and our connection to the world around us.

"An economically transcendental society might prioritize measures like work-life balance, environmental sustainability, and community engagement alongside traditional economic indicators. It would recognize that the wealthiest nation isn't necessarily the one with the highest GDP, but the one where citizens find the greatest meaning and purpose in their daily lives.

"Economic transcendentalism challenges us to elevate our understanding of value beyond the confines of the marketplace, encouraging a holistic approach to prosperity that nurtures both our bank accounts and our souls."

He watched as realization dawned on faces around him, the light bulb moments so bright they could've powered the city's grid—if only such things were transferable. Students questioned their own pursuits, pondering whether the chase for wealth was a race towards happiness or merely a treadmill powered by societal expectation.

In his lectures, William often quoted Emerson, but he lived like Thoreau—modestly, with purpose, and without the need for validation from brand names or bank balances. And while some might have found it ironic that a man who once gambled well beyond his means was now preaching authenticity, William knew that life was nothing if not filled with contradictions that made for the best stories.

His books, lined up like dominos on the shelf of every self-help enthusiast, weren't just paper and ink; they were roadmaps to fulfillment without greed. *From Addiction to Inspiration* wasn't merely a title—it was a promise, one that he had kept to himself and now offered to others.

"Professor William," another student interjected, her eyes alight with a mix of reverence and mischief, "if we follow Thoreau's principles, wouldn't we all just end up living in the woods alone?"

"Ah," William smirked, the corners of his mouth curling upward with the grace of a Cheshire Cat in academia's clothing, "but then you'd miss out on my delightful company. And who would want that?"

Laughter followed him out the door, a less tangible but no less significant testament to his influence. As he headed out to run—his second run of the day—he reflected on how the most profound con had been on himself. Convincing a man once tethered to addiction that he could inspire others to find freedom in simplicity. Indeed, the greatest heist was stealing back one's own life from the clutches of excess, and what a sweet victory that was.

Stealing Clarity From Chaos

William's arrival at the Penn Center reminded him of toeing the line at the start of a race—his pulse quickened, anticipation lacing his every stride. The Beaufort sun cast a warm glow over the historic venue as he pushed through the double doors, the murmurs of the gathered literati swirling around him like leaves in an autumnal gust. He nodded at some familiar faces, his shaved head gleaming under the foyer's lights—a beacon of stoic intent in a sea of intellectual bustle.

• • • ● • ● • ● • •

Penn Center, on St. Helena Island near Beaufort, South Carolina, is a testament to African American resilience and the pursuit of education. In 1862, Pennsylvania Quakers and Unitarians founded Penn School, an early Southern institution educating freed slaves. The school's establishment came in the wake of the Civil War, when Union forces captured St. Helena Island, prompting plantation owners to flee and leaving behind a population of formerly enslaved people eager for education and opportunity. For nearly a century, Penn School provided academic instruction and vocational training and served as a vital educational institution for the island's Gullah community.

The Gullah people are a distinct African American subgroup, primarily living in the Lowcountry coastal regions and Sea Islands of the Southeast. Blending African and American influences, their unique culture developed because of their relative isolation on plantations and islands during slavery and post-emancipation periods. They have preserved significant elements of their African heritage, including linguistic features, cultural practices, crafts, cuisine, and folklore. Their language, Gullah, is an English-based creole with strong influences from various West and Central African languages. Scholars debate the origins of the term *Gullah*; they have connected it to Angola, the West African Gola people, and the Dyula ethnic group. Despite historical challenges, they have maintained a distinct identity and continue to play a crucial role in preserving and celebrating their rich cultural heritage in the American South.

In 1948, the state took over public education on the island, and Penn School transformed into Penn Center, continuing its mission through adult education programs, a museum, and cultural preservation efforts.

Penn Center played a significant role in the Civil Rights Movement of the 1960s. As one of the few places in the segregated South where interracial groups could meet, it hosted retreats for Dr. Martin Luther King Jr. and the Southern Christian Leadership Conference. Today, Penn Center's focus on cultural preservation and social justice is an important part of preserving and promoting Gullah culture and history, while also providing educational programs and serving as a conference center.

· · · ●· ● ● · ·

The panel discussion was part of a wellness conference in nearby Beaufort: *The Power of Physical Pursuits: Overcoming Addiction and Finding Purpose.*

This panel was scheduled to explore the intersection of physical activity, mental health, addiction recovery, and personal growth. Other panelists included:

- A psychologist specializing in addiction treatment
- A professional athlete who has overcome personal struggles
- A mindfulness coach
- A neuroscientist studying the effects of exercise on the brain
- And William

William navigated through the crowd during the break, dodging egos that seemed to take up more space than their owners. He caught snippets of conversation about market projections and investment strategies that made a root canal sound entertaining. As he watched the suits jockey for position near the coffee station, he couldn't help but think Thoreau would have had a field day with this lot. Though the philosopher probably hadn't imagined quite this much designer wool and overpriced cologne when he wrote about the mass of men sleepwalking through their lives.

As attendees fluttered between discussions like moths to varying flames, one flame flickered into the room with a presence that demanded attention without demanding it at all. The woman sauntered in, her dark skin radiant against the backdrop of eager intellects clamoring for enlightenment. Her long, dark, straight hair swayed as she moved with the grace of one who had mastered the art of existing loudly in silence. Standing at 5'8", Amelia possessed an athletic build, a testament to her dedication to fitness and her background in amateur bodybuilding. Her dark brown eyes were intelligent and observant, twinkling with humor and flashes of determination. She carried herself with a natural grace and confidence.

William was thunderstruck.

But before he could get nervous, the Q & A portion of the discussion began.

The first question—"What gives you the right to discuss running and exercise as a *cure* for addiction?"—was to the point.

William was the first to respond.

"I appreciate your question, and it's an important one. I want to clarify that I've never claimed running or exercise is a *cure* for addiction. It's a tool, a powerful one, but not a panacea.

"My right to discuss this comes from my lived experience, but I'm far from alone in recognizing the potential of physical activity in addiction recovery. Countless researchers, healthcare professionals, and recovered addicts have explored and promoted this approach.

"Dr. Nora Volkow, director of the National Institute on Drug Abuse, has spoken extensively about how exercise can help rewire the brain's reward system, which is crucial in addiction recovery. The work of Dr. John Ratey, author of *Spark: The Revolutionary New Science of Exercise and the Brain,* provides compelling evidence for exercise's role in mental health and addiction treatment.

"Organizations like Phoenix Multisport, founded by Scott Strode, have built entire communities around the concept of physical activity as a support for recovery. Their success stories are numerous and inspiring.

"Moreover, the principles I discuss aren't new. Henry David Thoreau wrote about the spiritual and mental benefits of physical activity in nature over 150 years ago. More recently, Haruki Murakami's *What I Talk About When I Talk About Running* beautifully explores the meditative aspects of running.

"So, while I don't claim to have all the answers, I believe my experience, combined with the wealth of research and shared experiences of others, gives me not just the right, but the responsibility to discuss this powerful tool in the fight against addiction. It's not about preaching a cure, but about sharing a path that has helped many, including myself, find strength, purpose, and a way forward."

While the questioner and the rest of the audience attempted to recover from his detailed response, another hand shot up. The woman who caught his eye earlier. Her gesture alone sliced through the pretentious chatter like a well-aimed philosophical quip. "William," she began, her voice resonating with a confidence that perked up even the most jaded ears, "my name is Amelia. Your book beautifully weaves together Thoreau's concept of self-reliance with your journey through running. How do you reconcile the solitary nature of long-distance running with the Transcendentalist idea of the *oversoul* connecting all beings? And how has this balance contributed to your personal growth and recovery?" A collective inhale seemed to suck the very oxygen from the room, followed by a ripple of knowing chuckles.

William's eyes twinkled with appreciation; his fondness for transcendental musings found its match in her incisive probe. As she spoke, her deep brown eyes scanned the room, alighting upon his with a spark of recognition—a meeting of minds across the crowded space. They shared a momentary bond, a silent acknowledgement of the comedy playing out in this microcosm of societal grandstanding.

"Thank you for that insightful question. It's one that cuts to the heart of my journey.

"At first glance, long-distance running might seem to be the epitome of solitude, a pursuit that isolates us from others. And in many ways, it is. When I'm out there on a 20-mile run, it's just me, the road, and my thoughts. But paradoxically, it's in this solitude that I've found my deepest connection to the *oversoul* Emerson spoke of.

"You see, as I run, I strip away the layers of societal expectations, personal doubts, and the noise of everyday life. What's left is a pure, unfiltered version of myself. And in that state, I've found that I'm most open to experiencing the interconnectedness of all things.

"There's a moment in long runs—runners call it the *flow state*—where the boundary between self and surroundings begins to blur. Your breath syncs with the rhythm of your footfalls, your heartbeat seems to pulse in time with the world around you. In those moments, I've felt more connected to the universal spirit than in any crowded room or social gathering.

"This balance between solitude and connection has been crucial to my recovery and growth. Even when surrounded by chattering people, the isolating grip of addiction left me profoundly alone. Running taught me to be comfortable in solitude without being isolated. It allowed me to find myself, and in doing so, to find my place in the greater whole.

"The discipline of running—the daily choice to lace up my shoes and hit the pavement—has been an exercise in Thoreau's self-reliance. Yet, the strength I've gained from this practice hasn't led me away from others, but toward them. It's given me the stability and self-understanding to form deeper, more meaningful connections.

"So, to me, the solitary nature of running isn't at odds with the Transcendentalist idea of the *oversoul*—it's a pathway to it. By knowing ourselves deeply, by finding comfort in solitude, we open ourselves to a more profound connection with all beings. And that balance, that interplay between solitude and connection, has been the cornerstone of my recovery and personal growth."

The audience was impressed.

Amelia just smiled.

In those minutes, they formed a connection—one that promised engaging runs through the philosophies of life, punctuated by the sarcastic wit of two souls seasoned by their own tribulations. And as William prepared to navigate the post-panel mingling, he sensed this encounter would be anything but pedestrian.

Though knowing his track record with philosophical discussions, she was probably just being polite. Most people's eyes glazed over by the second Emerson quote.

· · · ● ● · ● ● · · ·

Backstage, the air hummed with private victories and intellectual sparring—a battleground of egos posturing under fluorescent lights. William navigated through the sea of bookish peacocks, his eyes set on the refreshment table, but it was Amelia who intercepted him, a smirk that danced on the edge of mischief and knowing.

"Mr. Marathon Man . . . ready for a victory lap, or shall we skip straight to the philosophical wind-down?"

"Only if it involves less metaphysical hot air and more of your sharp wit," William parried, snagging two waters from the dwindling spread. He offered her one, the plastic bottle a cold peace offering between minds.

"Careful, I might just accept your offer." Amelia's smile was as disarming as her intellect, and they both knew it.

"You're a bit of a modern-day Margaret Fuller, huh? Lead the way!"

"Today a reader, tomorrow a leader."

Their conversation became a dance of words as they moved away from the noise, weaving through corridors lined with history and ambition. With each step, their banter volleyed back and forth with the ease of old friends—or skilled adversaries sizing each other up.

"Ever consider that running is just philosophy in motion?" William tossed the idea into the mix as they exited into the embrace of the South Carolinian twilight, the Penn Center sprawling before them like a testament to endurance and legacy.

"Ah, the body achieving what the mind envisions," Amelia responded, her tone playful yet thoughtful. "I prefer to think of it as the ultimate con against one's own limitations."

"Spoken like someone who's outrun more than just the competition," he said, catching the flicker of a deeper story in her gaze.

"Perhaps, but let's save the tragic backstories for another chapter, shall we?"

"Agreed."

He appreciated her deft avoidance. They continued their stroll, the fading light casting long shadows across the grounds, wrapping around them like an intimate shroud.

"Philosophy, though," Amelia wondered aloud, changing lanes without signaling, "isn't that just the art of questioning everything until nothing makes sense anymore?"

"Or until everything does. The greatest heist, stealing clarity from chaos."

"Sounds like a motion worth arguing," Amelia replied, her legal mind showing through.

"Sounds like our topic for a run," William said, the promise hanging between them, neither tangible nor fleeting—just another secret handshake sealed by kindred spirits in the dusk of Southern charm.

"Let's not jump the gun. After all, every good argument requires proper preparation."

Must be a lawyer, William thought, recognizing the precise way she chose her words. It suited her somehow.

"Then consider this the groundwork," he assured, his eyes alight with the thrill of the chase—the run, the philosophy, and the undeniable pull of whatever lay ahead.

Amelia offered a soft, conspiratorial laugh. "Groundwork . . . just make sure you can keep up."

As the sky deepened to indigo, they found themselves at her car and at the edge of understanding. After exchanging contact information, Amelia got in her car and backed out of her parking stall; she lowered her window, "until next time Marathon Man!"

"Next time indeed," thought William.

• • • ● • ● • • •

The next morning, William met Amelia at her hotel and they ran along Depot Road until they arrived at the Spanish Moss Trail. They turned right and continued into the wetland, just as the pink and orange sun was just rising low over the coastal marsh. Their conversation flowed as they ran along the *Lowcountry's Rails to Trail*. The soft, hypnotic sound of their footsteps on the paved path became the steady backdrop to their exchange, punctuated occasionally by the roar of jet planes from the nearby Marine Corps Air Station Beaufort. They were fleeting reminders of the world beyond this secluded stretch of tranquility.

Amelia's stride was confident, her body moving with the grace of someone accustomed to pushing limits. Beside her, William ran with a purposeful gait, the kind that told of countless miles and marathons conquered, each step a testament to his endurance—not just in body, but emotionally as well.

The air was rich with the scent of brackish water mingling with earth—a pungent reminder of life's raw, untamed essence. Spanish moss hung like ancient drapery from the arms of live oaks, the morning light filtering through in slivers, casting an ethereal glow upon the trail. It was here, in the embrace of nature's muted spectacle, that their armors dissolved, layer by layer.

"Running," Amelia said, her breath measured against the rhythm of her pace, "it's the only time my mind goes silent. No arguments, no cases, no contract . . . just the heartbeat and the breath."

William glanced at her, appreciating the simplicity of her words as they resonated with his own truth. "For me, it's a form of meditation," he confessed, voice steady despite the exertion. "Each run is like shedding the skin of my past mistakes. With every mile, I'm reborn."

Grand pronouncements and lengthy discussions proved unnecessary; their shared understanding transcended the spoken word. For once, William found himself without the urge to quote any dead philosophers. Some moments, he realized, were profound enough on their own.

The conversation shifted, as natural as the trail winding before them, to delve into the scars they bore beneath their resilient surfaces. William spoke of the nights lost to vice and the mornings found in regret, the relentless cycle that once threatened to consume him whole. Running had been his salvation—a physical manifestation of his journey from addiction to authorship.

"Philosophy," he said, more to the surrounding vegetation than to Amelia, "taught me the value of struggle. The Stoics, they understood pain is inevitable, but suffering? That's a choice."

"Sounds like you've stolen more than clarity," Amelia said, her eyes catching the last glints of daylight. "You've pilfered hope from despair."

"Isn't that the ultimate scam?"

"Perhaps. But it's one thing to know the path and another to walk it."

Their laughter was short-lived as silence settled between them like an unspoken pact. Each lost in reflection yet anchored by the other's presence, they turned around near a parking area and headed back to town.

William matched Amelia's pace, a comfortable rhythm that seemed to echo the pulsing heartbeat of the natural world around them. Their feet fell in sync, a silent language of camaraderie shared between two seasoned runners.

They pushed forward, and the banter continued, a dance of words and wit that drew them closer in spirit. They shared stories of runs gone hilariously wrong: William recounted a marathon where he'd taken a wrong turn and ended up leading a pack of confused runners through a farmer's market, Amelia countered with a tale of a local 5K where she'd accidentally become tethered to a dog leash and finished the race with a borrowed poodle in tow.

"Maybe running is the universe's way of teaching us humility," he said, his smile visible even in the dimming light.

"Or its way of showing us who we really are," she added, her gaze lingering on him a second too long, a soft challenge flickering in her eyes.

Each joke, each story, each glance wove a thread of intimacy, binding them in a shared understanding of life's absurdities and beauties. It was this connection—forged in sweat, sealed in humor—that promised more than just a fleeting run.

As they approached a bench in the middle of the swampy grounds, the chemistry between them was undeniable. As they paused, catching their breaths and stealing glances, the anticipation of what might come next charged the surrounding air. The sun was higher now . . . warmer, too. Their breaths slowed after miles of shared pavement. The silence was comfortable, punctuated only by the occasional splash from the swampy waters nearby—a lurking alligator's ritual jaunt.

He found his gaze drawn to her profile, the morning light casting her strong features in a soft glow. In this quiet moment, William could appreciate the subtle curve of her lips, the way her eyelashes fluttered like the wings of a dark moth against the impending night sky. Amelia turned her head slightly, catching him in the act, and a playful smirk danced across her face.

"See something you like?" she asked, the corners of her mouth turning up in amusement.

"Nature is quite the artist," William said in reply, deflecting smoothly with his own brand of dry humor, while gesturing ambiguously towards the marsh before them . . . or to Amelia herself—he left it deliciously unclear.

Her chuckle was a low melody that mingled with the rustling leaves around them. "You're not so bad yourself, M Squared," she said.

"M Squared?"

"Marathon Man, of course."

"Well . . . oh, ok."

Referencing one of the many philosophers he had quoted during their run, Amelia said, "I doubt Thoreau would approve of all this idleness."

"Thoreau never had the pleasure of your company," he noted, his voice a half octave lower than usual.

They let the joke hang between them, a banner of their banter. As the sky brightened, the world seemed to shrink until it was just the two of them and the rhythmic breathing of the marshland. Her hand lay inches from his on the weathered wood of the bench—an expanse of uncharted territory begging to be claimed.

But then, the tranquility shattered. Somewhere down the trail, a branch snapped—a harsh crack in the quietude of their sanctuary. Both William and Amelia tensed, turning toward the sound. Their eyes met, and the charge between them shifted, an electric current of awareness that spoke of dangers more primal than any lurking reptile.

"Race you back?" she whispered, the challenge lighting up her eyes with the thrill of the unknown.

"Only if you can keep up," he said, his words laden with double meaning.

In a single fluid motion, they rose from the bench, adrenaline replacing serenity. While they ran off, the sky transformed into twilight blues, carrying whispers of what could have been on the breeze, signaling the end of one chapter and the beginning of a new mystery, and possibly, a fresh start.

Expose, Depose, Dispose

William hadn't planned on being in Boston, but when Amelia mentioned she was speaking at a healthcare law symposium at Suffolk University, it seemed like fate. Or at least a good excuse to leave Salem for a day. The conference focused on emerging trends in medical liability—not his usual fare, but something about Amelia's sharp wit and keen insights made even the driest legal precedents sound intriguing.

Their feet stumbled over the cobblestones as they threaded their way through the narrow streets of Boston's North End. Amelia sidestepped a steaming manhole cover and glanced over at William, whose shaved head gleamed under the Boston sun like a lighthouse beacon for the philosophically lost at sea.

After a quick stop at *Bova's Bakery* for cannoli, they continued up Salem Street to the Old North Church—*one if by land, two if by sea*—and marveled at the sanctuary's boxed pews that congregants purchased to give them a vote in church matters. They made their way up the hill and walked amongst the thin, aging markers of Copp's Hill burying Ground. They paused before a marker near the Charter Street entrance indicating the Mather Family Tomb.

"Cotton Mather . . . why do I know that name?" she asked as she swept her hand toward the marker, her dark locks swaying with a hint of defiance against historical follies.

William chuckled to himself, remembering the oversimplified quip he'd once heard. Someone once told him, *Here lies the man who thought smallpox could be cured by prayer.*

But living in Salem had taught him the folly of such reductive thinking. Mather, he'd learned, was a far more complex figure. True, the Puritan minister had been embroiled in the infamous witch trials, but he was also a man ahead of his time.

"Cotton Mather was a Puritan minister. His father—Increase Mather—was as well. Increase eventually became president of Harvard College . . . Cotton, though he tried, never did. They were both avid writers, but Cotton's prolific writing defined his era.

"During the 1700s smallpox outbreak here, Cotton had advocated for inoculation; that's the norm now, but it was a radical and controversial idea then. He'd learned of the practice from an enslaved African named Onesimus. Cotton saw no conflict between his faith and this medical advancement; to him, prayer and practical action went hand in hand."

The irony struck William. Here was a man often remembered for religious zealotry, yet he'd faced fierce opposition for promoting a life-saving medical treatment. Cotton's contemporaries had seen inoculation as dangerous and unnatural, much like how some viewed William's unconventional approaches to addiction recovery. And yet, this same man who advocated for scientific progress in medicine had also been a driving force behind the Salem witch trials, fervently believing in and prosecuting supposed practitioners of witchcraft. It was a stark reminder of how even the most forward-thinking individuals could be blind to their own contradictions, persecuting the misunderstood while simultaneously championing misunderstood causes. William couldn't help but draw parallels to his own journey—how he had once judged and been judged before finding a path that embraced both science and spirituality in recovery.

As they continued their walk, he reflected on how history, like recovery, was rarely black and white. It was a tapestry of contradictions, missteps, and unexpected progressions—much like the path that had led him from addiction to the tranquil streets of Salem.

• • • ● • ● • • •

As they walked along the cemetery's path that paralleled Charter Street, William's stoic gaze traced the lines of history etched into the stone of each gravestone. They looked through the trees and around the buildings to see the *USS Constitution* in the

Charlestown Navy Yard, where the Charles River meets Boston Harbor; here, the air smelled faintly of the ocean, mixed with the aromas of Italian restaurants they had passed earlier.

"Before I decided that health was more than a commodity, I danced to the tune of corporate litigators," Amelia said, folding her arms as if to shield herself from the ghosts of her past. "Lawsuits as foreplay, mergers as consummation. It was all very . . . stimulating."

"Until?" William prompted, leaning against an ancient oak near the middle of the cemetery, its roots likely as entangled as the healthcare system Amelia now navigated.

"Until I realized I was courting the devil in a pinstripe suit." Amelia's laugh was short, a staccato note punctuating the seriousness of her revelation. "I transitioned to healthcare, took up the mantle at Coastal Beacon Health System. General Counsel."

"From devils to angels?" William asked, quirking a brow as he watched her face, searching for the punchline in her career plot twist.

"More like exchanging one set of horns for another," she replied. "But at least at CBHS, I thought I could make a difference. That was before I saw the books—before I knew I was dining with wolves."

"Sounds like a feast you're ready to walk away from," he observed, straightening up, his body coiled and ready.

"Let's just say I'm sharpening my knives, William. And I'm not talking about the steak variety." Amelia's smile was sharp, a glint of strategy in her gaze. "Care to join me at the table?"

"Amelia, I think I'd join you just about anywhere."

She blushed. "Now let's find one of those Italian restaurants!"

With the old cemetery behind them, they descended the hill, leaving the dead to their eternal rest.

• • • ● • ● • • • •

The crisp morning found them in Manhattan a few days later, where William had agreed to give a talk at the New York Running Club later that evening. His publisher was already excited about his next book—tentatively titled *From Running Away to Running Toward: A Journey of Recovery*—even though he'd only drafted the first few chapters. When he'd mentioned his trip to Amelia during their Boston dinner, she'd suggested meeting early to walk across the Brooklyn Bridge. These chance encounters were becoming less chance and more choice, though neither was quite ready to acknowledge it.

As she approached the Manhattan entrance of the Brooklyn Bridge, Amelia's footfalls tapped out a rhythm on the pavement, a metropolitan metronome in sync with the pulse of New York City. There she found William leaning casually against a lamppost, the lines of his runner's body unconsciously mimicking the bridge's taut cables. The early evening sun caught the shaved plains of his head, turning him into a lighthouse beaconing her arrival.

"Always on time," William said, pushing himself off the bridge's armature to greet her. "The punctuality of a Swiss watch with the style of an Italian sports car."

"Trying to keep up with you," Amelia shot back, a smirk playing on her lips as she took in his attire—casual, yes, but meticulously chosen. "I see you've dressed for the occasion. Is that the new marathon runner chic?"

"Only the best for a walk across the East River," he replied, matching her tone. "Besides, who knows when we might need to sprint from corporate raiders or dash after runaway justice?"

Their banter was a verbal dance they had become adept at—a weave of sarcasm and wit that somehow drew them closer without crossing unspoken boundaries. They began their stroll across the bridge, steps falling in an easy cadence, each aware of the other's presence like a new melody blending with a well-known chorus.

The city, behind them now, a canvas of ambition and dreams sketched out in concrete and glass. The bustle mirrored the energy between them—lively, unpredictable, tinged with the thrill of something still undefined. Side by side on the wooden path, they shared fleeting glances that held promises neither was quite ready to voice, each look a subtle acknowledgment of the delicate web of attraction being spun.

"Mind the tourists," Amelia said, deftly navigating around a cluster of camera-wielding visitors. "I'd rather not end up as an unwitting photobomb in someone's vacation memories."

William laughed, matching her pace. "Come now, where's your sense of adventure? A surprise appearance in a stranger's photo album could be the start of an intriguing story."

"Or the end of my anonymity," Amelia said with a wry smile. "I prefer my narratives a bit more . . . curated."

They stopped near the first of the bridge's two grand gothic towers, and William reflected on his journey across the Brooklyn Bridge, a pilgrimage he'd made countless times. For him, it represented something beyond a simple walk; it was a transition between worlds. "There's something transformative about this trek from Manhattan to Brooklyn. With each step, the frenetic energy of Manhattan seems to ebb away, replaced by Brooklyn's more languid rhythm. It's like watching the city exhale."

He paused, gazing back at Manhattan's skyline. "But it's not just about decompression. This walk gives you a real sense of Brooklyn's scale, its vastness. You start to understand why it was once its own city. From up here, you can almost feel the borough's heartbeat, distinct from Manhattan's, yet unmistakably part of the same urban organism."

The wind toyed with Amelia's hair as they continued their walk. She felt William's presence beside her, unmistakable even without glancing his way.

"Ever think about what secrets hover just beneath the surface?" she asked, watching a barge slice through the river below. "All these people scurrying back and forth, each one a closed book."

"Occasionally," William replied, the lines around his eyes deepening as he squinted into the sunlight. "But then I remember I've read enough tragic tales for one lifetime."

"Ah, but some stories must be shared." A smirk played on Amelia's lips, her gaze still fixed on the horizon. "Especially when they're non-fiction and could make Robin Hood consider a comeback."

His eyebrows arched, curiosity piqued. "You've stumbled upon something?"

"Stumbled, crashed, got buried under an avalanche of it," she corrected, her tone light despite the gravity of her words. She was ready to return to the conversation they began at the cemetery in Boston. "CBHS isn't the beacon of hope it pretends to be. It's more like a lighthouse with a bulb gone dark."

"Dark how?"

William's voice was steady, but she noticed the subtle stiffening of his posture, the telltale sign of gears shifting, thoughts racing.

"Let's just say our CEO, Vincent Blackwell, would have made a fine pirate in another life. Only instead of treasure chests, he prefers retirement funds. And his parrot? Well, it's a balance sheet that squawks lies."

"Embezzlement?"

"Among other indiscretions," she confirmed, feeling a surge of satisfaction at the shock etched on his face. "A veritable smorgasbord of corporate malfeasance."

"Damn," William breathed out, his gaze now locked with hers. "I suppose it makes some sense. Blackwell's always struck me as a man who'd sell his grandma for a nickel."

"Sadly, in this story, grandma's already been auctioned off." Her stride never faltered, even as the implications of her discovery loomed large beside them. "And they rigged the bidding war from the start."

William's jaw clenched, the stoic philosopher now replaced by an avenger in the making. The bridge, once a symbol of connection, now spanned the chasm between justice and corruption, with both of them poised to cross it together.

• • • ● • ● • • •

Amelia's strides matched the rhythm of revelation, her words painting an elaborate fresco of deceit across the Brooklyn Bridge's expanse. "Blackwell's greed doesn't end with a little creative accounting," she said, the sarcasm in her voice as sharp as the Manhattan skyline. "Our dear CEO—my boss—has been playing a high-stakes game far beyond us."

William's brow furrowed as he watched the play of determination on Amelia's face, each detail of corruption adding depth to the portrait of a man who would bleed dry his own empire.

"One of their first overseas ventures was acquiring a failing healthcare company in Montenegro," she said, her gaze locked on the horizon where skyscrapers met the sky in a cold handshake. "The deal stank from the start. They paid just one euro to take over three public hospitals—sounds generous until you learn the government actually paid them millions to accept the deal. The local doctors were up in arms, protesting the handover of their public healthcare system to a company with zero experience in the region."

"Let me guess, the promised renovations never happened?"

"Worse. They siphoned millions out of the country under the guise of consultancy fees while the hospitals crumbled. Medical workers went on strike, patients suffered in dilapidated wards, and when the courts finally investigated—" Amelia's lips twisted in disgust, "—they found evidence of collusion between company officials and government representatives. The whole thing was a sham from day one."

The river below mirrored William's growing fury, its current a tumultuous reflection of his thoughts. "They don't just prey on vulnerable hospitals," he said. "They prey on vulnerable nations."

"Exactly." Amelia's nod was solemn, her athletic frame cutting through the crowd with prosecutorial precision. "And stateside? It's a veritable ghost town of services never rendered. Imagine paying for a five-star meal and receiving a TV dinner, or rather, no dinner at all."

"Charming," William said, his head shaking slightly. A quote from Seneca danced on the tip of his tongue, something about virtue being sufficient for happiness, but the irony was too rich to taste amid the bile of betrayal.

"Surveillance, too. Big Brother Blackwell had eyes everywhere, keeping tabs on anyone daring to whisper dissent."

"Privacy is so last century. But, I imagine our modern-day Midas didn't stop at mere surveillance."

"Of course not. His golden touch extended to yachts, jets, and a ranch so big it'd make the Ponderosa look like a petting zoo." The disdain in Amelia's voice could've cut a diamond.

"Nothing screams *healthcare* like a fleet of private jets. I presume there's more?"

"Indeed. The masterstroke: selling hospital real estate to WRI at suspiciously high valuations, then leasing it back through complex arrangements that obscure the true financial burden." Her dark eyes blazed as they passed a group of tourists snapping selfies, oblivious to the corporate shell game playing out in their city's shadow. "WRI claims the deals are fair market value, based on their *internal appraisals*, but the numbers tell a different story. And conveniently, their executives' compensation seems to rise with every acquisition they make, regardless of how risky the tenant."

They continued their walk and officially entered Brooklyn, the wooden path now concrete. They continued on until the path split; the path veered to the left, which took them into DUMBO. As they descended from the bridge, they found themselves in DUMBO, a neighborhood whose very name spoke to the quirkiness of New York. "Down Under the Manhattan Bridge Overpass," William said, gesturing to the massive steel structure looming above them. "DUMBO. Whoever said urban planners lack a sense of humor?"

The area, once a ferry landing in the 1600s—long before the Brooklyn Bridge was built—had transformed over centuries into a manufacturing district, its imposing brick warehouses and factories a testament to Brooklyn's industrial past. But like so much of New York, DUMBO had reinvented itself. Starting in the 1970s, artists drawn by cheap rents and vast spaces colonized the abandoned buildings. What was once a backdrop of industrial decay became a canvas for creativity. By the late 20th century, tech startups and luxury lofts had joined the artistic community, turning DUMBO into one of Brooklyn's most desirable neighborhoods. The old warehouses now housed art galleries, boutique shops, and high-end restaurants, while keeping the area's gritty, artistic charm. As they walked the cobblestone streets, the juxtaposition of old and new, of industrial heritage and modern innovation, was clear at every turn.

• • • ● • ● • • •

As they wandered amongst the shoppers in the archway of the Brooklyn Flea, William paused at a vendor's stall, pretending interest in a collection of vintage books. One caught his eye—a weathered copy of *The Art of War.*

"Now there's an interesting find," Amelia said, picking up the book. "Strategy, timing, knowing your opponent's weaknesses . . ."

William nodded, understanding her unspoken meaning. "Speaking of strategy," he said, "have you given any thought to next steps with CBHS?"

"Expose, depose, dispose." Amelia's reply was crisp, her inner warrior stepping forth. "In that order."

"Sounds like my kind of trilogy," he responded, the glint in his eye now matching hers.

The wind picked up, carrying with it the briny scent of the East River and resolve as William and Amelia threaded their way through the throng of DUMBO's flea market, a tapestry of humanity that unfolded in vibrant bursts of color and sound. It was an artist's fever dream come to life, with every stall a frame for the peculiar and the profound. Vintage records spun tales next to handcrafted jewelry that glimmered like tiny galaxies caught in mid-spin. The scent of sizzling street food mingled with the dulcet tones of a jazz saxophonist pouring his soul into the afternoon air.

"Life's rich pageant," William said, watching a magician pull more than just rabbits from his proverbial hat. "And we're stuck on the chapter about corporate thieves."

"Thieves who wear ties instead of masks," Amelia added, her voice laced with a venom so smooth it could be bottled and sold as artisanal poison. Her eyes scanned the crowd, not unlike a general surveying the battlefield. She moved with the grace of a panther, each step deliberate, exuding both danger and allure.

"Vincent and his cohorts have made an art out of deception," she said, her words painting a picture more grotesque than any of the avant-garde pieces they passed. "They've bled the system dry while masquerading as its saviors."

A vendor hawked antique watches, promising timelessness; Amelia scoffed at the notion. Time, after all, was ticking away for the patients and employees whose lives had been pawned in CBHS's grand scheme. Her resolve was as tangible as the vinyl records nestled in crates, each groove a testament to trials endured.

"Every second counts when you're saving lives—or supposed to be," she continued, her voice carrying the weight of the world yet never breaking under it. "But Blackwell? He'd rather count seconds on his luxury watch collection than on a patient's heart monitor."

William's lips twitched upwards, the corners of his mouth betraying a smile that held more determination than humor. "Then let's wind back the clock on him, shall we?"

"Let's," Amelia said, her spirit undeterred by the gravity of their undertaking. They wove through the human mosaic, their presence a pair of silent meteors destined to collide with the corrupt constellation that loomed over Coastal Beacon Health System.

· · ● · ● · ● ● · ·

Stepping away from the sensory carnival of Dumbo's flea market, William glanced at Amelia with a sly tilt of his head, the sun casting a conspiratorial glow around them. "What say we drown our outrage in a cone of vanilla chocolate chunk?" he asked, nodding toward the Brooklyn Ice Cream Factory, its windows fogged with the promise of creamy indulgence.

"Because nothing screams *planning a takedown* like brain freeze," Amelia said, her eyes sparkling with mischief as she followed him into the cool embrace of the shop. They stood side by side, indecisively hovering over the flavors, while a scoop of dark chocolate ice cream flirted with the edge of a waffle cone, threatening to dive into oblivion before it reached eager lips.

With cones in hand, they found themselves perched on a bench that offered a view of the bridge, the East River flowing beneath it like a silent accomplice to their conversation. The ice cream began to melt, mirroring the facade of normalcy they both projected, knowing full well that behind Amelia's poised demeanor and William's casual stance lay a brewing storm.

"Vincent Blackwell's been playing Jenga with people's lives," Amelia said, her tongue darting out to catch a drip of vanilla bean. "If we pull the wrong block too fast, it won't just be his tower that topples." Her words were light, but the gravity behind them was as dense as the fudge ribbon swirling through her dessert.

William nodded, his shaved head reflecting the fading daylight. "And when it comes crashing down, we need to ensure we're not the ones buried under the rubble." He paused, considering the risks, his spoon carving methodical paths through a mound of mint chocolate chip.

"Subtlety isn't exactly my strong suit," she admitted, a half-smile curving her lips. "But I suppose we'll need more finesse than a sledgehammer to crack this nut."

"Perhaps a scalpel then? Precision can inflict a far deeper cut than brute force." The sarcasm in William's voice was a fine layer, almost imperceptible, like the sprinkling of sea salt atop his caramel confection.

Their banter was a dance, each step calculated yet effortless, a playful duel that masked the intensity of their shared purpose. They continued to dissect their plan with the precision of surgeons, their words weaving through the possibilities and pitfalls, even as their spoons scraped the last vestiges of ice cream from soggy cones.

"Whatever the plan is," Amelia said, tossing her empty cone into a nearby trash can with a flourish, "it better be as bulletproof as Blackwell thinks his alibis are."

"Bulletproof and watertight," William agreed, standing up and stretching his legs as if preparing for the marathon ahead. "After all, we're setting sail in treacherous waters. It wouldn't do to sink before we even spot the sharks."

Their laughter mingled with the sounds of the city as they walked away from the factory, leaving behind the sweetness of their treat but carrying with them the taste of determination . . . a flavor far more enduring.

• • ● • ● • • •

Halfway through their walk back across the bridge, Amelia leaned against the weathered railing of the Brooklyn Bridge, her gaze fixed on the East River below, where the water churned with the secret currents of the city. The sun painted the waves in hues of liquid gold and fiery orange, a spectacle of beauty that belied the darkness lurking beneath the surface.

"Empires crumble, you know," she said, more to herself than to William. Her fingers traced the intricate pattern on the railing, etched by time and a thousand other hands, seeking solace in the steady pulse of the river. "And when they do, it's the silent rot within that brings them down."

William watched her with an intensity that matched the dying light. He saw the fire in her eyes, the sort that could either warm a soul or burn it to cinders. It was clear which one fueled Amelia at this moment.

"Tell me about your vision, Amelia," he said, his voice a low rumble against the backdrop of the city's evening symphony.

She turned to face him, her athletic silhouette outlined by the skyline. "It's simple, really," she began, her voice a blend of steel and velvet. "We expose the festering wounds within CBHS and cauterize them with the truth. We don't just topple a corrupt CEO; we dismantle an entire empire of greed, piece by rotten piece."

The conviction in her words was palpable, a tangible force that seemed to ripple through the air between them. She spoke not just as a lawyer or an advocate, but as a guardian of justice, willing to fight tooth and nail for what she believed in.

"Restoring justice to a system that parasites have bled dry," she continued, "that's my vision. To see hospitals serving their true purpose, not as cash cows for the morally bankrupt."

William's lips quirked into a half-smile, the kind that suggested he appreciated the irony of the situation. Here they were, plotting the downfall of a healthcare empire against a cityscape that seemed to hold its breath—a tableau of anticipation—like two modern-day Robin Hoods with a taste for corporate blood.

"Count me in," he said, the words carrying the weight of an unspoken oath. "I've spent a lifetime learning to navigate treacherous paths, Amelia. Now, I'm ready to run this one with you—through every twist, turn, and dark alley."

"We're up against Vincent, Samantha, Kiran—the unholy trinity of CBHS," she said, locking eyes with him. "They won't go down without a dirty fight."

"Dirty is just how I like it," William replied, his voice tinged with the kind of sarcasm that danced on the edge of seduction. "Makes the victory all the sweeter, doesn't it?"

"Sweet as stolen honey. And we're going to pilfer the whole damn hive."

· · · · ● · ● · · ·

They walked in sync, the only sign of their internal frenzy: the occasional tap of Amelia's fingers against her thigh—rhythmic and precise like her legal arguments—and the way William's gaze swept their surroundings, ever the tactician, even amid the tourists and selfie-snappers.

Their conversation was sparse, but the silence was rich with shared intellect and the sizzle of forming camaraderie. A gentle ribbing here about the absurdity of their ice cream interlude juxtaposed against the gravity of their cause, an arched brow there at the notion that justice could be served cold and sweet—these were the undercurrents of their alliance.

As silhouettes against the bright blue sky, William considered the Stoics' musings on fate and virtue. Was it kismet? He smiled at the thought; fortune was something you seized, not something that serendipitously landed in your waffle cone.

The connection between them was no longer just the mutual appreciation for sarcasm or the thrill of the impending heist. It ran deeper, a current that carried the weight of their histories, their struggles, and the world they intended to set right.

"Look at us," Amelia said, her voice low, almost lost to the wind. "Two would-be avengers in the land of opportunity, finding common ground over corruption and dairy products."

"America really is beautiful, isn't it?" William said, though his eyes told a story of admiration—not for the view, but for the woman beside him who could appreciate the irony.

In the shadow of the city's towering monoliths, they pressed forward, their purpose as solid as the now concrete sidewalk beneath their feet. The bridge behind them spanned more than just the river; it was a metaphorical crossing from solitary warriors to a united front.

"Ready?" Amelia asked, her tone shifting to one of resolve.

"Since the day I was born," came William's response, half truth, half jest. It wasn't entirely clear which half was which.

And so, with the bond between them sealed in the crucible of a shared crusade, Amelia and William stepped off the Brooklyn Bridge, leaving behind nothing but the echo of their footsteps and the promise of a storm on the horizon.

The city's pulse thrummed through the soles of their shoes, a reminder of the lives entangled in the web of CBHS's greed. And yet, amidst the urban symphony of honking taxis and chattering pedestrians, there was a palpable sense of clarity.

"Here we are," Amelia said, more to herself than to William, "the precipice of something great."

"Or at least the precipice of making someone's day really, really bad." William's tone was dry, but his eyes sparkled with the kind of mischief that only comes when risk intertwines with righteousness.

They paused, allowing the gravity of the moment to anchor them before taking the final steps off the bridge. Tomorrow, they would gather their allies, plot trajectories, and prepare alibis. But tonight, it was about the electric charge of anticipation, the seductive dance of potentiality that hung in the air between them.

"Shall we?" William extended his arm, a gentleman's gesture marred only slightly by the hint of conspiracy that laced his words.

"Lead on," Amelia replied, slipping her hand into the crook of his elbow, her grip firm and unyielding.

Together, they walked into the city, their shadows merging into one as they disappeared into the urban maze. The chapter closed, not with an ending, but with the irresistible pull of a new beginning—one lined with the hope of justice and the sweet taste of revenge yet to come.

The Frosted Philosopher

P hone - Darby

His first call was to Darby. As the phone rang, he remembered her quick wit and adaptability from their previous heist. She answered on the third ring.

"William? This is unexpected." Darby's voice carried a mix of surprise and intrigue.

"Darby, I need you in Salem. It's time for another job," William said, his tone serious.

There was a pause before Darby replied, "I'll be there tomorrow."

The morning sun cast long shadows across William's Salem home as Darby's car pulled into the driveway. She stepped out, her platinum hair catching the light, a mix of curiosity and excitement in her eyes.

William opened the door before she could knock. "Darby," he greeted, a hint of a smile playing on his lips. "Glad you could make it."

"Well, well, if it isn't my favorite reformed gambling addict turned philosopher king," she smirked, stepping inside. "Missing the thrill of the con, or just couldn't resist my charming company?"

"Says the former enforcer," William said with a wry smile. "How's the life of a strategic communications advisor treating you?"

"Freelancing has its perks," she admitted, following him to his study. "I get to choose my battles now, help companies clean up their messes—the legitimate ones, anyway. But it's still boring as hell compared to our last venture. Though I have to say, taking down a porn empire was never on my bucket list."

William gestured for her to take a seat as he poured them both coffee. "Let's aim higher. It's about a healthcare conglomerate called CBHS, Coastal Beacon Health System," William began, his tone serious. "They've been buying up hospitals across the country, promising improved care and efficiency. But the reality is far darker."

Darby leaned forward, her interest piqued. "Go on."

"They're denying care to patients who can't pay, understaffing hospitals to cut costs, and running once-thriving medical centers into the ground for profit. A whistleblower named Amelia approached me. She's got evidence, but she needs our help to expose it all."

Darby's eyes narrowed. "And you want to take them down."

William nodded. "It's big, Darby. Bigger than anything we've done before. But if we pull it off, we could save lives and bring down a corrupt system that's hurting people when they're most vulnerable."

Darby was quiet for a moment, processing the information. Then a slow smile spread across her face. "Well, it sounds like you could use my particular set of skills. When do we start?"

"Right now," William said, standing up. "We need to assemble the team. Are you up for a road trip?"

Darby stood, a mischievous glint in her eye. "Always. Let's go round up the usual suspects."

• • • ● • ● • • •

New York City - Tommy

The neon glow of Guardian International's sign bled into Tommy's office, casting an array of distorted shadows across his desk. William and Darby stood in the doorway, taking in the sight of their old friend.

His office was just one building to the east of his home on W 37th Street in New York City's Garment District. Though he now had more money than he could ever spend, he never left his neighborhood. Tommy sat with the quiet confidence of a man who could disarm you with a smile or a swift uppercut—whichever the situation called for.

"Well, well," Tommy said, his voice as rough as worn leather. "If it isn't the dynamic duo. To what do I owe this pleasure?"

William stepped forward, his eyes scanning the office. "Nice setup you've got here, Tommy."

"Business seems to be booming," said Darby. "I guess I'm a little surprised you're still in this part of town. For some reason, I thought you'd move."

"The ghosts of Eleanor and Mark kept me here, I imagine." Tommy was referring to Eleanor Roosevelt and Mark Twain; Eleanor lived on the street while Mark's funeral was held nearby.

He leaned back in his chair; the leather creaking under his mass. "I love this area. I just couldn't see myself anywhere else.

"So I can't complain. Turns out there's always someone needing protection in this city. But somehow, I doubt you're here to discuss my client list."

Darby perched on the edge of his desk, her platinum hair catching the light. "You're right about that. We've got a proposition for you.

Tommy's eyes narrowed slightly. "I'm listening."

William took a seat across from Tommy. "What do you know about CBHS?"

"Big healthcare, big money, big trouble," Tommy replied. "What's your angle?"

As William outlined the situation with CBHS and Amelia's story, Tommy's expression grew increasingly grim. When William finished, Tommy stood up and walked to the window, gazing at Reichenbach Hall and the street below.

"So," he said, turning back to face them, "you're telling me this hospital conglomerate is not only denying care to patients but also running hospitals into the ground for profit? And you want to bring them to justice?"

Darby nodded. "That's the gist of it. We could use your expertise, Tommy. Your security knowledge, your ability to read people and situations—it would be invaluable."

Tommy was quiet for a moment, then a slow smile spread across his face. "Well, it's been a while since I've done anything truly exciting. Guardian International can run without me for a bit. Count me in."

As they prepared to leave, William paused. "By the way, Tommy, how's that youth boxing program you started coming along?"

A slight softening appeared on Tommy's face, his usual harsh lines relaxing. "Good. Really good. Keeping kids off the streets, teaching them discipline. It's . . . fulfilling."

Darby smiled. "Looks like you've found your calling."

Tommy nodded. "Maybe. But I wouldn't mind mixing it up a bit. When do we start?"

· · · ● · ● · · ·

Los Angeles - Justine

The California sun was an attention hog, but it had serious competition from the gleam of the sleek PR firm that Justine now called home. William and Darby found her in her corner office, red curls bouncing as she paced back and forth, phone pressed to her ear.

"No, absolutely not. We're not spinning this as a *youthful indiscretion*. Your client knew exactly what he was doing," Justine was saying, her voice firm but professional. She glanced up, seeing William and Darby together, and her eyes widened. "I'll call you back," she said, ending the call.

"Well, this is a surprise," Justine said, a smile playing on her lips. "What makes me so lucky as to see two of my favorite people?"

William stepped forward, taking in the view from her office window. "Impressive setup, Justine. Looks like you've been busy since our last . . . adventure."

Justine leaned against her desk. "Strategic Shield Communications has been a wild ride, and I was beyond thrilled to work with Darby to start it. Since that start, the company has grown, and—as I'm sure she told you—she's given it all to me, now. Turns out my particular set of skills translates well to crisis management. But something tells me you're not here to discuss my client list and past business dealings."

Darby grinned. "Sharp as ever. I miss working with you, Justine. But it turns out we might team up again. We've got a situation and we could use your help."

As William laid out the details about CBHS, Justine's expression turned serious. When he finished, she was quiet for a moment, drumming her fingers on her desk.

"So," she said finally, "you're talking about taking down a healthcare giant that's not only exploiting patients but also potentially causing harm through unethical practices? And you want me to help craft the narrative?"

"To start, yes, that's the idea," Darby confirmed. "Your ability to shape public perception, to control the narrative—it could be crucial in bringing CBHS down."

Justine stood up and walked to her window, gazing out at the Los Angeles skyline. "You know," she said, turning back to them, "I've been feeling a bit . . . unfulfilled lately. Don't get me wrong, the work we do is challenging, but sometimes I wonder if I'm really making a difference."

William nodded understanding. "And how's the pro bono work going? Still helping those wrongfully accused clear their names?"

A smile touched Justine's lips. "It's good. Great, really. It's the most rewarding part of what I do here. But this . . . this could be a chance to make an even bigger impact."

She looked at William and Darby, determination in her eyes. "I'm in."

• • • •**•**•**•**• • •

Los Angeles - Josh

Across town, in a gleaming Financial District high-rise, William and Darby found Josh in his corner office. His desk was a meticulous arrangement of dual monitors displaying endless columns of numbers and market data.

Josh spun in his chair as they entered, his eyebrows shooting up in surprise. "Well, if it isn't the troublemakers. To what do I owe this unexpected visit?"

William smiled. "Hello, Josh. Looks like legitimate banking agrees with you."

Josh gestured around his office. "Risk management for Fortune 500 companies. Turns out there's good money in keeping everything above board . . . for a change. But I doubt you're here for investment advice."

Darby sat on one of his office's leather chairs. "You're right. We've got a job that could use your particular brand of genius."

As William outlined the situation with CBHS, Josh's fingers stilled on his keyboard, his full attention captured. When William finished, Josh leaned back in his chair, a thoughtful expression on his face.

"So . . . you're talking about dissecting the financials of a major hospital conglomerate, uncovering their accounting tricks, and potentially redistributing some of their ill-gotten gains? Sounds like fun."

William nodded. "We thought you might see it that way. We need someone who can trace their money trails, spot the creative accounting, find where they've hidden the evidence of fraud. Your forensic skills could blow their entire operation wide open."

Josh was quiet for a moment, his fingers tapping a restless rhythm on his desk. "You know," he said finally, "I love what I do, but sometimes it feels a bit . . . soulless."

Darby tilted her head. "And how's that pet project of yours going? The one helping small businesses protect themselves from cyber threats?"

A smile touched Josh's lips. "Each of these businesses is like a person; helping people protect what they've built—often with all of their savings . . . well, it's the most satisfying part of what I do. But this . . . this could be a chance to help on an even bigger scale."

He looked at William and Darby, a glint of excitement in his eyes. "Count me in. What's our first move?"

Cambridge - Ella

The halls of MIT buzzed with activity as William and Darby navigated their way to the computer science building. They found Ella in a state-of-the-art lab, sprawled in her chair with her feet up on the desk, idly tapping away at her laptop.

"Look who finally wandered into my digital kingdom," Ella said without looking up. "MIT's hallowed halls must be desperate for visitors."

William raised an eyebrow. "How'd you know it was us?"

Ella rolled her eyes, finally glancing their way. "Please. I hacked the security cameras ages ago. Saw you coming a mile away."

"Of course you did . . ."

Darby grinned, unfazed. "And here we thought we'd surprise you. We've got a job that could use your particular brand of . . . genius indifference."

"Cute," Ella said, her tone flat but her eyes betraying a flicker of interest. "What kind of job? And make it good, 'cause I'm oh-so-busy with all this thrilling academic work." She gestured vaguely at her surroundings, sarcasm dripping from every word.

As William explained the situation with CBHS, detailing the hospital conglomerate's unethical practices and exploitation of patients, Ella's bored expression shifted into one of barely concealed anger.

"So," she said when William finished, her voice carefully controlled, "you're telling me this healthcare giant is basically treating patients like cash cows, denying care, and running hospitals into the ground for profit?"

William nodded grimly. "That's the long and short of it. We need someone who can slice through their systems like a hot knife through butter. Someone who can find the evidence we need and make sure we don't leave so much as a digital fingerprint."

Ella leaned back in her chair, crossing her arms. "And you thought of little old me? I'm touched, really."

Darby tilted her head. "Come on, Ella. We know you care, even if you pretend not to. What about that anonymous tip line you set up to report trafficking? The one that's been making waves in the media?"

For a moment, Ella's carefully crafted mask of indifference slipped, revealing a mix of surprise and something deeper—perhaps pride, or purpose. But it vanished in an instant, replaced by her usual sardonic half-smile.

"Been keeping tabs on me, have you?" she said. "Fine, you got me. Maybe I do care. Sometimes. So what?"

William's expression softened. "I know why this might hit close to home. But that's exactly why we need you. Your skills, your experience . . . you could make a real difference here."

Ella was quiet for a moment, her fingers tapping a restless rhythm on her laptop. When she spoke, her voice was quieter, stripped of its usual sarcasm. "You know, sometimes I wonder if anything I do here really matters. All this code, all these theories . . . sometimes it feels a million miles away from the real world. From real people getting hurt."

She looked up at William and Darby, a spark of determination in her eyes. "Alright, I'm in. But not because I care or anything. I just . . . I could use a challenge . . ."

Darby smiled knowingly. "Of course. When can you start?"

Ella stood up, closing her laptop with a decisive click. "No time like the present. Besides, these stuffy academics were starting to bore me to tears, anyway."

As they left the lab, William hung back for a moment. "Hey, Ella . . . where are we meeting for our next cupcake adventure?"

Ella's sarcastic facade cracked for just a moment. "Inman Square here in Cambridge. *The Frosted Philosopher*. I hear their *Existential Vanilla* isn't half bad."

"Nietzsche would be proud . . . contemplating the void never tasted so sweet."

As they walked out into the crisp Cambridge air, Darby looked at William. "Well, looks like we've got our hacker extraordinaire. What's next on the agenda?"

William smiled, a glint of mischief in his eyes. "Now, we plan. CBHS won't know what hit them. And with Ella on our side, they won't even see us coming."

The team was assembled, each member bringing their unique skills and experiences to the table. They were ready to take on CBHS and right the wrongs that had been done. As they headed back to Salem, the anticipation of the upcoming heist hung in the air. The team was back together, and CBHS wouldn't know what hit them.

Winter Street

William's Salem home stood quietly on Winter Street, awaiting its return visitors. He opened the black door, his bald head reflecting the dusky light as he greeted his team.

"Welcome to the den of enlightenment," he said dryly.

One by one, they filed in: Darby, her blonde hair now styled in a disheveled bob; Justine, her eyes bright with anticipation; Tommy, his military bearing unchanged; Josh, looking every inch the reformed banker; and Ella, her presence radiating muted confidence.

"Look what the philosophy department dragged in," Darby said, pulling William into a hug. "Still quoting dead guys to solve life's problems?"

"Only on days ending in y," William shot back, returning the embrace.

The room filled with greetings and laughter as the team reunited. Josh straightened his tie, ever the banker even in casual moments. "How's your voluntary imprisonment at MIT treating you, Ella?"

"Please," Ella rolled her eyes, but her grin gave her away. "At least real prisons let you out for good behavior. MIT's firewalls never sleep. Though their coffee is marginally better."

Tommy moved through the group, dispensing brief hugs that belied his military bearing. "Like herding cats, getting this crew back together."

"Expensive, well-dressed cats," Justine added, smoothing her designer blazer with mock pretension.

William watched his unlikely family reconnect, their easy banter filling his home with warmth. After CAYA, they'd scattered to their respective corners of legitimacy—banking, academia, security. Yet here they were again, drawn together by another chance to right some wrongs.

"As much as I'm enjoying this touching reunion," he finally said, his tone shifting to something more serious, "we should move this to the dining room. We've got work to discuss."

The dining room, converted to their makeshift headquarters, reflected William's dual nature—running medals and philosophical quotes sharing wall space with the evidence of his transformation from addict to mentor.

"Here's what we know," William began, gesturing to the documents spread across the table. "CBHS—Coastal Beacon Health System. They're buying up hospitals across the country, promising improvements while bleeding them dry."

"Less poetry, more details," Darby interjected. "If this is bigger than CAYA, we need specifics. What exactly are we walking into?"

Tommy nodded. "Agreed. Who are they, what have they done, what do they have, where are they?"

"Fair points," William conceded. "Our insider will be here soon with the full brief. But before she arrives, understand this isn't just another heist. As Thoreau said, *The price of anything is the amount of life you exchange for it.* Once you hear everything, you'll need to decide if you're willing to pay that price."

"Always the philosopher," Tommy said, but his tone held respect.

$$\bullet \; \bullet \; \bullet \; \bullet \; \bullet \; \bullet \; \bullet \; \bullet \; \bullet$$

A fire crackled in the hearth of William's Salem abode, throwing shadows that danced like specters over the faces of assembled masterminds, each one a connoisseur of chaos in their own right. They lounged across various pieces of antique furniture as they updated each other on their lives, teased about life choices—and Darby's newest hairstyle—and showed a genuine affection for each other.

Finally, the sound of a car repeatedly shifting gears—drive, reverse, drive, reverse—announced an arrival. William's face lit up, a smile tugging at the corners of his mouth as he watched Amelia parallel park in a rare open spot on Winter Street. He composed himself, clearing his throat. "She's here," he announced, moving to the door.

Moments later, William returned with a woman by his side. She was tall and elegant, with piercing green eyes that seemed to take in everything at once. Her dark hair was pulled back in a neat bun, giving her an air of professionalism that was softened by the warmth in her smile.

"Everyone, I'd like you to meet Amelia," William said, his voice carrying a note of admiration that didn't go unnoticed by the team. "Amelia is a friend and current executive at CBHS. She's the one who brought this case to our attention."

Amelia nodded to the group, her gaze lingering on each face. "It's a pleasure to meet you all. William has told me so much about your . . . unique skill sets."

The team couldn't help but notice the subtle glances exchanged between William and Amelia. There was a comfort between them, a familiarity that spoke of shared experiences and mutual respect—perhaps even something more. As introductions wound down, Darby nudged Josh, raising an eyebrow.

"So, Amelia," Darby said, a mischievous glint in her eye, "how long have you and our illustrious running machine been . . . collaborating?"

William cleared his throat, a faint blush creeping up his neck. "Darby, please. We're here on serious business."

"Oh, I'm sure it's very serious," Josh chimed in, grinning. "Seriously intense research sessions, no doubt."

Amelia, to her credit, took the teasing in stride. "I assure you, our collaboration has been strictly professional. Though I must say, William's skill at evading questions is second only to his talent for finding obscure philosophical quotes for every occasion."

"Hey, I resemble that remark," William protested, a begrudging smile tugging at his lips.

Tommy, who had been silently observing, finally spoke up. "As riveting as this middle school dance routine is, perhaps we could get to the matter at hand? Unless you'd like to pass some notes first?"

Amelia nodded, her expression shifting from playful to intensely focused. "Right you are, Tommy. As General Counsel for CBHS, I've had a front-row seat to their operations. What I'm about to share with you results from years of observation and investigation," she began, her voice steady but tinged with urgency. "Coastal Beacon Health System has been systematically destroying community hospitals across the country and beyond."

The room fell silent, all traces of earlier levity vanishing as the team prepared to hear the grim details of their next mission.

She pulled out her phone, tapping the screen a few times before holding it up for the group to see. "This is St. Nicholas Hospital in Podgorica, Montenegro," she said, showing them a photo of a dilapidated building. "CBHS expanded internationally, promising to revolutionize healthcare in developing nations. Instead, they've left a trail of neglect and broken promises."

Darby leaned in, her brow furrowed. "How bad is it, really?"

Amelia's expression darkened. "Worse than you can imagine. Let me give you some examples."

She swiped to another photo, this one of a crowded emergency room. "This is from Seaview General in Florida. Last month, a patient named Elena Rodriguez died in the hallway of this ER. She was having a heart attack, but there weren't enough nurses to monitor her. Ten nurses were scheduled for the ER that day. They had five."

The team exchanged grim looks as Amelia continued, swiping to another image.

"This is Riverside Community Hospital in Ohio. A patient named Marcus Thompson went into cardiac arrest while restrained in the psychiatric ward. He was supposed to be under constant observation, but the staff member assigned to him was juggling three other high-risk patients. By the time someone checked on him, it was too late."

Josh shook his head, his face a mask of disgust. "How are they getting away with this?"

"Money and influence," Amelia replied, her tone bitter. "While hospitals struggle, Vincent Blackwell—CBHS's CEO and a former neurosurgeon—and his executives are living large. They've prioritized expansion and personal luxury over patient care."

She pulled up another image, this one of a sleek private jet. "This is Blackwell's personal aircraft. He uses it to jet between CBHS locations and for personal trips. Meanwhile, hospitals can't afford basic supplies. In one location, nurses were bringing in their own pens and gloves because the hospital couldn't—or wouldn't—provide them."

Tommy's jaw clenched. "So they're choosing caviar over care?"

Amelia nodded grimly. "Precisely. And it gets worse. At Pinecrest Memorial in Maine, there was an outbreak of antibiotic-resistant bacteria in the NICU. It infected six infants. Three didn't make it. The investigation revealed that the hospital had been cutting corners on their sterilization procedures to save money."

Ella, who had been quietly absorbing the information, spoke up. "What about their technology? Security systems?"

"Outdated and neglected, like everything else. Most of their hospitals are running on systems from the early 2000s. They can't interface with modern medical equipment, leading to dangerous errors and delays in care."

William stood, his expression a mix of anger and determination. "This is why we're here. CBHS isn't just mismanaging hospitals—they're actively harming people. We have a chance to expose them, to bring them down, and potentially save countless lives."

He moved to stand beside Amelia, their shoulders almost touching. The team noticed how they seemed to draw strength from each other's presence.

"Amelia has risked everything to bring us this information," William continued. "She's not just a whistleblower. She's a hero, fighting from within a corrupt system to save lives."

Amelia's cheeks colored slightly at William's praise, but her voice remained steady. "I've done what I can from the inside. Now, I need your help to finish this."

The team looked at one another, a silent agreement passing between them. They had each taken on challenging jobs before—and CAYA was a tremendous team effort—but this . . . this was something else entirely. It wasn't just about the thrill of the heist or outsmarting the bad guys. This was about justice, about protecting the vulnerable, about righting a terrible wrong.

As Amelia continued her briefing, she pulled up a complex diagram on her tablet.

"To truly understand CBHS's web of deceit, we need to look at their financial structure. Coastal Beacon Health System wasn't always the behemoth it is today. It started in 2010 when a private equity firm, Hydra Capital, bought a struggling chain of community hospitals from a religious organization in New England."

William nodded, adding context for the team. "Hydra Capital is known for aggressive takeovers. They're not exactly loved in the business world."

Amelia continued, "CBHS encountered financial difficulties almost immediately. In 2016, they made a decision that would set the stage for their current crisis. They sold all their hospital properties to a real estate firm called Waterfront Real Estate Investments, or WRI, for $1.3 billion."

Josh leaned forward, his interest piqued. "Let me guess, they're leasing the properties back?"

"Exactly," Amelia confirmed. "CBHS used some profits from the property sale to expand outside their original region. But instead of investing in or updating their existing hospitals, they went on a buying spree, acquiring more struggling hospitals across the country."

Darby frowned. "So they're stretched thin, with a bunch of outdated hospitals and hefty lease payments?"

Amelia nodded grimly. "And it gets worse. The COVID pandemic hit their surgery numbers hard, which had been a reliable source of income. It was a financial gut punch."

"But surely they had reserves?" Ella asked.

"They might have weathered it better if they weren't already drowning in debt," Amelia said. "To make matters worse, they've avoided submitting required financial information to state regulators for years."

William's expression darkened. "And I bet I know where some of that money went."

Amelia pulled up another image, this time of a luxurious yacht. "Meet *Artemisa*, the super yacht owned by Vincent Blackwell. He also has the private jet I mentioned earlier."

The team exchanged disgusted looks.

"Using money from struggling hospitals for personal luxuries? That's beyond reprehensible," Tommy said.

Amelia continued, "They pitched the deal with WRI as a way to give CBHS more flexibility and capital for growth. Edward Marlowe, WRI's CEO, said at the time, *We look forward to expanding our relationship with CBHS in the years ahead.* They even bought a 10% equity stake in CBHS."

"So WRI is profiting from this too," Josh said.

"Exactly," Amelia confirmed. "The deal allowed WRI to participate in up to $1 billion of CBHS's future hospital acquisitions. It looked good on paper—a way for CBHS to serve broader populations. But in reality, it's been a disaster for patient care."

William stepped in. "CBHS has been playing fast and loose with the numbers for years. In 2015, they posted a profit, but only because of changes to employee pensions. Without that, they would have lost money, following four years of losses."

Amelia nodded, "Their revenue has been stagnant, growing only about 1% year over year. Yet Blackwell keeps expanding, keeps buying, keeps promising growth and efficiency."

"All the while, patients suffer," Darby said softly.

"Exactly," Amelia said, her voice filled with determination. "That's why we need to stop them. We need to expose the truth about CBHS, about Blackwell, about this whole corrupt system."

The team sat in silence for a moment, absorbing the magnitude of what they were about to undertake.

Finally, William spoke, his voice steady and resolute. "This isn't just about money anymore. It's not even just about justice. It's about saving lives. Are we all in?"

One by one, the team members nodded their assent. They were ready to take on CBHS to unravel the complex web of deceit and greed that was costing innocent lives.

As the meeting broke up and the team dispersed to prepare for their roles, William and Amelia found themselves alone for a moment. Their eyes met, a silent understanding passing between them.

All heads turned toward Amelia. "There's one more story you need to hear. It's why I'm here. Why I can't walk away from this fight."

The team paused, turning back to listen.

"Two months ago, a woman named Sophia Martinez gave birth at Coastal Bay Hospital, one of CBHS's facilities," Amelia began, her voice barely above a whisper. "The delivery seemed routine at first, but then Sophia started hemorrhaging severely."

William moved closer to Amelia, offering silent support as she continued.

"The doctors tried everything they could, but they needed a specific medical device—an embolization coil—to stop the bleeding. It's a common tool, something every maternity ward should have on hand." Amelia's voice cracked slightly. "But when they went to get it, they discovered the vendor had repossessed their entire stock weeks earlier."

"Repossessed?" Darby asked, incredulous.

Amelia nodded grimly. "CBHS hadn't paid the bill. The supplier, MedTech Solutions, had been trying to collect for months. They finally took back their inventory."

"What happened to Sophia?" Ella asked, though her face suggested she already knew the answer.

"They transferred her to Central City Hospital," Amelia said, her eyes glistening with unshed tears. "But by then, it was too late. Sophia died, leaving behind a newborn daughter and a devastated family."

The room fell silent, the weight of Sophia's story hanging heavy in the air.

"One unpaid bill," Tommy said, his fists clenched. "One woman's life."

"And it's not an isolated incident," Amelia added. "This is happening across the CBHS network. Lives are being lost because of their mismanagement and greed."

William placed a hand on Amelia's shoulder, his touch gentle but firm. "This is why we're doing this," he said, addressing the team. "Not for the thrill, not for the challenge, but for Sophia. For every patient who's suffered because of CBHS's negligence."

The team nodded, their resolve strengthened by Sophia's tragic story.

"We'll fix this," Darby said, her voice filled with determination. "We're going to make sure no one else dies because of an unpaid bill or a missing medical device."

As they filed out of the room, each team member carried with them the weight of Sophia's story. It wasn't just a mission anymore. It was a moral imperative.

William and Amelia remained behind for a moment. Without a word, William pulled her into a comforting embrace. They stood there, drawing strength from each other, united in their determination to bring down CBHS and prevent more tragedies like Sophia's.

The battle against Coastal Beacon Health System was about to begin, and they were ready.

· · · ● · ● · · ·

"Vincent," Darby began, tossing a glossy photo onto the mahogany coffee table. "His god complex might be his downfall. He's so busy strutting around like a peacock, he doesn't notice the foxes at the gate." Her eyes shone with the thrill of the hunt, her sleek silhouette outlined by the flickering flames.

"Speaking of foxes, Samantha's paranoia is her Achilles' heel," Justine continued, her voice smooth as silk with an undertone of steel. "She sees threats in every shadow—let's make sure she finds them."

"Kiran," Ella added, leaning forward to examine the intel strewn before them, "she's got the bedside manner of a king cobra. But she's sloppy with her emails. I've seen fourteen-year-olds with better password security."

"Perfect," Tommy said, a spark of determination lighting his battle-worn gaze. "Arrogance and complacency, our favorite cocktail, but let's not get too cocky. They're slippery, and we need more than sass and bravado to pin them down."

"Agreed," William nodded, suppressing a smirk. "We exploit their vices, leverage their egos against them. Pride goes before the fall, and these three are perched on a high wire without a net."

As the fire dwindled to embers, talk turned to lives lived in the shadows of their last caper. Darby and Justine recounted days of sun-soaked beaches and the vicious underbelly of PR, where they spun stories with the finesse of puppeteers.

"California's nice this time of year," Justine said, a wry smile tugging at her lips. "But nothing beats the adrenaline of the game."

"Especially when the stakes are this high," Darby agreed, her eyes meeting William's—a silent understanding passing between them.

Josh hadn't lost his edge, despite his return to legitimate banking. "You know, helping millionaires move their money around legally isn't quite the rush it used to be when I worked for the other side. This . . ."—he gestured to the room—"this is where I find worth."

"Guarding the globe hasn't dulled your senses, I hope?" William asked, glancing at Tommy.

"Protecting the weak is what I do best," Tommy said, the shadow of a former life etched into his features. "And with this lot, I actually sleep better at night, knowing we did good—even if it's outside the lines."

"Speaking of sleep, I've mastered the art of power naps between coding marathons," Ella interjected with a lopsided grin. "MIT doesn't teach you that."

"Life hacks from the young and restless," William said, earning a roll of Ella's eyes but a chuckle from the rest.

· · · ● · ● · ● ● · ·

As dawn's light tiptoed through the blinds, casting long shadows across William's home office, Amelia commanded the room's attention. She spread her evidence across the table like a general planning a campaign—charts, diagrams, and financial records that painted a damning picture of CBHS's operations. The team leaned in, their collective focus sharp as a surgeon's blade.

With methodical precision, Amelia walked them through CBHS's labyrinthine financial structure. Her fingers traced paths through flowcharts more intricate than spider webs, mapping how money disappeared into shell companies only to emerge, laundered and legitimate, on the other side. The complexity of offshore accounts and international banking regulations became clear under her guidance, transformed from impenetrable financial jargon into a blueprint for justice.

Darby and Justine exchanged knowing looks as the familiar patterns of corporate fraud emerged. This was their element—the careful dismantling of seemingly impregnable systems. Ella's eyes narrowed as she absorbed the technical details, no doubt already planning ways to penetrate CBHS's digital defenses. Tommy maintained his watchful stance, while Josh's banker's mind dissected the financial weaknesses in their target's armor.

William observed his team's reactions with muted satisfaction. The initial levity of their reunion had given way to focused determination. They'd faced impossible odds before with CAYA, but this . . . this was different. Lives hung in the balance, not just profits and reputations.

As the sun climbed higher, casting the room in golden light, their mission crystallized. They weren't just planning another heist; they were preparing for war against an enemy who had turned healing into profit, compassion into commodity. The dragon they faced might wear a suit instead of scales, but, as Amelia fiercely noted, it remained vulnerable to the right weapons wielded skillfully.

· · · ● · ● · ● · · ·

William leaned back in his leather chair, the creak of the aged material mimicking the stretch of his lips into a smirk. Around him, the team was a mosaic of resolve and restless energy. Darby lounged against the oak-paneled wall, her fingers absently twirling a lock of today's hairstyle—a platinum braid cascading over one shoulder, a silent banner of her adaptable nature.

"Alright," William said, his voice cutting through the room like a finely-tuned violin in a rock concert. "We've got brains, brawn, and beauty. A veritable triple threat to corporate greed."

Josh, seated at the table, was tapping a rhythmless beat with a pen on his notepad, a symphony of numbers swirling in his head. The specks of gray in his dark hair caught the light as his head bobbed in agreement, an unspoken melody of schemes yet to unfold.

"Can't forget the charm," Justine chimed in, her red curls bouncing as she threw a wry glance toward Darby. Her chuckle held the weight of shared secrets and the lightness of inside jokes yet to come.

"Charm," Josh echoed, deadpan as ever. "Because nothing says 'trustworthy' like a crew of reformed criminals playing Robin Hood."

"Ex-financiers," corrected Darby, without missing a beat. "Let's at least pretend we're reformed characters."

"Speak for yourself," Tommy interjected, a grin threatening to break through his stoic façade. He adjusted his posture, the protective instinct within him a silent sentinel among the jesters.

Ella, perched on the edge of the desk, her fingers dancing across the keys of her laptop, glanced up from her screen. "This reads like the start of a bad joke. Five con artists and a hacker walk into a bank—"

"Correction, they virtually walk into a bank," Amelia cut in, her smile a brief flash of lightning. "And walk out with more than just free pens."

"Assuming we get that far," Darby pointed out, her tone laced with enough sarcasm to flavor the tension hanging in the air.

"We will," William said, standing up to signal the end of the gathering. "And CBHS won't know what hit them."

They rose, a phalanx of unlikely heroes bound by a shared quest. Their laughter mingled with the hum of determination, the sound echoing off the walls, a testament to their unity despite—or perhaps because of—their eclectic pasts.

"Let's go make some noise," Amelia said, her voice carrying the final note of the prelude to their grand performance.

"Quietly," William reminded them, his eyebrows raised in mock severity. "Preferably without any actual explosions."

"Where's the fun in that?" Justine asked, but her hand rested on the doorknob, ready to step into the fray that awaited them.

"Trust me," William replied with a conspiratorial wink. "There'll be fireworks."

As they filed out of William's Salem home, the chapter closed on a band of misfits turned avengers, their steps synchronized to the rhythm of revenge and retribution. A heist unlike any other lay ahead—an intricate dance of deception where they calculated every move, choreographing every gesture in the name of justice.

And so, with the stage set for action and excitement, the curtain rose on their most daring mission yet.

The Moral Minute—Episode 1

ANIE: I'm Anie Chen.

LUCAS: And I'm Lucas Rodriguez. Welcome to The Moral Minute, a brand-new podcast where we examine the day's most egregious ethical failures in corporate America.

ANIE: While we're still reporting the news for TechTruth, this format also gives us a chance to look closer at certain stories. Today we're following up on our deeper investigation into Coastal Beacon Health System, or CBHS. Lucas, every villain has an origin story. Tell us about Vincent Blackwell.

LUCAS: [dry] Ah yes, our Harvard-educated hero turned healthcare horror show. Stanford Med grad, UCSF surgical residency—

ANIE: [interrupting] Sounds like the American Dream.

LUCAS: More like the American Nightmare. We first introduced our TechTruth viewers to Dr. Blackwell months ago, during an investigative report. The *good* doctor started as a neurosurgeon with a mission to "revolutionize healthcare." Spoiler alert: the only thing he revolutionized was creative accounting.

ANIE: Wait, didn't he start some kind of foundation early on?

LUCAS: [sarcastic] Oh, you mean the Blackwell Foundation for Accessible Healthcare? The irony is chef's kiss perfect. Used it as a springboard to buy up struggling hospitals while paying himself consulting fees that could fund a small country.

ANIE: Classic either-die-a-hero-or-live-long-enough-to-become-the-villain situation.

LUCAS: More like never-was-a-hero. His former colleagues at UCSF say he was always more interested in the business side than patient care. One called him "a shark in surgical scrubs."

ANIE: Time's almost up. What's our moral of the minute?

LUCAS: Sometimes the most dangerous predators wear white coats and carry MBAs.

[Theme music fades out]

Efficiency Is Godliness

Vincent Blackwell's hands were steady, his focus absolute in the sanitized sea of white and blue. The operating room was his stage, the scalpel his baton, and with each slice, he worked his precision on the gray matter.

Born to Japanese-American parents in San Francisco, Vincent had grown up with medicine in his blood. His mother, a pharmacist, and his father, a renowned oncologist at UCSF Medical Center, had instilled in him a drive for excellence and a taste for the finer things in life. The family's history of perseverance through internment camps during World War II had left them with a fierce determination to succeed, and Vincent's parents had worked tirelessly to ensure their son would have every opportunity they had fought so hard for.

Vincent's brilliance was clear from an early age. He blazed through the University of Southern California with a biomedical engineering degree, but the siren call of medicine—perhaps echoing his father's influence—proved irresistible. He found himself at Stanford Medical School, emerging with an MD, before pursuing a master's in public health at UC Berkeley. His surgical training at UCSF Medical Center honed not just his skills, but his ambition.

"Dr. Blackwell," a nurse whispered, her voice betraying awe, "you've done it again."

"Of course," Vincent replied, not even bothering to look up from the suture he was tying off. It wasn't arrogance; it was fact. Like saying the sky was blue or taxes were inevitable.

Such triumphs marked the early years of Vincent's career, each one a stepping stone paved with ambition and the kind of talent that didn't apologize for itself. He was a maestro in the theater of neurosurgery, crafting miracles with gloved hands while peers watched with envy poorly disguised as admiration.

But beneath the veneer of success and under the microscope of his own scrutiny, Vincent saw the cracks in the system—the way money flowed like IV fluids, nourishing some parts and neglecting others. He noticed how insurance companies played God, deciding who got a chance at life. It was all a game of chess with human pawns.

At first, Vincent's reaction was one of righteous indignation. He threw himself into *pro bono* work, established a foundation to help underprivileged patients, and became a vocal advocate for healthcare reform. He testified before state legislatures, wrote op-eds, and appeared on news programs, all in the name of making healthcare more equitable and accessible.

But as the years wore on, Vincent's idealism waned. He watched as bureaucracy, special interests, and the sheer inertia of the system stymied his efforts. Promising initiatives were watered down or killed outright. Patients he fought for still died waiting for treatments they couldn't afford. The very insurance companies he railed against seemed to grow more powerful with each passing year.

Frustration turned to cynicism, and cynicism to a cold, calculating anger. If the system wouldn't change, Vincent reasoned, perhaps it was time to play by its rules—and win.

"Healthcare," he had said one evening to no one in particular, "is ripe for the picking."

It was like the moment when a lock clicks open, the tumblers aligning with a satisfying snick. Vincent realized he was playing small, saving one brain at a time, when he could shape the entire body of healthcare. It wasn't an epiphany born under the surgical lamp—it was the gleam of opportunity.

He began to see the potential for profit in every aspect of the healthcare system. Where once he saw patients in need, now he saw revenue streams. Where he once saw dedicated staff, now he saw overhead to be optimized. His brilliant mind, once devoted to healing, now turned to the intricate dance of mergers, acquisitions, and financial engineering.

His ambition, coupled with his charm and medical expertise, caught the eye of influential figures in the healthcare industry. When the struggling Coastal Beacon Health System needed a new CEO, Vincent saw his chance. He leveraged his connections, dazzled the board with his vision, and secured the position. It was time to operate on a grander scale.

"Coastal Beacon Health System," he declared with the smoothness of a man used to getting what he wanted, "will redefine the industry." And by redefine, he meant exploit every loophole, pressure every weak link, and squeeze the system until it hemorrhaged profits.

He crafted his plan with the meticulous care of a surgeon planning an incision. CBHS would be the façade of philanthropy hiding the machinery of greed. It would be his magnum opus, composed not of flesh and bone, but of cold, hard cash.

Vincent justified his actions to himself, rationalizing that by making the system profitable, he was ensuring its survival. If a few people had to suffer for the greater good, wasn't that a price worth paying? Besides, hadn't he tried to change things the *right* way? Hadn't that failed spectacularly?

"Remember," he'd often say, a smirk playing on his lips, "in this business, it's not about healthcare. It's about who holds the scalpel." And Vincent always held the scalpel, even if he had to twist a few arms—or ethics—to keep it that way.

The idealistic young surgeon was gone, replaced by a hardened healthcare tycoon who saw the world not as it should be, but as it was—a place where only the strong survived, and where compassion was a luxury he could no longer afford.

· · · ● · ● · ● · · ·

Vincent Blackwell's office, high above the city, was a chessboard of power plays and checkmates. The king on this board, however, didn't wear a crown; he wore tailored Italian suits.

Vincent's empire rested on the shoulders of two formidable women, each a master in her own domain. Samantha Bowen, the Chief Financial Officer, was a fiscal alchemist who could turn red ink into black with a few keystrokes and creative accounting. Her razor-sharp mind and even sharper instincts had made her indispensable to Vincent's grand scheme. As CFO, she orchestrated a complex dance of numbers, juggling budgets, manipulating reports, and finding innovative ways to maximize profits while minimizing scrutiny.

Kiran Devi, on the other hand, ruled the clinical side of CBHS with an iron fist in a latex glove. As Chief Nursing Officer, she wielded her power like a scalpel, precise and often ruthless. Kiran had climbed the ranks from bedside nurse to CNO through a combination of clinical excellence, political savvy, and an unyielding drive for efficiency. She saw the nursing staff not as caregivers, but as assets to be optimized, squeezed for every ounce of productivity. Under her watch, CBHS hospitals ran like well-oiled machines—efficient, streamlined, and devoid of the human touch that once defined nursing care.

Together, Samantha and Kiran formed the backbone of Vincent's operation, turning his vision of a profit-driven healthcare empire into a cold, hard reality. They were the perfect complement to his grand strategy—Samantha ensuring the money kept flowing, and Kiran keeping the hospitals running at peak efficiency . . . patient satisfaction be damned.

• • • ●• • ● • • •

Samantha—Sam—didn't need to knock; doors opened for her as if they recognized the rustle of money in her stride. She glided into Vincent's office, charts and graphs under one arm—a financial warrior priestess ready to sacrifice ethics at the altar of profit.

Sam's journey from Chicago middle-class to CBHS's financial mastermind had been methodical and deliberate. She'd proven her talent for numbers early, parlaying a Wall Street career into healthcare finance when she realized where the real power lay. At 35, she became CBHS's youngest CFO, bringing her cutthroat mentality to an industry she saw as an untapped goldmine.

Now in her early 40s, Sam was known for her designer suits, blood-red manicures, and the cold, piercing gaze that reduced everything—and everyone—to numbers on a balance sheet. She drove a Tesla, lived in a luxury penthouse, and viewed relationships as potential liabilities. In CBHS, she'd found the perfect playground for her talents and ruthless ambition. As CFO, she wasn't just moving money around—she was shaping the future of healthcare, one spreadsheet at a time.

"Vincent," she greeted, voice cool as polished marble, "the numbers don't lie, but we can certainly make them dance."

"Music to my ears, Sam," Vincent replied, his eyes taking in the flickering candle of paranoia that always seemed to burn in hers.

Together, they surveyed CBHS from their glass tower, seeing not patients, but profits; not care, but capital. Where others saw a *healthcare* system, they saw a *healthscare* system ripe for manipulation—after all, fear was just another revenue stream.

"Imagine if we could charge every trembling heart for the peace of mind we provide."

"Let's make sure it's only peace of mind we're selling. Actual peace would put us out of business."

· · · ● · ● · · ·

As Vincent and Samantha plotted, another player maneuvered herself on the board below. Kiran, with her charisma wrapped tight like the bun atop her head, walked the halls of CBHS with the air of someone who had places to be and people to subordinate.

"Walk with me," she commanded more than requested. Nurses and doctors parted before her like the Red Sea, her presence bringing both awe and anxiety.

"Kiran," a nervous intern ventured, clipboard hugged to his chest as a shield, "there's a problem with—"

"Problems are just opportunities wearing ugly outfits," Kiran cut him off, her gaze piercing enough to sterilize surgical equipment. "Dress it up and bring it back to me."

She continued her march, leaving behind a wake of scurried whispers and hurried nods. Kiran treated CBHS not as a hospital, but as her kingdom, and she was its self-anointed deity in tailored professional attire.

"Efficiency is godliness," she said without irony to anyone within earshot.

· · ● · ● · · ·

Kiran Devi was born in Mumbai, India, the only child of a prominent physician father and a mother who was a respected professor of nursing. From an early age, Kiran immersed herself in the world of healthcare, often accompanying her parents to the hospital and watching in fascination as they worked.

At 18, Kiran moved to the United States to pursue her education, earning her BSN from Johns Hopkins University. Her intelligence and drive separated her from her peers. While other students struggled with homesickness, Kiran thrived, viewing every challenge as an opportunity to prove herself.

After graduation, Kiran began her career in the ED of a busy urban hospital. Kiran's efficiency and calm under pressure impressed hospital administration, leading to her quick promotion to charge nurse. Here, Kiran discovered the power of leadership and forged her philosophy of ruthless efficiency.

Driven by ambition, Kiran pursued her MSN in Nursing Administration from the University of Pennsylvania. Her master's thesis on optimizing nurse-to-patient ratios for maximum efficiency (with little regard for nurse burnout or patient satisfaction) became required reading in several hospital management courses.

Kiran's rise through the ranks was meteoric. By 32, she had become the youngest Chief Nursing Officer in her hospital's history. Her methods were controversial—she viewed nurses as resources to be optimized rather than caregivers to be nurtured—but her results were undeniable. Under her leadership, the hospital's efficiency metrics soared, even as staff turnover reached record highs.

It was at a healthcare leadership conference that Kiran first met Vincent Blackwell. Her vision of a hyper-efficient healthcare system immediately impressed him; it was a system that prioritized throughput over patient comfort. When he offered her the position of CNO at CBHS, Kiran saw it as the opportunity she had been waiting for—a chance to reshape nursing on a grand scale.

Now in her early 40s, Kiran is a striking figure in the halls of CBHS hospitals. Always impeccably dressed in tailored suits, she moves through the wards like a general inspecting her troops. She usually wears her dark hair pulled back in a severe bun, and her sharp eyes miss nothing.

Kiran's management style is often described as *military-like* by her staff. She demands perfection and is quick to reprimand those who fall short of her exacting standards. Yet, she also has a knack for identifying and nurturing talent—those nurses who share her drive and willingness to prioritize efficiency over empathy.

Despite her outward success, Kiran struggles with the cost of her ambition. She's estranged from her parents, who are horrified by what they see as a betrayal of the caring principles of nursing. She has few close friends, viewing most relationships as potential weaknesses. Her one indulgence is a weekly yoga class, where she pushes her body to the limits of flexibility and control—a physical mirror of her professional life.

Kiran justifies her harsh methods as necessary for the survival of the healthcare system. She truly believes that by maximizing efficiency, she's serving the greater good. In her worldview, individual patient experiences are less important than the overall functioning of the healthcare machine.

At CBHS, Kiran has found the perfect environment to implement her vision. As CNO, she's not just managing nurses—she's reshaping the very nature of healthcare delivery, one optimized workflow at a time.

· • • ●•●● • • ·

Back in the tower, Vincent watched Kiran's progress with a smile that was equal parts pride and predator. She was a force of nature he had harnessed, a storm contained within CBHS walls—a tempest in a teapot that brewed a potent concoction of control and ambition.

"Kiran believes she's the lifeblood of this hospital," Vincent remarked, leaning back in his chair and looking down at the orchestration of his empire. "Little does she know, she's just another cell in the body of CBHS. And I," he said, fingers steepled, "am the brain."

"Careful, Vincent. Brains can get blood clots if the circulation gets too ambitious."

"Then it's a good thing we have such skilled surgeons, isn't it?" Vincent replied, the ghost of his past life winking from behind his calculating gaze.

And so, the game continued—pieces moving, strategies unfolding. The air was thick with sarcasm and the subtle scent of treachery. In the world of CBHS, where greed donned a white coat and deceit wielded a scalpel, it was just another day in the operation.

The Moral Minute—Episode 2

[Theme music—short, serious but with an edge]

ANIE: I'm Anie Chen.

LUCAS: And I'm Lucas Rodriguez. Welcome to The Moral Minute, where we examine the day's most egregious ethical failures in corporate America.

ANIE: Lucas, CBHS has been busy shopping lately—and I don't mean for medical supplies.

LUCAS: [sardonic] No, they're more interested in collecting hospitals like some people collect Pokemon cards. Their latest acquisition? Addison Gilbert Hospital in Gloucester.

ANIE: Tell our listeners about AGH.

LUCAS: Picture this: a community hospital serving the same families for generations. Struggling financially, sure, but still providing good care. Then CBHS swoops in like a corporate vulture, promising improvements and efficiency.

ANIE: Let me guess—those improvements never materialized?

LUCAS: [dry laugh] Unless you count laying off half the nursing staff as an improvement. One nurse told me they're now handling double the patient load with half the resources.

ANIE: But CBHS claims these acquisitions save struggling hospitals.

LUCAS: Oh, they're saving something alright—just not patients. Since taking over AGH, they've cut three service lines, closed the maternity ward, and somehow still managed to increase executive bonuses by 300%.

ANIE: Time's almost up. What's our moral of the minute?

LUCAS: When a healthcare company cares more about acquisitions than patients, it might be time for a second opinion.

[Theme music fades out]

Salem Marine Society

The team headquartered themselves in the heart of Salem, in the grand ballroom of the historic Hawthorne Hotel. Built in 1925 and named after Salem's native son, novelist Nathaniel Hawthorne, the hotel stood as a testament to the city's rich history and enduring allure.

William's house had served well for their initial reunion, but with surveillance equipment to set up and plans spanning multiple states to coordinate, they needed more space. The Hawthorne's grand ballroom, with its elegant chandeliers and ornate moldings, offered both the room they required and the privacy they demanded. The hotel's reputation for hosting corporate events meant their presence would raise no eyebrows, and its proximity to William's house on Winter Street made it an ideal command center for what would become a coast-to-coast operation.

The hotel itself had a storied past. Once home to the Franklin Building, which housed the Salem Marine Society, the location had witnessed its share of drama—from devastating fires in the mid-1800s to its rebirth as a modern hotel in the Roaring Twenties. Frank Poor was the founder of the Sylvania Lighting Company; he saw the need for a sophisticated establishment to accommodate Salem's growing number of visitors and spearheaded the hotel's construction.

Over the years, the Hawthorne Hotel had played host to an eclectic mix of guests, from business travelers to television stars. In 1970, it famously housed the cast and crew of the popular sitcom *Bewitched*, including Elizabeth Montgomery, as they filmed episodes in Salem. Today, her bronze likeness still rides her broomstick down Essex Street, a whimsical tribute to the city's ability to embrace both its haunting history and its playful present.

But it wasn't just its Hollywood connections that made the Hawthorne Hotel famous. Whispers of supernatural occurrences had long swirled around the building. Guests reported furniture moving of its own accord, sightings of a mysterious woman's ghost, and unexplained noises echoing through the halls. These tales of the paranormal culminated in 1990 when the hotel hosted a séance in the very grand ballroom the team now occupied, attempting to contact the spirit of the legendary escape artist Harry Houdini.

As the team gathered in this historic space, they couldn't help but feel the weight of the past around them. The Grand Ballroom, with its elegant chandeliers and ornate moldings, seemed to hold secrets of its own. It was a fitting location for their clandestine operation—a place where history, mystery, and the promise of the impossible converged.

· · · · ● · ● · · · ·

The evening draped over the Salem like a velvet heist, all deep blue mystery and sparkling danger. Darby leaned against the window frame, her gaze as sharp as the silhouette of the skyline. Below, Salem Common sat, with its several paths staring back up at her.

"Taking down a healthcare behemoth isn't your usual grab-and-dash," Darby said, twirling a strand of today's hair choice—a sleek, platinum bob—around her finger. In the gambling underworld, she learned that sometimes she needed to play dirty to get what she was owed. CBHS had spread through the veins of the country like a cancer, and she was here to perform the excision.

Josh stood by, looking every inch the GQ cover model he wasn't, his eyes scanning equations invisible to the rest. He had crunched more numbers than a blackjack dealer on a hot streak, but this . . . this was personal. His years of cooking books for the mob had taught him that finance was just another form of warfare—and he intended to balance this ledger. "They say revenge is a dish best served cold," he said, not looking up from his gadget du jour. "But I'm partial to lukewarm with a side of fiscal ruin."

Justine sauntered over, her red mane a fire warning of past battles fought and won. "Nicknames are for friends and lovers," she remarked dryly, eyeing the building below. "To them, we'll be nothing but a collective nightmare." She knew corporate manipulation better than most, and CBHS's brand of exploitation left a bitter taste in her mouth that no amount of PR spin could sweeten.

In the shadows, Ella fidgeted with the hem of her new shirt, one that screamed hacker chic. Her eyes, dark pools of untold stories, were fixed on the villainous institution. Childhood traumas didn't come with an escape key, but she had found liberation through lines of code. CBHS would soon learn what it meant to be on the wrong side of her keyboard.

"Let's not kid ourselves," Darby said, her voice cutting through the night air with a seductive edge. "We're not just doing this for kicks. This is for every time they thought they could get away with bleeding people dry."

"Every penny hidden, every book cooked, every fraud they thought was buried too deep to find," Josh added, clenching his jaw.

"For every story they've silenced, every truth they've buried," Justine chimed in, her tone laced with venom.

"And every digital footprint they thought they'd erased," Ella concluded, her fingers itching to start their digital dance.

Tommy stood watch near the ballroom doors, his imposing 6'4" frame and military bearing a grounding presence for the team. Born in Cuba and raised in West New York, New Jersey—an area affectionately known as Havana on the Hudson—Tommy had found a new purpose with the team after his dishonorable discharge from the military. After their last adventure in Los Angeles, his loyalty to the group was unwavering, a stark contrast to the complicated theft in Afghanistan that had ended his military career. Even now, in his early 40s, he carried himself with the discipline of a soldier, his muscular frame and watchful eyes a testament to his role as the team's protector.

"The hotel staff knows not to disturb us," he reported, his voice tinged with a hint of his Cuban accent—a quirk that emerged when he was focused. "We're clear to work."

· · · ● · ● · · ·

Meanwhile, in Boston's financial district, William and Amelia claimed a secluded table in the Boston Athenaeum's historic reading room. They were early for their meeting with Dr. Haley Chen, a former CBHS hospitalist who had reached out through encrypted channels.

"How well do you know her?" William asked, arranging papers as casual camouflage. His eyes drifted to the magnificent arched windows, a strange comfort in a building that had housed secrets for nearly two centuries.

"She worked at three different CBHS hospitals. Left after reporting critical staffing short-ages that led to patient deaths. Officially, she took a position at Mass General. Unofficially . . ." She let the implication hang.

William nodded, scanning the room with practiced caution. The Boston Athenaeum, founded in 1807, had long been a sanctuary for America's intellectual elite—a fact that wasn't lost on William as he adjusted his decidedly non-elite posture.

"Fitting place for a clandestine meeting," he said. "Nothing says *we're not plotting anything* like sitting in a 200-year-old private library surrounded by first editions and marble busts of dead philosophers."

"Says the man who once lost twenty grand betting on a racehorse named *Sure Thing*," Amelia whispered, a hint of a smile breaking through her professional demeanor.

William's retort died on his lips as he noticed a man in a dark suit enter the reading room, scanning methodically before selecting a seat with clear sightlines to their alcove.

"Don't look now, but I think we have company," William said, casually reopening his notebook. "Three o'clock, corporate type, terrible tie. Either he's CBHS security or he's auditioning for *Obvious Surveillance: The Musical*."

Amelia didn't turn. "Could be coincidence."

"And I could be Ernest Hemingway's long-lost grandson. The way my luck runs? That's Vincent's bloodhound."

Just then, Haley Chen appeared at the entrance, her gaze sweeping the reading room. She spotted them but hesitated when the man in the suit glanced her way. Without missing a beat, she veered toward the rare manuscript section, pretending to examine the display cases while subtly checking her phone.

William watched as she navigated through the stacks, taking a circuitous route that brought her past the Athenaeum's famous King's Chapel Collection—America's first public library, housed here since 1807. She paused to examine a glass-enclosed first edition, giving the suit time to lose interest before finally approaching their table from an angle that kept the massive columns between her and the observer.

"Creative entrance," William said as she slid into her seat. "You've done this before."

"When you work for people who consider basic healthcare an optional luxury, you develop certain skills," Haley replied, her voice carrying the precise combination of exhaustion and determination that William recognized from his own mirror. "Had to double back twice on the way here. Pretty sure I lost the tail at Park Street, but better safe than explaining to my former colleagues why I'm meeting with investigative journalists."

"Well, they found us anyway," William said, his eyes briefly flicking to the side. "Check out the guy in the suit across the room. He doesn't belong here; poorly fitting suit aside, his demeanor screams, *I'm following you and trying not to be seen.*"

Haley stiffened, but didn't turn to look. "Dark hair, bad tie, pretending to read Emerson?"

"That's our guy," Amelia confirmed, casually opening a folder. "Let's keep this brief, then. We'll handle him when we leave."

After a brief introduction, Haley pulled out her tablet, keeping it below table height.

"I started documenting everything," Haley said, her voice tight with controlled anger. "Screenshots of nurse-to-patient ratios, equipment maintenance logs, incident reports that got buried. We lost three patients in one week because our CT scanner was down and administration wouldn't approve repairs." She swiped through images. "Here's an email thread where I begged for more ED coverage. The next night, we had a code blue in the hallway because we were too short-staffed to monitor critical patients."

As she spoke, William noticed the man in the suit rise and begin a casual circuit of the room, pausing to examine the collection of historic Boston maps on the far wall—a collection that provided a better view of their alcove.

"Our friend is getting restless," William said, sliding a book across the table. "Let's admire the architecture for a moment."

They shifted positions, using the massive columns and book-lined walls as visual barriers while appearing to discuss the building's historic features.

"You know, this place has remained private for over two centuries," William noted loudly enough to be overheard. "One of the oldest independent libraries in the country. Makes you appreciate tradition."

"And when you reported this?" Amelia prompted Haley, their voices now lowered.

"I went through proper channels—straight to the CMO. But he was useless, completely under Vincent's thumb. Then Kiran Devi started showing up on my rounds, talking about *resource optimization* and *efficiency metrics*. She was supposedly there to help with workflow issues, but the message was clear—stop making waves." Haley's laugh was bitter. "When I threatened to go to the medical board, suddenly there were questions about my clinical judgment. Patient complaints appeared out of nowhere. I got the message."

The suit had moved closer, pretending to browse nearby shelves. William reached for his water glass, *accidentally* knocking it over with a crash that echoed through the quiet reading room. All eyes turned their way.

"Terribly sorry," William announced with exaggerated contrition. "My editor would say this is why I shouldn't be allowed near first editions. Clumsy hands, you know."

While attention focused on the minor commotion, Haley slipped a thumb drive to Amelia, who pocketed it. The suit, momentarily distracted, returned to his seat, now watching them with thinly veiled interest.

They spent the next hour reviewing Haley's evidence—a damning collection of real-world consequences of CBHS's cost-cutting measures. While Ella and Josh might be able to expose the financial fraud, Haley's documentation put human faces to the numbers.

When they finally rose to leave, William took a circuitous route through the stacks, pausing by a glass case containing first editions of Hawthorne and Emerson. The suit followed at a discreet distance.

"Looks like you've got an admirer," Amelia said as they descended the grand staircase. "Think we should introduce ourselves?"

"Not today," William replied, glancing at a marble bust of George Washington watching them from its perch. "But I'd bet old George here has seen worse conspiracies in his day. At least ours is for a good cause."

At the exit, William wheeled and headed for the men's room, forcing their shadow to either reveal himself by following or lose them momentarily. The man hesitated, then pretended interest in a nearby bookshelf.

"Meet you outside," William whispered to Amelia and Haley. "Give me two minutes, then take separate exits. East for you, Amelia. South for Dr. Chen."

As the women departed, William emerged and marched toward the suit, who stiffened in surprise..

"Fascinating place, isn't it?" William said. "I'm researching for my next book. *Corruption in American Healthcare*. Perhaps you'd like to be interviewed? I didn't catch your name . . ."

The man mumbled something unintelligible and quickly exited, leaving William alone in the sunlight streaming through those magnificent arched windows.

The train ride back to Salem was quiet, both of them processing what they'd learned. Spreadsheets could show where money disappeared to, but Haley's evidence showed where it should have gone—and who had paid the price for its absence.

"You know," William finally broke the silence, "I used to think my gambling debt was rock bottom. But some people bet with other people's lives and still sleep at night." He stared out the window. "Makes me feel almost virtuous by comparison."

Amelia said nothing, but her hand squeezed his shoulder—a silent acknowledgment that sometimes redemption came in unexpected forms.

• • • ● • ● • • •

Vincent leaned back in his leather chair, watching through one-way glass as Sam walked the halls below. The boardroom, all sleek lines and cold efficiency, mirrored its occupants' hearts.

"The Massachusetts numbers are concerning," Sam said as she entered, not bothering with pleasantries. She placed a tablet in front of Vincent. "Three hospitals showing significant losses this quarter."

"Kiran has some thoughts on that," Vincent replied, just as Kiran strode in, impeccably dressed and radiating authority.

"We can optimize staffing further," Kiran said, taking her seat. "Cut another fifteen percent of nursing hours. Move to team nursing instead of primary nursing."

Sam's eyes narrowed. "The last cuts led to four sentinel events. The state's already watching us."

"Then we need better documentation," Kiran said. "Train the staff to chart defensively. No incident, no problem."

Vincent smiled, the expression never reaching his eyes. "Why not both? Cut the staff, document carefully, and if something goes wrong . . ." He shrugged. "We'll blame human error. After all, it's not the system that's broken. It's the humans trying to work within it."

The women exchanged glances—not quite approval, not quite distaste. Just acceptance of another move in their endless chess game of profit over people.

A sharp knock interrupted their strategy session. The door opened without waiting for an answer, and a man in an ill-fitting suit stepped in, his expression a mixture of satisfaction and discomfort at being in Vincent's inner sanctum.

"Your hunch was right, sir," he said, addressing Vincent while carefully avoiding eye contact with the two women. "Dr. Chen did meet with someone at the Boston Athenaeum today. Two people, actually."

Vincent leaned forward, suddenly interested. "And?"

"A man and a woman. The woman was Amelia, our former legal counsel. I'm certain it was her. The man with her was older, academic-looking. They spent nearly two hours in the reading room, examining documents."

"Did you get photos?" Sam asked, her voice sharp.

The security man shifted uncomfortably. "Limited. The Athenaeum has strict policies about photography, and they were seated in one of those alcoves with the columns. The man made me—deliberately caused a distraction and then they separated. I tried to follow them."

"Tried?" Kiran's voice could have frosted glass.

"They split up at the exits," the man said, a bead of sweat appearing at his temple. "I followed the man, thinking he had whatever they exchanged, but he walked straight up to me and asked if I wanted to be interviewed for a book about healthcare corruption. Called my bluff."

Vincent's laugh was as warm as a morgue drawer. "Sounds like someone who's played the game before. Did you follow them back to wherever they came from?"

"No, sir. They all separated. I lost the man and Amelia in the crowd, heading toward North Station. Chen had mentioned to someone she had to get to her shift at Mass General, so I assume that's where she went, but I couldn't follow all three at once."

Vincent drummed his fingers on the polished table. "So Chen met with our former counsel and an unknown man. And you lost all of them."

The security man flinched slightly. "Yes, sir. Sorry, sir."

"Find out where Amelia's been since she left us," Vincent said, his tone deceptively calm. "And put someone on Chen at Mass General. I want to know everyone she talks to."

Samantha left Vincent's office and her feet hit the floor with the precision of a metronome, each tap a countdown to another dollar in CBHS's coffers. She slipped into the finance department's war room, where spreadsheets wallpapered the space like modern art only she could appreciate. Numbers danced under her gaze, twirling in a ballet of creative accounting that would have made even the most jaded IRS agent reach for anxiety medication.

"Sam," called out a junior analyst, his voice quivering like a tax auditor at a biker bar. "The offshore accounts are ready for the . . . reallocation."

"Of course they are," Samantha said, her eyes not leaving the screen. The numbers didn't lie, but under her touch, they did more than dance; they pirouetted on the edge of legality, spinning a web of transactions so complex it could turn money laundering into an Olympic sport.

She pulled up personnel records, searching for both Dr. Haley Chen's and Amelia's files.

"Troublemakers. We should have buried both their careers when we had the chance."

Sam's fingers flew across the keyboard, searching for any connection between Chen, Porter, and potential whistleblowers. She pulled up Amelia's last known address—a condo in Cambridge—and her current employment status: "Independent Legal Consultant."

Independent, my foot. Let's see who's paying you these days, Amelia.

Meanwhile, Kiran prowled the corridors of CBHS like a panther in designer heels, stalking through her jungle of steel and antiseptic. With each step, her Italian leather pumps whispered threats to the linoleum beneath. Nurses scattered at her approach, their scrubs rustling like autumn leaves before a particularly well-dressed hurricane.

"Charting needs to be done yesterday!" she barked at a passing nurse, her tone dripping with the warmth of a February morning in Maine. "I am the lifeblood of this hospital. Without me, the entire system would flatline."

Her phone buzzed—a text from Vincent: "Amelia and Chen connected. Pull all files related to Amelia's last six cases with us. Priority."

Kiran froze mid-stride. During Amelia's last months with CBHS, she had been asking uncomfortable questions about resource allocation and patient outcomes. Nothing had come of it then—they'd ushered her out with a generous severance package and ironclad NDA. But if she was meeting with Chen . . .

"Cancel my afternoon meetings," she snapped at her assistant. "And get me everything we have on Dr. Chen's patients from the last six months. Every chart, every outcome, every complaint. And pull Amelia's exit documentation."

As she stalked away, her assistant whispered to a colleague, "Amelia was the one leader who actually cared about patients, right?"

"Yeah," the colleague replied. "No wonder she's on Kiran's hit list."

• • • • ● • ● • • • •

Back in the safety of Salem, William and Amelia were reviewing their security protocols. The crowded commuter train from North Station provided cover, but they still took precautions—changing cars at one stop, doubling back briefly at another.

"Do you think they made you?" William asked, pouring coffee from a French press that had seen better days.

"Definitely," Amelia said, accepting the mug gratefully. "That security guy at the Athenaeum—I've seen him before at CBHS headquarters. If Haley noticed she was being followed, Vincent already knew she was meeting someone. Now they know that someone was me."

"And they know about the mystery man with the terrible poker face," William said with a self-deprecating grimace. "Though they don't know who I am yet."

"That changes things," William continued, frowning. "You signed an NDA when you left, right?"

Amelia's smile was grim. "Yes, but it doesn't cover criminal activity. And what they're doing crosses that line."

"Still, they're onto us sooner than we expected. Haley was right about being followed. She said she lost the tail at Park Street, but obviously not early enough."

William's phone buzzed with a text from Ella: "Dr. C reached work safely. No obvious tails now. Running background on security guy now."

He showed the message to Amelia. "Ella works fast."

"Let's hope she works anonymously too," Amelia said. "The one advantage we still have is that they don't know where we're based or about the rest of the team. If they think it's just you and me working with Haley, we might use that to our advantage."

William nodded, texting back: "Meeting at usual spot, 7 PM. Bring everyone. We've got a new player on the board."

As he pocketed his phone, William couldn't help a small, grim smile. "You know, when Haley said she was being followed, I thought we were being paranoid, taking all those precautions on the way back."

"Paranoia is just good planning when you're dealing with CBHS," Amelia said. "They may have found their way to Haley, but as long as they don't know about Salem and the others, we still have the high ground."

William raised his coffee mug in a mock toast. "To staying one step ahead, then."

"And to Haley," Amelia added. "She knew she was being watched and met with us, anyway. That takes courage."

· • ● • ● • ● • ● • ·

By seven, the team had assembled in the hotel space that served as their headquarters. As William recounted their Athenaeum encounter, Tommy's expression grew increasingly grim. The former marine stood with his back to the wall, arms crossed—a habit from years of securing perimeters and watching for threats.

"Corporate security," Tommy said when William finished. "Not ex-military, definitely not law enforcement. The way you describe him handling the situation—following Chen first, then splitting his attention when you separated—that's amateur hour. A professional would have called for backup or stuck with the primary target."

"Is that good news or bad?" Justine asked, perched on the edge of the conference table.

Tommy shrugged. "Both. Good, because they're not sending their best. Bad because amateurs are unpredictable. They panic, make mistakes, overcompensate."

"And now they know Amelia's involved," Darby added, her fingertips drumming restlessly on the tabletop. "They'll be watching for you."

"Let them look," Amelia said, her attention focused on her laptop, where she was carefully extracting data from Haley's encrypted thumb drive. The physician had provided what she couldn't access remotely—internal memos, staffing audits, and most critically, patient outcome data that had been scrubbed from the main system but still existed in offline backups.

Ella hovered nearby, watching the data transfer with the intensity of someone who lived and breathed in the digital realm. "This is why we needed the physical handoff," she said, noting William's questioning look. "CBHS upgraded their security protocols last quarter. Their internal networks are now segmented behind military-grade firewalls. I can get into their public-facing systems, but the real data—the financials, the patient records, the communication between executives—that's all air-gapped from external access."

Josh adjusted his cuffs, his eyes scanning the numbers already appearing on Amelia's screen. "Smart move. From what I've learned, Samantha is paranoid about digital footprints. When I was consulting for similar operations, we'd keep the most damning evidence isolated on private servers, usually at the corporate headquarters."

"Or at their data center in Nevada," Ella said. "That's where CBHS keeps their primary servers. I've been mapping their network architecture for weeks. If we want a complete picture of what they're doing, eventually we'll need physical access to that facility."

"One step at a time," William said. "Let's see what Haley's files tell us first."

Amelia was typing with a rhythm that could almost pass for a flirty tango . . . if one thought data breaches had a sultry side. The glow of the screen illuminated her face—a portrait of focus and a touch of mischief—as she sifted through the labyrinthine financial records of CBHS. It was like playing cards with the devil; you knew the game was rigged, but oh, the thrill of calling the bluff.

"Gotcha," she whispered to herself as another piece of the puzzle clicked into place. Darby leaned over her shoulder, her hair today in a playful pixie cut that somehow looked both innocent and mischievous. Her eyes sparkled with barely contained triumph.

"Breaking and entering?" Darby joked, her voice low and velvety. "I thought we were upstanding citizens now."

"Consider it . . . proactive community service," Amelia said without looking up, her fingers never missing a beat. "We're about to give Mr. Blackwell and his merry band of profiteers a taste of their own medicine."

Josh leaned forward, his perfectly pressed cuffs sliding up just enough to reveal platinum cufflinks—a reminder of his more questionable financial endeavors. His eyes scanned the numbers with the practiced ease of someone who'd once made millions disappear with a few keystrokes. "Well, well," he said, a humorless smile playing at his lips. "Looks like Samantha learned her creative accounting from the same school I did. Though I have to say, her technique lacks . . . finesse. It's like watching someone try to pick a lock with a sledgehammer."

"At least Wall Street pretends to be legitimate," Darby said, arching an eyebrow.

"Point taken," Josh conceded, straightening his tie with practiced precision. "I must admit, the mafia's expense reports were a lot more straightforward. No one tries to hide a yacht under *office supplies*."

Justine sauntered in, her red hair a fiery banner of rebellion against the sterile corporate backdrop. She dropped a stack of papers on the table with the dramatic timing of someone who knew how to command attention. "What's this?" Darby asked, rifling through the pages.

"Kiran's playbook," Justine said, her voice carrying the kind of disdain usually reserved for bad acting. "Turns out our goddess of efficiency likes her nurses silent and her patients compliant. Though I'm not sure she remembers the *care* part of healthcare."

"Ah yes, Kiran's famous staff optimization protocols," Amelia said, her voice dry as desert sand. "I remember trying to make these sound legitimate in board meetings. *Streamlined patient care* sounds so much better than *skeleton crew and prayer*." She continued scrolling through the files, her expression hardening. "Though I see she's gotten even more . . . creative since I left."

Together, they huddled around the evidence they'd amassed—a mosaic of greed, negligence, and outright corruption. It was time to turn the tables on CBHS, to use their unique expertise for something bigger than themselves.

"For every patient who got a bill instead of a bedpan," Amelia said, her voice carrying the weight of years spent watching the system fail.

"For every number they fudged," Josh added, adjusting his tie with practiced precision. "And believe me, they fudged a lot."

"For making an industry of suffering," Justine said, eyes blazing with the intensity of someone who knew about exploitation firsthand.

Darby's smile was sharp enough to cut glass. "And because sometimes karma needs a little . . . professional assistance."

• • • ● • ● • • •

Darby noticed Josh glued to his phone, his brow furrowed. "Earth to Josh. You still with us?" she called out.

Josh started, looking up from his phone. "Huh? Oh, yeah. Just . . . thinking."

Darby leaned over, curious. "About what? The meaning of life? The square root of infinity?"

Josh sighed, looking slightly embarrassed. "No, it's . . . it's this stock market simulator game. I'm trying to beat my high score, but the virtual market keeps crashing."

Darby burst out laughing. "The man who made millions disappear with a calculator is getting worked up over fake stocks?"

"Hey, it's a very sophisticated simulation!" Josh defended, straightening his perfectly pressed tie. "Besides, my virtual retirement is at stake here."

"Let me see that." Darby plucked the phone from his hands. Several taps later, a triumphant grin appeared. "There. I just made you a virtual billionaire."

Josh stared at the screen, dumbfounded. "How did you—"

"Sometimes the house always wins because it's rigged. Even virtual ones."

"I should've known better than to doubt your . . . creative problem-solving skills."

"Next time, just ask. Though I do charge a consulting fee. Say, 10% of your virtual fortune?"

They shared a laugh before turning back to their actual mission. Some things never changed—like Josh's obsession with numbers, even the fake ones.

To Be Compassionate

The chandelier's light and the glow from the wall sconces, combined with the windows' natural light, cast long shadows across the faces of the assembled team in the Hawthorne Hotel's Grand Ballroom. For the past week, they had methodically picked apart CBHS's empire—poring over bank statements that revealed systematic fraud, corporate documents exposing patient neglect, and insurance contracts designed to deny care rather than provide it. Josh had traced money through a labyrinth of offshore accounts, while Ella mapped their digital security vulnerabilities. They scrutinized every property deed, every internal memo, and every email, building an airtight case against the healthcare giant.

William sat at the head of the table, surrounded by organized stacks of evidence. He watched his team with pride—each brought unique skills honed from questionable pasts, now turned toward a worthy cause. The runner's medals hanging in his Salem home seemed a lifetime away from this opulent ballroom, but then again, life had a way of taking unexpected turns.

"As Thoreau said, *It's not what you look at that matters, it's what you see*," William said. "And I'm seeing a whole lot of gray area here."

"Gray area?" snorted Tommy. "More like black and white. CBHS is screwing people over left and right."

"I get it. But are we any better than them if we stoop to their level?"

Amelia placed a hand on his arm, her touch electric. "We're not stooping, William. We're rising to the occasion."

He met her gaze, seeing the fierce conviction there. Part of him wanted to run—not metaphorically, but literally. Lace up his shoes and hit the streets of Salem until his lungs burned and his thoughts cleared.

Instead, he took a deep breath. "Alright," he said. "Let's hear the plan. But I reserve the right to quote more philosophers if things get too morally ambiguous."

The team chuckled, the tension in the room easing. As they dove into the details, William couldn't shake the feeling that this mission might be his shot at redemption—or his fastest route back to rock bottom.

Amelia cleared her throat, drawing the team's attention. "Before we dive deeper, there's someone you need to hear from." She opened the ballroom's doors to present a man, his suit rumpled and eyes haunted by sleepless nights. "This is John Franklin, CFO of MedTech Solutions. He's been a friend for years, and he has a story that will shed light on just how far CBHS's corruption reaches."

John stepped forward, his shoulders hunched as if carrying the weight of his entire company. The fluorescent lights cast harsh shadows across his face, emphasizing the deep lines of worry etched there. "Thanks for having me," he said, his voice barely above a whisper, rough with emotion. "I never thought I'd be involved in something like . . . this. Exposing corruption, risking everything."

"Welcome to the dark side," Josh said, trying to lighten the mood. "We have cookies."

"John," Amelia said, her voice carrying the quiet authority of someone used to commanding boardrooms. "I think it's time they heard your story firsthand."

John took a deep breath, his hands trembling slightly as he adjusted his tie. "MedTech has been a CBHS surgical supplier for years. We're not a huge company, but we're good at what we do. Last quarter, we delivered over $2 million in state-of-the-art equipment. Lifesaving stuff—heart-lung machines, advanced surgical robots. But when it came time to pay . . ." He trailed off, swallowing hard, his eyes glistening with unshed tears.

William leaned forward, his marathoner's instincts sensing the importance of pacing in John's story. "They stiffed you?" he asked, encouraging John to continue.

John nodded, a bitter laugh escaping his lips. "Completely. It was like we'd vanished from their books. I called, I emailed, I even showed up in person and camped out in their parking lot for three days straight." His voice grew stronger, anger seeping through the cracks of his composure. "Vincent and Samantha, they . . ." His voice cracked, raw with betrayal. "They laughed in my face. Said if I didn't like it, I could sue them. As if a small company like ours could afford to take on their army of lawyers."

The room fell silent, the weight of John's words settling over them like a heavy fog. William's mind raced, imagining the ripple effects—dedicated employees laid off, families struggling to make ends meet, a small business that had poured its heart into saving lives now crushed under the heel of corporate greed.

Darby broke the silence, her voice uncharacteristically soft. "What happened to your company, John?"

John's shoulders sagged, defeat etched in every line of his body. "We're hanging on by a thread. Had to let go of half our staff—good people, with families to support. The rest of us haven't taken a paycheck in months. We're one missed payment away from bankruptcy."

Tommy, who had been quietly observing, spoke up. "And the equipment? The machines meant to save lives?"

John's eyes flashed with anger. "Sitting unused in CBHS warehouses, as far as we know. They have the tools to help people, and they're letting them gather dust while patients suffer."

John's voice trembled with barely contained fury as he continued, "They didn't pay us a single cent. Two million dollars' worth of lifesaving equipment, and we didn't see a dime. As I said, it's put us on the brink of bankruptcy."

The team exchanged shocked glances, but John wasn't finished. His next words sent a ripple of disgust through the room.

"And here's the kicker," he said, pulling out his phone and bringing up a news article. "Just a few months after I was begging—literally on my knees—in CBHS's parking lot, this happened."

He thrust the phone towards them, displaying a photo that made their blood boil. There was Vincent Blackwell, his million-dollar smile gleaming beneath a pristine white hard hat, gripping a golden shovel at a groundbreaking ceremony.

"This bastard had the audacity to pledge millions for a new math wing at his precious twin daughters' elite private school in Chicago. And guess where that money came from?"

"CBHS," Josh said as he exhaled in disgust, the pieces falling into place.

John nodded. "Exactly. The same company that claimed they couldn't pay their bills was somehow flush enough for Vincent's vanity projects."

Darby leaned in, her eyes narrowing. "How much are we talking about here?"

"The initial pledge was $5 million," John replied, his voice dripping with disdain. "But there's much more to it than that. I've done some digging, and it turns out Vincent's been treating CBHS like his personal piggy bank for years."

He swiped through more photos on his phone—Vincent on a gleaming yacht, hosting lavish parties, jetting off to exotic locations. "Private jets, luxury vacations, multimillion-dollar homes . . . all while hospitals are understaffed, patients are suffering, and suppliers like us are going under."

While they knew some of this, the team listened in horror as John laid out a first-person account of excess and exploitation that went far beyond simple corporate greed. Vincent Blackwell wasn't just mismanaging CBHS; he was bleeding it dry to fund his own extravagant lifestyle.

"The line between CBHS's finances and Vincent's personal expenses doesn't just blur," John concluded, his voice hoarse with emotion. "It vanishes completely. He's driving the company into the ground, and he doesn't care who gets hurt along the way—suppliers, employees, patients . . . as long as he gets his slice of the pie."

As John's words sank in, the atmosphere in the room shifted from shock to steely determination. This wasn't just about righting a wrong anymore. It was about toppling an empire built on lies, greed, and the suffering of countless innocent people.

William stood, his eyes blazing with a fire that made even Darby take a step back. "Thank you, John," he said, his voice low and dangerous. "You've just given us an important piece we needed. CBHS thinks they can crush small companies like yours without consequences. Time to show them how wrong they are."

The team nodded in agreement, their faces set with grim resolve. The game had changed, and CBHS was about to learn the true cost of their greed.

As Amelia walked John out, the atmosphere in the room shifted. The team's resolve hardened, their motivation no longer just about the thrill of the con or personal vendettas. They were now soldiers in a war against a system that valued profit over human life.

And with that, they turned back to their plans, John's story fueling their determination to bring CBHS down, no matter the cost.

Ella was the first to break the silence when she returned. "Well, I suddenly feel a lot less conflicted about hacking their systems."

Amelia's voice carried the weight of years spent watching CBHS's abuse from the inside. "Every story like John's confirms what we already knew. The corruption runs deeper than any of us imagined. It's not just vendors they're destroying—it's employees, patients, entire communities."

William nodded, his expression hardening. "We're long past the point of a simple heist. This is about dismantling a system designed to profit from people's suffering."

"And doing it with style," Darby added with a wry smile. "After all, if you're going to take down a corrupt empire, you might as well look good doing it."

As the team dove back into their planning, William felt the familiar surge of purpose that had first drawn them together. This wasn't about running from his past anymore—this was about fighting for a future where companies like CBHS couldn't prey on the vulnerable.

• • • ● • ● • • •

Tommy's low whistle abruptly broke the silence in the grand room. "My goodness," he said, eyes glued to his laptop screen. "You guys need to see this."

The team huddled around Tommy's computer, tension palpable in the air. William's muscles tightened instinctively, as if preparing for a sprint.

"Looks like our friend Vincent's been busy," Tommy said, as he scrolled through a Wall Street Journal article. "CBHS just made a new $2.5 million donation to his daughters' school in Chicago."

"So that's a total of $7.5 million now. I'm sure it's a great school—with a yearly tuition of $40,000, it better be." Amelia's eyes narrowed as she continued. "But that's . . . oddly generous for a company supposedly struggling to pay its vendors."

"Perhaps he thinks he's some sort of philanthropic genius?" William remarked, his tone dripping with bitter irony. "As if robbing from the sick to fund his vanity projects is a stroke of brilliance. Thoreau once said, *Goodness is the only investment that never fails.* Somehow, I doubt that's the returns Vincent is after."

The room crackled with even greater outrage and determination. William paced, his lean frame coiled with tension. He'd seen addiction destroy lives, but this? This was a different poison.

"We're talking about lives here," Tommy said, surprising himself with the intensity of his emotions. "People denied care, small businesses crushed, all so Vincent can play big shot philanthropist?"

William took a deep breath. "You're right. As Emerson said, *Nothing great was ever achieved without enthusiasm.* Let's channel this anger into something productive."

As the team dove back into planning, William allowed himself a small smile. For once, the rush wasn't about the con—it was about the cause.

• • • ● • ● • • • •

William stepped out of his modest Salem home, the crisp morning air nipping at his skin. The sun was just beginning to peek over the trees of Salem Common, casting a warm glow on the colonial-era buildings that lined the quiet streets. He set off toward the Hawthorne Hotel and stepped through part of the wrought-iron fence that encircled most of the Common. Strolling under the protective canopy the old trees provided, his feet fell into a familiar cadence as the crushed gravel crunched beneath his feet.

"Another day, another philosophical quandary," William said to himself, his voice gruff but tinged with wry humor. "Thoreau would have a field day with this one."

He decided to take a lap around the green before climbing the Hawthorne's stairs. As he passed by the Salem Witch Museum, its looming presence a stark reminder of past injustices, William's mind wandered to the impending heist. The peacefulness of his surroundings stood in sharp contrast to the turmoil within.

A jogger passed by, giving William a nod; it wasn't rude, but it wasn't friendly either . . . isn't that just the way of the New England runner? He returned the gesture, thinking, "If only they knew what kind of *run* I'm really on."

Pausing at one of the war memorials, William closed his eyes and took a deep breath. "Emerson said, *The purpose of life is not to be happy. It is to be useful, to be honorable, to be compassionate*," he recited softly. "But where's the honor in a heist, even if the cause is just?"

As he resumed his walk, the weight of his past seemed to press down on him. The teaching, the book, the speaking tours—all of it had led him here, to this moment of potential redemption or spectacular failure.

You've come a long way from Omaha, old man. What would your therapist say?

After his peaceful walk, the back of the Hawthorne Hotel came into view, its proud stature a silent witness to countless secrets. William squared his shoulders as he crossed South Washington Square and walked around the small valet stand in the rear. Across the street from *Moody's Home & Gifts*, the hotel has a side entrance, so he entered there for a change.

"Well, as Emerson also said, *Do not go where the path may lead, go instead where there is no path and leave a trail*. Let's hope this trail doesn't lead straight to a jail cell."

As William entered the Grand Ballroom, he was greeted by the sight of Amelia holding court, her presence commanding yet inviting. She was in the middle of explaining a complex legal maneuver, her hands gesticulating elegantly as she spoke.

"Think of it as unraveling a sweater," Amelia said, her eyes twinkling. "Pull the right thread, and the whole thing comes apart. We're not just looking for loose ends—we're going to unravel CBHS's entire empire, one carefully chosen strand at a time."

The team hung on her every word, even the usual leader Darby was leaning in with interest. William couldn't help but marvel at how quickly she'd become an integral part of their ragtag group.

"We need two trails," Amelia said, her years as general counsel evident in her measured tone. "One for the OIG investigators—subtle enough to make them feel like they're uncovering it themselves. And another for the SEC that'll set off every regulatory alarm in their system."

Ella nodded, already typing. "Like dropping breadcrumbs for bloodhounds while setting off flares for everyone else. I can work with that."

"Josh," Amelia turned to their financial expert, "this is where you come in. We need those SEC flags to look like they came from internal audits. Make the trail look like someone inside got sloppy."

Josh straightened his tie, a glint of anticipation in his eyes. "Please. Creating suspicious audit trails was practically my day job. It's truly for a worthy cause this time."

"And when the investigators start digging?" Darby asked, leaning forward.

"That's where I come in," Amelia said. "Every document they find will lead to three more, each more damning than the last. By the time they reach Vincent's personal files, they'll be salivating."

William watched his team, a surge of pride mixing with determination. "For Sophia Martinez . . . and everyone else CBHS has hurt along the way."

The team nodded, their focus sharp. No more needed to be said.

Before the team could disperse, the large ballroom doors opened and Justine strode in, her fiery hair windswept and her eyes gleaming with the thrill of a successful reconnaissance mission. The team, gathered around a table strewn with blueprints and surveillance photos, looked up expectantly.

"Ladies and gentlemen," Justine announced, her voice carrying a hint of triumph, "I come bearing gifts from the belly of the beast itself." She tossed a USB drive onto the table with a flourish. "CBHS's headquarters in Boston? It's a fortress, but every fortress has its weak points."

She pulled up a chair, leaning in conspiratorially. "They've upgraded their security system. It's now state-of-the-art, but it's got one fatal flaw—it's run by humans. And humans, my friends, are delightfully fallible." A wicked grin spread across her face. "I may or may not have convinced a rather gullible IT intern that I was from corporate, doing a routine security check. Let's just say he was very eager to impress the *new boss* with his knowledge of the system."

William raised an eyebrow, impressed. "And Gloucester?"

Justine's smile widened. "Ah, now that's where things get interesting. Addison Gilbert Hospital—it's small, it's understaffed, and it's our perfect entry point into CBHS's network." She pulled out her phone, swiping through photos. "I posed as a potential donor, got the grand tour. The place is a mess—outdated equipment, overworked staff, and a computer system that's practically begging to be hacked."

She paused for dramatic effect. "But here's the kicker—their backup generator is on its last legs. One well-timed *malfunction*, and we could have access to their entire system while they scramble to keep the lights on."

Amelia's eyes brightened. "Interesting, Justine. The town has condemned one of AGH's buildings; they literally chained the doors shut. We could use one of those areas as a staging point."

The team leaned in, their eyes alight with the possibilities Justine's intel and Amelia's insight presented. These two bits were the keys to the kingdom, and the anticipation of what they could do with this information was palpable in the room.

"Well done, Justine," William said, a rare smile crossing his face. "Looks like we've found our way in. Amelia, your insider knowledge . . . well it's essential. Now, let's make all of this count."

The Moral Minute—Episode 3

[Theme music—short, serious but with an edge]

ANIE: I'm Anie Chen.

LUCAS: And I'm Lucas Rodriguez. Welcome to The Moral Minute, where we examine the day's most egregious ethical failures in corporate America.

ANIE: Lucas, remember when CBHS promised to revolutionize healthcare? Turns out they're revolutionizing something else entirely—creative bankruptcy.

LUCAS: [sardonic] Speaking of bankruptcy, our sources just confirmed that MedTech Solutions had to repossess vital equipment from several CBHS hospitals. Apparently, someone forgot to pay the bills.

ANIE: Forgot? While Vincent Blackwell was buying a superyacht?

LUCAS: [dry] Ah yes, the *Artemisa*. Because nothing says "healthcare leadership" like a 190-foot floating palace with a wine collection worth more than most emergency rooms.

ANIE: What happened after the equipment was repossessed?

LUCAS: [serious tone] Two hospitals had to divert critical patients. One ER was operating with equipment from the 1990s. Meanwhile, Mr. Blackwell was shopping for a private jet - you know, for all those urgent golf meetings.

ANIE: [deadpan] Essential healthcare business, clearly.

LUCAS: Here's the kicker—the equipment they couldn't pay for? Cost less than the artwork in Blackwell's office.

ANIE: Time's almost up. What's our moral of the minute?

LUCAS: When your CEO's yacht is better equipped than your hospitals, it might be time for a leadership checkup.

[Theme music fades out]

Air Gapped

Darby reclined in her seat, long legs crossed as she surveyed the team gathered around the large oak table in the Hawthorne Hotel's Grand Ballroom. She twirled a lock of her glossy blonde hair, styled in sleek waves today. The chandelier cast shimmering light across their determined faces. She cocked an eyebrow. "Well, aren't we a merry band of misfits? Let's get this show on the road, shall we?"

Josh stood, fiddling with his cufflinks. Always impeccably groomed, that one. He cleared his throat. "Right. So here's the deal with Addison Gilbert Hospital—AGH to the locals. They used to be part of a larger system, but lost their Obligated Group status. Basically, they were hemorrhaging money like a patient with an aortic rupture." He smirked at his own metaphor.

Darby rolled her eyes. Trust Josh to make it sound like a financial soap opera. "Which left them ripe for the picking by dear old CBHS," she interjected. "Swooping in like vultures to *save* the day and line their own pockets in the process."

Josh nodded. "Bingo. So here's our play."

"Why AGH specifically?" Tommy asked, his security mindset kicking in. "Why do we need to be on site?"

Ella leaned forward, her dark eyes intent. "CBHS's network architecture is old school. They're paranoid about external threats, so they've built their system like a fortress—impenetrable from the outside, but vulnerable from within. Their main servers are air-gapped—physically isolated from unsecured networks."

"You mentioned that before—*air gapped*—what does that mean?" Darby prompted, though her slight smirk suggested she already knew the answer.

"Which means we can't do this remotely," Ella said. "We need to physically plug into their network to plant our little surprises. AGH is perfect—they're still integrating their systems with CBHS's main network, and their security is more . . . relaxed."

Ella gestured for Darby to continue.

She rose, almost gliding to the front. She leaned forward, palms flat on the table. "We're going to use AGH's outdated systems as our backdoor into CBHS's network. It'll be like taking candy from a baby. A very rich, very corrupt baby."

She explained the steps, her red lips curving into a devious smile. Exploit the vulnerabilities during the transition. Plant false financial data. Redirect funds. Watch the chaos unfold.

Justine elaborated, her fingertips pecked at the keyboard, each keystroke deliberate and measured. "We're going to create a series of phantom transactions within AGH's system. These will appear to be legitimate transfers between AGH and other CBHS facilities, but they'll actually be funneling money into accounts we control."

She pulled up a complex spreadsheet. "We'll backdate these transactions, making them look like routine inter-hospital resource sharing. But here's the kicker—we'll inflate the amounts. A $10,000 equipment transfer becomes $100,000. A $50,000 staff training program balloons to half a million.

"The beauty is in the merger's chaos . . . these inflated numbers won't raise immediate red flags. CBHS will assume it's just part of AGH's pre-existing financial mess."

Josh took over, his fingers jabbed at the keyboard, punctuating each point with a forceful keystroke. "Once these false transactions are in place, we start the real magic. We'll set up a series of smart contracts within their system. These will automatically trigger fund transfers based on certain conditions."

He brought up a flowchart on the screen. "For example, every time CBHS tries to move money from AGH to their primary accounts, our algorithm will intercept a percentage and redirect it to our offshore accounts. It'll look like normal processing fees or administrative costs."

"But that's not all," Josh grinned. "We're also going to create a few *ghost* departments within AGH's system. On paper, these will look like legitimate hospital wings or research units. In reality, they'll be funnels, siphoning off funds from every budget allocation CBHS makes to AGH."

Justine nodded approvingly. "And the cherry on top? We'll manipulate their payroll system. Create a few dozen fake employees, spread across different departments. Their salaries will be modest enough not to draw attention individually, but collectively, they'll be bleeding CBHS dry."

"By the time they realize what's happening," she concluded, "we'll have redirected millions. And the best part? It'll all look like it's CBHS's own mismanagement and corruption coming back to bite them."

"By the time we're done, CBHS won't know which way is up. Their accounts will be leaking money faster than they can say 'fraud'." Darby winked at Josh. "Time to plug the holes and make the cash flow our way for a change."

The team hung on her every word, electrified by the audacity of the plan. This wasn't just a heist. It was justice. It was redemption.

And damn if Darby wasn't going to look fabulous doing it. She straightened, smoothing her designer dress. "Any questions, class?"

"One, yes; and I think it's pretty important," replied Ella. "Who will get in there to plant this?"

The team fell silent until Amelia stood, her posture radiating confidence despite the tension crackling in the air. "I'll infiltrate AGH."

Silence descended, heavy with the weight of her words. Darby's perfectly sculpted eyebrow arched. "Sweetheart, you sure about this? If they catch you . . ."

"They won't." Amelia's voice was steel wrapped in silk. "I've got this."

Tommy leaned forward, concern etching lines into his forehead. "Amelia, the risks—"

She silenced him with a look. "I know the stakes. But this is our shot. Our chance to make them pay." Her eyes blazed with determination. "I'm not backing down."

The team exchanged glances, a silent conversation playing out in raised eyebrows and subtle nods. Finally, Darby sighed. "Alright, sugar. But you need to be careful in there. CBHS isn't playing around."

Amelia's lips quirked. "Neither am I."

. . . . ● . ● . . . .

Addison Gilbert Hospital stood before Amelia, its red brick facade a testament to its long history. The main building featured a classic architectural style, with arched windows lining the upper floor and a white-columned portico welcoming visitors at the employee's entrance. The name "ADDISON GILBERT HOSPITAL" was prominently displayed above the portico.

Amelia had come alone for this reconnaissance mission. As CBHS's former general counsel, she could no longer enter the front door—her face was too well-known to risk it. That's why today's approach required a different strategy altogether. Tommy had provided her with the nurse's scrubs she now wore, along with a detailed briefing on hospital shift changes and security protocols.

Earlier that morning, William's car had pulled up in the parking lot of the Salt Water Grille—delicious seafood, no real view—behind the iconic Welcome to Gloucester sign. As Amelia prepared to exit the vehicle, William reached out, gently grasping her hand.

"Be careful in there," he said, his voice low and tinged with concern. His eyes, usually twinkling with mischief or philosophical musings, were now serious and focused.

Amelia squeezed his hand reassuringly. "I've walked these halls a hundred times—just never dressed like this." She adjusted the unfamiliar scrubs. "I know where to go and who to avoid."

William nodded, a small smile tugging at the corners of his mouth. "I know you will. But still . . . watch your back. If anyone from the executive team spots you—"

"They won't. Night shift changeover is in twenty minutes. Perfect cover for slipping in with the crowd. Ella's temporary badge will get me where I need to go."

As Amelia stepped out of the car, she took a moment to appreciate the town's welcome sign. Its bold black background and gold lettering proudly proclaimed Gloucester as America's Oldest Seaport, established in 1623. The image of a stalwart fisherman at the helm, along with the silhouettes of cod and a majestic schooner, spoke volumes about the city's rich maritime heritage.

She turned back to William, who was still watching her from the car. "I'll see you at the rendezvous point," she said with a confidence she didn't entirely feel.

William nodded once more, then drove away, leaving Amelia to begin her half-mile walk towards Addison Gilbert. As she set off, the morning sun glinted off the golden fish on the sign, almost as if wishing her luck. The salty breeze from the nearby Atlantic Ocean tousled her hair, carrying with it the whispers of over 400 years of history—and the unspoken words of support from William.

Her walk had her cross the Grant Circle Rotary and through the outskirts of Gloucester; the scenery gradually shifting from the coastal charm near the welcome sign to the residential setting surrounding the hospital. Each step brought her closer to AGH and to the high-stakes game she was about to play. By the time the red brick façade of Addison Gilbert Hospital came into view, Amelia had shed her lawyer persona, adopting instead the hurried gait and tired eyes of a night shift nurse heading in for work.

Taking a deep breath, Amelia squared her shoulders. The familiar butterflies of anticipation fluttered in her stomach as she prepared to put their plan into action. With one last glance at the imposing yet somehow comforting facade of Addison Gilbert Hospital, she strode purposefully toward the employee entrance, joining a small cluster of actual nurses arriving for the night shift.

Surrounding the entrance, well-maintained flower beds added a touch of color and life to the scene. The combination of red brick, white trim, and greenery gave the hospital a warm, almost inviting appearance despite its serious purpose.

As Amelia approached, she noted the mix of old and new—the historic main building juxtaposed with more modern additions, visible to the side and rear. A parking lot in front held a scatter of vehicles, hinting at the activity within.

She slipped through the doors, just another face in the sea of scrubs and white coats. Her disguise was flawless—nurse's scrubs, ID badge, even the right shoes. Amazing what a little creative hacking from Ella could do.

"Long night ahead," she said to a passing nurse, who nodded with the weary camaraderie of the overworked.

"Tell me about it. Third double this week."

After she climbed the interior staircase, she began navigating the maze of corridors. Her heart raced. Every corner held the threat of discovery. Every passing employee was a potential enemy. But she moved with purpose, her steps confident; her smile easy.

Just another nurse on a mission. Nothing to see here.

The administrative wing beckoned, its hushed corridors a stark contrast to the busy patient floors. She knew where to go from her days reviewing acquisition documents—and more importantly, she knew which faces to avoid. Kiran occasionally made surprise visits to satellite facilities, and the hospital director would certainly recognize her.

The restricted section beckoned, its nondescript door a challenge. Amelia glanced around, then swiped her badge. A breathless moment. Then—click. The lock disengaged.

She slipped inside, adrenaline singing in her veins. The terminal sat in the corner, its screen a siren call. Amelia's fingers flew over the keys, her focus absolute. Backdoors and firewalls crumbled beneath her digital onslaught.

Almost there. Just a little more . . .

Footsteps. Voices. Getting closer.

Ugh.

As she began to call Ella for further instruction, Amelia's pulse pounded. She had little time to start and definitely had no time to finish. She had to go. Now.

Ripping the flash drive from the port, she darted for the door. Out into the hallway, trying to look casual. Like she belonged.

The voices rounded the corner. Security guards. Suspicious eyes landed on her. "Hey! You! Stop right there!"

Amelia ran.

The fluorescent lights of the hospital's corridors buzzed overhead as Amelia's footsteps echoed through the empty hallway. Her heart raced, pounding against her ribcage like a caged animal seeking escape. The familiar antiseptic smell that usually permeated the air was overshadowed by the acrid scent of her own fear-induced sweat.

Rounding a corner, Amelia's eyes darted frantically, searching for any means of escape. The stairwell was too risky—they'd expect that. The elevator was out of the question. Then, like a beacon of hope, she spotted a supply closet in a restroom. It was less than ideal, but it was her only option.

With a quick glance over her shoulder, Amelia slipped into the restroom and ducked inside the supply closet, easing the door shut just as the guards thundered past. She pressed her back against the cool metal shelving, willing her ragged breathing to quiet. The pungent smell of cleaning supplies filled her nostrils as she waited, every muscle in her body tense.

Minutes ticked by like hours. Finally, when the corridor outside fell silent, Amelia allowed herself to exhale. But her relief was short-lived. She knew it was only a matter of time before they found her. The question was, how much damage had already been done?

In the administrative wing of the hospital, Samantha Bowen sat behind her imposing mahogany desk, her manicured nails tapping an impatient rhythm on the polished surface. She prided herself on always being three steps ahead of everyone else. But this . . . this she hadn't seen coming.

Minutes earlier, her phone buzzed, the screen illuminating with a message that made her blood run cold:

Security breach. Amelia caught accessing restricted files in the server room.

Samantha's lips pressed into a thin line, her mind racing She had always been suspicious of Amelia; the woman asked too many questions—even for a lawyer—and always seemed

to hover on the periphery of conversations she had no business being part of. But this . .
. this was beyond mere curiosity.

With a fluid motion born of years of corporate maneuvering, Samantha rose from her
chair and strode towards Vincent Blackwell's AGH office. Her heels clicked faintly against
the linoleum floor, a sound that usually heralded trouble for someone. Today, that someone was Amelia.

She burst into Vincent's office without knocking, interrupting his meeting with two
board members. "We have a situation," she announced, her voice sharp enough to cut
glass.

Vincent looked up, annoyance flashing across his face before he registered the gravity in
Samantha's eyes. He excused himself from the meeting and closed the door behind the
departing board members.

"What's happened?" he demanded, his tone matching Samantha's urgency.

"Amelia," Samantha spat the name like it left a bad taste in her mouth. "She was just
caught in the server room, accessing files she has no clearance for."

Vincent's face darkened, the lines around his mouth deepening. "Bring her in. Now."

As Samantha relayed the order to security, Vincent paced the length of his office. This was
a disaster. If Amelia had managed to access certain files . . . he didn't want to think about
the implications.

Thirty agonizing minutes later, a disheveled Amelia was escorted into Vincent's office.
Her usually immaculate appearance was in disarray—hair mussed, blouse untucked, a
smudge of dirt on her cheek from her stint in the supply closet. But despite her appearance, her eyes burned with a defiant fire.

Vincent gestured for her to sit, while he and Samantha remained standing, a power play
not lost on Amelia.

"Amelia," Vincent began, his voice deceptively calm. "Would you care to explain what
you were doing in a restricted area, accessing files well above your security clearance?"

Amelia's mind raced. She had prepared for this possibility, had a cover story ready. But looking into Vincent's cold eyes, she knew it was futile. They had her dead to rights.

Before she could speak, Samantha cut in. "Save your excuses. We know you've been gathering intelligence. The only question is, who are you working with?"

Amelia's silence spoke volumes. She wouldn't betray her team, no matter the consequences.

Vincent leaned forward, his massive desk dwarfing Amelia's seated form. "Your silence is all the confirmation we need. You're fired, effective immediately. Security will escort you from the premises." His voice dropped to a menacing whisper. "And Amelia? If I were you, I'd leave town. Fast. CBHS has a long reach, and we don't take kindly to corporate espionage."

As security led Amelia out, Samantha turned to Vincent, her face a mask of icy determination. "We need to initiate a full security lockdown. If she's working with others, our entire system could be compromised."

Vincent nodded grimly. "Do it. And Samantha? I want to know who she's working with. Use whatever resources you need. We need to contain this before it spirals out of control."

Outside the hospital, Amelia stood on the sidewalk, the weight of her failure pressing down on her shoulders. Her phone buzzed in her pocket—a group text from William: "Rendezvous at my house ASAP. We need to reevaluate."

As she hopped in an Uber, Amelia's mind was already racing, analyzing where they had gone wrong, strategizing their next move.

What was it? Beefed up security staff? Additional rounds? Did increased security slow her time to access the system?

They had underestimated CBHS once. It was a mistake they couldn't afford to make again.

The Uber pulled away from the curb, carrying Amelia towards an uncertain future. Behind her, the CBHS building loomed, its windows reflecting the setting sun like a multitude of watchful eyes. They lost the battle, but the war was far from over. And Amelia was just getting started.

As the Uber driver navigated Salem's historic streets, he remained oblivious to the tension radiating from his passenger. Amelia sat in the back, her mind racing as she replayed the disastrous events at Addison Gilbert Hospital. As they turned onto Winter Street, she glimpsed William's house—her sanctuary in the storm that was about to break.

"You can drop me at the corner of Oliver Street and North Washington Square," she instructed the driver, her voice steady despite her inner turmoil.

As Amelia stepped out of the car, she took a moment to collect herself. The late afternoon sun cast long shadows across the street as she made her way up Oliver Street, her footsteps echoing off the centuries-old buildings. She passed a garage for John Story's house; he was a lawyer, politician, and at 32 years old, he remains the youngest ever US Supreme Court Justice. The weight of history in this neighborhood was palpable, a stark contrast to the very modern danger she now faced.

Continuing down the alley-like street behind William's property, Amelia slipped into the backyard. The space was a hidden oasis, with its brick patio and carefully tended gardens. A wrought-iron table and chairs sat beneath a gnarled old tree, its branches providing a natural canopy. Forsythia bushes added splashes of bright yellow to the scene, their cheerful color at odds with Amelia's somber mood.

William was already waiting for her, his thin frame silhouetted against the fading light. As she approached, his face etched with concern, Amelia felt a wave of relief wash over her. Here, in this tranquil garden just steps away from the bustling street, she could finally let her guard down.

"Amelia," William said softly, pulling her into a tight embrace. "Thank God you're safe."

For a moment, they stood in silence, the weight of the day's events hanging between them. Then, with a gentle squeeze of her shoulders, William stepped back.

"Come on," he said, gesturing towards the house. "The others are waiting inside. We need to regroup and figure out our next move."

Amelia nodded, taking one last look at the peaceful garden before following William into the house. The Greek Revival structure loomed above them, its red brick facade a testament to Salem's maritime past. As they entered through the back door, Amelia couldn't help but feel grateful for this haven—a place where history and present-day rebellion intertwined, much like the team gathered within its walls.

The warm glow from the chandelier in the entryway welcomed them, and as they made their way to the dining room where the others waited, Amelia steeled herself for the difficult conversation ahead. The pink walls of the dining room, usually so cheerful, now seemed to pulse with the urgency of their situation. The antique table, which had likely seen its share of clandestine meetings over the centuries, was about to host another.

With a deep breath, Amelia prepared to face her team and share the news of her capture and termination. The fight was far from over, but the stakes had just gotten much, much higher.

The team huddled around the table in their new makeshift headquarters; it wasn't the opulent Hawthorne Hotel they'd left behind, but it was nice. The air was thick with the musty scent of neglect, and the dim light cast long shadows across their faces.

Darby leaned forward, her blonde hair a tangled mess. "So, what now? We can't just give up."

"No one's giving up," Justine said, her eyes flashing with determination. "But we need a new plan, and fast. CBHS will be on high alert after this."

William sat back, his weathered face creased in thought. "We need to hit them where it hurts. Their reputation. Their bottom line."

Ella's fingers danced across her keyboard, her voice barely audible. "After that fiasco at Addison Gilbert, they'll lock down every hospital in their system. The data we need isn't accessible remotely."

Josh shook his head, his voice tight with frustration. "And then what? We've got nothing but a close call and Amelia nearly caught."

Tommy leaned against the wall, arms crossed. "We need to go to the source."

"The source?" Darby asked.

"Vincent's ranch in Nevada," Tommy replied. "Ella's intel shows that's where they keep their primary servers. If we can't get the data through the hospitals . . ."

"We get it from Vincent's backyard," William finished, understanding dawning on his face.

Ella nodded, her expression grave. "It won't be easy. The place is private property with security systems that would make Fort Knox jealous. But if we can get physical access to those servers . . ."

"We can download everything," Josh said, a hint of his old confidence returning. "Financial records, internal memos, patient data—all the evidence we need."

Darby leaned forward, her eyes gleaming with a newfound purpose. "We don't just release it to the media. We divulge it to their investors. Their patients. We make it so big, so damn ugly, that they can't sweep it under the rug."

The others fell silent, considering her words. It was a bold move, one that could either make or break them.

William nodded slowly, a glimmer of hope in his eyes. "It could work. But getting onto Vincent's property—that's not just breaking into a hospital. That's infiltrating his personal fortress."

"Good thing we've got the right skill sets for a heist," Darby said with a half-smile. "Between Tommy's security experience, Ella's tech knowledge, my . . . persuasive abilities, and Josh's financial expertise, we might have a chance."

The energy in the room shifted, the despair giving way to a tentative sense of purpose. They had a plan, a way forward. It wouldn't be easy, but then again, nothing worth doing ever was.

As they set to work, dividing tasks and plotting their next move, Darby couldn't shake the feeling that they were on the cusp of something big. Something that could redefine the game.

Hold on, Vincent, she thought, her jaw set with determination. *We're coming for you. And this time, we will not fail.*

The Moral Minute—Episode 4

[Theme music—short, serious but with an edge]

ANIE: I'm Anie Chen.

LUCAS: And I'm Lucas Rodriguez. Welcome to The Moral Minute, where we examine the day's most egregious ethical failures in corporate America.

ANIE: Today we're telling a different kind of story. Not about numbers or corporate dealings, but about Sophia Martinez.

LUCAS: [somber] Sophia was 28 years old, giving birth to her first child at Coastal Bay Hospital, a CBHS facility.

ANIE: The birth went well. Her daughter was healthy. Then Sophia started hemorrhaging.

LUCAS: The doctors knew exactly what they needed—an embolization coil. A common medical device that should've been in stock.

ANIE: [quietly] Should have been.

LUCAS: But it wasn't. Because weeks earlier, MedTech Solutions had repossessed their entire inventory. CBHS hadn't paid their bills.

ANIE: They transferred Sophia to another hospital.

LUCAS: [softly] She didn't make it. Her daughter will never know her mother. All because a billion-dollar healthcare company couldn't pay for basic medical supplies.

ANIE: The day Sophia died, Vincent Blackwell pledged $5 million to his daughters' private school.

LUCAS: Time's almost up. What's our moral of the minute?

ANIE: Some costs can't be measured in dollars and cents.

[Theme music fades out]

Stealing Lives

S ilver Sage Ranch sprawled across the high desert landscape of northeastern Nevada, a vast expanse of over 250,000 acres nestled between the rugged Ruby Mountains and the Tuscarora Range. Founded in 1941 by Gabriel Echeverria, a Basque immigrant turned successful hotelier and rancher, the property had grown to become one of the largest and most productive ranches in the state.

Vincent Blackwell had acquired the ranch a few years ago, drawn to its isolation and rich history. The main entrance, marked by a sturdy gate, opened onto a winding road that stretched for miles through the property. Two pristine trout ponds reflected the vast Nevada sky, their surfaces broken only by the occasional jump of a fish. Beyond the ponds, cattle grazed on lush pastures, carrying on the ranch's long tradition of agricultural excellence.

About three miles from the front gate, Vincent's house stood proudly on a mountainside overlooking the entire ranch. The imposing structure of timber and stone blended with its surroundings, its large windows offering panoramic views of the high desert landscape. This was more than just a retreat for Vincent; it was his fortress, a place where he could escape the pressures of running CBHS and, more importantly, keep his most sensitive information far from prying eyes.

As the team pored over satellite images and blueprints of the ranch, Ella let out a frustrated sigh. "This place is a digital black hole," she said, her fingers tapping restlessly on her laptop. "Vincent's paranoia helps him here. The entire ranch, especially his house, is completely off-grid when it comes to network connectivity."

"No internet?" Darby asked, her blonde hair whipping as she turned to face them. Today's 'do was a sleek French braid, though William suspected it would be something quite different come morning.

"Oh, there's internet," Ella replied. "But it's a closed system. No external access whatsoever. All the sensitive data—financial records, internal memos, everything that could implicate CBHS—it's stored on local servers in the house. There's no way to access it remotely."

William nodded grimly. "Which is why we need to be there in person. They will immediately detect any attempt to breach the system from the outside."

"Not to mention," Amelia added, "many of the most damning documents aren't even digital. Vincent's old school—he keeps hard copies of everything in a safe in his study. Contracts, handwritten notes, records of off-the-books transactions—it's all there."

Josh whistled low. "So we're talking about an actual, physical break-in? A real-deal heist? Breaking and entering, safecracking, the whole nine? Count me in."

Justine arched an eyebrow. "Easy there, Hondo. This isn't exactly a smash and grab at the local liquor store. It's not even what we pulled off in LA. We're talking state-of-the-art security, armed guards . . . we're used to that. It's the vast expanse that's the problem. It's big. It's open. One wrong move and we'll be enjoying a lovely stay at the Elko gray bar hotel."

William nodded, his gaze fixed on the distant house. "Justine's right. Vincent's no fool. He's turned this place into a veritable Fortress of Solitude. But every fortress has its weakness. And we're going to find it.

"This ranch isn't just Vincent's retreat. It's the lynchpin of his entire operation. Everything we need to bring down CBHS is hidden away there, protected by miles of empty desert and a security system that would make Fort Knox jealous."

The team fell silent, contemplating the enormity of the task before them. Silver Sage Ranch, with its breathtaking vistas and rich history, had become the ultimate obstacle in their quest for justice.

"So," Darby said finally, a determined glint in her eye, "how do we get in?"

William exchanged a glance with Amelia before responding. "We're working on that. But one thing's for certain—if we want to expose CBHS's corruption, we need to breach Vincent's sanctuary. Vincent thinks his isolation protects him, but that same isolation is going to be his undoing."

As the team continued to strategize, the image of Silver Sage Ranch loomed large in their minds. The sprawling property, once a symbol of the American West's pioneering spirit, had become the key to their mission. And for Vincent Blackwell, his high desert haven was about to become the stage for his downfall.

A charged silence settled over the group, each lost in their own thoughts. The stakes had never been higher, the odds never more daunting. But they had come too far to turn back now.

Darby was the first to break the stillness, a mischievous grin spreading across her face. "Well, then. Let's go steal ourselves a corporate empire."

As the team continued their strategy session, the Silver Sage Ranch loomed in the distance—a sprawling reminder of the challenge that lay ahead. Vincent Blackwell may have thought himself untouchable in his desert fortress, but he was about to learn that even the most impenetrable strongholds can crumble from within. And this band of unlikely allies? They were the ones holding the sledgehammer.

· · ● ● · ● · ● · ·

The crew gathered around the dining table. Darby leaned forward, her blonde hair cascading over her shoulder as she studied the blueprints spread before them. "So, this is it, huh? The belly of the beast."

Tommy nodded, his fingers tracing the intricate lines of the ranch's layout. "Vincent's got the standard high-tech security setup—motion sensors, thermal cameras, even drones patrolling the perimeter. But that's not what worries me."

"Let me guess," Darby said, leaning in. "It's all that open space?"

"Exactly," Tommy confirmed. "The house sits on high ground, with clear sightlines for miles in every direction. It's like trying to sneak across a football field, only this field is 250,000 acres."

Ella smirked, her fingers dancing across her keyboard. "The electronic stuff I can handle. Looping camera feeds, spoofing drone signals—child's play. But I can't make us invisible crossing all that open ground."

Justine leaned back, twirling a strand of vibrant red hair. "What about underground? Any old mine shafts or tunnels we could use?"

Tommy shook his head. "Nothing that gets us close enough. And digging our own would take too long and leave too much evidence."

"So we're back to the distraction play," William said. "But it needs to be big enough to draw attention away from a wide area, not just a single point."

"And perfectly timed," Tommy said, his expression grim. "One misstep, and we're caught out in the open with nowhere to hide. This entire operation could go south fast."

The team fell silent, the enormity of the challenge sinking in. The Silver Sage Ranch's vast openness, once a selling point for Vincent, had become their biggest obstacle. They needed a plan that could conquer not just technology, but space itself.

William stood at the head of the table, his gaze sweeping over the crew. "We've got one shot at this, and I think I've found our way in. Vincent's hosting a charity gala at Silver Sage Ranch next weekend. It's our golden ticket."

Josh leaned forward, intrigued. "A charity gala? At that isolated fortress?"

"Exactly," William nodded. "It's Vincent's annual *Healing Hearts* fundraiser. A lavish affair with CBHS's top donors, potential investors, and a handful of carefully selected patients with heartwarming stories."

Amelia frowned. "As much as I'd love to see Vincent's face when we bring him down, I can't be there. He and his team would recognize me immediately."

"You're right," William said. "I've got something else in mind for you. But your insider knowledge will be crucial for guiding us through the ranch."

Darby's eyes sparkled with mischief. "Well then, looks like everyone else has got themselves an invite to the party of the year. I assume you've got a plan for getting us on that guest list?"

William allowed himself a small, satisfied smile. "Already in motion. Josh will pose as a potential investor. Darby, you'll be our PR consultant. The rest of us will blend in with the event staff—caterers, valets, IT, security. It's our best chance to move freely across the property without raising suspicion."

Tommy nodded approvingly. "Smart. The commotion of a big event provides perfect cover. They will focus security on the perimeter and VIP guests, not the help scurrying around in the background."

"Exactly," William said. "We'll have a limited window, but with all the activity, we should be able to access areas of the house that would normally be off-limits."

Ella was already typing on her laptop. "I can create foolproof identities for all of us. Just need to hack the catering company's staff list, maybe plant a few last-minute *additions* to the guest roster . . ."

"Perfect," William said. "Remember, this isn't just about getting in. We need to locate Vincent's office, access his private servers, and find that safe—all while playing our parts to perfection."

The energy in the room was palpable, a mixture of excitement and nervous anticipation.

"Alright, team," William concluded, his voice firm. "We've got one week to prepare. Let's make it count. It's time to crash Vincent Blackwell's party—and bring the whole corrupt empire crashing down with it."

• • • ● • ● • • •

Darby's mind wandered to the first time she had met William, all those years ago. She had been a different person then—jaded, guarded, a shell of her former self. But something about his quiet strength, his unwavering sense of justice, had sparked a flame within her.

A flame that had grown into a burning desire to make things right, to use her skills for something more than just survival.

She glanced around the table, taking in the faces of her newfound family. Josh, with his quick wit and analytical mind. Justine, a survivor like herself, her cunning matched only by her fierce loyalty. Ella, a technical genius with a heart of gold. Tommy, a steadfast ally ready to put everything on the line for the greater good.

Her gaze lingered on Amelia, the newest addition to their tight-knit group. Darby couldn't help but admire the woman's resilience and determination. Fired from her cushy corporate job for trying to do the right thing, now risking everything to expose the truth—it was the kind of bold stance Darby respected. Despite losing her position, Amelia hadn't backed down. Instead, she'd doubled down on her commitment to justice, bringing her insider knowledge and legal expertise to their cause. And the way Amelia looked at William . . . well, Darby recognized that look all too well. It was the same one she used to see in the mirror, back when she first joined the team.

A twinge of something—jealousy? nostalgia?—tugged at Darby's heart. But she pushed it aside. This mission was bigger than any of them, bigger than old flames or new attractions. They needed Amelia's insights, her understanding of CBHS's inner workings. And if there was a spark between her and William . . . well, that was just another thing they'd have to navigate as a team.

And William. The man who had brought them all together, who had given them a purpose, a chance at redemption. The man who had stolen her heart without even trying, and who now seemed to be at the center of a complex web of loyalties and emotions.

Darby shook off these thoughts, refocusing on the task at hand. They had a job to do, a corrupt empire to bring down. She had always prided herself on her ability to keep her emotions in check, to let no one get too close. But with this crew, with this mission, she found herself letting her guard down, allowing herself to hope for something more.

As the planning continued late into the night, Darby felt a sense of calm settle over her. Vincent Blackwell may have thought himself untouchable in his desert fortress, but he was about to learn the hard way that even the most carefully guarded secrets have a way of coming to light. And when they did, Darby and her crew would be there, ready to watch his empire crumble to dust.

· · · ● · ● · ● · ·

Josh leaned forward, his eyes gleaming as he addressed the team. "I've been digging deeper into the financials. Vincent's not just stealing—he's flaunting it. Eight million euro apartment in Madrid, private jets for his yacht salesmen, a wedding on the Amalfi Coast. Meanwhile, hospitals can't even keep basic supplies in stock."

"Any of this traceable?" Darby asked, examining the documents.

"Better than that," Josh said, tapping a specific spreadsheet. "There's a federal grand jury in Boston already sniffing around some suspicious transactions. When we're done laying our trail, they'll find a lot more than they bargained for.

"This charity gala? It's just another smokescreen. But it's also our chance to nail this bastard once and for all. We get in there, find the proof, and we can bring this whole house of cards tumbling down."

William nodded, his jaw tight. "And that's exactly why we need to take him down. He's not just stealing money; he's stealing lives. Every day we wait, more people suffer."

Justine tapped her finger on the table, her brow furrowed. "I've been monitoring the chatter on the dark web, and it looks like Vincent's been making some shadowy deals with offshore accounts. Could be money laundering, or worse."

Ella's eyes locked on her laptop's screen. "I'll dig deeper, see if I can trace those transactions. If we can tie them directly to Vincent, it'll be the final nail in his coffin."

William's voice cut through the silence, low and determined. "We've all lost something to men like Vincent, whether it's our savings, our health, or the people we love. But now, we have a chance to fight back, to make sure no one else has to suffer the way we have."

As the team dispersed to make their preparations, William gathered the last of the documents. Breaking into a ranch in the middle of nowhere to steal evidence of corporate corruption . . . just another Tuesday for this crew.

North Square

The late afternoon sun cast long shadows across William's Salem home, its warm light softening the edges of the historic structure. Ella stood on the porch, her figure silhouetted against the fading day. Her long dark hair, touched by the golden hour, fell past her shoulders, framing a face that bore a pensive expression far too mature for her years.

She fidgeted with the delicate necklace at her throat, her fingers brushing against the thin straps of her black crop top. The exposed skin of her midriff betrayed a slight shiver—whether from the cooling air or her own nerves, it was hard to tell. Her loose-fitting black sweatpants hung low on her hips, a deliberate contrast to the fitted top, embodying the street-smart style she'd adopted since their last adventure.

Ella's hand, adorned with an assortment of bracelets that clinked softly together, hovered over the doorbell. In her other hand, she clutched her phone like a lifeline, her thumb idly swiping across the dark screen. She took a deep breath, steeling herself, before finally pressing the bell. The sound seemed to echo her quickening heartbeat, a staccato rhythm that betrayed her calm demeanor.

This moment, poised on the threshold of William's home, felt symbolic for the larger journey she was about to undertake—a step into the unknown, fraught with both danger and the promise of redemption.

William opened the door, his face lighting up with a mix of surprise and genuine pleasure. "Well, if it isn't my favorite hacker prodigy. To what do I owe this honor?"

Ella rolled her eyes, a hint of a smile tugging at her lips. "Your jokes haven't improved, old man."

William clutched his chest in mock pain.

"Ouch. And here I thought I was getting better with age, like a fine wine."

"More like a stale cheese," Ella replied, stepping inside.

As they entered the living room, Amelia looked up from her laptop, smiling warmly. "Ella, what a nice surprise."

William settled into his favorite armchair, studying Ella's face. "Alright, spill it. What's got you looking like you're trying to hack the Pentagon again?"

Ella's smile dimmed as she perched on the edge of the couch. "It's . . . it's about the trip to Nevada."

William's expression softened, understanding dawning in his eyes. "Ah. Bringing up some memories?"

Ella nodded, her gaze fixed on her fidgeting hands. "Yeah. I know the ranch is nowhere near Vegas, but . . ."

"But county lines don't matter when it comes to trauma," William finished gently.

Ella looked up, meeting his eyes. "Exactly."

William leaned forward, his voice low and earnest. "You know you don't have to go if you're not comfortable, right? We can figure out another way."

"No. I need to do this. I want to do this. It's just . . ."

"Scary as hell?"

Ella nodded, a wry smile touching her lips. "Yeah, something like that."

William's eyes crinkled with a mix of pride and concern. "You've come a long way, you know that?"

"Have I?" Ella asked, uncertainty creeping into her voice.

"Are you kidding? The Ella of a year ago would've rather eaten a bowl of coding errors than admit she was nervous about anything."

"Maybe I've just gotten soft in *my* old age."

"Nah. You've gotten stronger. There's a difference."

A comfortable silence settled between them before William spoke again. "So, how's life treating you these days? Still running circles around those MIT professors?"

Ella's eyes lit up. "You should see their faces when I correct their algorithms. It's priceless."

"That's my girl," William grinned. Then, his tone softening, "And how are you really doing? With everything else?"

Ella's smile faded slightly. "It's . . . a process. Some days are better than others. The money helps with some things, but . . ."

"But it can't buy peace of mind," William finished.

Ella nodded. "Exactly. I'm still working on trusting people, on not jumping at every shadow. But I'm getting there. Slowly."

Amelia, who had been listening quietly, stood up. "I'm going to grab some water. Ella, still lemon in yours?"

As Amelia left for the kitchen, Ella turned to William, her voice low. "William, I . . . I'm glad you've found happiness with Amelia. Really. I just . . . I don't want to lose this. Us. Our friendship. It's been . . . it's meant more to me than I can say."

William reached out, gently squeezing Ella's hand. "Hey, you're not getting rid of me that easily. No matter what happens, you'll always have me in your corner. Always."

Ella blinked back tears, nodding. As Amelia returned with the waters, William's expression turned thoughtful.

"You know, Ella," he began, "Margaret Fuller once wrote: *Very early, I knew that the only object in life was to grow.* You've been doing just that, facing your fears and growing stronger every day."

He paused, letting the words sink in before continuing. "She also said, *If you have knowledge, let others light their candles in it.* That's what you've been doing with your skills, your experiences. You're lighting candles for others, helping us fight against injustice. And in doing so, you're growing beyond what happened to you."

Ella listened, a mix of emotions playing across her face as William spoke.

"I know Nevada scares you. But remember, as Emerson put it, *What lies behind us and what lies before us are tiny matters compared to what lies within us.* You have more strength within you than you realize, Ella. And you won't be facing this alone. We're all in this together."

Ella nodded, a small smile forming on her lips. "Thanks, William. I . . . I needed to hear that."

As the conversation shifted to lighter topics, the warmth of William's words lingered, a balm to Ella's fears. In that moment, she knew that whatever challenges lay ahead in Nevada or beyond, she wouldn't face them alone.

She paused, then smirked. "Though I have to say, you were really on a roll with the quotes there. Fuller, Emerson . . . what's next? Planning to recite the complete works of Thoreau while we're at it?"

"Hey, I had to save something for the plane ride to Nevada."

"Oh god," Ella groaned, but her eyes sparkled with amusement. "Four hours trapped at cruising altitude with William's Philosophy Greatest Hits. Maybe I should hack the in-flight entertainment system instead."

• • • ● • ● • • •

William's backyard was a hive of activity, a maze of wires, gadgets, and enough cutting-edge tech to make MIT's computer lab look like a calculator convention. He surveyed his team, a motley crew of misfits who looked more suited to a comic book convention than a high-stakes heist. But then again, who needs biceps when you've got brains?

"Alright, listen up," William said, his voice cutting through the chatter like a knife through a conspiracy theory. "We've got two ops going down simultaneously. The ranch near Elko, obviously. But there's more—remember Vincent's precious yacht, the *Artemisa*? Time we paid it a visit down in Fort Lauderdale. Timing is everything. We screw this up, we'll be sharing a cell with Bernie Madoff."

Tommy snorted. "Madoff's been dead since 2021. We'd be sharing a cell with his ghost." His expression remained stoic, but his eyes held a glint of dark humor. "Besides, what we're doing actually helps people. The yacht's a risk we don't need."

"I'm handling the yacht operation," Amelia said coolly. "Please, like I'd ever let myself get caught twice."

William shot her a look. "Addison Gilbert wasn't your fault."

"Wasn't it? Either way, I'm not letting it happen again."

William couldn't help but smirk. That woman had more confidence than a politician at a fundraiser.

"Solo mission on a superyacht?" Darby raised an eyebrow, glancing up from the security specs she was studying. "And here I thought I was the ambitious one."

"The *Artemisa's* security system isn't going to hack itself," Josh said, his fingers flying across his keyboard with practiced precision. "Vincent's got the thing locked down tighter than his wallet at a charity auction."

"Going to need more than computers for this one," Tommy pointed out, ever the pragmatist. "A yacht that size normally has a crew of what, fifteen? Twenty?"

"Which is precisely why we need to coordinate these hits perfectly," William said, getting them back on track. "Now, about that equipment . . . Tommy, run us through the checklist," William said, turning to the ex-military man.

Tommy nodded. "We've got the latest in covert communication tech—earpieces, throat mics, encrypted radios. Lock picks that could make Houdini weep with envy. Hacking gear that'd make the NSA blush. Disguises so convincing, your own mother wouldn't recognize you. And enough non-lethal weaponry to take down a small army."

"Perfect," William said, his mind already racing ahead to the challenges they'd face.

"The ranch's security is tighter than most CEO's expense accounts—though not this one, apparently," he said with a smile, referring to Vincent's lavish spending. "We're talking biometric scanners, armed patrols, and an alarm system with a hotline to the local sheriff. And let's not forget about the floating palace. That yacht's got more security than some small countries—its own private army and enough high-tech gadgetry to make the NSA jealous."

But that was the thrill, wasn't it? The rush of pitting your wits against the best in the biz, of taking down the corrupt and powerful with nothing but your cunning and a few well-placed gadgets. This was what he lived for.

"Remember," William said, his voice taking on a gravitas that would make Morgan Freeman proud, "we're not just doing this for the money or the kicks. We're doing this because it's right. Because someone has to stand up to the Vincent Blackwells of this world and say *enough*. We're the underdogs, the long shots, but that's what makes us dangerous. They won't see us coming until it's too late."

He looked around at his team, saw the determination in their eyes, the readiness to put it all on the line for the greater good. This was more than a crew—it was a family. Dysfunctional as hell, sure, but bound by something deeper than blood.

Josh was thinking the same thing and said, his usual wry smile playing on his lips, "You know, in those *Fast and Furious* movies, they're always going on about family. But this?" He gestured to the group. "This isn't some high-octane, over-the-top action movie family. It's real. It's messy. It's us."

Darby, tossing her sleek platinum blonde bob with vibrant purple tips, chuckled at Josh's comment. The edgy cut framed her face, drawing attention to her mischievous eyes. She ran her fingers through the asymmetrical style, the shorter side tucked behind her ear revealing a row of small, glittering earrings. "Yeah, well, I'd take our brand of family over theirs any day. Fewer car chases, more wit."

"And significantly better dressed," Justine said with a smirk.

Ella, who had been quietly listening, spoke up. "You know, I actually like those movies. The fast cars, the adrenaline rush . . ." She paused, a rare smile softening her usually serious expression. "But this?" She gestured to the group, her Vans scuffing the patio as she shifted her weight. "This is real, like you said, Josh. Our family doesn't need high-speed chases or explosions to prove how much we mean to each other. We just . . . are."

Her words hung in the air for a moment, the sincerity in her voice catching everyone off guard. Then Josh grinned, breaking the tension

"Well said, Ella. Though I wouldn't mind a high-speed chase now and then, just to keep things interesting."

Darby swatted his arm. "Don't give William any ideas. Next thing you know, we'll be parachuting into Vincent's compound."

The group laughed, the sound echoing down Winter Street. As their chuckles subsided, William's voice cut through, warm and determined.

"Alright then," William said, a grin spreading across his face. "Let's go steal ourselves some justice."

· · · · ● · ● ● · · ·

The gentle clatter of keystrokes filled the air as Ella worked, her eyes flickering between the multiple screens arrayed before her like a digital symphony. The team had dispersed to different parts of the house to make their final preparations, but she knew her role was crucial. And then, like a record scratch in a cliché movie, she saw it.

"Guys, we have a problem." Her voice cut through the chatter on the comms, silencing everyone. "Vincent's got a Quantum Encryption Key. It's like a physical password for his most sensitive files. Without it, we might as well be trying to hack a stone tablet."

The stunned silence was broken by Josh's eloquent response. "Well, shoot."

"Shoot indeed," Ella said, her fingers flying over the keyboard as she tried to find a workaround. "I was hoping for a challenge, but this is like showing up to a knife fight and . . ."

"Please don't say *and the other person brought a gun*," said Justine.

Ella sighed, "no . . . finding out your opponent brought a tactical nuke. It's that bad."

Darby's voice crackled over the comm. "So, what are we talking about here? Some kind of futuristic USB stick? A retinal scan? Please tell me it's not his DNA. I draw the line at stealing bodily fluids."

Ella leaned back, her chair creaking in protest. "It's shaped like a pen. He carries it with him. Always from what I've learned. We're going to need to get up close and personal to swipe it or clone it without him noticing."

"A pen," Tommy deadpanned. "Of course it's a pen. Because why use something inconspicuous when you can weaponize office supplies?"

William's sigh was louder than usual. "Alright, new plan. Darby, you're on pen duty. Use that charm of yours to get close to Vincent at the gala. The rest of us will adjust accordingly."

"Fantastic. I always dreamed of being a cat burglar. Though I was hoping for diamonds, not overpriced stationery."

"Look on the bright side," Josh chimed in. "If we fail spectacularly, at least we can write Vincent a lovely concession note with his own pen."

"Your optimism is truly inspiring," Justine responded. "Now, can we please focus on not failing spectacularly?"

As the team bantered back and forth, formulating their new strategy, Ella couldn't help but smile—not something that comes naturally to her anymore, though being with her friends has made it easier than it had been. They were facing insurmountable odds, about to crash a high-society gala to steal a pen that could make or break their entire mission. Just another Tuesday for this crew.

• • • ● • ● • ● • •

As the team discussed the new strategy, each member's thoughts drifted to their own reasons for being here.

For Darby, this leveraged her past as an enforcer in the gambling underworld to strike against those exploiting the vulnerable. She'd spent years watching powerful men like Vincent treat people's lives like chips on a table. It was time to turn the tables. The thought of using her charm to steal Vincent's pen brought a wry smile to her face. *Time to show these amateurs what purposeful action looks like. Spoiler alert: it doesn't involve letting patients die.*

Josh saw this as his shot at redemption. He'd spent years cooking the books for organized crime, making dirty money look clean while turning a blind eye to the consequences. Now, he could use his skills to bring down a corrupt system from within. *Who knew all those years of creative accounting would come in handy for something other than hiding bodies in the ledger?*

Justine's motivation was a mix of professional pride and personal vendetta. She knew how to spin a story. But CBHS's façade of caring was an insult to her craft. They'd crossed a line, and she was determined to make them pay. *From adult film star to cat burglar . . . my resume just keeps getting more interesting.*

And then there was Ella herself. She'd been fighting her demons for as long as she could remember, using her intellect as both a shield and a sword. This mission was more than just another hack. It was a chance to turn her pain into purpose, to make sure no one else suffered as she had. *Who needs therapy when you can just take down a corrupt healthcare empire?*

William's motivation ran deep, rooted in his years of gambling addiction and subsequent redemption. He had spent years watching casinos and bookies prey on people's desperation, not so different from how CBHS exploited the vulnerable. He'd written books about his recovery, about finding purpose through running and philosophy, but this mission wasn't just about justice—it was about preventing others from falling into the same patterns of exploitation he'd experienced firsthand. *Guess I've traded one kind of high-stakes game for another. Though I doubt Thoreau would approve of this particular form of civil disobedience.*

Amelia's drive came from a place of righteous anger and professional betrayal. She had joined CBHS believing in its mission, only to discover the rot at its core. Now, she was determined to expose the truth, no matter the cost to her career. *I went to law school to uphold justice. Funny how that sometimes means breaking a few laws.*

Tommy's motivation was born from his military background and the stark realities he'd faced. He'd seen firsthand how systems meant to protect could be twisted to serve the powerful. This mission was his way of fighting back, of protecting those who couldn't protect themselves. *From soldier to vigilante . . . not exactly what they meant by 'career advancement' in the Army.*

· · · ● · ● · ● · ·

The warm afternoon sun cast a golden glow on the red façade of the Olde Main Street Pub as Darby and Josh settled into their seats on the outdoor patio. The red and black planters separated them from the bustling sidewalk and street, where tourists and locals alike strolled past, enjoying the quaint charm of Salem.

Darby's hair, a vibrant emerald green fading to turquoise at the tips, caught the sunlight as she leaned back in her chair. "You know, Josh, this place reminds me of that dive bar we used to frequent in LA. What was it called again?"

Josh laughed, his eyes crinkling at the corners. "The Broken Halo. God, that place was a dump, but shockingly, they made the chocolate cream pie in town."

"And the worst karaoke nights," Darby added with a smirk. "I still have nightmares about your rendition of *I Will Survive.*"

"Hey, I'll have you know that performance was legendary," Josh protested, feigning offense.

Their laughter faded into a comfortable silence as they perused the menu. The pub's atmosphere was a far cry from their glamorous past in Los Angeles, but there was something comforting about its simplicity.

"So," Darby said, her tone growing serious, "here we are again, about to dive headfirst into another high-stakes game. Feels like old times, doesn't it?"

Josh nodded, his expression thoughtful. "Yeah, but this time it's different. We're not just in it for the thrill or the payday. This is about making things right."

Darby reached across the table, giving his hand a squeeze. "I know. It's funny how life works out, isn't it? Who would have thought that our . . . colorful pasts would lead us here, planning to take down a corrupt healthcare empire?"

"Life's got a twisted sense of humor," Josh said, raising his glass of milk in a mock toast. "To second chances and unlikely heroes."

As they clinked glasses, Darby couldn't help but feel a surge of affection for her old friend. "You know," she said, a mischievous glint in her eye, "I've got a feeling this little adventure of ours is going to make our LA days look like a walk in the park."

Josh grinned, the excitement of the impending mission clear in his voice. "Bring it on. With you and the team by my side, Darby, I feel like we can take on the world."

As they dove into their meals, the conversation flowed, a mix of reminiscing about old times and strategizing for the task ahead. The Olde Main Street Pub, with its charming decor and the faint strains of Irish music drifting from inside, served as the perfect backdrop for this reunion of old friends and partners in crime.

Across the street, the Hawthorne Hotel—the historic hotel and their old headquarters—loomed, a silent reminder of the high-stakes game they were about to play. But for now, in this moment, Darby and Josh were content to enjoy each other's company, strengthening the bonds that would see them through the challenges to come.

· · · ● · ● · · · ·

William stared at the blueprints spread across his dining room table, his brow furrowed in concentration. "Alright, let's talk more security."

Ella, her dark hair pulled back in a messy ponytail, tapped the ranch layout with a slender finger. "We've already discussed the biometric scanners and armed patrols, etc.—"

Josh, ever the analytical mind, chimed in. "I know where you're going, Ella. The alarm system."

"Exactly. It's tied directly to local law enforcement. One false move and we'll have the entire Elko police force on our asses."

"Language," Justine chided, her red hair a vibrant contrast to her black turtleneck. "But she's right. We need to be surgical about this."

"What about the yacht?" Tommy asked, his military background obvious in his ramrod-straight posture. "The *Artemisa*. What are we looking at there?"

Ella pulled up a schematic on her laptop. "Luxury on the outside, Fort Knox on the inside. Advanced security system, onboard personnel, the whole nine yards. But if Vincent's hiding anything, it'll be there."

"Can we get in?"

"I think so; from what I see here, it should be a pretty standard hack."

"Along with enough champagne to fill a swimming pool," Darby said. "Rich people, am I right?"

A moment of silence fell over the group as they processed this information.

"We'll have CBHS cornered from land and sea," Darby finished, a mischievous glint in her eye.

· · · ● · ● · · ·

William's gaze drifted to Amelia, her dark eyes meeting his with a silent intensity. She was poring over the yacht schematics, memorizing every detail of the *Artemisa*. The weight of their mission and impending separation hung in the air, a bittersweet ache that lodged in his chest. He moved towards her, the rest of the team fading into the background as they prepared their gear.

"Amelia," he said, his voice rough with emotion. "I . . ."

She shook her head, a wry smile playing at the corners of her mouth. "Don't go getting sentimental on me now, William. We've got a job to do."

He laughed, the sound a low rumble in his chest. "Wouldn't dream of it. But I just wanted to say . . ." He paused, searching for the right words. "Be careful out there. And come back to me."

Amelia's smile softened, her hand reaching up to cup his cheek. "Always," she said. "But this goes both ways—no heroics from you, either."

William leaned into her touch, savoring the warmth of her skin against his. "No promises," he said, his eyes sparkling with mischief.

She rolled her eyes, but the affection in her gaze was unmistakable. "Incorrigible," she said, her thumb brushing over his jaw. "Just . . . don't do anything stupid, okay?"

He grinned, pressing a quick kiss to her palm. "Wouldn't be me if I didn't."

Amelia huffed a laugh, shaking her head. "Go," she said, stepping back. "Before I change my mind and handcuff you to the nearest radiator."

He turned, striding back to the group as they huddled around a table, eyeing the contingency plans spread out before them.

"Alright, let's go over this one more time," he said, his voice turning serious. "Emergency extractions, backup plans, the works. We're not leaving anything to chance."

Josh nodded, his fingers tapping against the table. "If the primary plan for the safe fails, we've got a secondary method. It's riskier, but it'll get the job done."

"And if we get made?" Darby asked, her brow furrowed.

"Backup disguises, cover stories, the whole shebang," Justine said, her PR expertise shining through. "We'll have contingencies for our contingencies."

William's eyes scanned the plans, his mind whirring with possibilities. *Scorched earth protocol . . . erase all evidence, leave no trace.*

"Rally points," Tommy said aloud, tapping a finger against the map. "If we get separated, we'll need predetermined locations to regroup. And communication protocols—coded phrases, encrypted channels, the works."

Ella grinned, her eyes alight with excitement. "Already on it, boss. By the time I'm done, we'll be harder to track than a ghost in a sandstorm."

William straightened, meeting each of their gazes. "We're as prepared as we'll ever be," he said, his voice ringing with conviction. "Let's eat."

· · · ● · ● · ● · ·

The sun dipped low over the Boston skyline, painting the city in a warm, golden glow as the team gathered at Mamma Maria, a cozy Italian restaurant nestled in the heart of the North End. Following what had become their pre-mission ritual since their CAYA heist—when they'd shared steak tips at Champion's Pub in Peabody—the familiar comfort of breaking bread together settled over them like a well-worn cloak. William stood by the window, his gaze drawn to the striking view of downtown and North Square, the city's energy pulsing through him like an electric current.

The restaurant overlooks North Square, a picturesque and historically significant place. As the oldest public square in America, it exudes an atmosphere of timeless charm and rich heritage. Intimate and quaint, the square is surrounded by narrow cobblestone streets that speak to its colonial past. Red brick buildings, some dating back to the 18th and 19th centuries, line the square, their facades showcasing the architectural styles of bygone eras. Many of these buildings feature bay windows, some with flower boxes, adding to the square's Old World feel.

Smaller than many expect, the square is more of a cozy urban nook than a sprawling plaza. This intimate scale contributes to its charm, making it feel like a hidden gem within the bustling city. Instead of scattered benches, the square features a recent renovation with modern stone seating areas and planters, blending contemporary design with the historical setting.

Surrounding the square are several notable buildings, including the North Square Oyster restaurant housed in a building with distinctive copper-green bay windows. While not visible in this view, the Paul Revere House is nearby, offering a glimpse into 17th-century architecture.

Old-fashioned street lamps, which cast a warm glow over the well-worn sidewalks in the evening, enhance the square's ambiance. The Freedom Trail, marked by a line of darker bricks, runs through the square, guiding visitors on a journey through America's revolutionary past.

North Square, despite its historical significance, remains a vital part of the neighborhood, seamlessly blending past and present. Italian restaurants like Mamma Maria and cafes contribute to the area's vibrant atmosphere, a reminder of the North End's heritage as an Italian-American enclave.

From their vantage point at Mamma Maria, the team observed the ebb and flow of locals and tourists in this historic setting as they plan their next move.

· · · ● · ● ● · · ·

William turned to face the team, their faces illuminated by the flickering candlelight. Amelia, Darby, Josh, Justine, Ella, and Tommy—each of them brought something unique, something essential to the mission. William cleared his throat, the weight of the moment settling on his shoulders.

"I know we've gone over the plan a thousand times," he began, his voice low and steady, "but I want to remind you why we're here, why we're taking this risk."

He paused, letting his words sink in. "Coastal Beacon has hurt people, exploited the vulnerable, and lined their pockets with blood money. But with this . . . we have a chance to make it right, to expose their corruption and bring them to justice."

William's eyes gleamed with conviction, his voice rising with passion. "As Thoreau once said, *I was not born to be forced. I will breathe after my own fashion.* When we get to Nevada, we'll breathe the air of freedom . . . and of justice. We'll take back what they've stolen."

The team nodded, their expressions a mix of determination and anticipation. Amelia stepped forward, her hand resting on William's arm, a gesture of support and solidarity.

"We're with you, William," she said, her voice soft but fierce. "Till the end of the line."

One by one, the others chimed in, their words a rallying cry.

"I've seen firsthand what exploitation can do," Darby said, her eyes flashing with anger. It's time to treat them as they've treated so many others.

Josh grinned, his fingers tapping against his leg, itching for action. "Let's show them what happens when they underestimate the underdogs."

Justine raised her glass, catching the candlelight. "To truth, justice, and the CBHS way," she said, her voice dripping with sarcasm.

Ella cracked her knuckles, a mischievous smirk playing at her lips. "Time to dance with the devil in the pale moonlight."

Tommy, ever the soldier, nodded solemnly. "We've got your back, boss. Always."

The team lingered a moment longer, savoring the camaraderie, the sense of purpose that hung in the air. But as the last drops of wine disappeared, so too did the spell of solidarity. Reality crept back in, reminding them of the monumental task ahead.

William watched as his team dispersed, each retreating to their own corner of the city to prepare for their role in the heist. Darby sauntered out, her hips swaying with a confidence that belied the nerves William knew she felt. Her hair, a vibrant cascade of emerald green fading to turquoise, caught the light from the streetlights, creating a halo effect that drew curious glances from passersby. She wore a form-fitting black jumpsuit, its tailored cut speaking of elegant precision rather than flash. She calculated and gracefully navigated every movement across the uneven cobblestones, each step a silent countdown to what lay ahead. As she paused to adjust her oversized glasses, William glimpsed the steely determination in her eyes, a look that said she was ready to con the world if that's what it took to bring down CBHS.

Josh followed, his fingers still tapping a restless rhythm, his mind no doubt already whirring with contingency plans. He cut a dashing figure in his tailored charcoal suit, the fabric subtly shimmering under the streetlights—a nod to his life in high finance. His hair—usually styled perfectly—was slightly disheveled, betraying the hours he'd spent poring over financial records. In one hand, he clutched a sleek tablet, its screen still glowing with complex algorithms and data streams. As he stepped onto the sidewalk, he paused, his dark eyes scanning the square with the sharp gaze of a man used to spotting patterns in chaos.

Justine and Tommy left together, their whispered conversation fading as the door swung shut behind them. Justine's fiery red hair was pulled back in a sleek ponytail, emphasizing her sharp cheekbones and the intensity of her green eyes. She wore a crisp white blouse tucked into high-waisted black trousers, an outfit that screamed *power publicist* while allowing for quick movement if needed. Her tablet was tucked under one arm, likely filled with crafted press releases and crisis management strategies.

Tommy towered beside her, his muscular frame straining against his dark blue henley and well-worn leather jacket. His military buzz cut and the set of his jaw gave him an air of constant vigilance, his eyes scanning their surroundings for potential threats. Every movement spoke of coiled strength and tactical awareness, a reminder of the very real dangers they faced. As they moved down the street, their contrasting appearances—Justine's polished professionalism and Tommy's rugged intensity—created an intriguing dynamic that turned heads.

As Ella stepped out of Mamma Maria onto the cobblestones of North Square, she cut a striking figure against the historic backdrop. Her outfit was a sleek, modern contrast to the centuries-old architecture surrounding her. She wore a fitted black mini dress that hit mid-thigh, its long sleeves and crisp white cuffs giving it a polished, almost collegiate air. The dress hugged her figure, accentuating her lean silhouette. Her legs were bare, leading down to a pair of chunky black knee-high boots that added an edge to the ensemble. The boots' thick soles looked ready to tackle both the uneven cobblestones and whatever challenges lay ahead in their mission. Slung across her body was a small black handbag on a chain strap, its compact size belying the tech gear hidden within. Her long hair, usually pulled back for practicality, was styled in loose waves that caught the late afternoon light.

As she paused on the steps, Ella's gaze swept across the square, her expression a mix of determination and calculation. In that moment, she looked less like a skilled hacker and more like a fashion model on a photo shoot—a disguise that would serve her well in the coming days. The juxtaposition of her contemporary outfit against the historic North End created a striking image—a visual representation of their mission to use modern methods to right long-standing wrongs.

As the door swung shut behind them, leaving William alone with his thoughts, he couldn't help but marvel at the unlikely team they'd assembled. Each member brought their own unique skills and experiences to the table, a motley crew united by a common purpose. The weight of their impending mission settled on his shoulders as he watched his team disappear into the bustling streets of Boston's North End, ready to take on the corrupt empire of CBHS.

He settled the bill, his mind already miles away, on a ranch in Nevada and on a yacht in Florida. The pieces were in motion, the game set. All that remained was to see how it would play out.

No turning back now.

He stepped out into the cool Boston night. The city hummed with oblivious activity, unaware of the storm brewing on its horizon. William tugged his collar up against the chill, his footsteps echoing off the cobblestones as he melted into the shadows. Tomorrow, the real work would begin. Tonight, he allowed himself a moment of relaxed reflection, of gratitude for the team he had assembled.

We're as ready as we'll ever be, he reassured himself, though a flicker of doubt persisted. In this game, there were no guarantees, only calculated risks and desperate hopes.

But wasn't that what made it worth playing?

· • ● ●•●• ● ● •

William's solitary footsteps led him to the tranquil expanse of Salem Common, the historic park a stark contrast to the bustling streets he'd left behind. The moon hung low in the sky, casting a silvery glow across the manicured lawns and ancient trees.

He paused at the edge of the common, his eyes drawn to the statue of Roger Conant, Salem's founder. The bronze figure stood imposing atop its stone pedestal, draped in a dramatic flowing cloak and wide-brimmed Puritan hat. The way the metal fabric billowed around him suggested movement against an eternal wind, yet Conant remained unmoved—a steadfast guardian surveying his domain with simple authority.

If only they knew the depths of corruption that lurk beneath the surface.

He wandered deeper into the park, his mind turning over the intricate details of their plan. The stakes were high, the risks immense, but the potential reward—the chance to expose the truth and bring down a corrupt system—was worth every ounce of danger.

As he walked, snippets of Emerson and Thoreau floated through his mind, their words a balm to his troubled thoughts.

What lies behind us and what lies before us are tiny matters compared to what lies within us.

And wasn't that the crux of it? The strength that lay within each member of his team, the unwavering determination to see this through no matter the cost?

He paused beneath a towering oak, its branches stretching towards the heavens. In the stillness of the night, he could almost feel the weight of history bearing down upon him, the echoes of those who had come before.

We're part of something bigger . . . a legacy of resistance, of standing up for what's right.

The thought buoyed him, chasing away the lingering doubts that had plagued his mind. They were ready for this, each and every one of them.

With a final glance at the moon-drenched common, William turned his steps towards home, his resolve hardened and his spirit renewed. Tomorrow and in the days to come, they would face the fire. Tonight, he would rest, knowing they were on the right path.

It is not what we get, but what we become, he thought, Thoreau's words a promise and a prayer.

The heist was on.

The Moral Minute—Episode 5

[Theme music—short, serious but with an edge]

ANIE: I'm Anie Chen.

LUCAS: And I'm Lucas Rodriguez. Welcome to The Moral Minute, where we examine the day's most egregious ethical failures in corporate America.

ANIE: Let's talk about the *Artemisa*, CBHS CEO Vincent Blackwell's floating palace.

LUCAS: [dry] You mean his 190-foot "mobile conference center"? That's how they listed it on the tax forms.

ANIE: Must be some interesting conferences. The wine cellar alone is worth $2 million.

LUCAS: [sardonic] Well, you can't expect executives to brainstorm cost-cutting measures without their vintage Bordeaux.

ANIE: Speaking of cost-cutting, while nurses are bringing their own medical supplies to work-

LUCAS: [interrupting] Wait, what?

ANIE: Oh yes. Nurses at three CBHS hospitals reported buying their own gloves and basic supplies. Meanwhile, Vincent just had gold fixtures installed in the yacht's master bath.

LUCAS: Don't forget the private jet. Or the new math wing at his daughters' school. Or the apartment in Madrid.

ANIE: [deadpan] Essential business expenses, I'm sure.

LUCAS: Time's almost up. What's our moral of the minute?

ANIE: When your CEO's wine cellar is worth more than your hospital's emergency supplies, something's very wrong with the prescription.

Casino Express

N estled in the northeastern corner of Nevada, Elko embodies the rugged spirit of the American West. This small city, with a population of around 20,000, is cradled by the stunning Ruby Mountains to the southeast, often referred to as the *Alps of Nevada* for their jagged, snow-capped peaks and pristine alpine lakes.

Elko sits along Interstate 80, midway between Reno and Salt Lake City. Six and a half hours northeast of Las Vegas, it feels like a world apart from the glitz and glamor of Sin City.

Elko has always been a place where fortunes are made and lost. The city's economy hinges on two industries that embody the essence of Nevada: mining and gaming. Massive gold mines in the surrounding hills, operated by companies like Barrick Gold, fuel the local economy and have earned the region the nickname *Gold Country*.

But Elko isn't just about striking it rich in the mines. The city embraces Nevada's gambling culture with several casinos dotting its landscape, offering visitors and locals alike a chance to test their luck. These gaming establishments, while smaller than their Las Vegas counterparts, provide a more intimate and authentically *Western* gambling experience. Gaming is so big in Elko that a revolutionary, now defunct, airline—Casino Express—offered innovative charter flights that combined air travel with casino junkets, providing a seamless and attractive option for the Red Lion Casino to draw in patrons from across the country.

In a nod to Nevada's unique legal landscape, Elko is also home to Mona's Ranch, one of the state's legal brothels. Located just outside the city limits, it's a reminder of Nevada's complex relationship with vice and regulation, standing as one of the few remaining legal brothels in the United States.

Despite its relatively small size, Elko serves as a cultural hub for northeastern Nevada. It hosts the National Cowboy Poetry Gathering each year, celebrating the area's rich Western heritage. The city also acts as a gateway to outdoor adventures, with the Ruby Mountains offering world-class hiking, skiing, and wildlife viewing opportunities.

From gold rushes to poker flushes, from cowboy poetry to high desert beauty, Elko embodies the contradictions and allure of the modern American West. It's a place where the old frontier meets the new, where fortunes are still made in the ground and on the felt, and where the spirit of adventure is as vast as the Nevada sky. With Silver Sage Ranch just a short drive away, Elko serves as the perfect staging ground for the team's daring heist, blending urban resources with the ranch's isolated grandeur.

• • • ● ● • ● • • • •

Ella's rented SUV sped down I-80 West, the endless Nevada desert stretching out before her. She'd flown into Salt Lake City International Airport earlier that day, opting for the longer drive to Elko to minimize her digital footprint. As she approached Elko, a faded sign welcomed her to town—population 20,304, elevation 5,060 feet. This dusty mining town was a far cry from MIT's hallowed halls back in Cambridge.

She pulled into the Baymont Inn parking lot, her sleek black rental SUV a stark contrast to the dusty pickups surrounding it. Grabbing her backpack from the passenger seat, Ella stepped out into the Nevada heat. Her outfit—a dark oversized t-shirt layered over a gray long-sleeved top, paired with baggy black cargo pants—was a perfect blend of comfort and anonymity. A silver chain necklace with a pendant added a touch of edgy flair.

As she entered the lobby, the faint smell of chlorine and industrial carpet cleaner assaulted her senses. Ella adjusted the small hair clips holding back sections of her dark hair, a nervous habit she'd picked up during long coding sessions. Her dark, almond-shaped eyes scanned the room, taking in every detail as she approached the front desk where a bored-looking middle-aged woman sat.

Ella's ensemble, complete with chunky black boots barely visible beneath her pants, screamed *disaffected youth* rather than *skilled hacker on a covert mission*. It was exactly the camouflage she needed in a town like Elko. She put on her best *tired traveler* face as she prepared to check in, knowing that blending in was the first step in staying off the radar. The long drive from Salt Lake City had left her exhausted, adding authenticity to her cover as she began her reconnaissance of Silver Sage Ranch.

"Welcome to the Baymont. Checking in?"

"Yep. Reservation for Ella Johnson." She drummed her fingers on the chipped formica counter. "There should be some packages for me, too."

The receptionist nodded, tapping away at her computer before going to a back room. She produced a cart with several nondescript brown boxes of various sizes along with a keycard. "Room 305. Packages arrived yesterday."

Ella nodded, snatched the keycard and cart, and headed to the elevator. Once inside her room, she dropped her bag on the bed and opened the package. Inside was all the electronic equipment she'd need for the mission—high-end laptops, portable servers, multiple monitors, and an array of surveillance gear. A slow smile spread across her face as she pulled out her personal laptop. Time to get to work.

• • • • ● • ● • • •

The next morning, after downing three cups of burned lobby coffee, Ella hopped into her SUV and headed towards Silver Sage Ranch. She drove past expansive rangeland dotted with sagebrush and native grasses, occasionally spotting groups of Black Angus cattle grazing in the distance. The rugged landscape of the high desert stretched out before her, broken only by the occasional irrigation pivot in the valley bottoms. Up ahead, the ranch's private exit off of I-80 came into view.

She slowed and turned off, following a short driveway past pastures protected by barbed wire and electric fences. As the sprawling ranch emerged over a gentle hill in the distance, Ella pulled off onto a dirt side road partially obscured by various buildings.

Grabbing her binoculars, she crept to the edge of the tree line to get a closer look at the property. The main house was a hulking stone and log mansion with picture windows and twin chimneys. A six-car garage jutted off one side. Manicured lawns rolled out in all directions. The house looked to be a mile from the front gate.

"Well hello there, rich people problems," she whispered. "Seriously . . . Olympic-sized horse troughs."

Closer to her, she noted the black wrought-iron fence encircling the low-slung houses and buildings near the gate; each had security cameras perched under the eaves and appeared to have reinforced steel doors. No guards posted outside at the moment, but there were definitely boots on the ground somewhere.

Ella cataloged the area's details—the winding gravel driveway that created a chokepoint, mature trees that could provide cover, the trimmed hedges that could conceal cameras or motion sensors. She'd need to bypass a hell of a firewall to knock out that security system remotely.

As she hiked back to her truck, the wheels in Ella's head were already spinning, formulating her next steps. This overblown lodge plunked down in the Nevada desert wouldn't know what hit it. Time to give those one-percenters a long overdue reality check.

• • • ● • ● • • • •

A week before the team's arrival, Ella stood in the parking lot of a nondescript warehouse on the outskirts of Elko, eyeing two sleek black Mercedes-Benz Sprinter vans. She'd arranged their purchase through a series of untraceable transactions—a necessary precaution for their upcoming operation.

With the hot northern Nevada sun beating down, Ella opened one of the van's rear doors and got to work. Her first task was installing a custom-built rack system to house their high-powered servers and networking equipment. She mounted each component, her nimble fingers making quick work of the complex wiring.

Next came the climate control system—essential for keeping the sensitive electronics cool in the desert heat. Ella installed a whisper-quiet air conditioning unit, integrating it with the van's existing systems.

The real magic happened with the communications setup. Ella outfitted the van with a state-of-the-art satellite uplink, ensuring they'd have broadband-speed internet access even in the most remote locations. She also installed a sophisticated signal booster and an array of antennas, disguised to look like standard roof racks.

For power, Ella set up a hybrid system of high-capacity batteries and a silent generator, giving them hours of off-grid capability. She even added solar panels to the roof for supplementary charging.

As the day wore on, Ella transformed the van's interior into a mobile command center. She installed ergonomic workstations with multiple monitors, a holographic display for 3D modeling, and a top-of-the-line biometric security system to protect their equipment.

By sunset, exhausted but satisfied, Ella stood back to admire her handiwork. The unassuming black van now housed enough computing power to rival a small tech company. She allowed herself a small smile, knowing that this mobile data center would be the backbone of their audacious plan.

With a final check of the systems, Ella locked up the van and headed back to the Baymont, her mind already racing with the possibilities their new mobile headquarters would provide.

· · ● ● ● ● ● · ·

After choking down her fourth cup of burned lobby coffee, Ella settled into her makeshift command center in the Baymont Inn room. The curtains were drawn tight, and the soft glow of multiple screens illuminated her determined face. Today's mission: crack Silver Sage Ranch's firewall and (maybe) avoid the need for a full-scale heist.

She started with a basic port scan, probing for any obvious vulnerabilities. Nothing. The ranch's IT team wasn't completely incompetent, it seemed. Undeterred, Ella moved on to more sophisticated methods.

First, she attempted a SQL injection attack, hoping to exploit any flawed web applications connected to the ranch's network. Her fingers flew across the keyboard, injecting malicious code into every input field she could find. After hours of attempts, she found only error messages and dead ends.

Frustrated but not defeated, Ella switched tactics. She set up a phishing campaign, crafting emails that looked like they came from the ranch's internet service provider. Why not? This worked during their last adventure in Los Angeles. The messages warned of an imminent service outage and urged recipients to verify their login credentials. It was a long shot, but sometimes the weakest link in any security system was the human element.

As the sun began to set, casting long shadows across her room, Ella's hopes dimmed along with the daylight. Not a single bite on her phishing lures. The ranch's employees were too savvy or too technophobic to fall for her tricks.

In a last-ditch effort, she attempted a brute force attack on the ranch's VPN, using a custom-built program to cycle through millions of potential passwords. The progress bar crawled along at an agonizing pace, each failed attempt chipping away at her confidence.

Finally, as the clock ticked past midnight, Ella had to admit defeat. She slumped back in her chair, rubbing her tired eyes. The firewall had held strong against every trick in her considerable arsenal. Silver Sage Ranch's digital defenses were far more robust than they had anticipated.

With a mix of frustration and grudging respect, Ella reached for her secure phone. It was time to call William and confirm that Plan B—the heist—was now their only option. As she dialed, she couldn't help but feel a twinge of excitement beneath her disappointment. After all, there was something to be said for doing things the old-fashioned way.

· · · ● · ● · · ·

Barrick Gold Corporation is one of the largest gold mining companies in the world. Its presence in Elko, Nevada, began in the late 1980s when it acquired the Goldstrike Mine, located 60 miles west of Elko. The company's rise to prominence in Elko was meteoric. Its Goldstrike Mine quickly became one of the most productive gold mines in the world. This success led to further expansions and acquisitions in the area, solidifying Barrick's position as a major economic force in northeastern Nevada.

Barrick's impact on the local economy was profound. The company remained one of the largest employers in the region, providing well-paying jobs to thousands of residents. This employment had a ripple effect, stimulating growth in various sectors, including retail, housing, and services.

A notable feature of Barrick's operations is its employee transportation system. Near Ella's Baymont Inn and a gas station (Maverik Adventure's First Stop), Barrick maintains a bus lot. This lot serves as a hub for the company's extensive bus system that transports workers to and from the mines.

Why buses? Is this a back-to-school thing?

Not quite. Barrick Gold's bus system in Elko is a Swiss Army knife of solutions. It's a safety net for weary miners, a green initiative on wheels, a money-saver for all, and a clever workaround for corporate territory issues. By ferrying workers *en masse*, Barrick cuts down on traffic mishaps, shrinks its carbon footprint, and keeps wallets a little fatter. It's also their golden ticket through rival Newmont Mine's land, part of a deal that keeps the mining wheels turning smoothly. In short, these aren't just buses—they're the lifeblood of Elko's mining operations, carrying workers and clever corporate strategies alike.

· · · ● · ● · · ·

The sun had barely crested the horizon when Ella stepped out of the Baymont Inn, eager to escape the hotel's abysmal excuse for coffee. She'd thrown on a faded black crop top, its vintage band logo obscured after years of wear. Her high-waisted, ripped black jeans hung loosely on her frame, the holes offering glimpses of sun-kissed skin.

As she made her way towards the Maverik store, her worn Vans scuffed against the sidewalk. The morning air was crisp, carrying the promise of another scorching Nevada day. Ella's hair, still wild from sleep, caught the breeze framing her face as she eyed the sprawling Barrick bus lot to her right. Even at this early hour, there was activity—miners in reflective gear boarding buses, engines humming to life. Ella slowed her pace, taking in the scene with keen interest.

After securing her precious cargo of actually drinkable coffee from Maverik, Ella found herself drawn back to the bus lot. She leaned against a nearby fence, sipping her coffee and observing the comings and goings. The rhythmic departure and arrival of buses, the ebb and flow of workers—it all painted a picture of Elko's lifeblood.

As she watched, her mind raced with possibilities. She made mental notes of the timing, the process, the security measures visible from her vantage point. As the last morning bus pulled away, Ella pushed off from the fence. Her coffee run had yielded more than just caffeine—it had provided valuable intel. With a satisfied smile, she headed back to the hotel, already planning how this new information might factor into their plans.

· · · ● ● · ● ● · · ·

For the next week, Ella fell into a new routine. Each morning, she'd make her way to the Maverik store, drawn as much by the prospect of decent coffee as by the opportunity to observe the Barrick bus lot. On her second day, while waiting for her black coffee, Ella noticed a woman in her mid-forties, dressed in Barrick work attire, ordering a hazelnut latte.

"You should try this," the woman said, noticing Ella's plain order. "Makes the morning shift a little sweeter."

Ella raised an eyebrow. "Sweet mornings? In this economy?"

The woman chuckled, appreciating Ella's dry humor. The next day, however, Ella took the plunge. "I'll try the hazelnut," she told the barista. "If I'm going to face the day, might as well do it with a sugar high."

"Ah, a convert!" The woman from yesterday grinned. "I'm Alice, by the way."

"Ella. And don't get too excited. I might just be having an early midlife crisis."

Over the next few days, their morning encounters evolved from brief nods to friendly chats. Alice worked in warehouse inventory, she explained, in a facility attached to a garage that serviced enormous Komatsu electric drive mining trucks.

"Those things are monsters," Alice said one morning, gesturing towards a poster of the trucks. "So big, they've driven over cars without the driver even noticing."

Ella's eyes widened, her mind racing with the implications. "Well, that's one way to avoid paying for parking," she said, masking her intense interest.

Alice laughed. "You've got a dark sense of humor, kid. I like it."

"Dark humor is like clean water in a mining town," Ella replied. "Not everyone has it, but those who do really appreciate it."

"So, what brings you to Elko?" Alice asked, still chuckling. "We don't get many young folks passing through, especially not ones with such sparkling personalities."

Prepared for this, Ella replied, "I'm here helping Raley's with some IT upgrades. Apparently, their system was so old, it still thought Y2K was a threat."

"Sounds thrilling," Alice said with a grin.

"Oh, you have no idea. Nothing gets the blood pumping like updating firmware on a dozen cash registers," Ella deadpanned. "Should be here for a few weeks, living the dream."

As they parted ways each morning, Alice heading to her bus and Ella back to the hotel, Ella couldn't help but feel a twinge of guilt. Alice was nice, and in another life, they might have been friends. But for now, every conversation was a potential goldmine of information, and Ella couldn't afford to lose sight of why she was really here.

"See you tomorrow, Alice," Ella called out. "Try not to let any giant trucks mistake you for a speed bump!"

Alice's laughter echoed across the parking lot as she boarded her bus, leaving Ella to contemplate the strange turns her life had taken. Here she was, in the middle of nowhere, planning a heist and making friends over hazelnut lattes. Life, it seemed, had a sense of humor as dark as her own.

• • • ● • ● • • •

Casino Express Airlines, born from a unique vision in the mid-1980s, revolutionized the gambling industry by offering innovative charter flights that combined air travel with casino junkets. Started by Tod McClaskey—co-founder of the Red Lion hotel chain—the airline aimed to lure high-rollers to Elko away from Reno and other border towns.

Starting with a single leased Boeing 737 in 1987, Casino Express quickly gained popularity. In less than three years, it had dealt the Red Lion Hotel and Casino a winning hand of over $15 million in revenue. The airline's success led to a full house of aircraft, each sporting distinctive playing card-themed liveries—the *King of Diamonds*, *Queen of Hearts*, and *Ace of Clubs*—turning the skies into its own version of a flying poker deck.

Casino Express carved out a niche market, flying to over 75 cities across the West and Midwest a decade later. Its colorful planes became a familiar sight in major cities and small towns alike, transporting around 40,000 annual pilgrims to Elko's altar of chance. The airline's unique operations included a no-checked-baggage policy because of Elko's high elevation, truly living up to its *express* moniker.

After nearly two decades of keeping Lady Luck airborne, Casino Express cashed in its chips and ended its Red Lion Casino charter program.

Now, years later, the team found themselves at the Maverick Hotel and Casino, formerly the Red Lion, where it all began. In one of those curious small-town coincidences, the hotel's name differed from Ella's morning coffee spot by just a single letter—Maverick versus Maverik. As they settled into their rooms, the echoes of Casino Express's colorful history and the ghosts of high-rollers past seemed to whisper through the halls, a reminder of Elko's unique place in the intersection of gambling and aviation.

· · · · ● · ● · · ·

Ella walked confidently into the Maverick Hotel and Casino, her outfit a striking contrast to the opulent surroundings. She wore a cropped white long-sleeved top that exposed her midriff, paired with loose-fitting light blue jeans. Her dark hair fell straight past her shoulders, and she walked with purpose in chunky black boots.

As she passed the registration desk with its warm wooden tones and intricate carpet, Ella's eyes darted around, taking in every detail. The casino floor beckoned ahead, a cacophony of lights and sounds from countless slot machines.

Weaving between the rows of blinking games and focused players, Ella made her way to the elevators. Her attire drew a few curious glances—she looked more like she was headed to a casual night out than a high-stakes gambling session.

Once in the elevator, Ella pressed the button for the second floor. She emerged moments later and marched to room 219. This large guest room, with its adjoining space, would serve as the team's base of operations for their audacious plan. She rapped twice on the door before letting herself in with the key card. As she entered, Ella felt a mix of excitement and apprehension about the challenge that lay ahead.

Inside, Darby and Josh were bent over a laptop, deep in heated discussion. Tommy leaned against the wall, arms crossed, while Justine paced like a caged tiger.

"Well, don't you all look like a Rockwell painting," Ella said as she tossed her backpack on the nearest bed.

William stood at the head of the table in their makeshift headquarters, his lean frame casting a long shadow across the room. His eyes, sharp and focused, swept over his assembled team. "Alright, people. Let's run through this one more time."

Darby leaned back in her chair, twirling a strand of her ever-changing hair color—today, a vibrant teal. A mischievous glint sparkled in her eye. "You mean the plan where I dazzle Vincent with my considerable charms? I do love a good distraction."

"Just don't get too carried away," William warned, his tone a mix of amusement and caution. "We need that encryption pen, not a date for the charity ball. Remember, Vincent's as slippery as a greased pig at a county fair."

Josh hunched over his laptop, his fingers flying across the keys with a rhythm that would make a jazz pianist jealous. He pushed his glasses up his nose, squinting at the screen. "Once I'm in the main house, I can tap into their local network. Those financial records won't know what hit them. It'll be like taking candy from a baby . . . if the baby were a multimillion-dollar corrupt corporation."

"And while you're playing digital Robin Hood," Ella chimed in, her voice dripping with sarcasm, "I'll be in server farm paradise, surrounded by the soothing hum of overworked cooling systems and blinking lights. Maybe I'll even get to name the servers. I'm thinking *Huey, Dewey, and Louie* for the main cluster."

William nodded, a hint of a smile tugging at the corners of his mouth. "Precisely. You and I will pose as the hospital's new IT team. Jenny, from the office complex, is our key to both entry and exit. Ella, you'll need to work your magic in that server room. And remember, if anyone asks, we're just there to update Adobe Reader."

"No pressure or anything," Ella said, rolling her eyes. "Just hacking into a fortress while pretending to be the Geek Squad. Piece of cake."

Tommy, built like a linebacker and twice as intimidating, cracked his knuckles. The sound echoed through the room like gunshots. "I've got Josh's back. Any trouble comes our way . . . they'll wish they'd stayed home nursing their kombucha and avocado toast."

"Easy there, Rocky," Justine said, adjusting her perfectly pressed shirt. "We're aiming for subtle, remember? We want to be more *gentle breeze* and less *category five hurricane*."

William held up a hand, commanding attention. "Let's not forget our contingencies. If Jenny's a no-show, we abort. No heroics, no last-minute improvisations. If the pen doesn't work or we can't get it to Ella in time, we fall back to Plan B—a partial data extraction that won't be as comprehensive but should still give us enough to work with."

The team nodded, the gravity of the situation settling over them like a heavy blanket.

"Now, timing is crucial," William continued, his voice steady and authoritative. "Darby, once you have the pen, you need to get it to Tommy immediately. He'll make the drive to Ella at the server farm near the front gate. We have a 15-minute window from the moment Darby gets the pen to when Ella needs to start the data transfer. Any longer, and we risk detection."

Tommy nodded, his face a mask of determination. "I'll make that drive in record time, boss. You can count on me."

"Good," William said. "Ella, you'll need to be ready the moment Tommy arrives. We can't afford any delays once the pen is in your hands."

Ella gave a mock salute. "Aye aye, captain. I'll be poised over the keyboard like a pianist at Carnegie Hall, just waiting for my cue."

"Please," Darby said, examining her perfectly manicured nails. "I'll have that pen before Vincent even realizes it's missing. Distraction is my middle name."

"Just remember," William said dryly, "the goal is to charm him, not give him a heart attack. We need him conscious long enough for our plan to work."

Darby flashed a wicked grin. "Don't worry. I'll keep him hanging on my every word. By the time I'm done, he'll be too dazzled to notice anything amiss."

"Good," William nodded. "Just make sure you get that pen to Tommy as soon as you have it. The clock starts ticking the moment it's in your hands."

"As for our exit," he continued, "once we're clear of the ranch, we split up. The vans take separate routes out of town, and the Aston Martin acts as a decoy. We rendezvous at the safe house in 48 hours. Questions?"

Josh raised a hand, like a schoolboy afraid of the teacher's wrath. "Yeah, um, what if everything goes sideways and we're totally screwed? Like *dogs and cats living together, mass hysteria* level of screwed?"

William's eyes hardened, his jaw set in determination. "That's not an option. We've planned for every contingency. This is going to work because it must. CBHS has hurt too many people for us to fail now. Remember why we're doing this—for every patient denied care, for every worker exploited, for every life ruined by their greed."

The room fell silent, the weight of their mission settling over them like a heavy fog.

"One last thing," William added, his voice softening slightly. "I know we've all got our parts to play, but remember—we're a team. If something goes wrong, if someone needs help, we've got each other's backs. No one gets left behind."

He looked at each member of his team, seeing the mix of determination, nerves, and excitement in their eyes. "Alright," he said, straightening up. "Get some rest. Tomorrow, we take down an empire. And who knows? Maybe we'll even have time for a victory lap around the casino floor."

As the team dispersed, a potent cocktail of determination and nervous energy filled the air. They were about to pull off the heist of a lifetime, a daring act of robin hood-esque justice in the heart of Nevada. As they filed out of the room, each lost in their own thoughts, the magnitude of what they were about to attempt hung heavy in the air. Tomorrow, they would make history—or become it.

· · · ● · ● · · ·

Justine's phone buzzed, breaking the momentary silence. She glanced at the screen, her brows furrowing. "Guys, we might have a problem."

"What kind of problem?" Josh asked, his voice tight.

"My contact at the catering company just texted me. Apparently, Vincent hired a new security team last minute. Ex-military, top of the line." Justine's lips twisted into a wry smile. "Seems like our dear Vincent is getting a little paranoid."

Darby laughed, the sound sharp and sardonic. "Paranoid? More like he's finally realized what a scumbag he is." She shook her head, blonde hair cascading over her shoulders. "This changes nothing. We stick to the plan."

Ella, lost in her own computer world, chimed in. "I'm running background checks on the new security team now. If there's anything we need to know, I'll find it."

William nodded, his gaze distant as he considered this new information. "Justine's right. Vincent's paranoia could help us. He'll be so preoccupied with external threats that he won't notice us."

Tommy, who had been quietly cleaning his gear, spoke up. "What about the encrypted pen? If Vincent's beefing up security, he might be more cautious about who he lets near him."

Josh's eyes narrowed, his mind already working through the problem. "We'll need to create a bigger distraction, then. Something that will force Vincent to let his guard down, even for just a moment."

Darby grinned, a wicked gleam in her eye. "Leave that to me. I've got a few tricks up my sleeve that will have Vincent eating out of the palm of my hand."

As the team continued to strategize, adapting their plan to these new challenges, Ella couldn't shake the feeling that there was something else at play. Some unseen threat lurking in the shadows.

• • • • ● • ● • • •

The final hours before the gala were a whirlwind of activity. Each team member moved with purpose, their actions precise and calculated.

Justine, her fiery red hair tucked beneath a sleek black wig, practiced her Russian accent in the mirror. "Caviar, sir?" she said, her voice low and seductive. "Or perhaps you'd prefer something sweeter?" She winked at her reflection, satisfied with her transformation.

In the adjoining room, Tommy checked and rechecked his equipment. "Comms check," he said, his voice gruff. "Everyone online?"

"Loud and clear," Josh said. "Ella and I have eyes on the security cameras. We're good to go."

Darby emerged from the bathroom, her blonde hair swept up in an elegant updo, her dress a shimmering gold. "How do I look?" she asked, twirling for effect.

"Like a million bucks," Ella replied, her eyes never leaving the screen in front of her. "Or should I say, like a billion?"

Darby laughed, the sound rich and confident. "Vincent won't know what hit him."

As the team made their final preparations, Ella couldn't shake the feeling of unease that had settled in her gut. She scanned the blueprints of the gala venue for the hundredth time, searching for any weakness, any vulnerability they might have missed.

"Relax, Ella," Josh said, appearing at her side. "We've got this."

Ella nodded, forcing a smile. "I know. It's just . . . something doesn't feel right."

"We've planned for every contingency. Whatever happens, we'll handle it. Together."

Ella took a deep breath, willing herself to focus. Josh was right. They were a team, and they had each other's backs.

As the sun set over the Nevada desert, the team gathered in the center of the hotel room, their eyes locked on William.

William tapped his earpiece. "Amelia, you set on your end?"

"All good here," came the reply, tinged with the sounds of Florida's coast. "Ready to crash Vincent's nautical party."

Ella glanced at the separate monitor tracking Amelia's position in Fort Lauderdale. Their general counsel turned nautical thief was poised and ready, waiting to infiltrate the *Artemisa* while they created chaos at the gala. They'd staff the yacht minimally tonight—Vincent's paranoia about security maintenance had inadvertently given them the perfect window of opportunity.

"Two-pronged attack," Josh said, following Ella's gaze to the monitor. "While we keep Vincent distracted here, Amelia gets full access to everything he's hidden away on that floating palace of his."

"Alright, everyone," William said, his voice steady. "It's showtime. Remember the plan, stick to your roles, and above all else, stay safe. We're in this together."

With a final nod, the team dispersed, each member slipping into the night like shadows. The gala awaited, and with it, the promise of justice and revenge.

The clock was ticking, and the game was about to begin.

Grand Theft Artemisa

Amelia stepped out of the taxi, her designer heels contacting the sun-drenched pavement—each step a calculated reminder she wasn't here for the tourist traps. The sultry Florida air wrapped around her like a damp cashmere blanket as she surveyed the opulent high-rises and gleaming yachts of Fort Lauderdale. She adjusted her oversized sunglasses and smirked. *Just another playground for the rich and shameless,* she thought wryly. *Where even the palm trees have trust funds.*

She strode purposefully toward the Pier 66 Marina, her tailored linen suit impeccable despite the humidity. The sea breeze tugged at her hair as she approached the entrance, flashing a dazzling smile at the security guard.

"Good afternoon, sailor," Amelia said with a playful wink. "I'm here to scope out the slips for my boss's new floating palace. Any chance you could point a girl in the right direction?"

The guard, a burly man whose biceps strained against his uniform, looked her up and down appreciatively. "Well now, that depends. Who's your boss?"

Amelia leaned in, her voice low and smooth as silk. "Let's just say he's a man who appreciates the finer things in life. And he always gets what he wants."

The guard chuckled, shaking his head. "Don't they all. Alright then, miss. The big boys park their rides down that way. Slips 120 through 164. Can't miss 'em."

"Much obliged," Amelia said, slipping past him with a wink.

As she sauntered down the marina's polished walkways, the pungent smell of saltwater mixed with diesel fuel and the creaking of moored boats against their lines reminded her of her youth. Amelia's keen eyes darted from yacht to gleaming yacht, mentally cataloging the floating fortunes. *The Yankee Clipper*, 240 feet of Oceanco excess. Next to it, *The Sterling Dream*, all chrome and hubris. And there, the *Golden Ratio*, compensating for something with its helicopter pad and infinity pool. Each vessel a testament to wealth beyond reason, each owner a case study in conspicuous consumption.

She paused at Slip 147, noting the sleek lines and opaque windows of the *Artemisa*.

Bingo.

Amelia leaned against a nearby bollard, pulling out her phone. To the untrained eye, she was just another wealthy socialite checking her Instagram. In reality, she was discreetly snapping high-res photos of the yacht's exterior, her thumbs flying across the screen as she cross-referenced the details with her intel. The *Artemisa*, at 190 feet, is a 2007 custom superyacht from German luxury yacht builders Eisenberg & Müller.

· · · ● · ● · ● · ·

Artemisa—Cuba's answer to the question "What if we made a city out of coffee and revolution?"—has been brewing trouble since 1818. This scrappy municipality in western Cuba got a promotion in 2011 when some bureaucrat decided La Habana Province was getting too big and designated Artemisa as the capital of its own namesake province. Known as the *Villa Roja* or *Red Village*—not for its political leanings, mind you, but because of its soil's ruddy complexion (though the former aided its street cred during the revolution).

For two centuries, Artemisa has perfected the art of producing three things: amazing coffee, tobacco that would make a health inspector weep, and enough notable revolutionaries to staff a small army. It's like the city's soil is spiked with caffeine, nicotine, and a dash of rebellious spirit. Home to Celia Sánchez, a revolutionary who probably took her coffee as strong as her anti-imperialist sentiments, Artemisa proves that sometimes the most potent things come in small, red-soiled packages. Between its colonial architecture that screams *Instagram me!* and its agricultural prowess, Artemisa is like Cuba's own little time capsule—if time capsules grew tobacco and occasionally sprouted provincial capitals, that is.

• • • ● • ● • ● • • •

Amelia and the team had done their homework. They knew the *Artemisa* typically carried a crew of 15, but tonight, the yacht was deserted. Vincent had scheduled a complete overhaul of the ship's systems, and he had given the crew shore leave while a specialized maintenance team was supposed to come aboard. Of course, that team was currently enjoying an all-expenses-paid trip to the wrong marina, courtesy of some creative rescheduling on Amelia's part. *Thanks for making this easy, Vincent*; she appreciated the irony of how the billionaire's own paranoia about ship security had played right into her hands.

Now, if I were a slimy hospital tycoon trying to hide my dirty laundry, where would I stash it? Amelia's gaze traced the yacht's decks, pausing at a small, tinted window near the waterline. *Bingo again. Your subconscious betrays you, Mr. Blackwell. Always under cover in the dark.*

Amelia slipped her phone back into her pocket, a plan already forming in her razor-sharp mind. She turned away from the *Artemisa*, her lips curving into a Cheshire grin.

Enjoy your reign while it lasts. This queen is about to steal your crown jewels right from under your nose.

• • • ● • ● • ● • • •

Amelia sauntered towards the marina's security office, each step precisely measured against the polished wooden boardwalk. She adjusted her oversized sunglasses and smoothed the front of her tailored white pantsuit, a look that screamed *I belong here* with every fiber of its designer fabric. *And if you think otherwise,* she thought, *that's your problem, not mine.*

As she approached the office, she spotted two different security guards engrossed in conversation, their laughter carrying across the marina. *Typical rent-a-cops. More interested in swapping stories than actually watching the boats.*

She cleared her throat, drawing the guards' attention as she entered the office. "Gentle-men," she said, flashing a dazzling smile.

The guards straightened, their eyes widening as they took in the vision before them. "Ma'am," the taller one managed, his voice cracking slightly. "How can we assist you?"

Amelia leaned against the counter, her posture relaxed, yet undeniably in control. "Well, I seem to have misplaced my VIP pass for the *Artemisa*. You know how these things go—one too many mimosas at brunch, and suddenly your Chanel clutch is a black hole." She punctuated her words with a conspiratorial wink.

The shorter guard frowned, consulting a clipboard. "I'm sorry, ma'am, but I don't see your name on the guest list for the *Artemisa*."

Showtime. Amelia let out a tinkling laugh, shaking her head. "Oh, honey, of course you don't. Vincent always lists me under a pseudonym. He's so protective of his favorite girl." She lowered her voice to a stage whisper. "It's Natasha Romanoff. You know, like the Black Widow? Vincent's idea of a little joke."

The guards exchanged a glance, clearly unsure how to proceed. Amelia pressed on, her tone turning more serious. "Now, I know you boys are just doing your job, and I respect that. But I also know that Vincent wouldn't be too happy if he knew his special guest was being given the runaround. So, how about we make this easy for everyone? You let me through, I won't breathe a word to Vincent, and we all go on with our day. Deal?"

The taller guard hesitated, then nodded slowly. "Of course, Ms. Romanoff. My apologies for the confusion. Please, go right ahead."

Amelia favored him with another megawatt smile. "Thank you, sugar. I knew you were a smart one." She turned on her heel and strode out of the office, fighting the urge to laugh at the absurdity of the situation.

Natasha Romanoff. Really, Amelia? You're losing your touch. But as she made her way down the boardwalk, her eyes fixed on the Artemisa, she couldn't deny the thrill of the game. *Then again, if it's stupid, and it works, it's not stupid. Time to see just how smart Vincent Blackwell really is.*

As she approached, the sleek lines of the superyacht cut a striking figure against the azure sky, a floating fortress of wealth and secrets. *And somewhere in there lies the key to bringing down CBHS.*

She pulled out her phone, her fingers flying over the screen as she accessed the marina's network. A few deft keystrokes, and she was in, the yacht's security schematics unfolding before her eyes.

"Well, hello there," she said to herself, a smile playing at the corners of her mouth. "Aren't you just a tangled web of circuits and code?" Her gaze flicked over the display, taking in the array of cameras, motion sensors, and alarms. *Time to unravel you, piece by piece.*

Amelia's mind raced, calculations and strategies whirring behind her eyes. She needed to create a blind spot, a chink in the *Artemisa's* digital armor the team could exploit. *But how to do it without tripping any alarms?*

An idea struck her, and she grinned. *The old Trojan Horse play. Classic.*

Her fingers danced over the phone, crafting a deceptively simple piece of code. *A little gift for Vincent's security team. One that will keep them chasing ghosts while we make off with the goods.*

She hit send, watching as her digital creation wormed its way into the yacht's system. *Now, let's see how long they take to realize they've been hacked.*

Amelia pocketed her phone, her eyes still fixed on the *Artemisa.* She could almost feel the weight of the incriminating files in her hands, the evidence that would expose years of patient neglect, staff exploitation, and corporate greed. Soon, CBHS would face justice for all the lives they'd destroyed in pursuit of profit.

Soon, she thought, *the truth will come out. And not a moment too soon for all those counting on us.*

Amelia walked around the *Artemisa,* a sleek shadow gliding across the polished teak deck. The yacht was a floating palace, all gleaming chrome and pristine white surfaces, but she hadn't come to admire the decor.

Focus, Amelia. You're here for the files, not the Feng Shui.

She paused, her hand resting on the polished railing. For a moment, the weight of what she was about to do hit her. She remembered her first day at CBHS, fresh out of law school, idealistic and eager to make a difference. "How far I've come," she whispered, a mix of pride and regret coloring her voice. "From corporate attorney to yacht thief. Not exactly the career path I had in mind." She shook her head, steeling herself. "But sometimes, you have to work outside the system to fix it."

She crept towards the main cabin, ears straining for any hint of movement. The security team would be discovering her little digital surprise right about now, but there was no telling how long it would keep them occupied.

Better make this quick.

Amelia approached the biometric scanner guarding the main cabin. "Retinal scan, fingerprint, and voice recognition," she said. "Cute." She pulled out a small device, attaching it to the scanner. Within seconds, the system beeped, granting her access. "Thanks for the security upgrade, Vincent. It's almost like you wanted to give me a challenge."

She was in. *State-of-the-art security system. Right. And I'm the Queen of England.*

The interior of the *Artemisa* was just as opulent as its exterior, all plush carpets and glittering chandeliers. Amelia allowed herself a moment of appreciation. *Not bad, Vincent. Shame about the whole 'criminal empire' thing.*

She slipped down a narrow hallway, mentally reviewing the yacht's layout. If her intel was correct, Vincent's private office would be just ahead, likely hidden behind one of these innocuous-looking doors.

Decision, decisions . . . she thought, her lips curving into a knowing smile. *Though somehow I doubt Vincent keeps his skeletons in the coat closet.*

She stopped before a door that looked no different from the others, but something in her gut told her this was the one.

Jackpot.

The lock was no match for the skills Tommy taught her, and in seconds, she was sliding into the darkened room. *Hello, beautiful,* she thought as she took in the soft give of the plush carpet underfoot, the faint scent of expensive cologne lingering in the air and eyed the sleek mahogany desk. *I've seen smaller museums. Guess corruption pays well these days. So, what secrets are you hiding?*

As she navigated the office, Amelia's mind raced. *If I were Vincent, where would I hide my darkest secrets? The obvious safe is probably a decoy. Think, Amelia. What would I overlook if I were investigating myself?* Her eyes landed on an innocuous-looking bookshelf.

Ah . . .

On the shelf was a slim black external hard drive, disguised as an innocuous-looking bookend, but undoubtedly holding the key to bringing down CBHS. Amelia palmed the slim device, a triumphant smirk tugging at her lips. *Too easy. Someone's getting sloppy in their old age.*

She pulled out a compact laptop from her bag and connected the drive. As the files loaded, her smirk faded. The drive contained years of incriminating evidence—far more than she'd expected. But as she tried to access the files, she hit a wall. A sophisticated encryption system, unlike anything she'd seen before.

She realized she couldn't crack this on the spot, and there was too much data to transfer quickly. The realization hit her like a punch to the gut: she'd have to take the entire yacht to ensure she had enough time and resources to access all the evidence.

"Well," she said to herself, a wry smile forming, "I guess I'm about to add *grand theft boat* to my resume." Amelia's mind flickered back to her sailing experiences—summers spent on her uncle's sailboat, navigating the choppy waters of the Atlantic, and even a long ago stint as a deckhand on a luxury charter. But this? This was in a whole different league. "Though certainly nothing like this," she said, her hands confidently grasping the helm. "I mean, how many people can say they captained one of the largest yachts in the world? Time to put those skills to the test."

But as she turned to leave, a floorboard creaked behind her. Amelia froze, her hand instinctively tightening on her bag.

"Well, well," a familiar voice said. "Look what the cat dragged in."

Amelia turned, coming face-to-face with the last person she'd expected to see. *Of course he's here. Because this heist was going too smoothly.*

"Hello, Steve," she said coolly, mind racing. "Fancy meeting you here."

Steve Harrington, CBHS's head of security, leaned against the doorframe, his expression a mix of amusement and annoyance. "Amelia. I'd say it's a pleasure, but we both know that's a lie."

Amelia kept her tone light, despite her racing heart. "Oh, I don't know. Unexpected reunions can be so . . . thrilling."

Steve snorted. "Cut the crap, Amelia. What are you doing here?"

She shrugged, the picture of nonchalance. "Just taking in the sights. You know, admiring the decor. I hear mahogany is making a comeback."

"Right." Steve's eyes narrowed. "And I suppose that hard drive just fell into your pocket?"

Damn. Amelia's mind whirred, searching for a plausible explanation. "This old thing? I was just borrowing it. Needed to update my resume, you see. Unemployment is such a bore."

Steve pushed off the doorframe, taking a step into the room. "Enough games. Hand it over, and maybe I'll forget this little . . . indiscretion."

Amelia laughed, the sound sharp and humorless. "Oh, Steve. You always were a terrible liar." She took a step back. "I think we both know that's not going to happen."

They stared at each other for a long moment, the tension crackling between them. When Steve moved toward her, Amelia was ready. She sidestepped gracefully, simultaneously pressing a small device against his neck. There was a soft hiss, and Steve's eyes widened in surprise before rolling back. He crumpled to the floor, unconscious.

"Sweet dreams, Steve," Amelia whispered. "Don't worry, you'll wake up with one hell of a headache, but you'll be safe on dry land. Can't say the same for this yacht, though."

She secured him with zip ties, dragged him off the yacht, then used her phone to call in an *anonymous tip* about an unconscious man on the docks. By the time security came to investigate, Amelia would be long gone with the yacht.

With that, she slipped back aboard, making her way through the yacht's corridors to the bridge. *One obstacle down,* she thought, adrenaline humming through her veins. *Now to expose a corrupt system and help all those CBHS has hurt.*

The cool ocean breeze flowed through the bridge's windows as Amelia approached the helm controls, the incriminating hard drive tucked away in a waterproof pouch beneath her sleek, black wetsuit. She moved with feline grace towards the yacht's controls, her mind already racing ahead to the next steps.

Get this floating mansion out of the marina, contact the team, then find somewhere safe to dock where we can extract the data. Nothing like a little grand theft yacht to spice up a Tuesday evening.

Amelia's hands flew over the helm controls. She engaged the bow thruster to ease the yacht away from the dock, then gently increased throttle. The twin diesel engines rumbled to life, propelling the *Artemisa* into the channel. She kept a wary eye on the depth finder, knowing one wrong move could ground the vessel on a sandbar. She'd need to think fast about where to take this behemoth—somewhere close enough to reach before anyone raised the alarm, but secure enough to let them work.

She guided the yacht onto the Stranahan River, the dark water rippling in the vessel's wake. As they approached the 17th Street Bridge, Amelia called ahead to the bridge tender. The yacht's powerful engines thrummed, their deep rumble echoing off the concrete pillars of the award-winning drawbridge—Fort Lauderdale's stately entrance marker and, at the moment, Amelia's first obstacle to the open sea. The harsh glare of streetlights above illuminated the deck, creating a dazzling dance of shadows and reflections on the dark, rippling water as she passed underneath. Just past the aptly named Superyacht Village, the scent of salt and diesel mingled in the air as Amelia reminded herself to, *Stay focused. One mistake, and this whole operation could sink faster than the Titanic.*

Her eyes darted from the radar to the riverbank and back again, alert for any sign of trouble. As the *Artemisa* approached the inlet to the open ocean, Amelia spotted a Coast Guard cutter on the radar. Her pulse quickened. *Routine patrol, or are they onto me?* She reduced speed, trying to appear casual. The cutter grew closer, its searchlight sweeping the water. Amelia held her breath, hand hovering over the throttle, ready to gun it if necessary. After an agonizing minute, the cutter veered off, continuing its patrol. Amelia exhaled slowly. "That was too close," she said under her breath, increasing speed as she pointed the bow towards the open sea.

As she neared the Atlantic, Amelia felt a surge of adrenaline. *Almost there.* The inlet narrowed, funneling the yacht between rocky jetties on either side. Waves crashed against the stone barriers, sending plumes of white spray into the air. Amelia gripped the helm tighter, carefully steering the *Artemisa* through the choppy waters where the calm intra-coastal met the restless sea.

She could taste the salty air now, feel the fine mist on her face as the yacht crested each swell. The lighthouse at the inlet's mouth blinked its steady warning, a silent sentinel marking her escape to the open ocean.

And then she was through. The vast expanse of the Atlantic stretched out before her like a blank canvas, ready for her to paint her masterpiece of justice. The yacht's bow rose and fell with the deeper ocean swells, a rhythmic motion promising freedom and the thrill of the open sea.

Ocean, meet Artemisa. Artemisa, meet your new captain. I'm sure we'll all get along swimmingly.

Amelia pushed the throttle forward, the engines roaring in response. The *Artemisa* surged ahead, cutting through the waves like a hot knife through butter.

As the coast disappeared behind them, Amelia felt a sense of exhilaration, of purpose. She couldn't wait to see William's face when she told him how she'd spent her Tuesday evening. Somehow, she doubted even Thoreau had written about this particular form of civil disobedience.

The Moral Minute—Episode 6

[Theme music—short, serious but with an edge]

ANIE: I'm Anie Chen.

LUCAS: And I'm Lucas Rodriguez. Welcome to The Moral Minute, where we examine the day's most egregious ethical failures in corporate America.

ANIE: The walls are talking at CBHS, Lucas, and they're telling quite a story.

LUCAS: [wry] More like the staff is finally talking. After years of silence, whistleblowers are coming forward.

ANIE: Like Dr. Haley Chen—no relation—who reported critical staffing shortages that led to patient deaths.

LUCAS: And what happened to Dr. Chen when she spoke up?

ANIE: [sardonic] Oh, you know, the usual. Suddenly there were mysterious patient complaints, questions about her clinical judgment . . .

LUCAS: Classic intimidation playbook. But she's not alone anymore. We've got nurses, technicians, even administrators speaking out.

ANIE: One nurse reported working 20-hour shifts because there was literally no one to relieve her.

LUCAS: [grim] While Kiran Devi, the Chief Nursing Officer, called it "resource opti-mization."

ANIE: Time's almost up. What's our moral of the minute?

LUCAS: When your staff starts breaking their silence, it might be time to start listening.

[Theme music fades out]

Vivian Ward

S ilver Sage Ranch.

Their target.

The vast expanse of golden grassland stretched out under an impossibly blue sky, broken only by the winding ribbon of the main road. In the distance, snow-capped mountains soared, their peaks brushing against scattered white clouds. The ranch's isolation, miles of open country surrounding it, was both its beauty and its danger—offering little cover if anyone discovered them.

Black Angus cattle dotted the landscape, dark silhouettes against sun-bleached grass, grazing with lazy indifference to the high-stakes drama about to unfold. The air hung heavy with the pungent scent of sagebrush, nature's own camouflage for their covert operation.

As the sun began its descent, painting the Nevada sky in vibrant hues of orange and purple, William maneuvered the van behind a cluster of sagebrush near a cattle guard. His eyes scanned the sprawling ranch, taking in every detail. With a deep breath, he tapped his earpiece and asked, "Everyone in position?"

A chorus of affirmatives crackled through the comm.

"Ella, you ready to dazzle them with our IT expertise?" William asked, adjusting his fake employee badge.

"Oh, absolutely. I can't wait to explain why they need to update their Adobe Reader for the fifteenth time this week."

William smirked. "Just remember, if anyone asks, we're here to optimize their CPU cycles and defragment their RAM."

"Got it. I'll throw in some buzzwords about blockchain and AI for good measure."

Meanwhile, Josh's voice chimed in, "I'm in position near the service entrance. These catering uniforms are a crime against fashion. I feel like I should be serving overcooked chicken at a budget wedding."

"Focus, Josh," Tommy said. "I've got eyes on the security patrols. They're about as observant as a bunch of sleepwalkers, but let's not push our luck."

• • • • • • • • • • •

The air was thick with the pungent scent of sagebrush, the silvery-green plants covering the hillsides and providing ample cover for the team's covert movements. Darby stepped out of the sleek black Aston Martin Vanquish, her entrance turning heads faster than a whiplash injury. Her hair, usually a cascade of blonde waves, was now styled in an elegant updo with intricate braids woven throughout, small diamonds nestled within the plaits like stars in a night sky. The hairstyle, both regal and edgy, complemented her shimmering gold gown.

As she sashayed towards the entrance, Darby couldn't help but smirk. "I feel like I'm wearing the GDP of a small country on my head," she said into her concealed mic.

"Just don't sneeze," came Ella's reply. "We can't afford to rain diamonds on Vincent's fancy floors."

Darby's laughter, low and throaty, drew appreciative glances from nearby guests. She flashed a dazzling smile at the security guard, who was trying (and failing) to maintain his professional demeanor.

"Name?" he asked, fumbling with his tablet.

"Vivian Ward," Darby said, leaning in conspiratorially. "But you can call me Viv."

As she swept past the flustered guard—who obviously knew his movie history—Darby's eyes locked onto her target. Vincent Blackwell stood across the room, holding court amidst a group of sycophants.

"Showtime," she whispered, her smile turning predatory. "Let's see if this *Pretty Woman* can work her magic on our very own Edward Lewis. Minus the heartwarming redemption arc, of course."

"Just remember," William's voice crackled in her ear, "we're here to fleece him, not fall for him. No matter how charming his corrupt little heart might be."

"Please. I've dated gym bros with more depth than this guy. Trust me, my heart is as safe as his conscience is nonexistent."

With that, she glided across the room, every step calculated to draw Vincent's attention. Heads turned as she moved through the room with feline grace, the embodiment of elegance and allure. She locked eyes with Vincent across the ballroom, flashing a coy smile that promised secrets and temptation.

Vincent excused himself from a group of sycophants and glided over to Darby, his eyes raking over her curves. Without warning, Vincent asked, "Have we met before? You seem familiar."

Darby improvised, "Oh, you must have seen me in that charity gala in New York last month. I was there with the Astors."

"No. No, that's not it . . . I wasn't there, but you look so familiar," he said, taking her hand and brushing his lips across her knuckles.

Darby arched an eyebrow. "Vivian Ward. And you must be the infamous Vincent Blackwell. Your reputation precedes you."

"All lies and slander, I assure you. Though I'm sure you're no stranger to whispers and rumors yourself."

Darby laughed, a husky sound that sent a shiver down his spine. "Guilty as charged. But where's the fun in being predictable?" She snagged two glasses of champagne from a passing waiter and handed one to Vincent. "To living dangerously."

"I'll drink to that," Vincent replied, clinking his glass against hers. "So, Ms. Ward, what brings you to my humble soirée? Besides the obvious allure of overpriced champagne and forced small talk."

Darby took a sip, her eyes never leaving his over the rim of her glass. "Oh, you know, the usual. Boredom, curiosity, a burning desire to see how the other half lives." She leaned in, her voice dropping to a conspiratorial whisper. "And I heard a rumor that you throw the best parties this side of the Mississippi. I simply had to see for myself."

Vincent laughed, moving closer. "And? Does the reality live up to the hype?"

"Well," Darby said, pretending to consider, "the champagne is excellent, the company . . . intriguing. But I'm reserving judgment on the entertainment. The night is still young, after all."

"Perhaps I could provide a more . . . personal tour?" Vincent said, his hand ghosting over the small of her back. "I assure you, there's much more to see beyond this ballroom."

Darby's lips curled into a mischievous smile. "Dr. Blackwell, are you proposing we sneak away from your own party? How delightfully scandalous."

"What can I say? You inspire me to break the rules," Vincent replied, his eyes darkening with desire.

"Careful now," Darby teased, trailing a finger down his lapel. "A girl might get ideas. And I warn you, my ideas tend to be rather . . . ambitious."

Vincent leaned in, his breath hot against her ear. "Ambitious ideas and dangerous women are my weakness."

"How fortunate," Darby said, her lips barely grazing his cheek as she pulled back. "Because *dangerous* is my middle name. Right after *high-maintenance* and before *heartbreaker*."

Vincent laughed, genuinely amused. "I think I'm willing to take that risk, Ms. Ward. Shall we find somewhere more private to continue this . . . discussion?"

Darby's smile was equal parts invitation and challenge. "Lead the way, Dr. Blackwell. I'm dying to see what other surprises you have in store."

As Vincent guided her away from the crowd, Darby caught Josh's eye across the room. She gave an imperceptible nod. Phase one was complete. Now, the real game could begin.

· · · ● · ●· ● ● · · ·

Across the ranch, near the entrance, William tugged at the collar of his crisp white dress shirt, tucked into pressed khaki slacks. He adjusted his navy blue blazer, complete with an embroidered "IT Services" logo on the breast pocket. "I feel like I'm cosplaying as a corporate drone," he grumbled. "Like I should be selling overpriced toner cartridges instead of saving the world."

Ella, walking beside him in black ankle boots, snorted. "Please. You look like every middle manager's fantasy of corporate success. At least your outfit breathes." She tugged at her dark slim-fit pants, which she'd paired with a crisp white blouse and a tailored blazer that matched William's. She hid her usual edgy style beneath layers of corporate camouflage, but she kept a hint of rebellion with subtle, dark nail polish and a small, fake, silver nose stud.

"Fair point. Though I have to admit, you clean up nice. Very *rebel hacker goes corporate*."

"Thanks. I was going for *could hack your system or file your taxes, depending on the pay grade*." She adjusted her laptop bag on her shoulder. "Let's just get to those servers before someone asks us to turn their computer off and on again."

"Save the snark for after we've gotten what we came for. For now, let's just focus on getting to that server trailer without arousing suspicion."

They approached the isolated building, their steps purposeful and assured. Just beyond it, the Humboldt River flowed, its surface mirroring the azure sky. As they neared the entrance, both adjusted their posture, melting into their roles as IT professionals. Though the disguises felt foreign, their determination to pull off the heist overshadowed any discomfort.

Jenny, the office manager, greeted them with a harried smile. "Thank goodness you're here. The servers have been acting up all week. I'll show you to the trailer."

As they navigated the cramped space, dodging wires and humming equipment, William couldn't help but marvel at Ella's composure. For someone who had endured unspeakable horrors, she moved with a quiet strength that belied her years.

"I'll leave you to it," Jenny said, heading for the door. "Holler if you need anything."

The moment they were alone, Ella's fingers hit the keyboard, her eyes locked on the screen. "I'm in," she announced after a few tense minutes. "Got access to their network. But there's another layer of security protecting the sensitive files—looks like some kind of encryption key. We definitely made the right call coming here in person."

William kept watch at the door, his mind drifting to the philosophical quandaries that had consumed him for years. Was this mission a shot at redemption, or merely another chapter in a life marked by moral ambiguity? He shook his head. Emerson would have a field day with this one.

· • • ● • ● ◗ • • ·

In a dimly lit office in the main house, Josh hunched over his laptop, his fingers dancing across the keys with a rhythm that belied the surrounding chaos. The chatter of the guests and the clink of champagne glasses faded into the background as he lost himself in the familiar dance of code and encryption. With practiced ease, he connected a small, innocuous-looking device to an ethernet port, physically tapping into the mansion's network. The device, no larger than a USB drive, was their digital skeleton key, granting him unfettered access to CBHS's most guarded secrets.

The firewalls put up a valiant fight, but they were no match for Josh's analytical mind and relentless determination. With each keystroke, he felt a surge of adrenaline, the thrill of the hunt coursing through his veins.

"I'm in," he said into his comm, a hint of satisfaction coloring his voice. "You'd think a guy with billions would invest in better cybersecurity. This is almost too easy."

Data cascaded across his screen in an emerald waterfall, and Josh couldn't help but smirk. He was in his element, invisible to the glittering crowd outside, yet wielding more power than any of them could imagine.

The soft creak of the door made his heart skip. A security guard, face etched with suspicion, swept his gaze across the office.

Josh's fingers faltered for a split second as he ducked under the desk. *Just another puzzle to solve,* he thought, his lips twisting into a wry smile.

The guard moved on, oblivious to Josh's presence. Josh waited until the footsteps faded down the hall before letting out the breath he'd been holding. He quickly finished his work, closed his laptop with a satisfying snap, and slipped it into his bag.

· · · ● · ● · ● · · ·

Meanwhile, William stepped outside the trailer, the cool night air a welcome respite from the stuffy confines of the hot servers. He leaned against the wall, his mind drifting to the words of Thoreau. *The mass of men lead lives of quiet desperation.*

"William? William Prescott?" a voice called out, startling him from his reverie.

He turned to see a middle-aged woman in a sequined gown, her eyes wide with recognition. "I thought that was you!" she gushed, moving closer. "I loved your book. It changed my life."

William's heart sank. Of all the people to run into, it had to be a fan. Jenny looked up from her clipboard, her face expressing obvious confusion.

He plastered a smile on his face, his mind racing to come up with a way to extricate himself from the situation without blowing his cover.

"I'm flattered," he said, his voice taking on a practiced charm. "But I'm afraid you have me mistaken for someone else. I get that a lot, though. Must be my rugged good looks."

The woman blinked, confusion etched on her face. "But I could have sworn . . ."

William laughed, the sound low and conspiratorial. "Between you and me," he said, leaning in close, "I'm actually here undercover. Researching my next book. But don't tell anyone. It's all very hush-hush."

The woman's eyes widened, a flush creeping up her neck. "Of course," she said, clearly thrilled to be in on the secret. "Your secret is safe with me."

William winked, the gesture equal parts charming and mischievous. "I knew I could count on you," he said, straightening up. "Now, if you'll excuse me, I have some more, ah, research to do."

As he walked away, William couldn't help but shake his head in amusement. "The things we do for the greater good," he said under his breath, his lips twitching with the ghost of a smile.

In the server room, Ella's fingers darted from key to key in a blur of motion, her mind laser-focused on the task at hand. She'd already accomplished the first critical step—gaining undetected access to the system. Now came the real challenge: downloading Vincent's incriminating information. For this, they needed his encryption key, a unique and formidable security measure that had necessitated their physical presence at the ranch.

First things first, Ella. Get in unseen.

Her eyes locked on the screen as lines of code scrolled by at a dizzying pace. The familiar thrill of the hack coursed through her veins, but she forced herself to remain calm and methodical. One wrong move, and the entire operation could go up in smoke.

A blaring alarm sliced through the silence, jarring her from her focus. Ella's heart leaped into her throat, her fingers freezing over the keys.

"Shit," she said, the rare expletive escaping her lips before she could stop it. Ella rarely cursed, but the gravity of the situation warranted it. This wasn't just a setback; it could be catastrophic for their entire mission.

Not now. Not when we're so close.

After a tense minute, she killed the sound, but the system remained locked down, preventing her from moving forward with the hack.

"Guys, we've got a problem," Ella whispered into her comm. "I've silenced the alarm, but this security measure is like nothing I've seen before. I can't crack it alone, not in the time we have."

There was a moment of tense silence before William's voice came through. "What are our options?"

Ella bit her lip, weighing the risks. Then, with a resigned sigh, she made a decision. "I need to make a call."

Pulling out a secure phone, she dialed a number she knew by heart. After two rings, a familiar voice answered.

"Zack? It's Ella. I need your help."

Zack was a hacker extraordinaire Ella had befriended after her return to Omaha years ago. Together, they'd become a digital dynamic duo, targeting high-profile miscreants and serving up justice one destroyed hard drive at a time. While Ella was the undisputed Mozart of malware, Zack had a particular talent that bordered on the supernatural—he could sniff out flaws in internal security systems like a bloodhound on the scent of fear. His uncanny ability to silence alarms and slip past firewalls had saved their virtual bacon more times than Ella cared to admit. Right now, she needed that expertise like she needed her next breath.

"Ella?" Zack's voice was a mix of surprise and concern. "What's going on?"

Ella explained the situation; her voice low and urgent. "Can you help me bypass this thing?"

There was a pause, then Zack's voice came back, all business. "Alright, talk me through what you're seeing."

For the next few minutes, Ella and Zack worked in tandem, their expertise combining to tackle the unexpected security measure. Ella orchestrated a symphony of keystrokes, following Zack's instructions and adding her own insights.

"Try this," Zack said, rattling off a string of code.

Ella input the sequence, holding her breath as she hit enter. For a moment, nothing happened. Then, like magic, the security measure crumbled.

"We're in," Ella said, relief flooding her voice. "Zack, you're a lifesaver."

"Anytime, El," Zack replied, the smile clear in his voice. "Just . . . be careful, okay?"

"Always am," Ella said, then ended the call.

She looked back at her screen, a fierce grin spreading across her face. "Alright, CBHS," she said. "Let's see what secrets you're hiding."

With renewed determination, Ella turned back to her screen. What she'd thought was a completed hack had turned into a two-phase operation, but she wasn't complaining. Sometimes the best plans were the ones that evolved on the fly. And thanks to Zack's help, she'd silenced that alarm and complete the first crucial step.

Now she waited for phase two—and for that, she'd need help from other friends.

Darby.

Tommy.

* * *

While Ella worked in the server farm, Darby maintained her performance at the gala. She laughed, the sound musical and enchanting. She leaned into Vincent, her hand resting lightly on his arm, her every movement calculated to keep him enthralled.

But beneath the sparkling facade, her mind was whirring, analyzing every shift in his expression, every inflection in his voice. She could sense his suspicion, the way his questions probed a little too deep, a little too sharply.

"So, Vivian," Vincent said, his smile not quite reaching his eyes, "what did you say you do for a living?"

Darby's heart skipped a beat, but her expression never faltered. "Oh, darling," she said, her voice dripping with honey, "I'm in the business of making dreams come true. But let's not talk about work. Tonight's about pleasure, not business."

She trailed a finger down his lapel, her touch light and teasing. Vincent's gaze followed the movement, his focus momentarily diverted.

Darby seized the opportunity, steering the conversation to safer waters. "Speaking of pleasure," she said, her lips curving into a wicked grin, "have you tried the canapés? They're simply divine."

She plucked one from a passing tray, holding it to Vincent's lips. "Open wide," she cooed, her voice rich with innuendo.

Vincent complied, his teeth grazing her fingertips as he accepted the morsel. Darby suppressed a shudder of revulsion, masking it with a tinkling laugh.

"Delicious, isn't it?" she asked, her eyes sparkling with mirth. "Almost as delicious as the secrets I'm sure you're hiding."

It was a risky move, but Darby knew the best defense was often a good offense. Keep him on his toes, keep him guessing, and maybe, just maybe, they'd make it out of this unscathed.

Vincent's eyes narrowed, but then he threw his head back and laughed, the sound booming across the room. "Oh, Vivian," he said, his voice rich with amusement, "you are a delight. I think this is the beginning of a beautiful friendship."

Darby smiled, the gesture all teeth and sharp edges. "I couldn't agree more," she lied, her mind already racing ahead to the next move in this deadly game of cat and mouse.

As Vincent's laughter subsided, Darby's fingers again danced along his lapel, her touch light and teasing. Her eyes caught a glint of metal—the encryption pen nestled in his breast pocket. The key to unlocking his secrets lay near.

She leaned in, her breath hot against his ear. "Dance with me," she whispered, her voice a siren's call.

"How could I refuse such a tempting offer?"

He guided her to the dance floor, his hand on the small of her back. *Ugh, his hand on my back makes my skin crawl. But I can't let him see my disgust. The entire mission depends on me keeping him distracted.*

As they swayed to the music, Darby pressed herself against him, her movements fluid and seductive. Her hand slid up his chest, fingertips grazing the pen.

Just a little closer, she thought, acutely aware of every breath, every subtle shift of her body against his. The thrill of the con sang through her veins, a heady mixture of adrenaline and anticipation. *Focus, Darby. Don't get sloppy now.*

Vincent spun her out, then pulled her back in, her back now flush against his chest. Darby's eyes locked with Tommy's across the room, a silent communication passing between them.

As Vincent's hand slid lower, Darby leaned into him, using the movement to mask her true intention. Her fingers, light as a feather, slipped into his pocket. She felt the smooth surface of the pen and suppressed a triumphant smile. With a pickpocket's finesse, she extracted it in one fluid motion, palming it as she spun out of his embrace.

"Oh my," she said, her voice breathless and eyes wide with feigned embarrassment. "I'm feeling a bit flushed. Would you excuse me? I need to powder my nose."

She sashayed away, hips swaying hypnotically, leaving a dumbstruck Vincent in her wake. Her heart raced, but her exterior remained cool and collected. As she passed Tommy, disguised as a waiter, she pressed the pen into his hand. The exchange was quick and sub-tle—to any onlooker, it would have appeared she was simply taking a glass of champagne.

Darby didn't look back as she headed for the ladies' room, but she could feel Vincent's eyes on her. *Mission accomplished,* she thought, allowing herself a small, satisfied smirk.

Tommy nodded and slipped out of the ballroom, his movements smooth and unobtru-sive. Once outside, he made a beeline for the ATVs, his heart racing.

No time to waste.

He swung a leg over the vehicle, the engine roaring to life beneath him. With a twist of the throttle, he sped off into the night, the pen clenched in his hand. He navigated the terrain with ease, his military training kicking in. He hugged the shadows, avoiding the sweeping spotlights and patrolling guards.

Almost there.

The server farm loomed ahead, a nondescript trailer near the low-slung office buildings just inside the front gate. These plain looking trailers housed a treasure trove of secrets. Tommy killed the engine, sliding off the ATV with catlike grace.

He slipped inside, his footsteps echoing in the cavernous space. "Ella," he called softly, his voice carrying in the stillness.

"Here," came the reply, Ella emerging from the shadows. Her face was pale, her eyes wide.

"Did you get it?"

Tommy held up the pen, a triumphant grin splitting his face. "Was there ever any doubt?"

Ella snatched it from his hand, turning it over in her fingers. "Vincent's personal encryption key," she said, awe coloring her voice. "With this, we can grab everything."

Tommy nodded, his expression grim. "Then let's not waste any more time. Crack that bad boy open and let's steal all the skeletons Mr. CEO has in his closet."

"With pleasure."

She plugged the pen into her console, her fingers flying across the keys. The screen flickered to life, lines of code scrolling past.

Tommy watched, his heart in his throat. This was it. The moment of truth.

Ella's eyes locked on the scrolling lines of code. The world around her faded away, leaving only the hum of the servers and the thrum of her own heartbeat.

Come on . . . give me something, anything.

The screen flashed red, a new warning klaxon blaring from the speakers. Ella's heart stopped, her breath catching in her throat.

"What is it?" Tommy asked, his voice tight with tension.

Ella shook her head, her fingers never stopping their frenzied dance. "I'm in," she said, her eyes wide with disbelief. "I'm in Vincent's personal files."

Tommy leaned in, his eyes scanning the screen. "What do you see?"

Ella's brow furrowed, her mouth twisting into a frown. "Financial records, emails, memos . . . oh my God."

She turned to Tommy, her face ashen. "It's all here. Every dirty deal, every bribe, every cover-up. Vincent's been embezzling millions from CBHS, funneling it into offshore accounts."

Tommy's jaw clenched, his eyes hardening. "That absolute vulture."

Ella nodded, her fingers trembling as she typed. "And that's not all. A quick look confirms what we already knew: patient neglect, false insurance claims . . . CBHS is rotten to the core."

Tommy's hand came down hard on the desk, making Ella jump. "We have to get this out there," he said, his voice shaking with barely contained rage. "The world needs to know what kind of monster Vincent really is."

At breakneck speed, Ella copied the files and documents onto a secure drive. Her heart raced, adrenaline surging through her veins.

This is it. This is what we've been fighting for.

A flashing icon caught her eye, a file marked "Project Lazarus." Ella's brow furrowed, her curiosity piqued.

"What the hell is Project Lazarus?" she asked, clicking on the file.

The screen filled with images and documents, each more horrifying than the last. Illegal drug trials, cover-ups of patient deaths . . .

Ella's stomach turned, bile rising in her throat. "Oh my God," she whispered, her voice trembling. "This is . . . This is beyond anything we could have imagined."

Tommy's face was a mask of stone, his eyes blazing with fury. "Vincent's not just a thief," he said, his hands clenching into fists. "He's a cold-blooded parasite."

Ella's fingers closed around the drive, the weight of their mission settling onto her shoulders. "Let's finish this," she said, her eyes flashing with determination.

They turned to leave, the stolen data clutched tightly in Ella's hand.

• • • • • • • • • •

William's eyes narrowed as he watched the security guards converge near the server trailer, their radios crackling with urgent chatter.

They're onto us . . . if this goes wrong, I'm putting the entire team at risk. But if I don't act now, we'll lose everything we've worked for.

He glanced at his watch, his mind racing. Ella needed more time to finish the download, but with each passing second, the risk of discovery grew. *Think, William,* he chided himself, his jaw clenching with frustration. *What would Thoreau do?*

A sudden spark of inspiration ignited in his mind, and he grinned, a mischievous glint in his eye. *All good things are wild and free,* he said, quoting his favorite philosopher.

Time to unleash a little chaos.

With a deep breath, William strode purposefully towards a nearby utility pole, his eyes locked on the transformer mounted high above. *Here goes nothing,* he thought, steeling himself for what came next.

In one swift motion, he grabbed a rock from the landscaping and hurled it at the transformer. The resulting explosion was more dramatic than he'd expected—a blinding flash, followed by a thunderous boom. Sparks rained down as the entire area plunged into darkness. Screams of shock and confusion filled the air as guests and staff alike found themselves blinded. Security guards rushed to the scene, their attention diverted from the server trailer as they tried to assess the situation.

"Oh my God!" William said, feigning panic as he rushed back to Jenny. "I-I saw something climb up there—I think it was a raccoon! Did it cause this?"

Chaos erupted as people scrambled in the darkness, security frantically trying to restore order and light.

That ought to buy a few more minutes, William thought, fighting back a smirk as he watched the pandemonium unfold. *Thoreau would be proud.*

• • • ● • ● • ● • •

In the main house, Josh finished navigating through the labyrinth of Vincent's financial records. *Come on, come on,* he urged, his brow furrowed in concentration. *Faster,* as he continued his search.

A flashing red icon caught his eye, and he grinned, a triumphant gleam in his eye. *Jackpot,* he thought.

The screen filled with rows of numbers and account names, each one more damning than the last. Josh let out a low whistle, shaking his head in disbelief. "Looks like Vincent's been a very naughty boy," he said, his voice dripping with sarcasm. "Embezzlement, money laundering, tax evasion . . . he's hit the trifecta of financial skullduggery."

He inserted a flash drive into the computer and started the download. As the progress bar crept forward, Josh's eyes darted between the screen and the door, acutely aware of every second ticking by. *This ought to be enough to bury Vincent and his whole corrupt empire,* he thought, a grim satisfaction settling in his chest.

Josh crafted encrypted backups and erased any trace of his presence in the system. "You think you're clever, don't you, Vincent?" he said to the screen. "But you've never met a hacker quite like me."

As the progress bar inched towards completion, he hears footsteps approaching. He quickly hid under the desk, holding his breath as a guard entered and did a sweep of the room before leaving.

Safe for the second time tonight—*would a third time be necessary?*—Josh's mind wandered to the future, to the day when they would finally bring Vincent to his knees. *It's like compound interest . . . the longer we let this corruption fester, the bigger the payoff when it all comes crashing down.*

The computer beeped, signaling the end of the download, and Josh—his heart pounding with adrenaline—yanked out the flash drive, tucking it into his pocket. *Time to make like a tree and get the heck out of here.*

He tapped his earpiece, his voice low and urgent. "Darby, Justine, I've got the goods. Let's blow this popsicle stand before Vincent's goons wise up."

Justine and Josh met out front and hopped into the beautiful Vanquish. "Come on Darby," Justine implored.

After what seemed like an hour—but was closer to three minutes—Darby came out and walked to join them, heels in her hands. She opened the passenger door of the two-seater and sat on Justine's lap. "I'm in, let's go!"

Barrick and The Buses

William, Ella, and Tommy piled into the van, their faces taut with tension. The Aston Martin with Darby, Justine, and Josh kicked up rocks and dust as it sped past them. They fell in behind and together, the two vehicles tore out of the ranch, across the cattle guard, and onto the interstate, heading east back towards Elko. Ahead, Darby could see the flashing lights of police cars and security vehicles heading to the ranch, their sirens piercing the night air.

They raced down the highway, the Aston Martin leading the way, its sleek lines cutting through the darkness. In the van behind them, William's mind raced with possibilities, calculating their next move.

"Looks like we really stirred up the hornet's nest," Josh said, a hint of pride in his voice. "Vincent's going to be losing his mind when he realizes what we've done."

Ella nodded, her eyes fixed on the receding lights. "I'd pay good money to see his face right about now."

William's voice cut through the moment of levity, his tone serious. "Let's not celebrate too soon. We're not out of the woods yet."

His words sobered the group, and a sense of unease settled over the team. They had taken a tremendous risk, and now they were hurtling towards an uncertain future, with no way of knowing what lay ahead.

No turning back now, Darby thought, her jaw set with determination. As if sensing her thoughts, Tommy placed a reassuring hand on her shoulder. She met his eyes and saw her own resolve mirrored there.

The ranch disappeared from view, and the team settled into a tense silence, each lost in their own thoughts about the challenges that lay ahead.

As they approached the outskirts of Elko, William finally broke the silence. "We need to ditch these vehicles. They're too recognizable."

Tommy nodded, already scanning the road ahead. "I've got a spot. The hotel Ella stayed at—the Baymont—it's just across the bus parking lot. We can leave them there and proceed on foot to the pickup point."

"And our IDs?" Josh asked, pulling a slim folder from his jacket pocket.

"All set," Ella said, handing out meticulously crafted identification badges. "According to these, we're all maintenance contractors headed to the Goldstrike Mine for the night shift. The bus picks up the morning shift at the lot in fifteen minutes."

Darby examined her badge with an appreciative whistle. "Impressive work as always, Ella. Though I'm not sure Janet Goldstein really captures my essence."

"Sorry I couldn't make you a duchess or something," Ella said with a roll of her eyes. "Next time, you can design your own alias."

They parked the vehicles in the hotel's lot, wiping down surfaces and removing any trace of their presence. The walk to the bus pickup zone was tense but uneventful, the team splitting up as they approached the Maverik parking lot where dozens of miners in reflective gear gathered around multiple Barrick Goldstrike buses.

"Remember, Bus 17," William said under his breath as they dispersed into the crowd.

The team members melted into different clusters of workers, their practiced body language mirroring the weary, pre-shift demeanor of the surrounding miners and support staff. Josh slouched his shoulders, abandoning his usual perfect posture. Tommy adopted the wide-legged stance of someone used to physical labor. Darby pulled her cap lower, avoiding eye contact while maintaining spatial awareness of her teammates.

When Bus 17 opened its doors with a pneumatic hiss, they boarded among the flow of legitimate workers, each flashing their fake IDs with the casual indifference of people who'd done this hundreds of times before. Once inside, they scattered to different sections—Tommy near the emergency exit, Ella toward the middle, Josh and Darby near the front, William and Justine taking seats toward the rear, none making eye contact with each other.

The bus rumbled onto Interstate 80, heading west. Inside, the team maintained their cover identities, some pretending to doze while others scrolled through phones or stared blankly out windows—perfect imitations of workers settling in for their daily commute. After about twenty minutes, the highway signs for Carlin, Nevada appeared, and the bus took the exit. William caught Justine's eye in a fleeting glance, giving an almost imperceptible nod. As the bus slowed and turned onto Newmont Road, leaving the interstate behind, Justine's hand shot to her mouth. Her face paled convincingly as she stumbled to her feet, lurching toward the front of the bus. Their timing had to be perfect—far enough from the main highway to avoid immediate detection, but before they reached the security checkpoints near the mine entrance.

As the bus rolled down the narrow mining road, Justine leaned forward, her mouth to the bus driver's ear, her voice low and urgent. "Listen, I need to get off the bus. I'm going to be sick."

The driver, a grizzled man with a salt-and-pepper beard, shot her a skeptical look in the rearview mirror. "Lady, I've got a schedule to keep. I can't just be making unplanned stops."

Justine fixed him with a steely gaze, her tone brooking no argument. "Trust me, you want to make this stop. Unless you'd like to explain to your bosses why had a very messy accident all over the bus."

The driver's eyes widened, and he quickly signaled to take the next exit. As the bus pulled to a stop at a deserted off ramp, Justine exited, and the team disembarked with her, their hearts pounding with adrenaline.

"Wait, why are all of you leaving?"

They didn't answer and instead headed to the on-ramp on the other side of the unnamed road as the bus slowly pulled back onto the interstate.

Waiting for them in the shadows was a nondescript black Sprinter van, the same one Ella had equipped two weeks earlier. They piled in, taking comfort in the familiar setup of servers, monitors and high-end communication equipment. Tommy claimed the driver's seat and hit the gas, sending them hurtling into the early morning dawn.

While the van sped towards Reno, Ella and Josh settled into the custom workstations Ella had installed. The soft glow of multiple monitors illuminated their faces as they connected to the powerful servers humming in their rack mounts. The air in the van was thick with tension, broken only by the rhythmic purr of the engine and the occasional tap of keys. Outside, the Nevada desert stretched endlessly, a sea of darkness punctuated by the occasional glimmer of distant lights.

Ella's brow furrowed in concentration as the gentle clatter of keystrokes filled the air. "Alright, I'm running a final check on the virus," she said, more to herself than the team. "It's a beauty, if I say so myself. Multi-layered encryption, self-replicating, and with a few surprises thrown in. It'll keep Vincent's tech team chasing their tails for weeks."

Josh nodded approvingly, glancing at the sophisticated equipment surrounding them. "Nice work—both on the virus and this mobile command center. How long before it fully deploys?"

"Should be fully integrated into their systems within the hour," Ella replied, a hint of pride in her voice. "After that, every time they try to access their files, it'll scramble them further. It's like a digital Hydra—cut off one head, two more appear."

As they pulled up file after file from the stolen data, the team's expressions ranged from shock to disgust. William leaned forward, his eyes narrowing as he scanned a particularly damning spreadsheet. "Look at this," he said, his voice low and angry. "They've been systematically overcharging patients for medications. Some of these markups are over 1000%."

Darby let out a low whistle. "And here's a list of *problem employees*," she added, scrolling through another document. "Looks like anyone who tried to blow the whistle got quietly shuffled out . . . or worse."

Tommy's grip tightened on the steering wheel, his knuckles turning white. "Scum," he said. "How many lives have they ruined?"

Justine, who had been uncharacteristically quiet, suddenly spoke up. "It's not just the patients and employees," she said, her voice tight with controlled fury. "Look at this email chain. They've been bribing officials, manipulating research data. The entire healthcare system in these areas is compromised."

The van fell silent as the weight of their discovery settled over them. The Nevada landscape outside seemed to mirror their mood—vast, harsh, and gradually awakening under streaks of amber and lavender as the sun began its slow ascent. In the distance, the lights of a small town dimmed against the growing daylight, a reminder of the lives affected by CBHS's corruption.

William broke the silence, his voice steady despite the anger simmering beneath. "This is bigger than we ever realized," he said, echoing Ella's earlier sentiment. "We've got to get this information out there. People need to know what's been going on."

Ella nodded, her eyes still fixed on the screen. "And they will," she said, determination evident in her tone. "Once this virus fully deploys, CBHS won't be able to hide or destroy anything. Every dirty secret, every corrupt deal—it'll all be there for the world to see."

As the van continued its journey through the night, each team member considered the magnitude of what they'd uncovered and the challenges that lay ahead. The desert night stretched before them, a canvas of possibilities and dangers, much like the path they now found themselves on.

Just then, a notification popped up on the screen. Darby's eyes narrowed as she read the message, a mixture of disbelief and admiration washing over her features.

"Well, I'll be damned," Darby said. "Looks like our resident wild card has pulled off a little heist of her own. Amelia just informed me she's *borrowed* Vincent's yacht."

William's eyebrows shot up. "The *Artemisa*? That wasn't part of the plan."

"Since when do our plans ever go according to plan?" Josh asked, but his nervous laugh betrayed his unease.

Ella leaned in, her brow furrowed. "This complicates things. We'll need to adjust our escape route, our timeline . . ."

"And our cover story," Justine added. "A missing yacht isn't exactly low profile."

Tommy's hands tightened on the steering wheel. "We'll make it work. We always do."

The team spent the next hour brainstorming contingencies, weighing options from ditching the yacht after extracting its data to using it as a high-stakes decoy. William pulled up nautical charts on his tablet, studying potential routes and safe harbors, while Justine began drafting cover stories. Even Tommy contributed, drawing on his military experience to suggest offshore rendezvous points.

They were in the middle of debating the merits of a Bahamian port versus a secluded Caribbean cove when the radio crackled to life.

"Guys, I've got a situation." Amelia's voice came through, tension clear beneath her controlled tone. "I'm about 60 miles off the coast and the yacht's autopilot is malfunctioning."

"Amelia?" They all replied in unison, conversation forgotten.

"I'm ok, but piloting a yacht. Solo. On a boat normally staffed by a dozen crewmembers. Yeah, it's a bit much."

Tommy, though he was driving, was familiar with the area. "Can you make it another 25 miles? Freeport, in the Bahamas, isn't too far away."

"I think so, but then what?"

"Get there, check into the Paradise Cove Resort. We'll meet you there in time for a late dinner."

"I can do that. See you then."

As the call ended, the team exchanged glances, a mix of excitement, trepidation, and determination crackling in the air.

"Alright," William said, taking charge. "Change of plans. Josh, start looking for private charters out of Reno. We need to be in the air as soon as we hit the city."

Josh nodded as he pecked at the laptop's keys with deliberate focus. "On it. I might know a guy who owes me a favor. And Ella, make sure you cover our digital tracks. We can't have Vincent or his team following us."

"Consider it done," Ella replied, cracking her knuckles before diving back into her work.

"Darby, Justine," William continued, "start working on our cover story. We need a reason for a group of strangers to be chartering a plane to the Bahamas on short notice."

The two women nodded, already putting their heads together and murmuring ideas.

As the van sped towards Reno, the Nevada desert flying by outside the windows, William couldn't help but feel a surge of pride. They had pulled off the impossible, stealing right out from under Vincent's nose. And now, Amelia's unexpected move sent them toward a rendezvous that could change everything.

He allowed himself a small smile. They had come this far, risked everything to bring CBHS to justice. The finish line was in sight, but the race wasn't over yet. As the lights of Reno began to glimmer on the horizon, William knew one thing for certain: they couldn't afford to let their guard down now.

The real adventure was just beginning.

FakeAccountMcStealy

The Sprinter van hurtled down the Nevada highway, its occupants a curious mix of tension and excitement. William's fingers drummed an impatient staccato beat on the dashboard, his casual button-down and khaki shorts chosen specifically for this mission. His eyes, hidden behind aviator sunglasses, scanned the horizon restlessly.

Tommy, still in his catering uniform with the bowtie hanging loosely around his neck, gripped the steering wheel with laser focus. "You know . . . when I signed up for this, I didn't realize *wheelman* would be such a literal part of my job description."

In the back, the rest of the team had spread out, each engrossed in their own crucial tasks. Josh sat with perfect posture on one of the bench seats, his laptop balanced on his knees as he chatted animatedly on his phone. Despite the getaway circumstances, he'd maintained his sartorial standards with a tailored linen blazer over a crisp button-down—though he'd conceded to their *tourist* cover with a subtle tropical pocket square. The overall effect was that of a wealthy financier on vacation, which wasn't far from the truth.

"Yeah, we need a Falcon 2000EX for a direct flight from Reno to Freeport, Bahamas. Pronto," Josh said into the phone, giving a thumbs up to William. "Oh, and make sure it's fully stocked. We've got a long journey ahead."

Beside him, Ella hunched over her own laptop as she attacked the keys with furious intensity, thoughts racing ahead of her fingers. She'd changed into a striking color-block sweater—soft pink on top, transitioning to a vibrant yellow—paired with relaxed-fit jeans and sleek black ankle boots. Her dark hair fell in casual waves, framing her face as she scrutinized the screen through stylish cat-eye sunglasses.

Ella's focus was laser-sharp as she worked to cover their digital tracks:

- She deployed a series of complex VPNs and proxy servers to mask their online activities, muttering, "Try following this breadcrumb trail, Vincent. It'll lead you straight to Nowhere, Population: Your Ego."

- Creating and scattering fake digital footprints across the internet, she simulated travel plans to various locations. "A little vacation in Bali, a business trip to Tokyo, maybe a quick jaunt to Antarctica . . . Let's see them try to pin us down now."

- She initiated a cascading deletion protocol for all their temporary accounts and login credentials used during the heist. "Goodbye, FakeAccountMcStealyFace. You served us well."

- Implementing a series of time-delayed malware programs designed to corrupt and erase any potential evidence left on CBHS systems. "Here's a little parting gift, Vincent. Hope you like digital confetti."

- Setting up an intricate alert system to monitor for any signs of pursuit or investigation. "If anyone so much as googles *CBHS scandal*, we'll know before they hit Enter."

Darby and Justine sat opposite them, deep in conversation. Darby's blonde hair whipped wildly from the open window, her white linen shirt and high-waisted jeans giving her a carefree look. Justine, in a flowy sundress with a vibrant tropical print, scrolled through her phone, her fiery red hair pulled back in a messy bun.

"Alright," Darby said, her voice carrying a hint of mischief. "We need a cover story so airtight it could survive a deep-sea dive. Any brilliant ideas floating around in that PR-savvy brain of yours, Justine?"

Justine's lips curled into a sly smile. "Well, we could always go with the classic *impromptu bachelor party* excuse. Nothing says *last-minute charter flight* quite like a group of friends whisking the groom away for one last hurrah."

As the team worked, bantered, and planned, the van sped towards Reno and their awaiting escape plan. They were a curious sight—part vacationers, part business group, all united in their mission to outrun a billionaire's wrath and expose a corrupt empire. The thrill of uncertainty hung in the air like an intoxicating perfume, driving them forward into whatever fate awaited in the Bahamas.

· · · ● · ● · ● · · ·

The Sprinter van pulled up to the small private airport with a screech of tires. Tommy hopped out and headed to chat up the pretty clerk at the desk to hurry along with their travel arrangements. William surveyed his team as they gathered their few bags. Anticipation thrummed in the air, along with a giddy sense that anything was possible.

As the shining Falcon jet taxied into view, Darby let out a low whistle. "Hello gorgeous," she said, eyeing the sleek plane.

"I call dibs on the window seat!" Justine announced, shouldering past the others to climb aboard.

William caught Ella's eye, and they shared a smile. She looked more alive than he'd seen her in years, eyes sparkling with purpose.

· · · ● · ● · ● · · ·

Meanwhile, many miles away, Amelia maneuvered the stolen yacht *Artemisa* into port at Bradford Marine in Freeport. The 190-foot vessel glided through the crystal-clear waters, its sleek lines drawing admiring glances from other boaters. Amelia's hands were steady on the controls, her posture relaxed but alert, exuding the confidence of a seasoned sailor.

As the yacht approached the dock, she called out instructions to the waiting crew with the authoritative tone of someone born to command. The dockworkers, impressed by her skill, secured the lines. Amelia stepped onto the dock, her sea legs adjusting effortlessly to solid ground. She took a moment to breathe in the salty air, relishing the feel of the warm Bahamian breeze tousling her hair. A satisfied smirk played on her lips—she was back in her element, and it felt damn good.

Without missing a beat, Amelia strode towards the marina office, her eyes scanning for a familiar face. She spotted Rick, the manager, a burly man with sun-weathered skin and a no-nonsense demeanor. As she approached, she was already planning her request—a full servicing for the Artemisa, including a fix for the temperamental autopilot.

"Rick," she began, her voice carrying across the dock, "I need a full—"

But Rick held up a hand, cutting her off mid-sentence. "No need to explain, Amelia. Tommy already filled me in on everything." A knowing look passed between them, a silent acknowledgment of shared history and trust.

Amelia's eyebrows rose, impressed by her team's efficiency. "Tommy always was one step ahead," she said, a hint of admiration in her voice.

Rick nodded, his expression serious but not unkind. "We've got you covered. The boys are already prepping to give your lady a full once-over. And don't worry about accommodations—I've set you up with a villa on the Bell Channel Waterway in Lucaya. Private, secure, and with a view that'll knock your socks off."

Relief washed over Amelia, though she kept her composure. "Appreciate it, Rick. I owe you one."

"Just doing my job," Rick said gruffly, but there was a glimmer of warmth in his eyes. "We'll have the *Artemisa* shipshape and delivered to you when the work's done. Now go get some rest—you look like you've been through hell and back."

Amelia chuckled, the sound tinged with exhaustion. "You have no idea."

With a final nod of thanks, Amelia headed towards the waiting car that would take her to the Scarborough Villas. The drive was a blur of lush tropical scenery and pastel-colored buildings, but Amelia's mind was already racing ahead to the next steps of their plan.

Arriving at the villa, she took a moment to appreciate the luxurious surroundings—all funded by Vincent's ill-gotten gains. There was a certain poetic justice to it that brought a smile to her face.

After a quick but thorough security check of the premises (*new* habits die hard), Amelia finally allowed herself to relax. She shed her salt-stained clothes and stepped into a steaming shower, letting the hot water wash away the stress and grime of the past few days.

Clean and refreshed, Amelia slipped into the outdoor hot tub, the warm jets working magic on her tense muscles. As she soaked, her mind drifted to the challenges ahead. They had pulled off the impossible, but the game was far from over.

Glancing at her waterproof watch, she noted the time. The others would land soon, bringing with them a treasure trove of stolen data and a host of new complications.

"Bring it on," Amelia said to herself, her voice barely audible over the bubbling water. She was ready for whatever came next—after all, she'd just captained a stolen superyacht across international waters. How much harder could the rest be?

As the sun began to set, painting the sky in brilliant hues of orange and pink, Amelia allowed herself a moment of quiet satisfaction. Phase one was complete. Now, the real work would begin.

· · · ● · ● · · ·

The team entered the villa, marveling at the luxurious surroundings. Darby let out a low whistle. "Damn, Amelia. You sure know how to pick a hideout."

"Only the best for this crew of maritime felons," Amelia said with a smirk. "I figured after temporarily liberating a multimillion-dollar vessel, we deserved at least a thousand thread count."

They gathered around the expansive dining table, the ocean breeze drifting through open French doors. William surveyed his ragtag band of thieves-turned-justice-seekers with something like pride.

"So," he said, leaning back in his chair, "we've stolen this yacht, outrun the Coast Guard, and have enough incriminating evidence to sink CBHS. Thoreau would be so disappointed I didn't just build a simple cabin in the woods."

Darby snorted. "Speaking of simple solutions, why don't we just charter another plane and fly back to the US? We can get what we need from the boat and be done with it."

"I don't think it will be that easy," said Tommy. "I know how the military hides information in boats; it could take us days to extract all we need."

"Ok," Darby said, "can we just take it with us?"

Josh pulled out his laptop, his fingers flying across the keys with practiced precision. "I've been crunching the numbers. If we pilot the *Artemisa* at a speed of 14 knots, we can reach New England in about four and a half days. That should—hopefully—give us enough time to grab what we need from the boat."

"Well, I always wanted to be a sailor. How hard could it be? It's not like we're trying to navigate the Bermuda Triangle . . . oh wait."

Ella raised an eyebrow. "Ha ha, Darby. But seriously, four and a half days on the open ocean? That's no pleasure cruise."

"No, it's not," Justine said, her red hair glinting in the sunlight streaming through the windows. "We'll need to be prepared for anything. Storms, mechanical issues, you name it."

Tommy nodded, his expression serious. "We'll need to work in shifts, keep a constant watch. It's going to be grueling."

William stood up, his presence commanding attention. "But we can do it. We've all faced worse than a little seasickness and sleep deprivation."

Darby leaned back in her chair, a sly grin on her face. "Plus, think of the tan we'll get. Nothing like a little ocean voyage to give you that perfect glow."

The team chuckled, the tension easing. Ella turned to Josh, her dark eyes serious. "What about supplies? We can't exactly stop at a grocery store in the middle of the Atlantic."

Josh nodded, already hammering at the keys. "I'm on it. I'll make sure we're fully stocked before we leave. Food, water, medicine, the works."

Amelia stood up, her eyes glinting with determination. "Salem, here we come."

As the team dispersed to make their preparations, William caught Amelia's eye. She gave him a small smile, a silent acknowledgment of their closeness and of the challenges ahead. They were in this together, come hell or high water.

• • • ● • ● • ● • •

Josh approached the team just before dinner on their first night. "Ella and I have looked at all we've done over the past couple of days. We thought you'd like a summary."

Josh laid out what they had:

Vincent's Personal Finance Ledger

- $5 million in "consulting fees" to a shell company owned by his brother-in-law

- $2 million for a "team-building exercise" that suspiciously resembled a week-long yacht party in the Mediterranean

- $500,000 for "office supplies," which included a gold-plated stapler and diamond-encrusted paperclips

- Receipts for several high-end purchases, including a $200,000 watch that Josh said "could probably tell time on Mars, not that Vincent would ever need to know that"

CBHS Cash

- $10 million in "petty cash" hidden in a safe behind a portrait of Vincent himself

- A series of checks made out to various politicians, with memo lines like "for your consideration" and "golf lessons"

- A stack of gift cards to luxury retailers, totaling over $1 million, earmarked for "employee appreciation" but never distributed

Artemisa

- The yacht itself, which Amelia noted was "a bit much, even for a man compensating for something"

- A collection of rare wines valued at over $2 million, which Tommy suggested they use "to disinfect any wounds we might get while escaping"

- A state-of-the-art communication system that Ella remarked was "probably used more for insider trading than maritime emergencies"

Hard Drive

- Details of 17 offshore accounts in various tax havens, holding a total of $357 million

- A list of shell companies with names so ridiculous that Darby wondered if Vincent "got them from a random corporate name generator while drunk"

- Encrypted files revealing a network of bribed officials and blackmailed competitors, which Josh described as "a Who's Who of corruption, or as Vincent probably calls it, his Christmas card list"

Additional CBHS Documents

- Internal memos outlining strategies to deny insurance claims, which William dubbed "a masterclass in corporate empathy"

- A detailed plan for artificially inflating drug prices, complete with a chart showing "optimal price points for maximum profit and minimal conscience"

- HR files on whistleblowers who were quietly "relocated," prompting Justine to mutter, "I guess CBHS has a very broad definition of 'employee wellness program"

As the team reviewed their haul, Ella summed it up with a wry smile: "Well, folks, we've just inherited enough dirt to start our own corrupt corporate empire. Who's in for CBHS 2.0?"

· · · ● · ● ● · · ·

The *Artemisa* cut through the waves like a knife through butter, the salty spray misting the deck as they sailed past the South Carolina coast. William stood at the helm, his weathered hands gripping the wheel, eyes fixed on the horizon. A sense of purpose coursed through his veins, mingling with the thrill of the open sea.

Darby lounged near the yacht's bow, her blonde hair whipping in the sea breeze. She stretched languidly, a wry smile playing on her lips. "Ah, nothing like a leisurely cruise up the East Coast," she said, loud enough for everyone to hear. "Just us, the ocean, and the looming threat of federal prosecution."

The team chuckled, their laughter carried away by the wind. Suddenly, the satellite phone crackled to life, its harsh ring cutting through the peaceful atmosphere. Darby snatched it up, her posture shifting from relaxed to alert in an instant.

"Well, well, if it isn't the motley crew," Vincent's smooth voice oozed through the speaker, dripping with false charm. "Enjoying *my* boat on your little pleasure cruise?"

Ella, hunched over her laptop nearby, said under her breath, "Great, just when I thought we'd run out of opportunities for things to go horribly wrong."

Darby's grip on the phone tightened, but her voice remained playful. "Oh Vincent, I was truly hoping you'd call. How are you?"

"*Vivian*, or should I say Darby," Vincent said, his tone a mix of amusement and menace. "It's great to hear your voice. I heard through the grapevine that you're headed up the coast. I thought we could have a little chat, maybe come to an arrangement. Perhaps meet. Negotiate."

Ella couldn't contain herself. She snatched the phone from Darby's hand, her voice sharp. "We're not making deals with you, Vincent. You've taken enough from the world already."

"Ah, this must be Ella, the feisty IT pro." Vincent's condescension was palpable. "Let's be realistic here. You're out of your depth. I have resources, connections. What do you have? A stolen yacht and a ragtag bunch of misfits?"

Josh leaned in, his voice low and intense. "We have something you'll never understand, Vincent. Loyalty. And a burning desire to see you pay for what you've done."

Vincent's laughter echoed through the phone, cold and mirthless. "And Josh, is it? You speak of loyalty? In this business? That's cute. Let me make one thing clear. I can make your lives painful. But let's not let it get that far. Meet with me and my team. Let's chat. Work this out."

Darby reclaimed the phone—a little surprised he knew who they were—her voice was steady and still playful. "One week, Vincent. Gloucester. We'll settle this once and for all."

"I look forward to it." Vincent's tone was icy. "Don't disappoint me."

The line went dead, and Darby tossed the phone aside with a flourish. "Well, that was dramatic," she said, eyebrow arched.

Tommy, leaning against the railing, shrugged his broad shoulders. "What did you expect? The man's got a flair for theatrics."

Justine joined them, the wind whipping her fiery hair around her face. "He's scared. He knows what we have."

Darby nodded, a grim smile spreading across her face. "Damn right he is."

William and Amelia emerged from the cabin, their expressions serious but determined. William's voice carried across the deck. "This meeting was inevitable, really. We'll meet with him in Gloucester, down the road from Addison Gilbert. A reminder for him that harming small communities has consequences. We won't let him off the hook. Instead, we'll set that hook deeper."

Darby couldn't resist. "And could there be a more fitting place for such a fishing analogy? Well played, William."

As the *Artemisa* sailed on, the team settled into a determined silence. The sun began to set, painting the sky in brilliant shades of orange and pink. William looked out over the water, a sense of anticipation building in his chest. One week. One final showdown. And then, finally, they would have their revenge.

With its unlikely heroes aboard, the yacht continued its northward journey towards an inevitable confrontation. The gentle lapping of waves against the hull and the steady hum of the engines provided a soothing backdrop to their swirling thoughts and steely resolve.

The Moral Minute—Episode 7

[Theme music—short, serious but with an edge]

ANIE: I'm Anie Chen.

LUCAS: And I'm Lucas Rodriguez. Welcome to The Moral Minute, where we examine the day's most egregious ethical failures in corporate America.

ANIE: Follow the money, they say. Well, we followed CBHS's money, and guess where it led?

LUCAS: [dry] Let me guess—not to patient care.

ANIE: Documents obtained by our team show a labyrinth of offshore accounts, shell companies, and suspicious transactions.

LUCAS: My personal favorite? A $2.5 million "consulting fee" to a company owned by Vincent's brother-in-law.

ANIE: [deadpan] Must be some consultant.

LUCAS: Then there's the $10 million in "petty cash" hidden in a safe behind—get this—a portrait of Vincent himself.

ANIE: [amused] Nothing says subtle like hiding money behind your own portrait.

LUCAS: But here's what's really interesting—federal investigators are starting to connect the dots. Sources say a grand jury in Boston is already looking into some suspicious transactions.

ANIE: Time's almost up. What's our moral of the minute?

LUCAS: When your financial records read like a crime novel, the next chapter might be written in a courtroom.

[Theme music fades out]

The Invisible Hand of
The Market

The sleek *Artemisa* glided through Gloucester's Harbor Cove, navigating past weathered fishing trawlers, whale watching charters, and gleaming pleasure boats. The yacht slipped by industrial buildings and seafood processing plants that lined the waterfront . . . structures that celebrated the town's rich maritime heritage. Josh stood on deck, the salty sea breeze ruffling his perfectly coiffed hair as he surveyed the twinkling lights of their destination—the Beauport Hotel—as they cruised past. He couldn't help but smile wryly. If only the unsuspecting CEO of CBHS knew the storm that was about to hit them . . .

Ella emerged from below deck, her usual casual demeanor replaced by a focused intensity that matched her sleek black attire. Josh noticed the transformation—she was all business tonight. The girl was a chameleon . . . from skater girl to runway model to chic spy; she could easily adapt to any situation. A useful skill in their line of work.

"Looking sharp," he said as she took her place beside him at the railing. "Ready to give CBHS a lesson in cybersecurity?"

"Oh, I've been ready. Their firewalls are about as effective as a chain-link fence against a tank." She cracked her knuckles. "It's like they're begging to be hacked."

Josh chuckled, shaking his head. The girl's wit was as sharp as her coding skills. Together, they made a formidable team. The *Artemisa* glided up to the private dock, and the crew swiftly secured her. Josh took a deep breath, the crisp night air filling his lungs. This was it. The calm before the storm.

As they made their way from the dock, past a large ice supplier and multiple seafood companies, and then up the street to the hotel, Josh's mind raced with calculations and contingencies, running through the plan like a complex equation. There could be no margin for error. Not with the stakes this high.

· · · ●· ● ·· ·

The Beauport Hotel's lobby exuded an air of casual elegance, blending coastal charm with a sophisticated design. A spacious area greeted guests, its high ceilings adorned with a series of gleaming brass lantern-style light fixtures that cast a warm, inviting glow throughout the space.

The lobby floor was a striking pattern of navy blue and cream, with geometric designs that evoked both nautical themes and modern aesthetics. Comfortable seating areas were strategically placed and featured a mix of striped armchairs, plush sofas in neutral tones, and accent chairs with bold patterns. The tufted leather ottoman served as a central coffee table, its rich caramel color adding warmth to the cool blues dominating the space.

The lobby's design balanced nautical elements with contemporary luxury, creating an atmosphere that was both relaxing and refined. It was a space that invited guests to linger, whether to admire the carefully curated maritime artwork or to sink into one of the inviting chairs and watch the world go by. But Josh and Ella had no time to linger. Instead, they stepped onto the nautical-inspired carpet and marched past the front desk. Just another wealthy couple on a romantic getaway. If only they knew.

The door to the lavish suite clicked shut behind them, revealing a space that echoed the maritime charm of Gloucester. More navy and white striped carpeting complemented the pale blue walls, while strategically placed lamps cast a warm glow over the carefully curated nautical accents. Josh got to work at the small wood desk, pulling out his laptop and connecting to the hotel's Wi-Fi via secure VPN. Ella flopped onto the king-sized bed, her own computer already whirring to life on her lap; her task was to hack into CBHS to monitor what they were doing to prepare for their upcoming meeting. Josh focused on gaining access to the hotel's system. They needed this to execute a future part of the plan.

There was a knock on the door; William and Amelia were there.

Fifteen minutes later came another knock came as Darby, Tommy, and Justine joined them.

Josh leaned back in his chair, watching the moonlight play over the harbor outside their window. The pieces were falling into place. CBHS wouldn't know what hit them during their *negotiations*. And he couldn't wait to watch them squirm.

• • • ●•●• • •

In a separate part of the suite, Amelia paced, her mind whirring with strategies and contingencies. William sat in a patterned armchair, his eyes locked on the computer screen as he reviewed their plan for the upcoming confrontation.

"We need to anticipate their every move," Amelia said, her voice tight with determination. "Vincent's not going to make this easy for us."

William glanced up, his gaze sharp. "We've got him cornered, Amelia. With the setup we have, he won't be able to wriggle out of this one."

Amelia nodded, but the crease between her brows remained. "I want to make sure we're prepared for anything if Vincent tries to pull any last-minute stunts."

"We'll be ready," William assured her, his tone unwavering. "We've got the truth on our side. And when we're done, the whole world will know exactly what kind of operation they've been running."

Amelia's lips curved into a smirk, her eyes glinting with anticipation. "I can't wait to see the look on Vincent's face when he realizes he's walked right into our trap."

William laughed, leaning back in his chair. "It's going to be a thing of beauty. CBHS won't know what hit them."

• • • ●•●• • •

Tommy moved silently through the hotel corridors, his eyes scanning every nook and cranny for potential security risks. The plush carpets and gilded fixtures of the Beauport

Hotel seemed at odds with his military precision, but Tommy knew better than to let his guard down.

"Place is locked up tight," he said under his breath, his gaze flicking to the security cameras tucked discreetly in the corners. "At least we won't have to worry about any unwanted guests crashing the party."

He paused outside the team's suite, his hand resting lightly on the doorknob. This was a different kind of mission, Tommy reminded himself. A battle fought with words and wits instead of brute force.

· · · ● · ● · · ·

In the elegant conference room of the Beauport Hotel, Ella moved with focused intensity, her dark hair pulled back in a sleek ponytail. She wore a fitted black blazer with subtle leather trim over a flowing white top, paired with dark slim-fit jeans. The room exuded a refined maritime charm, with its cream-striped wallpaper, ornate brass chandeliers, and large windows offering a breathtaking view of Gloucester Harbor and the Atlantic Ocean beyond.

"We need eyes and ears on every angle," she said, adjusting a camera's position with deft fingers. "Can't risk missing a single incriminating moment."

Josh nodded, his hands busy with a tangle of wires beneath one of the navy blue table-cloths. "Got it covered. These babies will pick up everything from a whisper to a shout."

Ella glanced over at him, a smirk playing at the corners of her mouth. "Just make sure you don't accidentally broadcast any of your lame jokes. We want to take down CBHS, not bore them to death."

"Ouch." Josh clutched his chest in mock hurt. "You wound me, Ella. My jokes are the stuff of legend."

"Yeah, legendary for clearing a room faster than a nor'easter," Ella said, her gaze drawn to the Fisherman's Memorial statue visible on Stacy Boulevard.

As they worked, the gravity of their mission settled over them. This room, with its picturesque view and refined decor, would soon become the final stage for CBHS's downfall. Ella couldn't help but appreciate the irony—such a beautiful setting for such an ugly truth to be revealed.

"All set on my end," Josh announced, straightening up. "I wired this room tighter than a lobster trap."

Ella nodded, doing one last sweep. "Good. Let's hope Vincent and his comrades take the bait."

As they stepped back to survey their handiwork, the late afternoon sun glinted off the harbor waters, casting a golden glow across the room. It was almost time. Soon, this serene space would become the epicenter of a storm that would shake CBHS to its core.

$$\cdot \; \bullet \; \bullet \; \bullet \; \bullet \; \bullet \; \bullet \; \bullet \; \cdot$$

Back in their suite, Ella's fingers hit the keyboard at her characteristic rapid-fire pace, her eyes locked on the screen as she set up the secure livestream. The rest of the team gathered around her, their faces tense with anticipation.

"We're almost ready," Ella said, her voice tight with concentration. "Just need to make sure the feed is untraceable. Can't have CBHS finding out where we are."

William nodded, his gaze fixed on the monitors displaying the conference room. "They won't know what hit them. We've got enough evidence to bury them ten times over."

"Let's hope so," Amelia said, her arms crossed tightly over her chest. "We're taking an enormous risk here. If this doesn't work."

"It'll work," Ella said, her fingers never slowing their relentless pace. "It has to. We've come too far to fail now."

As the final pieces of the livestream fell into place, Ella sat back in her chair, a sense of grim satisfaction settling over her. "We're live in three, two, one."

The screens flickered to life, the conference room awash in the harsh glare of hidden cameras. The trap was set, the bait laid out for CBHS to stumble into.

And as Ella watched the three executives file into the room, their faces smug with un-earned confidence, she felt a thrill of anticipation run through her.

"Showtime," she whispered, a predatory smile curving her lips. "Let the games begin."

• • • • • • • • • • •

The door to the conference room swung open, and Vincent strode in, his Brioni hand-made Italian suit hanging just right, his silver hair gleaming under the fluorescent lights. Sam and Kiran followed close behind, their expressions a mix of smug superiority and barely concealed nervousness.

Darby leaned forward, her eyes glued to the monitors. "Well, well, well," she said, her voice dripping with sarcasm. "If it isn't the unholy trinity of healthcare fraud. Vincent looks like he just stepped out of a Forbes magazine photoshoot."

Josh snorted, his fingers tapping restlessly on the table. "More like a wanted poster. I'm surprised he's not wearing a black hat and twirling a mustache."

Darby grinned, her eyes sparkling with mischief. "Give it time. I'm sure he'll break out the evil laugh any minute now."

On the screen, Vincent took his seat at the head of the table, his posture radiating confidence. Sam and Kiran flanked him on either side, their gazes darting around the room as if searching for hidden threats.

"Paranoid much?" Darby said. "You'd think they were expecting an ambush or some-thing."

William leaned forward, his eyes narrowed. "They should be. They just don't know it yet."

Darby nodded, her gaze never leaving the screen. She watched as Vincent leaned back in his chair, his hands steepled in front of him like a cartoon villain.

"Let's get started, shall we?" he said, his voice smooth as silk. "We have a lot to discuss."

Darby rolled her eyes. "Oh, I'm sure you do, Vincent. Too bad it's all lies and bullshit."

She glanced over at Ella, who was monitoring the livestream with a fierce intensity. "How's our audience looking?"

Ella grinned, her fingers flying over the keyboard. "We've got viewers from all over the world. Media outlets, government agencies, even a few healthcare watchdog groups. Word is spreading fast."

Darby nodded, a sense of satisfaction washing over her. "Good. Let's make sure they get a front-row seat to the downfall of CBHS."

She turned back to the screen, her gaze fixed on Vincent's smug face. "You're going down," she whispered, her voice filled with a muted fury. "And the entire world is going to watch."

On the conference room screen, a video flickered to life, casting an eerie glow on Vincent's face. His self-assured smile faltered as images of CBHS's misdeeds played out before him.

"What the hell is this?" he demanded, his voice losing its smooth edge.

The video cut to a shot of the team, their faces obscured by shadows. "This, Vincent, is the truth," a distorted voice announced. "The truth about your company's crimes, your greed, and your utter disregard for human life."

Vincent's eyes widened, his composure slipping. "This is outrageous! You have no proof—"

The screen split into multiple windows, each displaying damning evidence. Internal emails, financial records, and secret recordings of Vincent himself, discussing the company's unethical practices with a callous indifference.

"No proof?" the voice mocked. "We have everything we need to bring you down, Vincent. And the world is watching."

Vincent's gaze darted around the room, as if seeking an escape. He leaned forward, his voice low and menacing. "Listen, whoever you are, we can make a deal. Name your price, and I'll make this all go away."

In their suite, Josh snorted. "Wow, he's actually trying to bribe us. How cliché."

Amelia shook her head, her eyes never leaving the screen. "He's desperate. He knows he's trapped."

The voice on the video laughed, a harsh, grating sound. "You still don't get it, do you, Vincent? This isn't about money. It's about justice. It's about exposing the truth and making sure you pay for your crimes."

More evidence flooded the screens, each revelation more shocking than the last. Vincent's face paled, his hands clenching the table until his knuckles turned white.

"This can't be happening," he said, his voice barely audible. "I'm untouchable. I'm—"

"You're finished," the voice interrupted. "Your empire is crumbling, Vincent. And there's nothing you can do to stop it."

Vincent's composure shattered, his carefully crafted mask of confidence crumbling away. He looked small, defeated, like a man who had finally realized the magnitude of his own hubris. The team watched with a mix of satisfaction and anticipation. They had done it. They had exposed the truth and brought a corrupt corporation to its knees. But their work was far from over.

Unexpectedly, CFO Sam rose from her seat, her eyes darting between Vincent and the screens. "I can't do this anymore," she said, her voice trembling. "I won't be a part of this."

Vincent's head snapped towards her, his eyes narrowing. "Sam, what are you doing?"

Sam ignored him, stepping forward and facing the hidden cameras. "I have additional information." She pulled an encrypted phone from her jacket pocket, her fingers moving swiftly across the screen. "Financial records, emails, even recorded conversations. Everything you need to prove Vincent's guilt."

In the adjacent room, Ella leaned forward, her fingers flying over the keyboard. "She's accessing CBHS's servers," she said, her voice tinged with disbelief. "She's sending us the files."

Josh let out a low whistle. "Looks like someone grew a conscience."

"We already had them, by the way, but it's nice to see genuine remorse," said Ella.

"Or fear," countered Amelia.

On the screen, Vincent's face contorted with rage. "You traitor," he said, lunging towards Sam. "I'll destroy you for this."

But before he could reach her, the doors burst open, and a team of OIG agents swarmed the room. "Vincent Blackwell," the lead agent said, his voice booming. "You're under arrest for Medicare fraud, embezzlement, securities fraud, money laundering . . ."

Vincent's eyes widened, his mouth opening and closing like a fish out of water. "This is a mistake," he blustered, even as the agents cuffed his hands behind his back. "I'm innocent. I'm being set up."

". . . kickback schemes, HIPAA violations, tax evasion, obstruction of justice . . ."

Vincent just sat there now, the reality of the situation becoming more tangible.

". . . patient neglect, violation of the False Claims Act."

"But I wanted to help people. I never meant to hurt anyone."

The agent smirked. "Tell it to the judge," he said, dragging Vincent towards the door.

As the team watched, officers took Kiran into custody; shock and resignation were etched on her face. She remained silent. Sam stood to the side, her shoulders slumped, her eyes haunted.

"I'm sorry," she whispered, her voice barely audible over the chaos. "I should have done this sooner."

Amelia leaned back in her chair, a sense of satisfaction washing over her. "We did it," she said, her voice soft. "We actually did it."

William nodded, a small smile playing at the corners of his mouth as he watched the corrupt empire crumble before him. He'd once studied Adam Smith's theories about the invisible hand of the market; now he and his team had become that hand, redistributing wealth back to those who deserved it. "CBHS is finished," he said. "And Vincent will finally face the consequences of his actions."

But even as they celebrated their victory, they knew that their work was far from over. There would be fallout from this, questions to answer and loose ends to tie up. For now, they could savor the moment—and perhaps a well-earned nap.

As the chaos of the arrests filled the conference room, the team seized their opportunity to slip away unnoticed. Josh, his eyes gleaming with mischief, led the way through the hotel's labyrinthine corridors, his steps as silent as a cat burglar's. Amelia followed close behind, her heart pounding with adrenaline and the thrill of their victory.

They emerged into the bright sunlight, the salty tang of the ocean air filling their lungs. Josh scanned the horizon, his keen eyes taking in every detail. "Coast is clear," he said, a smile playing at the corners of his mouth. "Looks like the OIG has their hands full with our friends from CBHS."

Amelia couldn't help but grin. "I almost feel sorry for them," she said, her voice dripping with sarcasm. "Almost."

They made their way to the rendezvous point, where the rest of the team was waiting. Tommy, ever the vigilant security expert, kept watch, his eyes constantly moving, searching for any signs of trouble. Ella monitored the recording, ensuring that the evidence of CBHS's crimes continued to spread like wildfire across the internet.

As they gathered, Josh clapped his hands together, a mischievous glint in his eye. "Well, team," he said, his voice filled with barely contained glee, "I'd say that was our Ocean's Eleven moment, minus the Vegas glitz and the Brad Pitt eye candy."

Amelia rolled her eyes, but she couldn't help but laugh. Leave it to Josh to find humor in even the most serious of situations. "More like Ocean's Six," she said, her voice dry. "But I'll take it."

"What do you mean, Six? I count seven here."

Amelia blushed. "Thank you Josh. I'm honored to be one of you."

William, ever the strategist, was already looking ahead. "We need to monitor the fallout," he said, his brow furrowed in thought. "The rest of the CBHS Board won't go down without a fight, and we need to be prepared for any counterattacks."

Josh nodded, his expression sobering. "Agreed," he said, his mind already churning with calculations and contingencies. "But for now, I say we take a moment to celebrate. We just took down one of the biggest corporate sharks in the game and exposed their dirty laundry for all the world to see. That's no small feat."

As they stood there, watching the distant figures of the OIG agents loading the CBHS executives into waiting cars, Amelia felt a sense of pride and accomplishment wash over her. They had done it. They had struck a blow against the corrupt and the greedy, and had emerged victorious.

SPECIAL REPORT: The Fall of CBHS

TechTruth News Special with Anie Chen

Transcript from broadcast

[Theme music—dramatic, news-like opening]

ANNOUNCER: This is a TechTruth News Special Report. Live from Boston, here's Anie Chen.

ANIE: Good evening. I'm Anie Chen, and this is a TechTruth News Special Report: "The Fall of CBHS: How America's Healthcare Giant Crumbled." For the past week, we've been following the unprecedented collapse of Coastal Beacon Health System, once the fifth-largest healthcare provider in the nation. Tonight, we examine the far-reaching consequences of what federal prosecutors are calling "the most egregious case of healthcare fraud in American history."

[Montage of news headlines appears on screen]

- "CBHS CEO Vincent Blackwell Arrested on 47 Counts of Fraud"

- "Healthcare Giant's Stock Plummets 87% in Wake of Scandal"

- "Federal Authorities Seize CBHS Assets in Multi-State Operation"

- "OIG: 'Just the Tip of the Iceberg' in Healthcare Corruption Case"

ANIE: The spectacular downfall began with what appeared to be a routine business meeting at Gloucester's Beauport Hotel. Instead, Vincent Blackwell and his executive team found themselves facing Office of Inspector General agents, armed with what sources describe as "meticulously organized evidence" of years of systematic fraud.

But perhaps most remarkable is what happened next. Just days after the arrests, reports began emerging of mysterious payments to former patients and employees—restitution from an anonymous source.

We begin tonight with TechTruth correspondent Lucas Rodriguez at Addison Gilbert Hospital in Gloucester, where the community is still reeling from the revelations.

LUCAS: Anie, I'm standing outside Addison Gilbert Hospital, one of the many community hospitals acquired by CBHS in recent years. Just behind me, workers are already removing the CBHS signage from the building entrance.

The mood here is a complex mixture of shock, vindication, and cautious optimism. For many, the collapse of CBHS feels like liberation.

JENNY MARKHAM (Office Manager): [Emotional] They gutted this hospital from the inside out. Cut staff, cut services, cut corners on everything. Equipment that didn't work, supplies that never arrived. We were constantly told to do more with less. Now we know where all that money was really going.

LUCAS: Jenny Markham has worked at Addison Gilbert for 17 years. She tearfully told me that last week, she received an anonymous payment—money she says will help her pay off the medical debt she ironically accrued while working for CBHS.

JENNY MARKHAM: I'm not the only one. All across the hospital, people are getting these payments. It's like... it's like someone is making things right when the system failed us.

LUCAS: Similar reports are coming in from CBHS facilities across the country. Back to you, Anie.

ANIE: Thank you, Lucas. The question of who is behind these mysterious payments remains unanswered. Federal authorities acknowledge they're investigating but say their primary focus remains on the CBHS executives now facing charges.

Joining me now is Dr. Haley Chen, a former CBHS physician who was among the first to raise concerns about patient safety. Dr. Chen, thank you for being here.

DR. HALEY CHEN: Thank you for having me, Anie.

ANIE: Dr. Chen, you left CBHS last year after reporting critical staffing shortages. What happened when you raised these concerns?

DR. HALEY CHEN: [Sighs] I was systematically pushed out. Suddenly, there were "concerns" about my clinical judgment, patient complaints that appeared out of nowhere. It was textbook retaliation.

ANIE: And you believe this was orchestrated by CBHS leadership?

DR. HALEY CHEN: I know it was. The documents that have come to light confirm what many of us suspected—there was a playbook for silencing whistleblowers. My name was on a list labeled "Problem Employees."

ANIE: Yet despite the risks, you continued to speak out. Why?

DR. HALEY CHEN: [Emotional] Because people were dying, Anie. Sophia Martinez died in childbirth because basic medical supplies weren't available. A man went into cardiac arrest while restrained because there wasn't enough staff to monitor him. These weren't abstract budget numbers. These were human lives.

ANIE: I understand you've also received one of these anonymous payments?

DR. HALEY CHEN: Yes. A substantial amount with a simple note: "For your courage." But it's not about the money. It's about validation. For years, we were gaslit, told we were exaggerating, that the problems weren't real. Now everyone knows the truth.

ANIE: After the break, we'll look at the broader implications for America's healthcare system, hear from patients who suffered under CBHS's care, and examine the mysterious digital trail that led to the company's downfall. I'm Anie Chen, and this is a TechTruth News Special Report.

[Commercial break]

ANIE: Welcome back to our TechTruth Special Report on the collapse of CBHS. We're joined now by Marcus Thompson, whose story became a rallying cry for reform after his experience at Riverside Community Hospital, a CBHS facility in Ohio.

MARCUS THOMPSON: I lost my wife because they didn't have enough staff to monitor her. They had her restrained—standard procedure, they said—but no one checked on her for hours. By the time someone did . . . [voice breaks] it was too late.

ANIE: I'm so sorry for your loss, Marcus. What was the hospital's response?

MARCUS THOMPSON: They called it an "unfortunate incident." Said they'd "review their procedures." But nothing changed. Until now.

ANIE: You've been vocal about holding CBHS accountable. What do these recent revelations mean to you?

MARCUS THOMPSON: Vindication, but it's bittersweet. The documents show they knew—they knew they were dangerously understaffed. They calculated the risk of lawsuits versus the cost of proper staffing and chose profit. They put a dollar value on my wife's life.

ANIE: And now, the mysterious payment?

MARCUS THOMPSON: [Shakes head] No amount can bring Helen back, but I'm using what I received to start a foundation in her name. We'll advocate for patient safety standards with real teeth.

ANIE: Across the country, similar stories are emerging. Former CBHS employees and patients report receiving payments seemingly calibrated to the harm they suffered. Families who lost loved ones due to alleged negligence report the most substantial sums.

Financial analyst Jordan Kim joins us now. Jordan, what can you tell us about these payments?

JORDAN KIM: Anie, what's remarkable isn't just the amount—which is substantial—but the precision. Each payment appears carefully calculated based on specific factors: length of employment, severity of harm suffered, personal financial impact. Whoever is behind this has detailed knowledge of each recipient's situation.

ANIE: And no one has claimed responsibility?

JORDAN KIM: No one. The funds are being routed through an elaborate network of international transactions that's proving impossible to trace. It bears all the hallmarks of a highly sophisticated operation.

ANIE: Some have dubbed this "The Robin Hood Effect." Do you think that's an apt description?

JORDAN KIM: In many ways, yes. This appears to be a deliberate redistribution of wealth from CBHS back to those who were harmed by their practices. It's as if someone decided the legal system moved too slowly and took justice into their own hands.

ANIE: The question on everyone's mind: who could pull off something this elaborate?

JORDAN KIM: That's the billion-dollar question, isn't it? We're talking about someone with extraordinary technical skills, insider knowledge of CBHS's operations, and a moral compass that pointed them toward this form of justice.

ANIE: The digital breadcrumbs that led to CBHS's downfall are equally mysterious. Federal investigators reportedly received anonymously uploaded files containing years of internal communications, financial records, and evidence of systematic fraud—all meticulously organized and annotated.

Cybersecurity expert Mira Patel is here to help us understand how this might have happened. Mira, in your professional opinion, what are we looking at here?

MIRA PATEL: This has all the hallmarks of a sophisticated hack, but with unusual characteristics. Typically, hackers breaking into corporate systems are after financial gain or creating chaos. This was different—surgical, precise, and with a clear moral objective.

ANIE: Could this be the work of a single person?

MIRA PATEL: Unlikely. The breadth of skills required—from sophisticated network penetration to financial forensics to physical security bypasses—suggests a team. A very talented team.

ANIE: A team of digital vigilantes?

MIRA PATEL: [Smiles slightly] That's one way to put it. Whoever they are, they've certainly changed the landscape of corporate accountability overnight.

ANIE: Federal authorities have remained tight-lipped about potential connections to other high-profile cases.

MIRA PATEL: [With slight skepticism] Officially, they're treating this as an isolated incident. Off the record, I'm hearing comparisons to the CAYA situation last year. The surgical precision, the redistribution aspect, the moral component . . .

ANIE: Are you suggesting the same people could be responsible?

MIRA PATEL: [Dry smile] Let's just say certain investigative teams are working late nights comparing notes. The odds of two completely different groups pulling off operations this sophisticated, with such similar . . . philosophical underpinnings? That's quite a coincidence.

ANIE: As we conclude our special report tonight, I'd like to share something personal with our viewers. Dr. Haley Chen, who courageously spoke out about CBHS's practices, is my sister-in-law. Her experience opened my eyes to this story long before it made headlines, and I'm grateful that TechTruth gave me the platform to bring these issues to light. While I've maintained journalistic distance throughout our reporting, I want to acknowledge this connection in the interest of full transparency. Some stories find us because they're meant to be told. This was one of them.

Meanwhile, in boardrooms across America, executives are reportedly ordering urgent security reviews and compliance audits. One Wall Street analyst described it as "a seismic shift in corporate risk assessment."

The message seems clear: in an age of digital transparency, no secret stays buried forever.

For the patients and families affected by CBHS's actions, like Marcus Thompson, the road to healing continues. For whistleblowers like Dr. Haley Chen, vindication has finally arrived. And for the thousands of healthcare workers who struggled under CBHS's regime, there is cautious hope for a new beginning.

This has been a TechTruth News Special Report. I'm Anie Chen. Good night.

[Theme music fades out]

Leave a Trail

As the sun dipped below the horizon, casting long shadows across Winter Island in Salem, the abandoned buildings of the former Coast Guard Air Station Salem stood as silent sentinels to a bygone era. Once a bustling hub of maritime rescue operations, the island now lies quiet, its structures slowly reclaimed by nature.

Established in 1935, Air Station Salem played a crucial role in coastal defense and rescue operations for decades. From World War II submarine patrols to daring sea rescues, the station's aircraft and brave crews were a constant presence in the skies over Salem Harbor.

Now, these weathered buildings stood as archeological treasures, their peeling paint and rusted fixtures telling stories of heroic rescues and wartime vigilance. As visitors gaze due south across the Salem Harbor, they can imagine the pilots of yesteryear using the town's iconic landscape as a navigation point on their return from harrowing missions.

Across the harbor lies Marblehead, one of the oldest seaports in the United States. In the town's Historic District lies the Barnacle, which has been a Marblehead institution since 1935 and is a living testament to the town's maritime heritage. This charming, weathered establishment—originally a humble clam shack—has evolved into a beloved restaurant perched on the water's edge. Its shingled exterior and cozy, nautical-themed interior speak to decades of serving both locals and visitors. Large windows and a small outdoor deck offer breathtaking views of Marblehead Harbor, with boats bobbing gently in the distance.

The golden glow of the sunset on the water created a warm light on the team as they gathered on The Barnacle's outdoor deck, taking a moment to reflect on the generations of coastal life that have unfolded here, including the brave aviators who once soared over these waters from the nearby Air Station Salem. The weathered wooden planks beneath their feet have witnessed countless sea tales and celebrations. Surrounded by the gentle lapping of waves and the faint clink of rigging from nearby boats, the team settles in, ready to discuss their next moves. The Barnacle, with its rich history and stunning vistas, provides the perfect backdrop for this crucial meeting, blending the town's storied past with the team's ambitious plans for the future.

The worn deck creaked as William shifted in his chair, taking a sip of his water. The musty scent of old fishing nets and stale beer hung in the air. He glanced around the table at the team assembled before him—Amelia, her dark hair pulled back in a sleek ponytail; Justine, absently twirling a lock of red hair around her finger; Tommy, his intense dark eyes fixed on the door, reluctant to shed his protective instincts; Josh, well-groomed as always, this time in a bespoke light gray suit; and Darby, her hair, styled it with a slight tousle, giving it an effortless, windswept look that seemed perfectly at home in the seaside setting of The Barnacle.

As the team settled into their discussion on the deck, Ella made her fashionably late entrance. She strode confidently towards the group, her attire a striking contrast to the casual seaside setting. Ella wore a sleek, black strapless top that highlighted her shoulders, paired with a flowing skirt in a vibrant pattern of green, blue, and yellow hues. Her hair, usually pulled back for practicality, fell in soft waves around her face, elegantly framing her features.

As she approached, the team couldn't help but notice her transformed presence. The focused intensity of their technical mastermind had given way to something lighter, more relaxed. Ella's eyes, usually locked on a computer screen, sparkled with a mix of mischief and determination as she joined her teammates at the table.

"Sorry I'm late," she said with a hint of a smirk. "I was stuck debugging some MIT freshman's attempt at coding. Turns out, teaching a goldfish to tap dance would've been easier."

She slid into her seat, giving William a subtle nod that promised more information later.

He chuckled and shook his head. Same old Ella—brilliant, sarcastic, and always full of surprises. Some things never changed.

· · · ● · ● · ● · · ·

William cleared his throat, drawing the team's attention. "So, let's recap. Operation Corporate Takedown was a resounding success. We infiltrated CBHS, exposed their dirty dealings, and made off with enough evidence to bury them six feet under."

Josh nodded, a grim smile on his face. "They're done."

"Eloquent and straight to the point as always, Josh," Amelia said, rolling her eyes. "But he's right. The documents we stole are damning. Fraudulent billing, kickbacks, substandard care—it's all there in black and white. The OIG has some of this, but I doubt they have it all."

William leaned back in his chair, a sense of satisfaction washing over him. They'd done it. Months of meticulous planning, sleepless nights, and close calls had all led to that moment in Gloucester. CBHS's reign of greed and corruption was crashing down, and they were the ones wielding the wrecking ball.

But even as he savored the sweet taste of victory, William knew their work was far from over. They still had to figure out how to get the stolen documents into the right hands, how to ensure justice was served without implicating themselves. And then there was the small matter of the millions they'd siphoned from both Vincent and from CBHS's slush fund. Somehow, he didn't think *finder's keepers* would hold up in court.

He glanced at Ella, who was absently fiddling with the silver thumb drive containing the stolen files. Her focused determination reminded him why he'd always believed in her. Some people ran from their demons; Ella was learning to make hers work overtime.

"So," William said to everyone, leaning forward and clasping his hands on the table. "What's our next move?"

Ella tucked the thumb drive into her pocket, her dark eyes flickering with determination. "We need to make this right," she said quietly.

Amelia said, "More than a dozen patients died at one of CBHS's hospitals because of malfunctioning—or non-existent—equipment or inadequate staff, and more than 2,000 other patients were put at serious risk. That's not right. And at least 10,000 were over-billed for the services they did receive. They should be compensated for the chaotic environment CBHS created."

"But CBHS didn't just screw over their patients," Darby added. "They screwed over their own employees, too."

Amelia nodded, her perfectly manicured nails tapping against the table. "The nurses, the therapists, doctors, environmental services, security . . . they're all collateral damage in this mess. We can't just leave them high and dry."

Darby added, "and don't forget the thousands who were laid off and the service lines they closed."

"And the patients?" Justine asked, her voice tight with emotion. "What about all the people CBHS overcharged? Or given substandard care? Or died?"

William's jaw clenched, a familiar anger rising in his chest as he recalled Sophia Martinez's story. Her death—and leaving a newborn without a mother—was a powerful example of the real-world consequences of CBHS's corrupt practices and mismanagement. How many more Sophias were out there, suffering needlessly because of corporate greed?

"We'll make it right," he said, his voice low and fierce. "We'll go through the records, identify every patient who was wronged, and we'll find a way to help them. Whether it's reimbursing their expenses or connecting them with the care they need."

Ella nodded, a small smile tugging at the corner of her mouth. "Hacktivism at its finest," she said, her fingers twitching as if itching to get back to her keyboard.

The team's discussion turned to the practical challenges of distributing the stolen funds to employees and patients. Darby drummed her fingers on the table.

"The package delivery method we used in LA won't work this time. We can't just deliver a big box to them," she said. "Too risky, given the scale of the operation. We need a more secure way to transfer the money without raising red flags."

Justine leaned back in her chair, a sly grin playing on her lips. "What about offshore accounts? Create a bunch of shell companies, move the cash through a series of transfers."

William shook his head. "Too complicated. We need something simpler, more direct."

As if on cue, a familiar figure strode onto the outdoor patio. Chase, Justine's father and their ally from the LA heist, flashed a confident smile.

"I can help with that," he announced, pulling up a chair and joining the group.

Justine's eyes lit up, a mix of surprise and delight. "Dad! What are you doing here?"

Chase reached over and squeezed his daughter's hand. "Couldn't miss out on all the fun, could I? Besides, William called and I have a few ideas about how to handle the distribution."

• • • ● • ● • • •

Chase Harrison, Justine's father, had once been the picture of corporate success—an investor and co-CFO at the LA studio. But beneath the polished exterior lay a man grappling with the shocking revelation of his daughter's ordeal in the porn industry.

When the scales fell from his eyes, Chase's world tilted on its axis. The boardroom warrior transformed into an undercover operative, driven by a potent cocktail of paternal rage and an unquenchable thirst for justice. He became the team's ace in the hole, a wolf in sheep's clothing within the very den of iniquity they sought to bring down.

Chase's financial wizardry and corporate connections proved to be the skeleton key that unlocked CAYA's fortified secrets. He walked a tightrope between his public persona—the respected businessman—and his clandestine role as the team's inside man. His insider knowledge was the compass that guided the team through the labyrinth of corporate corruption, leading to their audacious multi-billion dollar heist and the subsequent implosion of the company's house of cards.

In the aftermath, Chase traded in his power suits for Hawaiian shirts, embracing a retirement filled with new pursuits. Yet, he remained tethered to Justine and the unlikely family forged in the crucible of their shared mission. Now, as he approached the table at the Barnacle, there was a glint in his eye that suggested he wasn't quite done with the game of high-stakes justice.

• • • ● • ● • • •

The team leaned in, eager to hear his proposal. Chase, with his business savvy and connections, had been instrumental in their previous success.

"We set up a secure online platform," he said, his voice low and conspiratorial. "Encrypted, untraceable. We can transfer funds directly to the affected staff and patients, all under the guise of a legitimate charity operation."

William nodded slowly, considering the idea. It was bold, but it just might work.

Chase continued, his eyes gleaming with the thrill of the challenge. "To avoid raising red flags, we'll distribute the funds gradually. Small, consistent payments that won't trigger any alarms in the banking system."

"Smart," Darby said, impressed.

"We'll establish a legitimate charitable foundation as our front," Chase said. "I've already drafted the paperwork. Our mission statement focuses on supporting healthcare workers and patients affected by corporate malpractice. It's vague enough to cover our tracks, but specific enough to be believable."

Amelia nodded approvingly. "That should provide solid legal cover."

"As for the long haul," Chase went on, "I've set up a small team of trusted individuals to manage the foundation and distribution process. They think it's a genuine charity, and their involvement will keep it running smoothly for years to come."

"And if something goes wrong?" Tommy asked, ever the pragmatist.

Chase's lips curved into a knowing smile. "I've got contingencies in place. If our primary method is compromised, we have backup distribution channels through international micro-loan organizations and healthcare worker unions. They'll act as additional layers of obfuscation."

William leaned back, a mix of admiration and relief on his face. "Chase, you've thought of everything."

"That's why you brought me in, isn't it?" Chase replied with a wink. "Now, let's make sure these funds get to the people who truly need them."

Justine beamed at her father, a newfound respect gleaming in her eyes. Though improving, their relationship had been strained, fractured by the weight of her past. But now, seeing him here, risking everything to help them, she felt a surge of gratitude and love.

"Thanks, Dad," she said, her voice thick with emotion. "For being here, for having our backs."

Chase smiled, a rare moment of genuine warmth breaking through his usually stoic exterior. "Always, kiddo. We're in this together, no matter what."

As the team finished discussing the distribution plan, Tommy leaned forward, his eyes narrowing slightly.

"Anyone catch the TechTruth special report?" he asked, voice low. "They're calling it 'The Robin Hood Effect.' Even had some cybersecurity expert on breaking down how sophisticated the operation was."

Ella snorted softly, a mixture of pride and concern crossing her face. "Yeah, I saw it. Apparently, we're *digital vigilantes* now." She made air quotes with her fingers.

"What about the CAYA connection?" Josh asked. "Think anyone's putting those pieces together?"

An uncomfortable silence settled over the table. The CAYA takedown had been their first major operation—different circumstances, but similar enough in execution to raise eyebrows.

William took a careful sip of his water before responding. "Law enforcement agencies rarely broadcast their investigative connections to the public. If they're seeing patterns, they're keeping it quiet for now."

"Feds are compartmentalized," Darby added, her voice carrying that matter-of-fact tone from her days as an enforcer. "Right hand rarely knows what the left is doing. But give it time—someone will eventually connect the dots."

"So what you're saying is," Justine said with a sardonic smile, "we should enjoy our seafood dinner while we can?"

Chase chuckled, shaking his head slightly. "No need to panic yet. These investigations move at glacial speed. Besides, we've been careful."

"Exactly," Amelia said. "We stick to the plan, keep our heads down, and remember that our mission is more important than the risks."

The team nodded in silent agreement, the weight of their choices—past and present—hanging in the air between them.

· · · ● · ● · ● · · ·

As the team began to hash out the details of the plan, a sense of excitement and purpose filled the air. They had done the impossible, had struck a blow against the corrupt and powerful. And now, with Chase's help, they were going to make sure that justice was truly served.

Amelia leaned forward, her gaze intense as she scanned the faces of her co-conspirators. "Now, about those documents we lifted from CBHS. We need to get them into the right hands, and fast."

William nodded, his brow furrowed. "OIG's the obvious choice. But how do we make sure they don't get *lost* along the way?"

"Leave that to me," Amelia said, a sly smile playing at the corners of her mouth. "I know a few tricks to ensure a secure delivery. But first, we need to catalog everything, build an airtight case."

She turned to Ella, the tech wizard of the group. "Think you can work your magic? Cross-reference the files, highlight the juiciest bits?"

Ella grinned, her fingers already dancing across her laptop keys. "Consider it done. I'll have this evidence singing like a canary in a coal mine."

As the sun set, fully behind them now, the team settled into a comfortable rhythm. A thoughtful silence descended upon the group as they pondered the moral implications of their actions. Josh leaned back in his chair, his eyes distant as he spoke. "We're walking a fine line here. Yes, we're exposing corruption, but at what cost? Are we any better than the people we're fighting against if we resort to illegal means?"

Darby shook her head, her blonde hair catching the fading sunlight. "We're not doing this for personal gain, Josh. We're doing it because it's the right thing to do. These people need someone to fight for them, and if we don't, who will?"

Justine nodded in agreement, her green eyes flashing with determination. "We've all seen firsthand the damage that greed and corruption can do. We have a chance to make a real difference here, to help people who have been exploited and forgotten."

Amelia listened to her team, her heart swelling with pride at their conviction. She knew the risks they were taking, the lines they were crossing, but she also knew that sometimes, the only way to fight injustice was to step outside the bounds of the law.

William cleared his throat, his eyes reflecting the wisdom of his years. "We're treading in the footsteps of Robin Hood here, no doubt about it. But let's remember what Emerson said: *A foolish consistency is the hobgoblin of little minds.* Sometimes, to adhere to a higher moral law, we must break the letter of the written one."

He paused, letting his words sink in. "The *Robin Hood effect* isn't without its complications. By redistributing wealth, we're making a judgment about who deserves what. It's a heavy responsibility."

Chase nodded thoughtfully. "True, but as your favorite, Thoreau, put it, *Under a government which imprisons any unjustly, the true place for a just man is also a prison.* We're choosing to act rather than be complicit through inaction."

Ella, who had been quietly listening, finally spoke up. "I've seen firsthand what happens when people with power abuse it. Sometimes, you have to work outside the system to change it."

William smiled, a mix of pride and concern in his eyes. "Indeed. Emerson also said, *Do not go where the path may lead, go instead where there is no path and leave a trail.* We're forging a new path here, one that I believe leads to justice."

• • • • •• • • • • ·

As the conversation lulled, William sat up, his eyes scanning the faces of his teammates. A wave of emotion washed over him as he reflected on his journey—from a man battling his own demons to someone who had dedicated himself to helping others. He thought of Justine during their last heist, of Ella's remarkable recovery, of the countless runners he'd inspired, of Lexi's challenges at school, and now of Amelia and this mission.

"You know," he began, his voice soft but steady, "when I started this journey—years ago, really—I was a broken man trying to piece myself back together. I never imagined I'd be here, surrounded by such remarkable people, fighting for a cause greater than myself."

He paused, his gaze settling on each team member in turn. "Each of you has taught me something valuable about resilience, about hope. And I've realized that in helping others, I've found my own healing. So, what's next for us? I think we continue on this path of making a difference, of being the change we want to see in the world."

Josh leaned back, a thoughtful expression on his face. "So, we'd be like . . . modern-day Equalizers? Not just Robin Hoods stealing from the rich, but actively working to level the playing field?"

Justine grinned, her eyes sparkling with mischief. "I like that. We could be the underground justice league, taking on the big guys and giving the little guys a fighting chance."

Amelia felt a thrill of excitement run through her at the thought. She knew it was a dangerous path, one that could lead them down a rabbit hole of moral ambiguity. But the idea of using their skills to address systemic inequalities? It was too compelling to resist.

"We'd have to be careful," she said, ever the pragmatist. "We can't let our emotions cloud our judgment. We need to stay focused on the mission, on doing what's right."

The team nodded in agreement, their expressions a mix of determination and anticipation. They knew the road ahead would be challenging, but they also knew that together, they could face anything.

As the light from the setting sun faded, Amelia grabbed William's hand and squeezed. She felt a sense of purpose settle over her. Whatever the future held, she knew she was exactly where she was meant to be, fighting alongside the people she trusted most in the world.

The Moral Minute—Episode 8

[Theme music—short, serious but with an edge]

ANIE: I'm Anie Chen.

LUCAS: And I'm Lucas Rodriguez. Welcome to The Moral Minute, where we examine the day's most egregious ethical failures in corporate America.

ANIE: Breaking news from Gloucester, where federal agents just raided a CBHS conference at the Beauport Hotel.

LUCAS: [satisfied] Looks like Vincent Blackwell's house of cards finally collapsed.

ANIE: OIG agents arrested Blackwell, along with CNO Kiran Devi. The charges include Medicare fraud, embezzlement, tax evasion . . .

LUCAS: [interrupting] Don't forget the kickback schemes and HIPAA violations. But here's what's fascinating—somebody gave the feds a roadmap.

ANIE: [intrigued] What do you mean?

LUCAS: Anonymous sources say the evidence was handed to them on a silver platter. Financial records, emails, internal memos—all meticulously organized.

ANIE: Almost like someone was working behind the scenes . . .

LUCAS: Time's almost up. What's our moral of the minute?

ANIE: Sometimes justice arrives in mysterious ways—but it always arrives.

[Theme music fades out]

The Twelve Lanterns Legacy

W illiam arrived at Marblehead's Devereux Beach wearing a faded t-shirt with *26.2* emblazoned on it.

Of course.

He always has to remind everyone he's a marathon man. His eyes scanned the shoreline for Ella. The beach, once a bustling hub of early 20th-century seaside activity, now lay peaceful in the soft morning light. He could almost imagine the scene from a century ago—Model T Fords lining the dirt road, their occupants spilling out onto the sand, while Usher's refreshment stand bustled with beachgoers seeking respite from the summer heat.

Looking out at the horizon, William smiled at how far he'd come from that eager grad student who thought reading *The Wealth of Nations* twice would unlock the mysteries of economic behavior. It turned out some mysteries required more than theoretical knowledge—they required action, courage, and a team of reformed criminals with hearts of gold.

He spotted Ella standing near the water's edge, her gaze fixed on the horizon. She wore a vibrant yellow crop top that contrasted with her sun-kissed skin, paired with ripped blue jeans and a plaid shirt tied casually around her waist. Her wavy hair danced in the gentle breeze as she stood motionless, seemingly lost in thought.

"It's peaceful here, isn't it?" William said softly, not wanting to startle her.

Ella turned, a serene smile on her face. "It really is. There's something about the sound of the waves, the feel of the rocks beneath my feet . . . it grounds me. Makes all the chaos we've been through seem distant somehow."

William nodded, understanding. "Longfellow once wrote a poem inspired by this very beach, you know. *The Fire of Drift-wood.* He captured the essence of this place beautifully."

As they began their walk across the causeway to Marblehead Neck, William recited a few lines: "*We sat within the farm-house old, whose windows, looking o'er the bay, gave to the sea-breeze damp and cold, an easy entrance, night and day.*"

"That's lovely," Ella said, her eyes still drawn to the water. "I can see why he was inspired. There's a timeless quality to this place. It feels like . . . like I can finally breathe here, you know?"

William felt a swell of pride and affection. Seeing Ella find peace, watching her strength and resilience bloom in this new chapter of her life, was more rewarding than he could have imagined. As they continued their walk, the conversation flowed easily between them, touching on the past, present, and the promising future that lay ahead.

"So, catch me up, William. How's the exciting world of motivational speaking treating you? Motivated anyone to actually stay awake during your lectures?"

As they stepped onto the smooth concrete of the causeway, the sea breeze picked up, carrying with it the pungent scent of salt and seaweed. The rhythmic lapping of waves against the rocks provided a soothing backdrop to their conversation. William could taste the salt on his lips and feel the sun warming his skin as they walked, the sensations grounding him in the moment.

They began walking to the Marblehead Neck. The only sound was the distant cry of gulls. "As it happens, my lectures are quite invigorating. Why, just yesterday, an octogenarian only nodded off twice. A new record."

"Careful. With success like that, you'll have to beat the groupies away with a stick. How's everything else?"

"Great, really. Amelia and I have grown closer. A relationship I never saw coming, but it's one I'm thrilled to have found. She understands me in a way few others do, and her strength and determination continue to inspire me. It's like we've found a kindred spirit in each other, both committed to making a difference in our own ways.

"And I'm running, of course. *When you have worn out your shoes, the strength of the shoe leather has passed into the fiber of your body.*"

"Let me guess—Emerson?"

"Thoreau, actually," William corrected with a wink. "But close enough. I'm just grateful to have a people in my life now. You've been part of it for nearly a decade. There's our team, of course. And now Amelia." He bumped her shoulder with his. "So, what's this mysterious place you've asked me to see? It must be quite something to lure you away from your keyboard."

Ella flushed, the significance of what she was about to show him truly hitting her. After so long, she finally had a place that was just hers. A haven. She felt the prickle of tears and blinked them back. Damn it, when did she get so sentimental? Must be William's syrupy influence.

She took a fortifying breath of salty air and quirked a brow at him. "Oh, just a little fixer upper with a decent view. Figured a muscular Adonis like yourself could help me hang some curtains, maybe assemble an IKEA bookcase or two. I mean, if you can handle it in your advanced age . . ."

"Why you impudent whippersnapper!" William made to cuff her upside the head, but she danced away, laughing.

"Better keep up, graybeard!" Ella called over her shoulder as she scampered ahead on lithe legs. "Try not to throw out a hip!"

Still chuckling, William increased his pace, feeling lighter than he had in years.

As they rounded the bend, the Mediterranean-inspired villa of Twelve Lanterns came into view. Perched atop a rocky ledge, the stucco-clad house commanded unobstructed views of the vast Atlantic Ocean stretching out before it. The red-tiled roof and arched windows gave the home a distinctly Spanish flair, while the crashing waves and salty breeze filled the air, creating a sense of peaceful isolation for its inhabitants.

Beyond a small parking area, a charming entryway caught the eye. A tiled roof sheltered an arched doorway, flanked by wrought-iron lanterns and framed by lush greenery. Stone steps led up to this inviting entrance, promising a glimpse into the interior.

Ella felt a swell of pride and possessiveness. Home. She had a home.

William let out a low whistle as they approached the multi-level structure with its balconies and terraces. "Well, I'll be. When you said fixer-upper, I was picturing more of a quaint bungalow, not this majestic Spanish villa. How many rooms does this place have?"

Ella shrugged, feigning nonchalance even as a grin tugged at her lips. "Oh, a few. Plenty of space for when the rest of the gang visits. Maybe I'll even let you crash on the pullout couch if you play your cards right."

She bounded up the steps, pulling the antique key from her pocket. The heavy oak door swung open with a pleased groan, welcoming them inside.

William stepped over the threshold and let out an appreciative hum, eyes roaming the gleaming hardwood floors and soaring ceilings. "I take it back. This is no fixer upper. This, my dear, is a grand dame just waiting for her debut."

Ella's heart swelled at his approval. She'd spent weeks painstakingly restoring every inch of the place, determined to bring it back to its former glory. Leading him into the sprawling great room, she spread her arms wide. "Welcome to my not-so-humble abode."

The massive fireplace commanded immediate attention, its craggy face stretching up to the exposed beam ceiling. Ella ran a hand along the mantle, fingers dancing over the pockmarked surface. "Can't you just picture it roaring away on a blustery winter night? Maybe even roast some chestnuts, seeing as we're leaning into the whole Hallmark movie vibe."

William smirked, gesturing to the raised alcove jutting out from the far wall. "Let me guess, that's where you'll put your piano? Serenade us with a little *Moonlight Sonata* while we sip hot chocolate and contemplate our lot in life?"

"Har, har." Ella rolled her eyes, but inwardly preened. He knew her so well. "For your information, I was planning on some rousing ragtime to match your doddering gait. Really set the mood."

They looked at each other, matching grins stretching their faces. This easy camaraderie, this unspoken understanding—it filled the soaring space as surely as music and firelight soon would.

Ella felt a sudden urge to hug him, to thank him for being here, for being him. But she tamped it down, defaulting to sarcasm as always. "So, ready to bust out the tool belt? Those curtain rods won't hang themselves, you know."

William held up his hands in mock surrender. "Lead the way, Boss. Let's make this place sing."

As they set off to explore the rest of the house, their good-natured quips echoing off the freshly painted walls, Ella felt something slot into place. She was home. And for once, that didn't feel like a four-letter word.

With a conspiratorial glint in her eye, Ella beckoned William towards the towering book-shelves lining the back wall. "You haven't seen the best part yet."

Her fingers danced along the spines, settling on a worn volume of Thoreau's *Walden*. With a deft tug, the book tilted forward, and the entire shelf swung inward, revealing a narrow spiral staircase.

William let out a low whistle. "Secret passages. Why am I not surprised?"

"Because you know I live for the dramatic reveal." Ella winked, starting up the steps. "It's like living in my very own Nancy Drew mystery."

The stairwell was tight, the stone walls cool against their shoulders as they climbed. William's voice drifted up from behind her. "If this ends with us finding a skeleton in the attic, I'm out."

Ella's laughter bounced off the curved walls. "Please, as if I'd be that cliché."

At the top, a wooden door greeted them. Ella paused, hand on the knob, savoring the anticipation. Then, with a flourish, she swung it open.

They stepped into a small room, windows on all sides offering a stunning 360-degree view. The ocean sparkled in the distance, sailboats bobbing like toys in the bath. Closer, the quaint streets of Marblehead unfurled, a patchwork of history and charm.

"Wow." William moved to the nearest window, pressing his forehead to the glass. "This is . . ."

"Quite the room with a view, right?" Ella joined him, their shoulders brushing. A comfortable silence stretched as they drank in the scenery, each lost in their own musings.

Finally, William turned to her, curiosity gleaming in his eyes. "So, what's the story? There's got to be a story."

Ella grinned, settling cross-legged on the floor and patting the space beside her. "You might want to sit. This could take a while."

As William lowered himself down, Ella began, her voice taking on a reverent hush. "It all started with Isabella Stewart Gardner. You know, the museum lady?"

William nodded. "The one who got robbed, right? Biggest art heist in history? I took you and the rest of the crew to her museum during our last escapade."

"The very same. But before that, she was a force to be reckoned with. A patron of the arts, a trailblazer. She used to summer here in Marblehead, and legend has it, she had a hand in designing this very room."

Ella leaned back on her hands, eyes dreamy. "Can you imagine? Isabella Freakin' Gardner, standing right where we are. Plotting her next grand acquisition or soirée. It's like a direct line to history."

William smiled softly, watching her face light up as she spoke. "She made quite the impact, huh?"

"That's an understatement. She shook things up, in the best way. Supported artists, collected works that others overlooked. She created something lasting, something bigger than herself. Isn't that what we all want, in the end?"

The question hung in the air, weighty with unspoken longing. For a heartbeat, they held each other's gaze, a flicker of understanding passing between them.

William reached out, placing a gentle hand on Ella's shoulder. "I think you're well on your way to doing just that, Ella. This place?" He gestured around the room, taking in the sweeping views and the sense of history that seemed to permeate the very walls. "It's a new chapter for you. A fresh start. And I couldn't be happier for you."

Ella ducked her head, a faint blush coloring her cheeks. "Thanks, William. That means a lot, coming from you." She nudged him with her elbow. "Look at us, getting all sentimental in our old age."

"Speak for yourself," William said, his eyes crinkling with mirth. "I'm like a classic book—I only get better with age."

"More like yesterday's newspaper." Ella shot back. "All wrinkled and outdated." Her grin was impish, her dark eyes sparkling with mischief.

William clutched his chest in mock offense. "You wound me, madam. And here I thought we were having a moment."

"Oh, we're having a moment alright. A moment of me putting up with your delusions of grandeur." Ella rose to her feet, offering William a hand up. "Come on, old man. We better get moving before Amelia sends out a search party."

William allowed himself to be hauled upright, chuckling softly. "Lead the way. These creaky bones could use a good stretch."

As they made their way back through the hidden passageway and down the stairs, their banter continued, filling the air with laughter and good-natured ribbing.

They stepped out into the fading light of day, the salt-tinged breeze tousling their hair and carrying the distant cries of seagulls. Ella paused, turning to face William with a smile that spoke volumes.

William returned the smile, his eyes soft with understanding. No words were needed; their shared journey and mutual respect were evident in the comfortable silence between them.

With a final nod, they set off down the path. As they walked from the causeway onto the beach, Amelia came into view, leaning against a sleek black convertible. William felt a warmth spread through his chest at the sight of her.

The three of them climbed into the car, the familiarity of their banter a comforting backdrop as they pulled away from the shore. As the wind whipped through his hair, William found his thoughts drifting, reflecting on the journey that had brought him here.

From the depths of addiction to the heights of redemption, from solitary runner to part of something greater than himself—it had been a long and winding road. He thought of Thoreau's words: *I learned this, at least, by my experiment: that if one advances confidently in the direction of his dreams, and endeavors to live the life which he has imagined, he will meet with a success unexpected in common hours.*

Glancing at Ella, then at Amelia, William felt a profound sense of gratitude. He had advanced towards his dreams, yes, but not alone. These remarkable individuals, and the others who had become his unlikely family, had been integral to his journey.

As the twinkling lights of the town blurred past, William realized his tale was far from over. There would be more challenges, more opportunities to right wrongs and make a difference. But now, he faced the future not as a solitary figure, but as part of a whole.

The road stretched out before them, a metaphor for the path ahead. And as they hurtled towards it, William couldn't help but think that perhaps this—this sense of purpose, this connection—was the truest form of transcendence.

Epilogue

William leaned back in his chair, a wry smile playing on his lips. "You know, Emerson once said, *Money often costs too much*. I think we've finally found a way to make it cost the right people."

The team had gathered in Ella's new Marblehead home, the ocean view a stark contrast to the gritty details of their recent escapade. As they settled in, Josh pulled out his laptop, ready to break down the numbers.

"Alright, folks," he began, his fingers flying over the keyboard. "Let's talk about our little redistribution of wealth, shall we?"

Darby snorted. "Redistribution of wealth? Is that what we're calling grand larceny these days?"

"I prefer *karmic rebalancing*," Justine chimed in, her eyes twinkling.

Josh cleared his throat dramatically. "If we're done with the semantics . . . let's start with our friend Vincent. We relieved him of a cool $357 million. I'd say he's probably feeling that pinch right about now."

"Couldn't have happened to a nicer guy," Tommy said.

"Then we've got CBHS itself," Josh continued. "We nabbed $180 million of their ill-gotten gains. Oh, and let's not forget the *Artemisa*. Sold back to Eisenberg & Müller for a tidy $40 million."

Ella piped up, "And the wine collection. $3 million from some pretentious collector who probably thinks box wine is a cardinal sin."

"Grand total?" Amelia asked, leaning forward.

"A whopping $580 million," Josh announced with a flourish.

William nodded solemnly. "Now, for the important part. How we're making it right."

Josh's expression sobered. "Right. We've allocated $2 million each to the families of the 15 patients who died because of CBHS's negligence. That's $30 million."

A heavy silence fell over the room, broken only by Ella's soft voice. "It doesn't bring them back, but I hope it helps somehow."

"For the 2,000 patients put at risk," Josh continued, "we've set aside $50,000 each. Another $100 million there."

"And let's not forget the 10,000 patients who were overbilled," Amelia added. "They're each getting $15,000 back."

Darby whistled low. "That's another $150 million. We're regular Robin Hoods, aren't we?"

"More like Robin Hood's tech-savvy, slightly unhinged cousins," Tommy said.

Josh rolled his eyes but pressed on. "For the 3,000 employees laid off, we've allocated $100,000 each. That's $300 million."

"And Alice?" William asked, his voice soft.

"Our insider at Barrick?" Josh nodded. "We've set aside $100,000 for her. A little thank you for unknowingly being our eyes and ears."

Ella leaned back, a satisfied smile on her face. "So that's it? $580 million, all accounted for?"

"Well," Josh said, his lips twitching, "we did go a bit over budget. That extra $100,000 for Alice? That's coming out of our pockets."

"A small price to pay for justice," William said. "As Thoreau said, *Goodness is the only investment that never fails.*"

"Oh boy, here he goes again," Darby said, but there was affection in her voice.

As laughter filled the room, William couldn't help but feel a sense of pride. They had taken on a corrupt system and won, redistributing wealth to those who truly deserved it. It wasn't a perfect solution, but it was a start.

"So," Amelia said, her eyes glinting with mischief, "anyone up for our next adventure? I hear there's a pharmaceutical company that could use a little . . . financial restructuring."

Justine leaned forward, her red hair catching the light. "Ooh, Big Pharma? Now that sounds like a challenge worthy of our talents. I can already taste the PR nightmare we'll cook up for them."

The team exchanged glances, a mix of excitement and determination on their faces. They had found their calling, and there was no turning back now.

Ella, however, remained quiet, her eyes distant. There was something else on her mind, a darker shadow from her past that she hadn't yet shared with the others. A potential target that hit much closer to home.

"Well," William said, rising to his feet, "as our friend Emerson would say, *Do not go where the path may lead, go instead where there is no path and leave a trail.* I say we blaze on."

As the team began planning their next heist, Ella's fingers twitched over her laptop keyboard. She had a lead of her own, one that made her heart race with a mixture of fear and determination. Maybe it was time to finally confront the ghosts of her past.

"Actually," Ella said, her voice barely above a whisper, "I might have an idea for our next target."

The room fell silent as all eyes turned to her. There was something in her tone that made even Darby's usual sarcasm die on her lips.

"Well, don't keep us in suspense, kid," Tommy said.

Ella took a deep breath. "It's . . . complicated. But I think it's time I told you about what really happened to me all those years ago."

And with that cryptic statement, the team knew their next adventure would be more personal—and potentially more dangerous—than anything they'd faced before. After all, they had a world to change, one corrupt organization at a time. And for Ella, it was time to face her own demons.

The End

· · · ● · ● · ● · · ·

Dear Reader,

Thank you for joining William, Darby, and the team on their journey to take down CBHS. If you enjoyed *Hippocratic Heist*, I'd be truly grateful if you'd take a moment to leave a review. Your feedback not only helps other readers discover this series but provides invaluable encouragement to me as I continue crafting these stories of righteous wrongs.

Even a few words can make an enormous difference to an author. Your reviews are the lifeblood that keeps independent writers like me creating the characters and adventures you enjoy.

Thank you for your support, and I hope to see you for the team's next mission!

· · · ● · ● · ● · · ·

YOUR FREE BOOK IS WAITING

Download your free copy of *The Transcendent Economist*—one of William's books mentioned in *The Hippocratic Heist*—and discover William's philosophical view of economics.

https://books.waldengray.com/35lmwerdt3

Afterword

Now that you've completed this journey with the *Righteous Wrong* crew, I wanted to take a moment to reflect on the themes we've explored. The world of gambling addiction and healthcare fraud may seem worlds apart from our previous adventure, but at their core, both involve systems that profit from human vulnerability.

While researching this book, I was struck by how gambling establishments and certain healthcare providers use similar psychological tactics to maximize profit—often at the expense of those they claim to serve. The characters in our story have each experienced exploitation from different angles, giving them unique insights into how these systems operate and, importantly, how they might be disrupted.

I believe fiction can be a powerful vehicle for examining uncomfortable truths about our society. By following these characters as they navigate their own complicated moral landscapes, perhaps we can better understand the complex factors that lead people into addiction and the predatory systems that make recovery so challenging.

Thank you for trusting me with your time and attention. I hope you'll join the *Righteous Wrong* team on their next mission, as they continue to seek justice in their own unorthodox ways.

With appreciation,

Walden Gray

Acknowledgements

I remain incredibly grateful for the constant and unwavering support of my family throughout my life's many adventures. Whether I was training for marathons, embarking on cross-country moves, or pouring my heart into my writing, my family has always been there, cheering me on and providing a foundation of love and encouragement.

To my wife, my partner in every sense of the word: your love, patience, and belief in me continue to sustain me through each writing journey. I am so grateful to have you by my side.

To my wonderful children: your love, laughter, and endless enthusiasm remain my greatest inspiration. Watching you grow and pursue your own passions has been one of the greatest privileges of my life.

To my mother: your guidance and unwavering support have shaped me into the person I am today. Thank you for always being there, through the good times and the challenging ones.

I also wish to acknowledge those who shared their personal stories of gambling addiction and healthcare industry experiences with me. Your courage and candor helped bring authenticity to these pages.

From the bottom of my heart, thank you.

About the Author

Walden Gray continues to explore the intersection of justice and redemption through the *Righteous Wrong* series. Like the transcendentalist thinkers who inspire their work, Gray believes in the power of individual action to effect meaningful change in the world, particularly in confronting those who exploit society's most vulnerable.

When not crafting tales of righteous wrongs and moral complexity, Gray can be found running along the shores of New England's beaches, seeking inspiration in the same region that moved Thoreau and Emerson. Their writing reflects a deep appreciation for both the darkness and light in human nature, and a belief that even the most damaged souls can find their way to redemption—while shining a light on industries and organizations that profit from human suffering.

The *Righteous Wrong* series represents Gray's ongoing exploration of how ordinary people with complicated pasts can become extraordinary forces for justice. Through these stories, Gray aims to expose those who corrupt legitimate enterprises for personal gain, believing that fiction can be a powerful tool in revealing uncomfortable truths. They divide their time between the North Shore of Boston and various urban centers, finding that the balance between solitude and society fuels their creative process.

Gray maintains a deliberate air of privacy, believing, as Thoreau did, that *the mass of men lead lives of quiet desperation.* Through their writing, they hope to show that there are always alternatives to desperation—even if those alternatives sometimes lie outside society's traditional moral boundaries.

Also by Walden Gray

Below are some of my other books. I'd be honored if you take a look.

The Righteous Wrong Series

- *The Emancipation Job* (Book1)

- *Perfect Fall* (Prequel)

For more information about these titles and upcoming releases, visit waldengray.com

www.ingramcontent.com/pod-product-compliance
Lightning Source LLC
Chambersburg PA
CBHW061918130726
47908CB00017B/1861